BEYOND MALICE

REBECCA FORSTER

WOLFPACK
PUBLISHING
— EST 2013 —

Paperback Edition
Copyright © 2020 (As Revised) Rebecca Forster

Wolfpack Publishing
6032 Wheat Penny Avenue
Las Vegas, NV 89122

wolfpackpublishing.com

Paperback ISBN 978-1-64734-339-2
eBook ISBN 978-1-64734-338-5
Library of Congress Control Number: 2020947037

Original copyright © 1994 by Rebecca Forster
Cover Design by Hadleigh O. Charles

BEYOND MALICE

Chapter 1

In 1892, Walter Dimsdale and Franklin Morris meticulously drew up a partnership agreement establishing the law offices of Dimsdale & Morris. They hung their shingle, which Walter carved himself, on the third floor of a Market Street office building in San Francisco. Conscientiously, quietly, they sought out the most prestigious clients the city had to offer, promised only what they could deliver, and delivered what they promised. Within ten years, Dimsdale & Morris had established itself as one of San Francisco's most respectable firms. Their clients pointed to the firm's traditional, low-risk approach to civil litigation as the predominant reason for D&M's success. Walter and Franklin credited their ability to make money for themselves and effectively defend against those who would take it away from their clients.

In 1906, the law offices of Dimsdale & Morris were leveled, along with the rest of San Francisco, by the great earthquake. The two partners packed their bags, bid adieu to their former clients, who were now sucking bricks, and moved on, settling in Los Angeles.

Initially, the going was rough. Los Angeles was little more than a lazy desert town. By the early twenties, though, a flourishing movie industry was making and breaking contracts with satisfying regularity. This suited the two old lawyers quite well. Once again, the firm began to flourish as it burrowed into this burgeoning market.

Sadly, neither man adapted well to the more casual attitude of their new home. They continued to wear their starched collars on a daily basis and preferred to meet moguls in suits at the office rather than in informal costumes by a pool filled with half-naked, frolicking starlets. Luckily, Dimsdale bit the dust before he could become totally outraged by such freewheeling posturing. Morris, alone and rich, was now in need of help. Mott, their associate of some years, was immediately made full partner. Two young associates were brought on board to replace him and they all settled into a fine routine.

Mott was forty and a native of Southern California. Working the field was his forte, despite his generally conservative bent. Fully understanding that luncheon at the Brown Derby was more appropriate than a meeting inside an office and that clients were more amenable to the advice of Dimsdale, Morris & Mott attorneys after a few drinks, Mott took the DM&M show on the road. Morris and Mott became richer as the firm entered this new era. More associates were hired, the office space was expanded, partnerships were bestowed, and Morris died.

In the natural scheme of the things, the legal community mourned during the funeral, then scrambled to steal Dimsdale, Morris & Mott clients only to find the firm's relationships solid and Mott staunchly at the helm.

In the intervening years, Mott died, senior partners were assigned, their names never gracing the letterhead in a show of some long-forgotten respect for the founders, and the conservative agenda established in 1892 was adhered to. The senior partners lived and died for the firm and its profits. Dimsdale, Morris & Mott would have been proud.

By 1993, the firm was a huge establishment, commanding three full floors and a partial in the Interstate Building in the heart of downtown Los Angeles. It represented clients, both corporate and private, of great wealth and notoriety. The contemporary DM&M handled its clients' affairs discreetly, intelligently, and, at times, brilliantly. Most of the ten million people in LA had no idea that DM&M existed, which suited the partners just fine. Scrutiny made them very uncomfortable. There were only two things in the contemporary firm that Dimsdale, Morris, and even Mott would not have condoned, even if the year was 2092.

The first was the partners' retreat: Each year since 1987, the four current senior partners of DM&M hosted three glorious days of professional intimacy for partners and associates. A few secretaries and paralegals came along to take notes and run errands. Partners and their wives were treated to rooms in that year's designated hotel but were expected to pop for their own food and drinks, including at least one dinner for the senior partners. The partners' wives shopped and played tennis, had their hair done and attended tea with the associates' better halves.

Associates were invited to the social festivities—which more often than not failed to live up to the adjective—and tedious seminars. They drove from the suburbs to attend since few could afford the price of a room in the places DM&M chose for this occasion, in a show of excessive good cheer, the senior partners approved all-day parking vouchers for the associates. In return, the associates were expected to bill at least twenty hours to various and sundry clients during the weekend.

The senior partners and their wives enjoyed full amenities during the three-day professional extravaganza. Their rooms were suites, their parking valet and their meals written off by the firm. The designated site this year was The Regency Hotel. Beverly Hills. *Tres chic.*

Though theoretically Dimsdale, Morris & Mott might have approved of the partners' retreat, the expense of three days at the Regency Hotel would have sent collective shivers down their conservative and miserly spines. Yet it was the second modification of their original charter they would have considered beyond objectionable. It was downright sinful.

In 1993, the firm of Dimsdale, Morris & Mott employed female attorneys and had done so for the past twelve years. The only saving grace was that these women ascribed to certain decorum. As associates, they worked hard, preferred discreet suits in blue and gray with skirts that skimmed well below the knee and spent less time on their makeup than they did brushing their teeth.

For the most part they were serious, intelligent young women who could be counted on to seek other employment without a fuss when it became clear the partnership track was peppered with almost insurmountable obstacles. Only handpicked associates were able to negotiate the road to glory with any degree of surety. Not surprisingly, those that triumphed were men. An exception had been made, however, in the case of Nora Royce. Obstacles, when they appeared, were conquered easily, as she was guided down the partnership path by her assigned mentor, Lucas Mallory. But then, Nora Royce had been the exception rather than the rule all her life. Things were no different now.

If Nora Royce wore gray flannel she had it fashioned into a skirt that rode her thighs and a jacket that fit snugly over what Dimsdale would have referred to as "fine bo-soms." She was tall. She stood out. She was beautiful. She was outspoken in that slightly disdainful way of hers. And Nora Royce was smart.

Her curriculum vitae boasted a finish of three in a class of five hundred and twenty Stanford undergrads; two in a class of one hundred and twelve Harvard Law graduates. Nora Royce clerked for the Chief Justice of the California Supreme Court. She was *Law Review*. She was an affirmative action dream: a woman who was easy on the eye and efficiently effective in the courtroom. Nora Royce was a sign of the times and most of the associates hated her guts. The partners, on the other hand, found her a definite asset to a firm that was considered incredibly dull even in a colorless industry.

The final night of the partners' retreat Nora outdid herself, surprising everyone with both her conspicuous costume and deportment. Nora Royce swept into the black-tie reception well after almost everyone was in place with the same drama she brought to a courtroom. Heads turned. She hardly noticed. The attention was expected. Her dress was royal blue, shirred at the waist, short and tulip skirted. Her beautiful shoulders were bare, and it was obvious that in those few hours when she wasn't giving every breath to DM&M, Nora managed to lift a weight or two. Her shoes matched her dress. Her bag matched her shoes. She stood in the doorway, indolently perusing the room as if she commanded everyone in it. Identifying her quarry, she headed straight toward Lucas Mallory, senior partner, slipping a drink off a silver tray as she went.

"At least she's not wearing that stupid scarf," one of the less-than-stunning female associates whispered to her companion.

"Oh, I don't know," her equally plain friend answered, picking at what was left of the first-class hotel's third-rate pate. "She might be on to something. Maybe if we wore the same thing day in and day out, Lucas Mallory might decide to notice us, too."

"Christ, I'd give my left tit if Lucas Mallory even remembered my name. On second thought, I'd kill just to have a partner say hello and mean it."

They laughed together, unaware their voices had a hard, hungry edge. Envious eyes darting to Nora Royce, both women wished they had the guts to walk up and vent at a senior partner in that controlled, righteous way she had. They wished they could make a powerful man like Lucas Mallory look pale and sick with chagrin, nervous in their presence. Maybe they'd be happier if they could. More than likely, though, they'd be unemployed if they gave voice to their frustrations in the presence of anyone other than mail room personnel. So the two women looked away from the oh-so-civilized altercation and did what they did best. They eased into a lively conversation with three of the nicer looking male associates. The topic was Constantine's repeal of the Roman law of Commissoria Lex. These were smart women, after all. They knew their allure lay north of their necks. But the subject couldn't hold their attention. Like everyone else, their eyes kept skittering toward Lucas Mallory and Nora Royce, their heads together as they argued. Lucas turned away first. Nora actually reached out and held him in place, her hand on the arm of his beautifully tailored tuxedo. He glared at that hand and said something. Nora seemed to struggle with herself. She released him and then walked regally, stiffly out the side door of the reception room. The warm-up act was over. The real show was about to begin.

Oliver Hedding, managing partner of Dimsdale, Morris & Mott, made his way through the crowd, leaving in his wake a silence born partially of respect and, overwhelmingly, of fear. Even Nora reappearing in the buff wouldn't have been competition for him.

Oliver Hedding was a frosty man who, in another time, would have made a fine pope, the kind of man who would pray to God, assuring spiritual brownie points, while relying on his own talents to guarantee more immediate, corporeal success.

Standing in front of his legal flock, Oliver seemed destined to be their infallible and immutable leader. Old, he never aged further. Intelligent, he never allowed his brightness to shine. Passionate, he kept his emotions in check, knowing only in his heart of hearts whether he was satisfied with that which was and that which he had wrought. Beside him, a bit behind, stood his wife, Kitty. In the fifties, when they married, Kitty Hedding would have been described as a cool drink of water, the cat's meow, the deb of the year. She was the kind who looked great in white tulle, whose widow's peak was a thing of envy, whose alligator bags were kept in velvet wrappings, her lingerie in tissue paper. She was a girl who made a good match and a woman who had learned to live with it. Life wasn't perfect, but Kitty Hedding had the uncanny ability to turn a blind eye to the things that made it that way—even though one of those things was Oliver. At one time Kitty Hedding had been the object of her husband's desire. Now she was a necessary accessory. So, as she did every time they appeared in public, Kitty looked attentively at Oliver, who expertly called attention to himself.

"Ladies and gentlemen," he began in that dry, close-to-a-whisper voice of his. They all leaned forward, having learned long ago they were not worth the effort of projection, understanding that, when Oliver Hedding spoke, there was a message to be attended to no matter how dispassionate the delivery.

The associates and partners closed ranks, creating a womb to selflessly nurture Oliver Hedding. As he raised a glass of champagne they fell silent. From lowered lashes, or behind the guise of catching the eye of a friend, they looked about the room to identify the positions of the generals. The four partners had all come quietly into the room, no one was quite sure when, and scattered themselves about, creating a power surge that was at once unnerving and exhilarating.

Don Forrester, amiable and open, his long face always just a bit pale, his perfectly ordinary brown eyes twinkling as though life was nothing more than a simply executed but morally satisfying two-party contract, stood with his arm around his wife, Min.

Peter Sweeney, more suited to the work of a mercenary than a lawyer, stood alone, hands clasped at crotch level, legs spread wide apart. He surveyed the indentured from his position just to the right of Oliver, his even-toothed smirk daring them to aspire to anything but the commonplace. His wife, Peg, drank, rather than sipped, from a tumbler of scotch as she stood near the window and watched the traffic inch along Wilshire Boulevard far below.

Only Lucas Mallory was alone, moving benevolently around the perimeter of the crowd. By far the most attractive of the senior partners, he put a hand out to shake that of the newest associate, lifted an eyebrow to acknowledge the woman who managed the office, smiled considerately at a partner who had just lost his wife to cancer. His hair was gloriously gray, silver sprinkled attractively and evenly over a bed of black. It was cut short, not so much in a nod to fashion as in a gesture of confidence. He had reached an age, and was of a temperament, that this style suited him. His features were even, almost patrician, and his complexion was pale, as though dedication to his firm and his clients kept him from seeing the light of day. Lucas's blue eyes were kind, yet lacked a certain depth of sincerity. This failing was ignored because of his graciousness. He would listen to your tale of woe for hours on end, only to forget your name the minute he looked away. But at least he listened and the associates liked him. The partners respected him. He alone was responsible for at least twenty percent of the billings. At fifty-seven, he was the youngest of the senior partners.

His eyes wandered over the crowd. He raised himself on the balls of his feet, peering over heads, looking for someone. The few who bothered to speculate figured he was trying either to steer clear of Nora Royce or to hook up with his wife. The latter option seemed the proper one, for it seemed that only a moment ago she was wending her way through the two-hundred-strong group of attorneys. He would find her soon. In the meantime, Oliver Hedding was beginning to speak in earnest. Ruth Mallory would, more than likely, be along soon.

"Kitty and I, Min and Don Forrester, Lucas and Ruth Mallory, Peg and Peter Sweeney are all delighted to see you here tonight. We are well aware that some of you have been putting in a few extra hours at the office today. It is appreciated. It is also hoped, in your excitement about this evening's gala event, that you managed to assign the correct billing codes. If not, you'll be receiving an invoice from the partners for your share of this little get-together." Oliver cast his old black eyes about the room and drew his lips back in his interpretation of a smile. Dutifully, a titter ran through the room. He drew a deep breath, dry like that of a dying man, and continued.

"Seriously, we do appreciate the dedication all of you have shown to Dimsdale, Morris and Mott. Whether a first-year associate"—he paused, impaling two or three of them with inky eyes,—"or poised on the edge of the partnership track…" These he ignored. A look might constitute confirmation of advancement. Oliver was not that generous. "…you have proven yourself to be DM&M material. For that we are grateful and proud. It is because of you we remain one of the finest law firms in this country and one of the largest in the state of California."

Another deceptive death rattle, another grimacing smile.

"As is the case on this last evening of our retreat, when we leave work behind and before we engage in frivolity, it is customary to report on the health of the firm. The other senior partners and I are pleased to announce…" Oliver paused, his attention caught by a movement at the edge of the crowd.

In that millisecond of silence, all eyes followed his gaze, in time to see Edward Ramsey slink through the door Nora Royce had so recently used to make her escape. Even the most ardent brownnoser couldn't stomach Edward. He had made a career—no, a science—of fawning. He was no great loss to the party but his defection in the middle of Oliver's speech was a point of interest. On cue, their unified attention slid back to the managing partner. In a blink, the old man's eyes narrowed, his jaw tightened, and his lips seemed to quiver for a split second with intense interest. Then the moment was gone, and he was smoothly making up for lost time.

"…happy to announce that our fourth quarter earnings for this year were solid, expenses after the renovation of the communications system have been brought back under control, and we enjoyed a passably secure end of the year. Next month, we will be closing our books on our fiscal year, and we hope to sign Andorack, the chain of superstores based in Milwaukee, by that time. We are negotiating to handle their western division civil litigation. We will, of course, keep you all informed of the progress made regarding this matter, through the normal channels."

Oliver took another deep breath, speaking a beat beyond his need for oxygen. It was an unnerving habit, one that made him seem in the constant throes of some terminal disease.

"I toast you for your good and constant work on behalf of DM&M." Oliver raised his glass, sipped ceremoniously before putting the glass down, then wrapped up the show. "Now I'd like to invite you all into the ballroom, where we will be dining and, for the next few hours, I order you to put any thought of work out of your minds."

Politely, the gathered attorneys put their hands together and clapped, more in homage to Oliver Hedding than in reaction to what he had to say, which wasn't really much, in the final analysis. But it was over, the close-to-the-vest report on the firm they all wanted to call home for the rest of their careers. The applause began to subside and with amazing accuracy, everyone executed steps in the dance of the pecking order.

Oliver remained where he was. Kitty moved up a step or two, almost parallel to her husband, close to becoming his social equal. Lucas Mallory, Don Forrester, and Peter Sweeney were suddenly animated, gravitating toward Oliver. Lucas and Don stopped now and again to make small talk. Their wives hung back. Associates stepped to the side, feeling more comfortable skirting the knot of powerful men that was forming. Partners remained in place, eagerly trying to catch the eye of one senior partner or another.

With the social migration in progress, just as the doors to the dining room were being opened by white-jacketed waiters, Lucas Mallory's wife upstaged them all, blowing the choreography all to hell.

Ruth Mallory was the most affable of all the senior partners or their wives and had been conspicuous by her absence. Tall, dark-haired and perfectly coiffed, she was a lady and a beautiful one at that. Almost ageless in her attractiveness, she preferred linen suits and silk blouses, and she eschewed high heels, opting for low-heeled spectators so she wouldn't tower over her husband. Her smile was gracious, her good words and wishes sincerely offered to any and all. They were accepted as manna from heaven by those employed by DM&M who knew themselves to be used, sometimes abused, and overworked.

So when, with a whoosh, the brass doors of the private elevator that served the concierge suites parted, more than one person grinned at the sight of so familiar and gracious a figure. The timing of her entrance was so uncanny that the laughter and conversation seemed magnified and re-directed toward the woman inside the wood-paneled box.

Yet something wasn't quite right. Ruth Mallory, wife of a senior partner of DM&M, had abandoned decorum and was playing a joke. Why else would she ride the elevator backwards? Laughter, mumbled exclamations, nervous titters ran through the crowd. More than one person admired the cut of her gown, gold and black, skimming hips that looked inviting, hiding legs they all knew to be long and shapely. She stood ever so still, as though waiting for everyone's attention. Dutifully, they fell expectantly silent. Imagination was not a collective strong suit, but curiosity was.

Though later everyone would swear it took more than a few minutes for Ruth to move, in reality no more than thirty seconds passed before she painfully presented herself. That face was as they all remembered: alabaster skin, a mass of short black hair teased into a rich woman's bouffant, arched brows, earlobes glittering with large, tasteful diamonds. Ruth's eyes, invariably bright, were more brilliant than usual. Yet, rather than smiling a greeting, her lips were rounded in an O of surprise, as though amazed to see such a crowd.

In the back of the room, someone laughed—a sharp, nervous bark. Others drew their breath in with hard, quick little gasps. Various reactions to information processed at differing rates, with divergent degrees of acceptance. The joke was an odd one. Many, who could tear their eyes away from Ruth, looked to Lucas hoping he would clue them in. He didn't. He couldn't.

Lucas Mallory stood stock still, staring at his wife. Don Forrester covered his face with his hands. Oliver Hedding moved a step - perhaps it was two - toward the elevator before Peter Sweeney put out a restraining hand just as Ruth Mallory fell through the gleaming doors, staggering, barely able to retain her balance.

The doors of the elevator closed before she had fully cleared them. Those gathered winced en masse as they struck Ruth's foot, bouncing open again with an irritated little pop as brass met bone. The audience empathized. Not for any hurt Ruth sustained because of this, but for the insult, the little pain was to the grave injury now so very evident on her person.

Ruth Mallory held one of her hands to her throat. Through her splayed fingers a raw, crimson welt could be seen. Her other hand, almost obliterated by blood, held tight to her chest in a gesture of mea culpa. Blood poured through her fingers, ran down the front of her gown, spilled onto the hardwood floor in bright, red, nickel-size drops.

Quizzically, Ruth considered her ankle. The doors tried to close again, pulled back, and were about to come at her once more when, with great effort, she managed to move out of harm's way, stumbling into the maze of people, each step an excruciating effort.

Escape from the elevator accomplished, Ruth tipped her hand, monitoring the ebbing of her life. When it lay against her breast again she raised her eyes, letting them light on Oliver Hedding. They rolled back in their sockets before focusing again, this time on Peter Sweeney. Those fragile lids fluttered closed, and then opened, her head bowing as though in prayer just before she caught sight of Don Forrester. It was then Ruth swayed. She swooned. She pulled herself upright and, as everyone watched, Ruth Mallory locked eyes with her husband.

In the stillness, Lucas took a step toward her. Ruth was able to match it. Her lips quivered. She tried to speak, managing only a rattle deep in her chest. Blood trickled from the corner of her mouth. A too-long-delayed scream erupted from a woman in the crowd. Eyes were shut in horror. Heads turned away. Only Ruth Mallory stirred in the freeze-framed room. The hand that clutched her wound cupped deeper. She examined the blood that filled it with a curious detachment, and then slowly, and with utter amazement, Ruth held that hand out to her husband, offering him her life. As their eyes met, a small sound bubbled deep in her throat. It was this sorrowful, pitiful mewling, almost a word, that drove him to action. Lucas Mallory sprung toward his wife howling: "No!"

They never connected. Timing was everything and Ruth was off a beat. She collapsed, sprawling at Lucas's feet, her eyes still locked onto his, her bloodied hand still held out to him. Ruth Mallory was dead.

Chapter 2

"Christl!" Amanda pulled her hand away and Consuelo yanked it back.

"*Madre de Dios! You are loca*, Amanda Cross. Now, stay still or I can' get thees thing off. See! You lose the tips of your fingers if you're not careful. Then how sexy will you be? A fingerless woman. Hah!" Consuelo shook her head, her waist-length hair a bouncing mass of blue-black frizz, her incredibly magenta lips pursed in concentration. Consuelo's eyes were lowered to her task and Amanda could see she'd managed to affix two pairs of lashes that morning. Inky eyeliner cracked on top of the glue strips and one edge was popping up.

Amanda laughed through the pain in her fingertips, "I wasn't shooting for sexy. I just wanted to make a minor improvement in my general appearance."

"Every six months you minor improve somethin', you gringa *loca*. You gonna kill yourself with so many improvements. They're all caca. You never do them right." Consuelo straightened, throwing her hair petulantly over one shoulder to get a better view and a bit more light before attacking Amanda's hand again. "First you go give yourself a permanent…"

Amanda bore the humiliation as best she could. "Okay, that wasn't one of my better efforts. But they wanted eighty bucks to do it at the salon, for Christ's sake. For six bucks I got the same thing in a box at the grocery store. It said No Mistake Formula in big red letters. I couldn't possibly make a mistake."

"You looked like those fuzz balls I find under my couch." Consuelo's comment dripped with disgust. Over went the hair to warm the other shoulder. She applied a cotton ball to Amanda's middle finger, rubbing gently so the smelly liquid could do whatever it was supposed to do. Amanda sat back considering her suite mate. Consuelo had definitely perfected the art of hair throwing. Amanda was as impressed with this as she was with all of Consuelo's affectations.

"Yeow!" Amanda jumped. "Jesus Christ!"

Consuelo ignored her. Triumphantly, the Chicana held up her trophy for Amanda's inspection. The false nail, so distressingly removed, looked utterly, repulsively perfect: pointed, painted, and porcelain-like. Under it, Amanda's real nail had shriveled almost to the point of extinction. She bent over her hand, looking closely at the damage. The operation was a success but the patient had expired. Consuelo slapped the top of Amanda's head. Amanda reared and glared.

"You wear those nails of yours like a badge now to show what an idiot you were. Go to court. Do your fancy talkin'. The judge, he will look at your nails and say, "There is a stupid woman. We won' let her win this case. A woman who can' even keep the most beautiful nails on her hands". What were you doin', Amanda, that you could break off two of these nails? They're like cement."

Consuelo tapped her own formidable extensions on the desktop for emphasis.

Amanda wiped away the residue and held out her hand. Five more to go. "I was trying to patch my driveway if you must know. I didn't think it would matter. The stick I was using to mix the mortar broke, so…"

Consuelo's little tongue clicked so fast, her head bobbed so passionately, Amanda thought she might swallow one and lose the other. "So you stick your hand in the cement to mix it! Dumb broad. Lawyer. Hah! I have more sense and make more money than you and I know how to keep my nails on."

Amanda shrugged. What could she say? The woman was one smart cookie.

Consuelo Hernandez's business, Maid for You, was operated out of the office next door. She and Amanda shared the sixth floor of the old brick building with an accountant, a freelance secretary who did precious little typing for the stream of clients that roamed in and out, and an office maintenance firm that consisted of a man in his eighties and his wife, who was the shy side of thirty.

The deal had seemed pretty attractive to Amanda when she happened upon the rental. Fresh out of the DA's office, she had a savings account that wouldn't buy two months in a high-rise. Here, in the old but clean building, the landlord was willing to provide a receptionist and a reception area to be shared by all. There was a reception area, as per their lease. Unfortunately, he had neglected to supply the promised furniture, making it an uncomfortable place to be received. His idea of a receptionist was the standard message on an answering machine hooked up in the corner of a very bare reception room. When Consuelo moved in she was outraged and demanded that

Amanda sue—class action and all that. Amanda refused the case but kept the friend. Amanda loved a lost cause but this one was beyond hope.

"Hah!" The next nail flipped off Amanda's hand. She felt lighter for it.

"Can you hurry that up?"

"What?" Consuelo drawled. "You got the press waitin' for you? Big case? Maybe somebody goin' to the 'lectric chair without you to defend them?"

"Consuelo," Amanda said with infinite patience, "why do you want me to be something I can't? I swear you're worse than a mother the way you harp on me. I'm perfectly happy doing what I'm doing. I wouldn't want to defend anyone in a capital case."

"I'm not talkin' capital. Money comes later." Amanda almost laughed but decided to wait until her hands were safely out of Consuelo's reach. "I'm talkin' gettin' other kinds of people to defend. Why aren't you tryin' to get big cases, get good clients, like I do? I get big, rich people comin' to me. They say, 'Consuelo, find me someone to clean my house that's honest. Find me a lady to watch my babies.' I do my work good then they pay me big money. But you go down and wait at the court 'till they give you the miserable crooks to defend. You just need to get rich people not those kind can' afford their own lawyer."

Amanda did laugh now. There were only two nails left. She could take anything Consuelo dished out.

"That's not the way things work. You don't hang out a shingle and say, 'I want rich clients'. Good God, there are ten thousand attorneys in Century City alone. Who knows how many downtown? We all want rich clients. I don't think there are as many rich people as there are poor attorneys. Besides, I'm not poor. I'm not downtrodden. I am perfectly happy." Amanda snapped her lids shut and stuck her nose heavenward for emphasis. "I do what I do. I do it well. Believe it or not, I'm actually quite proud of myself."

Consuelo made an appropriate snort of disbelief.

Amanda shook her head. Posturing was useless. "Ah, Consuelo, give me a break. I'm doing okay. I've got a house. I've got some nice clothes. I actually have helped some innocent people. Indigent defense is nothing to be ashamed of. Come on, my friend, say one nice thing. Just one," Amanda cajoled. She grinned. She would have chucked Consuelo under the chin but the other woman would have decked her, even though Amanda was twice her size.

"I won't. You deserve more. You're a nice lady."

"With a nice degree from a second-rate law school that, no matter how well regarded, is still second-rate. Big clients want big diplomas."

"You were a DA," Consuelo insisted.

"Assistant District Attorney who never once had a high-profile case," Amanda reminded her. "And, if it will shut you up, I'll tell you a secret."

Consuelo stopped working. Her orange stick was pressed into Amanda's cuticle, her eyes were narrowed. Knowing she better make it good, Amanda licked her lips, looked up, and stared straight into Consuelo's expectant black eyes.

"I didn't pass the Bar the first time I took it."

Consuelo balked. That secret wasn't worth spit. She worked the orange stick furiously.

"You're crazy, stupid woman. All excuses not to do what you can do. You don' even try."

"Consuelo, I do." Amanda barked a laugh. "What do

I have to do to convince you? I'm forty years old. Short of a miracle, I'm not going to be unmasked as a legal genius. Why can't you just pat me on the head and say 'good job,' when I get people off the hook. How about that little beauty one of your clients had, up on charges for stealing the madam's jewelry? Thought they were going to be shipping her back to Guatemala, didn't you? Without me they would have."

Reluctantly, Consuelo grunted her assent before crying, "Another!" Exultant, she deposited the nail that had once graced Amanda's thumb into the trash can at her feet. "What a waste of good money. Who you want to impress? The judge?"

"Don't be absurd," Amanda scoffed, swiveling her head to look out her one small window. Say what you would about her practice, she was proud of it. Her personal life? That was a sucker punch, she just didn't admit it to Consuelo.

Amanda considered the view. From her chair, she could look into the bank's executive gym across the street. A handsome VP type was running on the treadmill. Nylon shorts, tank top, great pecs, good legs, fabulous…

Her sights were just fine, thank you and they hadn't been set on the judge. That would have been too much to ask. Especially after she went to make a point at sidebar, tapped his desk with her new, plum-painted nails, and watched the one on her index finger lean precariously backwards.

Actually, the object of her interest had been the opposing counsel. But the assistant city attorney had been so appalled that one of her nails could do that, he scurried out of the courtroom without so much as a congratulations after she proved her client couldn't have been the one to run down a bicycle messenger at the corner of Sixth and Figueroa. Through the court interpreter, however, her client had managed to convey that he would like to see her socially. The nails weren't a complete waste but that was the end. No more nails, perms, or diets. Finis.

Amanda Cross wouldn't be trying any more fashion tricks, no siree. Her karma was to be a good Joe, a solid, dependable type. Not beautiful enough to fall for, not ugly enough to pity. Amanda Cross was nice to look at, nice to talk to, and had a nice little law practice. Nice could be pretty miserable but what the hey? Who was she to try and change what was preordained? From here on out it was do your best, get lots of rest, and drink eight glasses of water a day. God must have known what he was doing when he made her, so she might as well stick with the heavenly program.

"Can you hurry it up, Consuelo," Amanda snapped, suddenly itchy to have every last one of those things off her body. To be reminded of her fashion failure was to remember her husband—ex-husband—and the blond bimbo he'd found so alluring. Sure she was a successful realtor. Sure she had boobs that broke records. But where was her mind? Where was her soul? She lacked both, which might explain why she wanted Amanda's husband.

"So sorry, senorita." Consuelo drawled. "If only you'd made an appointment I could've got to you sooner."

"Okay. I appreciate the effort but I've got stuff to do." Amanda apologized stiffly, truly ashamed.

"Like I don'?" Consuelo's dropped Ts made her sound more street vendor than businesswoman. A shrewd woman, young and experienced, she found illegals to act as nanny, housekeeper, or general slave to Westside yuppies. These were the women who taught the next generation of politically correct citizens how to speak Spanish before they uttered their first word of English. The ladies worked for pennies on the dollar, while Consuelo collected a fat fee. That alone should have been enough to make Amanda hate Consuelo. But Amanda was practical. Someone was going to screw both the Westside ladies and the help so it might as well be someone as basically decent as Consuelo. Amanda was full of excuses today.

"I know you're busy but your work you can do from here. I've got to schlep down to the Criminal Courts Building and see if I can do a little pickup. My property taxes are coming due."

Consuelo sat back, her fingers still holding Amanda's lightly. It was a show of friendship that Amanda both recognized and appreciated. What she didn't appreciate was the lecture that followed.

"Amanda, you don' belong here. Look at us. We're a bunch of no-good misfits. You're a good looking' woman." Consuelo held up her hand and waffled it a bit as she gave Amanda the once-over. "Little big in the hips, but pretty, ya know? Nice dark hair. Real shiny. Good dark eyes. If you just did a little more with what you got. Shorten your skirt. I could show you how to tease your hair so it don' fall on one side like when you do it. You gotta make an impression, Amanda, if you're goin' to get along. Be sort of dramatic, you know, like me. In my business I make an impression…"

Amanda eyed her friend's cherry-colored dress, a size too small so the buttons pulled across her chest, her hips, her everything. Consuelo stood up to give Amanda an eyeful. Her stockings were sheer and black, her shoes stiletto heeled. No doubt about it, Consuelo made an impression. Consuelo ran her hand lovingly down the side of her body.

"Now, I don' say you can look like me. But you're a lawyer, you can' be *too* sexy. But hey, go get pretty. Find a lawyer man to open up shop with. It's no good, a woman all by herself. Take it from me. I know. You gotta have a man, otherwise, nobody takes you all that serious…"

Thankfully, before the lesson could continue, the phone rang. Deciding not to point out that Consuelo had never had a business partner—male or female—and she did just fine, Amanda dived for the phone, disengaging herself easily. Unperturbed, her friend shimmied back onto her chair, rearranged her rather substantial chest under her red, red dress, and checked her lipstick in the mirror on the desk while Amanda answered:

"Cross legal offices. Amanda Cross speaking."

Consuelo smiled at herself, turning her head to get the best light. Amanda was wasted here in the heart of downtown. She answered the call like she was meant to be—someone. With a quick glance, Consuelo offered Amanda a heartening smile, hoping the caller was telling her good news. Consuelo didn't need a second look to know something was up. She stopped her preening, tongue freezing mid-lick on her lower lip. Amanda's face was white and the hand holding the receiver was trembling. This wasn't good.

Consuelo propped her chin on her upturned palms, waiting, watching. But there wasn't anything else to hear. The conversation was over before it began. Amanda hadn't breathed a word, just sat in her chair like somebody had knocked her wind out.

"Amanda?" Consuelo ventured, daring to touch the hand that still held the receiver.

Amanda blinked as though surprised to find she wasn't alone.

"Consuelo," she whispered. "I'm sorry… my sister…"

That was all she managed to say before she grabbed her briefcase and half stumbled out the door. Consuelo carefully replaced the receiver that now dangled off the desk, turned off the light, and locked Amanda's office. Obviously, it was just one of those things. She couldn't wait to find out which one of those things it was.

~ ~ ~

Kitty Hedding wore a hat. She had chosen to do so in deference to Ruth who had loved hats but felt odd wearing them in Los Angeles. Ruth would have adored this one with its wide brim and short crown, a huge navy satin bow punctuating the black straw. It was almost too big, too much. Ruth would have thought it perfect. Few people understood Ruth's penchant for drama. What a pity she had just begun to indulge it before…

Kitty sighed, knowing Ruth would never have been flagrantly flamboyant. She was, after all, the wife of a very powerful man, wasn't she? An important man. Women gave up things for men like that. All the DM&M wives understood that. So the suppression of Ruth's theatrical bent in deference to Lucas's position was not to be mourned, rather, it was simply something to be remembered.

The final moments of Ruth's time on earth, however, would have made up for every time she bit her tongue against a witty remark or decided on dinner for eight rather than a balloon ride for twenty. Her own death and the pandemonium that followed would have delighted Ruth Mallory. Kitty almost laughed thinking of it. One hundred and seventy-five lawyers all highly educated and irreproachably intelligent, hadn't had the foggiest idea of what to do for a dying woman. Eventually, a waiter took matters into his own hands. He phoned for help, asking for an ambulance in broken English just before a pompous associate brushed him aside to summon the police and the hotel cleaning crew, in that order. The cleaning crew had arrived first, the police soon thereafter. The maids had to wait, of course, until the police completed their investigation, which was done with surprising nonchalance, to the dismay of the hotel management.

It wasn't until late that evening after it was determined there was no trace evidence to be found in the reception room, that it was cleaned. Photos had been taken, blood collected but that was about it downstairs. The cleaning crew had then worked backwards, following the police from the ballroom, to the reception room, to the elevator, where they were unceremoniously stopped. A Beverly Hills horror—real life sticking out like a sore thumb in the city's well-honed fantasy. The hotel would not be allowed to clean the elevator, the hall, or the suite in which Ruth Mallory had been attacked. In a day or two, perhaps, the crime scene tape would come down and rugs could be taken up. In the meantime, the maids were dismissed. What could be done had been done. It was time to vacate the premises.

One by one, the ineffectual, frightened attorneys were sent home. The police left feeling quite pleased, sure the case would be locked up in record time, given what they'd found. The coroner's pathologist and technicians were hard at work, called in the middle of the night because of the victim's social status. Lucas Mallory, declining any assistance, seemed in a state of shock. No one was sure when he left or if he did. The last anyone had seen of him, he was sitting in the middle of the murder scene holding Ruth's handbag, staring at a large, now dried patch of blood that a few of the cops thought looked like Bullwinkle.

Kitty shivered and blinked, almost surprised to find herself standing beside Ruth's casket, when three days ago she'd been hurrying a hysterical Min and a shocked Peg out of a hotel reception room. After that, Kitty had done the only thing she could. She'd left Oliver to do whatever it was men did in such a situation and did what any woman would: she went home quietly and mourned Ruth profoundly, her grief as deep as the wounds that had killed her friend. It was then, between the tears and the sighs and the long stretches of contemplative silences, that Kitty found Ruth's message on her answering machine. Over and over again, locked in the privacy of her bedroom, Kitty listened to the tape. When she'd heard enough, when she'd considered and negated the unthinkable, Kitty changed the tape. No one save for her would ever hear it, though she doubted it would matter even if they did.

Hours before her death, Ruth Mallory's world had looked so rosy. She and Kitty should have been laughing about that message, gossiping in whispers, making plans for the future like two expectant schoolgirls. What a pity. Now Ruth was dead. Soon she would be buried. The rest of them would go on, more sadly than ever, together. Indeed, they had done just that—calling each other back and forth, passing along news of the funeral arrangements and, of course, the latest information from the police until they had ended up here, at grave side.

To Kitty's left, Peg Sweeney stood rigid, her back straight, her muscles twitching as though inactivity pained her. Black didn't suit Peg half as well as tennis whites. Min Forrester, not a blond hair out of place, was to Kitty's right. She had swathed her lovely little body in a tasteful gray sheath, draped a black-and-gray scarf over one shoulder, and now stood stoically looking at the open grave. Beside Min was her daughter Marissa, teenaged and less sorrowed than intrigued that something so wicked could happen within the parameters of her parents' very dull lives.

The four men, the senior partners, were grouped as always —Oliver somehow in the center of a cluster that should not have had one. Peter was in his protective stance beside Oliver, just to the left of the old man. Every once in a while Peter would look up, scan the mourners and nod knowingly to the detective who, it was assumed, was there to watch for something sinister. Lucas, slightly forward near the grave, was to Oliver's right. His hands were clasped in front of him, his body intermittently jolted by almost imperceptible tremors. Don Forrester, a head taller than any of them, looking like an ill-favored son, stood, round-shouldered, just behind Oliver. To everyone's amazement, he was crying.

The DM&M higher-ups were by far the most interesting folks to watch but the mourners were far more diverse than that. Scattered about were various friends and acquaintances of Ruth and Lucas Mallory. The U.S. attorney was in attendance, as was the Los Angeles District Attorney. The U.S. attorney appeared properly somber. Leo Riordon, the DA, looked positively disrespectful. His silver hair had been well tended to and he raised his broad, fleshy face at such an angle he looked like a stylist's mannequin. He constantly shifted his considerable weight, tugging his very expensive suit into place, flashing the pinky ring that sported a perfect star sapphire. Thankfully, Leo's wife was stunningly successful otherwise the esteemed district attorney's ethics might be called into question, given his expensive tastes and county paycheck.

The women of the Junior League had turned out in force

for the memorial service only to dwindle at graveside. They would, more than likely, show up once more at the Lucas's home for tea and buffet, their makeup repaired, their spirits lifted. The Mallory's housekeeper kept her distance from the illustrious crowd and impressed no one by crying quietly into a rather large handkerchief. More than likely, other than Kitty Hedding's, hers were the most heartfelt tears shed that day.

Of note by their absence were the employees of DM&M, save for Edward Ramsey. Never a favorite of Kitty's, he was always on hand lately attempting to ingratiate himself. Oliver seemed not to mind, and that, in and of itself, was akin to being deemed indispensable. Perhaps, Kitty surmised, under the rather slick surface of Edward Ramsey, there actually lurked a legal mind of incredible proportions. If there didn't, Kitty would have to rethink Oliver's sanity. The rest, all one hundred seventy-four associates and partners, remained at work. This was not, after all, a national holiday but a moment of very private mourning and none grieved more deeply or sincerely than the partners' wives.

A sad little group, theirs. Women who had had the same hopes and dreams as their husbands, only to find that fulfillment was a men-only affair, leaving the women to cling to one another as they became not helpmates but image keepers.

Kitty lowered her head. How she had loved Ruth, the woman of courage in their tennis playing, grousing, disillusioned little group of women past their prime. Kitty mourned as the minister uttered the last, lying words of comfort. She no more believed Ruth was happy in heaven than she believed Oliver would come and take her in his arms and console her. That part of their marriage had ended long ago. How sad that the one small thing she needed was the last thing on this earth he could give her—or even imagine offering her.

Looking up, Kitty considered the men from behind her dark glasses, her face safely shadowed by the brim of her hat. The service was over and, as if they had been given permission to continue an interrupted discussion, they were talking. Peter's hand was on Lucas's shoulder. It seemed he was delivering command coordinates rather than words of comfort. Lucas appeared unimpressed. Oliver kept his distance. Just as well, there would be no solace in his touch. Don hovered, his face ashen, his neutral eyes red-rimmed. Lucas raised his head, murmured, his lips barely moving, and they all seemed intent on listening to this suffering man beside the open grave beside the bright white casket.

"I can't believe this—" Lucas's voice was low, monotone. His pale skin had turned the color of wet concrete. He looked as if he hadn't slept in the three days since the murder.

"None of us can. I don't think in our wildest imaginations we could have foresee—" Don interrupted.

"Don." Oliver stopped him with a look and a patronizing warning. Don had heard it so often before, he was immediately silent, deferring to Oliver. "It will be difficult, Lucas. Very difficult indeed. The memories of Ruth won't soon leave you. But you must try to escape them. Memories are nothing more than the workings of a mind not active enough. Concentrate on what is good for all of us, Lucas, as you have done for so many years. You'll see that I'm speaking the truth."

"But…" Lucas began to object, leaning into the men, seeking their counsel and reassurance. It was evident they had no more to give.

Peter glared. Lucas hadn't responded to his initial words of comfort or final call to brotherhood. He would have expected Lucas to be more pragmatic, less pitiable.

Oliver, quite simply, had nothing else to say. He had spoken and that should be the end of it.

Don resisted the urge to speak, knowing he could offer nothing of consequence and might prove himself even weaker than Peter and Oliver believed him to be.

Lucas looked at them all, his eyes charged with pain. But before Lucas could say another word, Min Forrester was on him, her tiny hands touching his arm, turning him into her. She hugged him gently.

"I'm so sorry, Lucas," she whispered before relinquishing her hold to Peg Sweeney, who grasped him in lean, muscular arms. Forever the outsider, Peg gave him a swift embrace then turned him to Kitty, who took both of his hands in hers.

"Lucas. If there is anything…"

"Thank you, Kitty. All of you." Eyes downcast, his body stiffened against the affection. Kitty accepted this. Lucas was not a man to show his emotions, assuming he possessed any. She only considered how deep his hurt must be and her own heart broke because she was sure it matched hers. She smiled gently.

"It's nothing for us to say how sorry we are Lucas. Don't be a stranger. Let us be your true friends. Don't hide now and grieve alone."

Lucas shook his head, "No, of course not," he murmured uncomfortable in her compassionate hold. He looked up, beyond the prying eyes of the women. "I think we should be going. The caterers are at the house. People will be arriving."

"Of course," Kitty acquiesced. She fell in line with Min and Peg. The men converged in front of them and walked on ahead, across the impeccably trimmed grass, their impeccably trim wives following, skirting the grave markers as they made for the waiting limousines. They were almost across when Min commented quietly, conspiratorially, "I still can't believe it."

"Neither can I. The whole thing is so outrageous." Peg spoke. Kitty thought it sounded as though she were forcing the words through clenched teeth. "What about her? The one who killed Ruth? What a waste. What an idiot. You know, Peter says she was brilliant. He also says it could have been any of us. It really could have been. She must have been crazy. What was her name?"

Kitty was about to point out that if Peg showed more interest in her husband's business she would know not only the name of the woman in question, she would know everything about her. But they had come to the limousines and there wasn't time to answer. None of their husbands wanted to be reminded of that woman.

Expertly, noiselessly, the three women settled themselves in the deep leather seats. There would be plenty of time to talk later, to speculate, and to meditate when they were alone. The heavy car doors closed, trapping them together behind the smoked glass. The moment the car began to move, the name Peg was searching for reverberated in her head with amazing clarity. She looked at Kitty, at Min, and knew that they, too, were thinking about the woman who murdered their friend. Peg shivered, wishing she could forget that name now that it was remembered.

Chapter 3

"Nora Royce. I'm her attorney, Amanda Cross."

"Over there."

The officer behind the grate lifted her chin, indicating a row of molded plastic chairs tied to one wall of the visitors' reception area. Amanda turned on her heel and headed right for them. She gratefully sank onto the orange one nearest the door. Swinging her briefcase onto her lap she wondered why she'd even brought it. She didn't need the police report from the Bergman petty theft trial, or the doctor's report on Mrs. Joseph, whose son beat her to a pulp one night because she didn't move fast enough to turn the television channels for him, or that Twinkie for those long days in court when her blood sugar took a dive, or breath mints or paper clips. All this stuff was useless as she sat in a prison in the middle of East L.A. waiting to see her sister.

Shit, when she'd heard Nora's voice, Amanda thought she had died and gone to heaven. It wasn't even Christmas and her sister was actually calling to chat. Chat! Dumb.

It took Amanda a couple of minutes to understand that

this was serious. Nora was at Sybil Brand Correctional Facility. No, no, she was *in* it. Nora had been arrested and charged with… what?

"Amanda Cross?"

The deputy, a huge woman who wore her holster like a baby on her hip, momentarily loomed in the doorway. Amanda stood instantly, pursed her lips, and exhaled. Out with the bad air, in with the good, and she'd be able to stop the fluttering in her heart. Christ, Nora had been arrested and she'd called Amanda for help. Hell!

Amanda managed to walk with some semblance of dignity toward the deputy, who turned and led her through another door and into a fishbowl of a room. The place was sparsely decorated, gray Formica partitioned tables, tiny round stools that swiveled like the ones at a soda shop but were never big enough for a normal behind. This was where attorneys met with their clients—usually. But nobody was there and Amanda wasn't staying. She was taken to the relative privacy of a room with a door, three walls that were made partially of glass. The other wall was concrete.

Amanda nodded to the deputy's back and then scoped the place. It was small, almost filled with a metal desk, two chairs. Amanda took the one that faced the door. She sat. She stood. Claustrophobia came to mind, paranoia was a close second. She was being observed through a double wall of glass—hers and the one that enclosed the deputy's office. Insulting. Intolerable. Inevitable in this place. Amanda actually wrung her hands until she realized what she was doing and stopped in disgust.

The minutes stretched toward infinity before snapping back into perspective. She thought of going to the bathroom just to assure herself she hadn't been forgotten and locked away. It was then, just as panic and worry were about to run away with her, that the door opened again. Amanda had just enough time to notice that this was not the same deputy who had ushered her in before Nora entered and Amanda's breath was taken away.

Even in the shapeless blue cotton shift, standard Sybil Brand issue, Nora was something to see. She was a fine example of nature at its peak of perfection. God had practiced creation with Amanda and gotten it right with Nora. Both had that long straight Royce nose. Amanda's tipped down just a bit, Nora's flared exotically. There was a likeness about the eyes, the way they dipped down at the outside corner, their lashes strung out from the inside in a perfect, graduated wave of lush sable. Around Amanda's, though, was a fan of fine lines; Nora's were deep set and surrounded by smooth, ivory skin. Amanda's face was square and broad; Nora's had been lengthened to allow for a sweep of perfectly defined, exquisitely proportioned cheekbones. Amanda's hair was dark brown, thick and straight, perfectly suited to bangs and a bob. Nora's swept dramatically away from her high forehead in fine strands of chestnut shot with gold. It hung past her shoulders and was usually caught in a loose chignon, making it seem as though she'd just awakened from sleep or emerged from a sudden and satisfying bout of lovemaking. It was all so natural, her beauty, so unstudied and unassisted. Amanda could have dealt with that if that's all there was to Nora.

Amanda, after all, had had her moment in the sun. When she was Nora's age, she'd looked pretty good. Not as good but no dog, either. What bothered Amanda about her sister was Nora's damned luck. Twenty-six, for God's sake, and everything had fallen into place: the best college, the best law school, *Law Review*, a clerkship with the California

Supreme Court, Dimsdale, and Morris & Mott. Lordy! Lordy! Shit. And Nora just accepted all this as if it were her due. Identifying her unreasonable twinge of jealousy, Amanda had to admit that maybe it *was* Nora's due.

Perhaps, in the twelve years it took their mother to conceive again the genetic recipe that produced Amanda had changed. Better food, more rest, more leisure, more bucks. Their parents had been a lot better off in '67 than they had been in '55. It must have been the vitamins, color television radiation, fluoride—something thoroughly modern had made Nora pop out of the womb perfect, while Amanda had fought her way out, perfectly normal.

Now they stood face to face and Amanda was ashamed to find herself searching Nora's beautiful countenance for some sign that this perfection was marred. God forgive her, she wanted to be better just once, even at the expense of Nora's distress.

"Amanda. Thank you for coming."

Nora dismissed the deputy like she would a servant. It was so subtle only Amanda seemed to notice. The uniformed woman gently closed the windowed door behind her as she left without a hint that she'd noticed the affront. Amanda shifted uncomfortably on her feet; Nora took a chair pretty as you please. Amanda followed suit and the two sisters faced each other as strangers.

Since their parents' deaths, they hadn't spent more than a snap of time together. Nora's annual Christmas jaunt to the Caribbean cut into seasonal sentimentality. Amanda didn't actually mind exchanging Christmas cards with a jotted note of all the news they had in common. It kept Amanda's self-esteem intact, along with the illusion that she and Nora had a wonderful relationship despite their disparate schedules, their unequal lives.

Given the circumstances of this meeting, however, Amanda had expected a more emotional greeting, a tad less arrogance, a momentary bout of hysteria expressed in a quick, yet highly communicative, hug. Obviously, this was not to be one of those Waltonesque moments of glory. Amanda dispensed with the greetings and got down to it.

"What in the hell is going on?"

Christ. She sounded more like the fat kid at a cheerleader's slumber party than a concerned sibling. Regroup. Amanda leaned back, affecting a posture of professional interest before she embarrassed herself further.

"It's ridiculous," Nora answered in that Bacallish voice of hers, doing something with her fingers, a sort of disdainful flicking away of the obvious import of her situation.

"Can't be all that ridiculous if they put us in this room. Only high-profile cases in here, Nora." Amanda looked at the scarred wall behind her sister's back, the one without a door or window and wondered how anyone ever managed the graffiti, given the guards and glass. "You don't book into Sybil Brand on a maybe." Amanda laughed, briefly, a frightened little sound made even more pathetic because there was hope in it. She talked because Nora wasn't.

"You know, after you called I just ran out of the office without thinking. But on the freeway I had the crazy idea you might be involved in that murder. The partner's wife? I thought that might be it." Amanda's fingers drummed on the metal desk. "Stupid, huh? To think you would be mixed up in that."

The ensuing quiet was Nora-driven, cool and full of things Amanda couldn't begin to fathom. At her leisure, Nora answered.

"Not stupid at all." Nora's hazel eyes were stony and focused steadily on Amanda. There wasn't a flicker of interest, or fear, or anything else in them.

Amanda chalked that calculating perusal down to shock and waited for the gory details. They were worse than expected.

"Her name was Ruth Mallory. She was murdered at the partners' retreat at the Regency Hotel. It made front page the day after it happened but the follow-up was minimal."

Amanda nodded as though she'd followed the story with intense interest. Far be it from her to inform a woman who read *Fortune* for pleasure that she barely managed "Dear Abby" and the comics in the morning. The paper depressed her and, considering her practice, she didn't need to feel any worse about the world than she already did.

Nora half smiled waiting until Amanda was nodded out. "She was stabbed." Nora leaned forward, closing the space between them ever so slightly, her hands splayed out on the table as though to prove there was no blood on them. "Actually, she was strangled, then stabbed." Hands down, they slid off the table, onto her lap.

Amanda could see the soft, shapeless jail slippers on Nora's long, slim feet. They should have made Nora appear vulnerable. They didn't.

"The authorities assume her attacker left her for dead in her suite but she managed to stagger down to the black-tie reception before she died. I hear she basically fell out of the elevator and made a valiant attempt to reach her husband before collapsing."

"You weren't there?"

Amanda finally managed an intelligent question. Reaching down, she flipped her briefcase open and was rewarded with the sight of a legal pad. It was on the table ready for notes a second later as her sister recited, her voice low, intimate, and not altogether inviting:

"No. I was on one of the patios off the ballroom. I'd been at the reception earlier." She paused, then added, "Actually, only a few minutes earlier."

"How long?"

"Ten minutes. Maybe fifteen." Nora paused before adding. "I didn't want to stay for dinner."

Amanda missed the verbal stumble, the guilty inflection. She didn't ask the right question.

"Any blood or hair or anything on you to indicate you were close to this woman at the time of her death?"

Nora shook her head. "Not a thing on me. There couldn't be." A beat. "I didn't do it."

Amanda ignored the last. She didn't think Nora was guilty, she simply knew there was more.

"Come on. Nora. The police don't just arrest the person with the most fabulous boobs."

"You're right, of course." Nora looked about and spotted the deputy. Her eyes flared a deep gold, the color of dying sunflowers. Her angry gaze snapped back to Amanda. "Do you have a cigarette?"

Amanda shook her head, "I quit a while back."

"Congratulations." Nora's voice was hollow.

"When did you start?" Amanda had the horrible urge to turn this into a reunion. Nora quelled it.

"I haven't, since you didn't bring any."

Amanda's blood boiled. Games. She hated them. Little nasty Nora things that made Amanda feel so stupid.

"As I was saying, the cops don't arrest people for the fun of it. What've they got on you?"

"Ruth Mallory was strangled with a scarf," Nora said slowly, distinctly, as if she were dictating to a person of diminished capacity. "The scarf was found stuffed in a potted plant outside my room."

"Oh, for God's sake!" Amanda laughed, relieved that it was only a scarf outside a room. It was so lame it would have been ludicrous if Nora weren't sitting in front of her dressed in a lousy shade of outlaw indigo.

"It was my scarf," Nora said quietly. Amanda's laughter faded. The muscles in Nora's jaw tightened. "I should say it appears to be my scarf, since mine was missing. That scarf was a trademark with me, you know."

"I wouldn't know." Amanda muttered but the complaint fell on deaf ears. Obviously, Nora was not needy enough of sibling intimacy to be receptive to subtle prodding.

"There was also the matter of my blood in the deceased's room, my fingerprints on the murder weapon, hair that I readily admit is mine found in the bedroom and sitting area of the suite."

That was it. Nora looked down, silently waiting for Amanda to process the information. An annoying little habit she'd had since childhood that made Amanda feel backward. She stood up, warding off the inevitable anger that came with the aggravation.

"You lied to me?" Amanda had the tacky urge to poke Nora on the shoulder and invite her into an alley.

"I didn't lie to you." Nora was kind. She was patient. She pissed Amanda off to no end when she said, "You asked me if they found any evidence *on me* to indicate I'd been near the woman. There was nothing on me. Not my dress, not my shoes, my fingernails-"

"Forget it!" Amanda waved her hands at shoulder height as though she might wave away the harsh, impatient sound of those words. More quietly now, she said, "I'm sorry. I wasn't exact. Sounds like they've got a bit, Nora." Amanda walked the few steps toward the corner where plaster wall met chicken-wired glass. She thought of the outside. A day that wasn't pretty. Neither bright nor gloomy. A no-color day. Better to see that than nothing at all. Amanda turned and leaned against the wall. "I'd think you did it, too if I were them but I'm assuming you have a reason for all of this. It's easily explained, I'm sure. The blood, the hair?"

"They say I was in his room because I was obsessed with Lucas Mallory. Someone told the authorities I'd been pulling a fatal attraction." Nora had done Amanda the courtesy of swiveling to face her but she had an odd way of avoiding Amanda's eyes. "The assumption is the obsession got out of hand when Ruth Mallory surprised me in their suite. She didn't. I had no such unhealthy attraction to Lucas Mallory, therefore I had no reason to want his wife dead."

Amanda was impressed. Nora sounded neither guilty nor frightened. Rather, she seemed simply inconvenienced. Such confidence. Such stupidity.

"Nora, come on, these people aren't idiots," Amanda objected trying not to think the unthinkable. But there it was. Young, privileged, arrogant. Why wouldn't Nora assume she could and have everything, including another woman's husband?

Thoughtfully, Amanda walked back to her chair. Movement did nothing to ease the tightness in her muscles but it gave her time to think. If Nora was guilty, Amanda would stand by her no matter what. Problem: she didn't have the foggiest idea how to say this to a woman who'd been six years old when Amanda left for college. Amanda knew her dry cleaner better than she did her own sister.

"I was not obsessed with Lucas Mallory," Nora said.

Amanda tried to resettle herself, unable to keep still, astonished at Nora's composure. Since their parents' deaths, their lives had seldom overlapped. Now that they infringed, the initial going was rough. Amanda tried a small smile of encouragement.

"Okay. I believe you. But that's not the whole truth. If you're protecting someone else, just tell me, so we can figure out how to beat this—together." Amanda cleared her throat, uncomfortable with even that degree of affection. "I am here to help, you know."

Nora's eyes narrowed, hazel slashes in an ivory face that scrutinized Amanda, assessing her worth. She looked Amanda in the eye. "I was sleeping with him. An affair, not a love match. I didn't want Lucas Mallory to leave his wife."

Nora's brief, informative speech had the ring of a little girl's protest. *I did it and it was fun and I'm not going to apologize.* To Amanda, Nora seemed very young indeed. In the heartbeat of silence that followed, Amanda formulated the kicker question:

"And what does Lucas Mallory say?"

With that Nora lost a little bit of everything: confidence, beauty, optimism. For Nora that was no great loss.

"Lucas hasn't said anything, as far as I know. That night—when his wife was killed—wasn't the time to approach him. After that everything happened rather quickly."

Nora shrugged and Amanda found this a strangely vulnerable gesture. Perhaps Nora was actually hurt by her lover's betrayal, for there was nothing else to call it. Lucas Mallory, first to be informed of the arrest, should have been the first to protest. Shouldn't he?

"Cute," Amanda muttered. Then, more directly, "Can you expect him to say anything?"

Nora raised a brow as if to say it didn't matter. Amanda knew it mattered a hell of a lot. A case was a case no matter who the defendant was—Nora Royce, beautiful young attorney or Jose Paniagua, head of a family of nine accused of murdering his wife. When it came to Lucas Mallory's word against hers, Nora's case wouldn't be easily defended, given what the cops had found in that room.

"Okay, what do you need me to do? Has bail been set? Can you make it? If you can't, I know a few people." Amanda kept going, leaving the offer hanging. Both of them knew it was hollow. "I can do leg work. I'll talk to Lucas Mallory on a personal level and try to figure out why he's not confirming your affair. If they're using obsession as motive, then he can nip that one in the bud right now. Sometimes it's better when a family member does these things anyway; he might open up and tell me what the problem is. I wouldn't dream of doing anything until I talk with your attorney, though." Amanda's laugh was self-deprecating. I understand I can't just go bombing around as your sister and not expect to impact his case. What's his number?"

"It's not a he, Amanda." Nora sighed. Amanda had that feeling again, the one she used to get when she went home and saw Nora so pretty and perfect, protected in the sheltering womb of their parents' much-changed home. It was a feeling of…the only word was contempt. As if Amanda could never measure up.

"A woman. That might be good."

"Whether it's good or not isn't the question," Nora murmured. "Unfortunately, I seem to be persona non grata in the legal community. It appears that I've offended their sensibilities. I'm an associate who screwed around—literally and figuratively—with the powers that be. Nobody wants to offend anyone at DM&M by being party to my defense. There are a few midsize firms willing to talk, with a hefty retainer up front. Even then, they're worried. If anyone believes me—believes I was sleeping with Lucas—that might mean he had a reason to murder his wife, too." Nora gave Amanda a moment to catch up. "Who on earth," Nora asked wryly, "would want to offend the president of the Los Angeles Bar? Midsize firms? Sole practitioners? Major players? They're scared and I'm an outcast."

Nora waved a hand in the air, a general gesture of amazement at the inane situation in which she found herself.

"So much easier to assume I was stalking Lucas than to imagine he and I were actually consenting adults pursuing a pleasurable relationship. So much more dramatic and realistic to believe that I lost my mind instead of Lucas or a bellboy or one of a hundred people who could have had access to that room."

"Do you think he did?"

Nora laughed, short and hard. She'd been banished by an entire industry in support of someone with more power, more history and a man. Rejection. This was a first for her.

"Hardly. He's a brilliant lawyer. A good lover. Highly physical without being dominant. But murder? I can't imagine Lucas getting his hands that dirty."

"So they've thrown you to the wolves because it's expedient?" Amanda rested her chin on her upturned palm. If it had been anyone else but Nora, Amanda would have asked for popcorn. The show was really getting good.

"That and the small problem of a great deal of circumstantial evidence. The DA isn't going to have to work terribly hard to prove opportunity." Amanda's spine stiffened at Nora's tolerant prompt. "Anyway, it seems I have very little choice regarding representation. I know next to nothing about criminal law but common sense tells me I should trust my attorney. Someone who stands outside the mainstream would be the ideal." Nora hesitated, her tiny tongue peeking out from between her lips as if there were some obvious thought on the tip of it waiting to be expressed. Behind her eyes, there was a light of indecision that faded quickly from necessity. "I can trust you, Amanda. I think it would be wisest if you represented me." She finished grandly albeit reluctantly. "I need you.

Stunned, Amanda stared at her sister. Nora didn't flinch. Nor did she laugh. The silence scared the hee-bie-jeebies out of Amanda. She stood up and pushed her chair away, petrified.

"Un-un. Nope. No way. That's ludicrous. I can't do this. Nope." She walked to the end of the table, trying to distance herself, though there was precious little space in which to do it, put her hand to her head, and pushed back her bangs.

"No, Nora. I'll help you some other way but not that. I can't be responsible for... this... your life. For God's sake! For close to fifteen years, I've been defending people who fall through the cracks. I know indigent defense like the back of my hand. I'm like a cement patch, fine in a light rain but watch out when it storms. I'd never hold up. And this! This is a goddamn typhoon. You're my sister. You're..." Her hands were going in circles as if that would describe Nora Royce, the indescribable,

"Money isn't a problem if that's what you're worried about."

Nora cocked her head a centimeter to the left, neither amused nor moved by Amanda's speech.

That was when Amanda lost it, unaware that it had been building up for years. All her self-serving, ineffectual motion ceased, and, in the sterile silence, Amanda went cold. Colder. Coldest.

"Damn you. Damn you, Nora. Shit."

She shot across the room in three great strides, landing in the corner as far away from the table as she could get. Whirling, Amanda planted her back against the graffitied wall, her mouth open, funny little puffs of breath pushing through her lips, huffing the way people do in a vain attempt to quell their nausea and its inevitable results.

"Nora, you are a piece of work. I can't believe you even said that to me." Amanda looked heavenward, studied the ceiling and talked to it because there was no talking to Nora. "I'm trying to tell you I'm terrified I'll screw up. I'm trying to clue you in that I'm just not good enough. All the while I'm feeling proud somewhere inside me because you thought I was good enough and that you could trust me with your life. Jesus, Nora, your life!" Her eyes were back down, riveted on her sister. Lord, even in jail, with not a ray of sunshine around to do its thing, Nora's hair glistened gold. "I'm trying to really talk to you for the first time in our incredibly separate lives and you're patting me on the head and stuffing money in my pockets like that's what all this boils down to. Like the only thing I care about is getting a fee. Come on."

Amanda was moving again. On her way to the north corner, she slammed the wall with the side of her fist.

"You know, Nora, I've always wondered who in the hell you think you are. For years I'd stop home, see Mom and Dad, hear about your latest accomplishments, sit down in the kitchen figuring you'd sit right down with the rest of us and shoot the breeze. But what did I get? That cool thing you do. You know, the eyes, the lips, the one-word answers. Like you're thinking something about me I don't want to know. Like you're pitying me. Well, let me tell you, there just isn't one thing to pity here. Not one damn thing."

"I never pitied you," Nora objected blandly.

"Okay, then you looked down on me. Nothing ever touched you. All the right words—thank yous and pleases—but no feeling. There was nothing to make me feel as if I was a part of you or even equal to you. Well, I'm damned glad to know exactly where I stand. Thank God I'm inferior, if that means being alive and making mistakes and every once in a while doing something right. You know, I've been out there running a damn good race while you've been waiting at the finishing line. Where's the satisfaction in that, Nora? Don't you think that's just so sad? No wonder everyone's turned against you. You never give them reason to be loyal to you. You never even give anyone reason to like you. Christ!" Amanda would have stomped her feet if she could have gotten away with it. "You just expect, expect, expect. Well, baby, you got and got and got. Now life's trying to teach you a little lesson. You can't buy the kind of help I was willing to give you. You can't—"

Amanda slapped the cold concrete wall with her open palms for emphasis. She closed her eyes against the arcing flashes of anger, pain, and humiliation that coursed through her. She wanted to cry and she'd be damned if she would. She heard the scraping of Nora's chair on the cold floor. If her sister dared to reach out, Amanda knew she would crumble. Opening her eyes, Amanda saw there was no need to worry. Nora, in her imperturbable way, was wearily disgusted, but not shamed.

"Lord above, you're funny, Amanda. Carrying around all this anger for so many years. If you feel shortchanged,

I'm sorry, but I wasn't the one who was at the till. I didn't take anything that belonged to you."

"Right."

"I didn't, for goodness sake. What do you want me to say? That I'm sorry you weren't the one working for Dimsdale? Okay, I'm sorry."

Nora's physical attitude wasn't enhanced by the apology. She was open to anything, affected by nothing. What a study in body language! Amanda had crossed her arms as if to protect her heart, Nora spread hers widely across the back of the chair, daring Amanda to take her best shot.

"That's not what I mean," Amanda said.

"Then what? Are you angry because I happened to be born when Mom and Dad could provide more? Or are you just mad because I was born?" Amanda's eyes were pinpoints of glinting darkness, narrowed, as if that could warn Nora off, explain that her stubborn silence was dangerous. Unaffected, unafraid, Nora wielded her words like a surgeon's scalpel cutting deep. "The only reason you're pissed, to use one of your favorite expressions, is that you're jealous."

"Like hell," Amanda snapped, outraged.

Nora blazed back with perfect timing, "Amanda, you wear blinders the way other people put on their clothes. The world is what Amanda can see in her line of vision and that's that. In and out of our lives you went: 'everything's dandy, haven't really got a whole lot of time for you. Don't worry, everything's fine.' That's the way you made things seem when you came home. Job is great, marriage is great, life is great.

"We were so stupid. I was so stupid! I thought you were sharing this big, wonderful world you lived in with us. Do you have a clue what that sounded like to a twelve-year-old kid? My sister the DA! My sister the attorney! My sister, married to that handsome guy! You made it seem so good. But you weren't really sharing anything with us, you were just telling us what you wanted us to hear. Everything was lousy for you, even back then. You didn't want us to help; you didn't even want us to know that you messed up. Now you're telling me I've failed you because I don't recognize your most sincere emotions? That's so rich, Amanda."

Nora finally became involved in the conversation, seeing the past, and Amanda was time traveling with her.

"Do you know I had to stay in my room while Mom and Dad tried to figure out how to help you? They never wanted you to know they were worried. Heaven forbid they should inadvertently humiliate you." Nora shook her head. Whatever disappointment she'd felt in her relationship with Amanda had long since ceased to exist.

"They were always talking about how smart you were, how pretty you were, what a good heart you had and how many hard knocks you'd taken. Impressive how you got back up and kept going. God, Dad was proud of you! They both worried about you. But me? Not a whole lot of worrying going on there. I was okay. It was always 'Oh, Nora, she'll be all right. Never a problem.'"

Nora allowed herself a conclusive sigh.

"Well, Amanda, they were right. I never was a problem. But that doesn't mean I wouldn't have liked to have been asked how I was, how I felt, whether or not I was happy. Just once I would have liked Mom and Dad to worry about me. I would have liked to lie in bed and hear that I was the topic of discussion instead of you. Or maybe you could have walked into my room and sat down. Maybe you could have asked me about—whatever."

Nora's fingers curled into her palm and lay loosely

there. A regal figure in blue cotton, a Madonna confined, an affront to her sister who, not as beautiful, not as stoic, not given to detachment, couldn't understand how Nora could ever hurt.

Nora was almost whispering. Unable to ignore the pleasing cadence of that deep, husky voice, Amanda leaned forward, straining to hear.

"You could have asked once. Or you could have waited for an answer after that little 'howareya' you threw at me. You didn't always have to turn away. Except, now I know you did have to turn away. You were afraid to hear everything was good in my life, weren't you? I didn't understand that when I was a kid. So, eventually, I didn't really care very much whether or not you ever stopped to listen. I wasn't hurt anymore. I just didn't care. And I stopped thinking you were so special."

"Marvelous. I disappointed you," Amanda responded in like tenor but she couldn't keep a cynical note from sounding. She did envy Nora one thing: her objectivity.

"It's true."

"Fine," Amanda was curt, her attitude nowhere near as impressively controlled as Nora's. "I believe you. I accept what you've been saying. I've done you wrong. You must be an amazing person to have overcome such mental abuse. I'm sure you go to bed every night questioning your good fortune; here I've thrown up all these psychological obstacles, I've been such an overwhelming force in your life, and still you've triumphed. Probably spent a mint on psychiatrists trying to figure out why I wanted to ruin your life by not hanging around and having a chat in the old pink, ruffled bedroom. Not to mention how I got that much power."

"Amanda, please."

"No, you please." Amanda boiled over and it wasn't a pretty sight. "I think it's really interesting that you feel the need to bring even more attention to yourself by putting me on the spot. You've dogged me all my life, you and your successes. It's like you couldn't wait to do exactly what I did, only better. Do you know how tough that is to watch when it's reversed? I didn't even have the opportunity to best you because I was older. No matter what I did, I couldn't start again. I could never try harder."

"You flatter yourself, Amanda. I never gave the parallels in our lives and careers that much thought. When I did, I actually had the audacity to believe it might be flattering to you that I wanted to follow your example. Obviously, that was the pipe dream of a very young, very naive girl. I'm no longer that young nor am I naive."

"Obviously," Amanda drawled. "But given your incredible savvy, your amazing intelligence, this desire that I represent you makes no sense. We're not talking running for class president anymore. Do you understand that?"

Amanda leaned her head on the wall, her hair obliterating the graffitied word 'screwed', changing the scrawl so it now read, "I'm for life." She was wearier than she had ever been in her life.

"I mean me. Why me? Things were going pretty well. I was happy defending my insignificant clients. Now you're setting me up to take the fall. I don't need it, Nora. I'm damned if I take this case and I'm damned if I don't. On the one hand I might blow it. You go to prison for the rest of your life, leaving me a mess of anxiety because I hadn't been up to the job in the first place. On the other hand, if I don't help you, I feel like a shit until the end of my days if you get a public defender that messes up and lands you with the max. You're screwed either way," Amanda said.

An almost dreamy cadence came into her voice. "So what is it, Nora? Have you suddenly gone soft in the head? Do you have a death wish?" Amanda looked at Nora. "Come on, sweet pea, talk to me. No more of this ice princess routine. Mysterious silences aren't going to cut it. The only reason you want me to defend you is that there's nobody—and I mean nobody—else."

A leaden silence hung between them. Amanda waited patiently for Nora, locking eyes with this sister of hers, watching when Nora's lips finally moved.

"There is no one else."

Amanda's eyes fluttered shut.

"Thank you for that."

She pushed herself away from the wall and walked toward Nora. Picking up her briefcase, Amanda rearranged her shoulders so they looked almost broad, fairly strong. "But I think you've been misled. Hector Jimenez is probably available. I'm sure your fee would floor him and a Hispanic attorney might be just the novelty you need. Or how about Susan Leiptzig? She usually handles workmen's comp but she's got a great chest and might manage to lean over the jury box far enough to sway at least a few of the guys. Maybe James Colburt? Marsha Payne? Oh, hell, I could go on and on. I'll send you a list of available attorneys from my neck of the woods, Nora. They won't worry about offending anyone at DM&M. Check 'em out, sis, because you don't need me. I'm not the only game in town." Amanda raised her chin. Her bottom lip was quivering a bit. "You'll do fine. Just remember to try and look contrite."

Amanda nodded to the deputy. The door was already open and Amanda halfway through when Nora called her back. It took a moment for Amanda to answer the summons. Turning, she looked at Nora without saying a word.

"Please," Nora said looking at the far wall, the one Amanda had been holding up not three minutes earlier. Her tone of humility was incongruent with her posture but she said what she must. "Help me."

Every bit of Amanda wanted to boogie. A pretty please wasn't enough to buy her or keep her. But the light played on Nora's profile just right and she couldn't help but see a reflection of their parents in her sister: the beautiful color of their mother's eyes, the narrowing of lips just like their father's when he was deep in thought. In the final analysis, it wasn't the comfort Amanda found in such resemblance that changed her mind, it was the fear she could trace just under Nora's perfect, perfectly composed face that tipped the scales. At least that was something the sisters had in common. Amanda, just afraid enough of being completely alone in the world, walked back to the table.

Chapter 4

Standing at the dock, Nora looked a bit like Joan of Arc. Her hands were clasped in front of her, cuffed at the wrist, her arms rested low on her hips. With stoic fortitude, she waited with four, more emotional, infinitely more verbal, less attractive women for her arraignment in Division 30 of the Municipal Court of Los Angeles in front of the Honorable G.A. Cotter.

The judge was bored from hours on the bench reading charges, accepting pleas. The one-man judicial assembly line was winding down and Amanda could tell he wanted to head for his three o'clock break in chambers. She checked her watch, anxious to get this over with too. Two-thirty. Samuel Blackwell, an actual paying client, was due for sentencing in Division Forty-two in the matter of accepting stolen merchandise. She felt a moral obligation to be there to catch him when he got the ax, poor kid. Amanda had no doubt he was innocent but the guy who really did it had fingered Sam and the merchandise was in Sam's hands and the system didn't really care which one of them went to jail, just as long as one of them did.

Nora's problems were a bit more complicated. Those who manipulated the system cared a great deal about whether she was prosecuted to the full extent of the law and most of them wanted that to happen as soon as possible.

Not that a murder was any great shakes in LA but in this case, the husband of the victim was an attorney of high standing, the accused as gorgeous as any movie star, and the victim the daughter of a retired, and recently deceased, senator. The press was hungry for drama and the DA's office eager for a slam-dunk. Against such a stacked deck, Amanda stood awed that circumstantial evidence could be whipped into a frenzied assumption of guilt. Amanda checked her watch again: two-thirty-eight.

The judge was almost finished with the case before him. A sixteen-year-old was pleading innocent to charges of murder even though four witnesses had seen him calmly gun down two people on a corner in South Central. Nora was up next and, in two minutes, the court would be waiting for the prosecutor. Judges hated to wait. One Brownie point for the ready-and-present defense attorney, Amanda Cross. The thought of that infinitesimal victory shored up her confidence, the next minute it took a dive when her opponent arrived in the nick of time.

Amanda's head swiveled. She expected to see either one of her old cronies from her days with the District Attorney's Office, one of the new kids, who looked less like an attorney and more like the captain of the football team dressed up for the prom, or the grim reaper. Instead, to her dismay, striding down the aisle, open palming the little swinging door as he stepped in front of the bar, came the district attorney himself—Leo Riordon.

Amanda's spine gave out under the weight of the world that plopped back onto those shoulders of hers.

Leo Riordan, perennial district attorney and Amanda's boss in those days before private practice. Year after year she'd wished him Merry Christmas, and year after year Amanda was rewarded with a practiced smile, a hearty handshake, and that dimming behind his eyes indicating he was searching his memory banks for her name. It was a big office and Amanda was a small part of it.

In the last few years, though, Leo's star had faded a tad. Leo had made some bad calls, prosecuting cases that never should have been tried, attacking when he should have retreated, spending taxpayers' money when it would have been wise to leave it in the bank collecting interest. Leo hadn't been very prudent of late. No, no. Leo needed a big score and this was the one that would do it for him.

Seeing his smiling face turned toward her now, Amanda knew Leo had done his homework. He knew exactly who she was—a woman who had never stood up to the likes of him in or out of the courtroom, a former employee who had sunk like a rock in the private practice pond. He was already tying her scalp to his belt, notching his gun, telling it to the guys in the locker room. Fearlessly, Amanda looked him in the eye and Leo Riordon dismissed her with a haughty little smile, a cynical little bow. It was just enough to make Amanda mad. She faced the bench, the butterflies still flapping but their wings clipped. Leo carefully placed his alligator briefcase on the prosecution table and flipped up the gold tabs, taking care to keep the sapphire on his pinky well out of harm's way. Amanda noted that the ring hadn't expanded in proportion to his weight. It cut what appeared to be a painful ridge into his chubby little finger.

Retrieving his meticulously typed notes, Leo cleared his throat, adjusted his silk tie, tried to button his jacket, remembered just in time that he hadn't been to the tailor to let out the seams, and smiled broadly, though the judge was thoroughly preoccupied with his docket and had no time to admire the fine figure the DA cut.

"Okay, folks." Judge Cotter took a deep breath and laced his fingers atop the bench. "Let's call number ten on the calendar. *The People of the State of California versus Nora Royce.* People's counsel, please make your appearances."

Leo's hand made one more quick pass over his ensemble, found himself to be acceptably turned out and announced, "Leo Riordan on behalf of the people, Your Honor."

Judge Cotter nodded, "Mr. Riordan, haven't seen you down here in a while. No black-tie affair to ready yourself for? No speeches to the mothers against crime? No editorial to write?"

Amanda gave Leo credit, his smile never faltered in the face of the judge's sarcasm but she was close enough to see his eyes cloud slightly with displeasure.

"There are a few things on the calendar, Your Honor, that I think are worthy of my personal attention," Leo responded.

Amanda, as usual, was impressed by the timbre of his voice. It was rumored that elocution lessons were on that very tight calendar of his. Pretty though it was to listen to him, her time to speak had come.

Left to their own devices, the men could drag out the insults until well past Sam's sentencing.

Amanda cleared her throat noisily while running a pencil through her fingers in an amazingly cowardly display of impatience.

"Amanda Cross for the defendant, Nora Royce, Your Honor."

Amanda almost grinned. She had the distinct feeling her announcement was akin to the local idiot calling out the town gunslinger.

Cotter cleared his throat, making sure the noise was a full octave deeper than Amanda's, underscoring his complete and utter control over his courtroom.

"Yes. Good morning to you, Ms. Cross. We see you regularly around here, don't we?"

"Yes, Your Honor," Amanda was pleased with his acknowledgment.

"Never on anything quite this weighty. Hope you're up to it." The last was muttered just loud enough to put Amanda in a very specific place. Though she tried to save herself, Amanda was powerless and slid right into the slot he had carved out for her. What God giveth, God taketh away.

Amanda chanced a glance at Nora. Her expression hadn't changed. In fact, she seemed to have a look of cool indifference that bothered Amanda greatly. An innocent woman would show something: fear, loathing, anxiety. A guilty woman might experience the same and face this trial with bravado or terror. But Nora, well, she left you thinking. The poker face perfected.

Possibly, she was analyzing the proceedings with a lawyer's eye. Perhaps her emotions were in such tight control she feared even acknowledging them. Maybe she was innocent and disdainful of the stupidity of those around her. Or, worse, she might be guilty and simply going through the motions prescribed by law. How was anyone to know? How was Amanda to know? And how was she to answer Cotter? The answer to that was easy—honestly.

"I imagine we'll know sooner than later if I'm up to it, Your Honor."

Cotter shot her a withering glance. Call him old fashioned but he liked women attorneys even less than he liked the DA.

"Shall we get to it," he commanded perfunctorily.

Leo Riordon obliged.

"Your Honor, we have today filed a one-count complaint charging defendant Nora Royce with murder in the first degree. We have further alleged special circumstances, that is, lying in wait, Your Honor." Leo symbolically bowed, waving his plumed chapeau, begging Cotter's leave. "And we will be seeking the death penalty."

"Ms. Cross, have you received a copy of the complaint?" Judge Cotter's attention was undivided now.

Amanda concentrated on him, unable to look at Nora to see if those hazel eyes of hers showed any sign of life. Amanda rose on surprisingly strong legs and said, in a more than surprisingly even voice, "I have, Your Honor. But may I say I am aghast and chagrined that Mr. Riordon has decided so quickly to seek the death penalty in this matter. I certainly don't view this as an open-and-shut case and, if the district attorney would review the documents to date, I'm sure you'll find that the case against my client is purely one of circumstantial evidence. He will, in no way, be able to prove beyond reasonable doubt that my client is the perp—"

"Ms. Cross." Cotter stopped her.

"Yes, Your Honor?"

"I would suggest you save that rousing speech for either your opening or closing arguments. I'm sure those remarks would be relevant in either situation." He leaned back in his high chair, checked his watch, and saw it was almost three. Cotter snapped, "Does your client waive reading and formal arraignment, Ms. Cross?"

"Yes, Your Honor," Amanda answered quietly, angry and scared.

"Fine. Let's set this matter down for preliminary hearing. Ten days from now is the twenty-seventh. We'll see it in Division Thirty. Mr. Riordon, how long is it going to run?"

"Your Honor, we may be proceeding directly to the grand jury for indictment," Riordon answered, as though it were a matter of course.

Cotter stopped jotting down notes, finally interested in something the DA had to say. He slid his eyes Amanda's way.

"Were you aware of that, Ms. Cross?"

"Your Honor." Amanda's voice was suddenly small. She willed it to strength but it wavered. Inspiration remained elusive. "No, Your Honor. The defense was looking forward to airing this matter in public rather than an ex parte hearing behind the closed doors of the grand jury room."

"Defense counsel rarely get what they want, Ms. Cross," Riordon shot back confidently, "and this case will be no exception."

Amanda responded to the sanguine chortle that punctuated his comment. "There's no reason, Riordon, to shove this through without a full hearing."

"I believe there is, given the circumstances of the act." Riordon was unruffled by her objection.

"Mr. Riordon. Ms. Cross," Judge Cotter called from the bench. Unruly children, they quieted, looking at him attentively, sorry to stop their finger pointing. It felt so good. "I think I'll play God and put an end to this discussion before it goes any further. I've been listening to bickering all day. I'm exhausted." He tipped his head toward the

DA. "Mr. Riordon, you know full well that a preliminary hearing must take place within ten days of the arraignment. So you have ten days to make up your mind how you'll handle this situation. If the grand jury does present a true bill, then the prelim will be vacated and the matter set for arraignment in superior court," He swung his head to the other side, "Ms. Cross, you will abide by the decision of Mr. Riordon and his office without further protest. Now, if there's nothing else—"

Judge Cotter was halfway out of his chair when Amanda stopped him.

"Excuse me, Your Honor. There is one more thing." She rounded the defense table almost as if she wanted to charge the bench. Instead, she held herself back with one hand on the table, the other was raised. "I'd like to have bail set now."

Riordon was on it in a flash, calling out in his most endearing whine, "I object. Judge Cotter. This is a death penalty case. No bail should be set. There is no question of it. I can't imagine—"

Amanda railed, indignation obliterating any trepidation. Anger at every prosecutor who had ever argued that a good person, a person who more than likely wasn't guilty, should be incarcerated in a place where no good and decent human being should ever be overcame her sense of courtroom propriety. Incensed by Riordon's pomposity, she was even more outraged that he should quarrel so vehemently against her sister!

"Your Honor, please. Nora Royce hardly poses a threat to our great society. Until the moment of her arrest, she was a respected member not only of this community but of the Bar itself. Her record is impeccable. It has only been proven that she was in the wrong place at the wrong time. We will happily surrender her passport if Mr. Riordon is afraid this woman will flee prosecution. I say she'll stay and see this through because she believes in the law. She has dedicated her whole life to it. If she felt differently, she wouldn't have been top of her class at Stanford. She would not have been tapped as clerk for Chief Justice Farnham and she sure wouldn't have been groomed by Dimsdale, Morris and Mott for a partnership fast track. Obviously, Ms. Royce has some degree of integrity or else she's spent a great deal of time and energy playing a tremendously black joke."

Riordon was ready and on the mark when Amanda ran out of breath and, knowing so little of her sister, out of character evidence.

"It is no surprise, Your Honor," Leo bellowed, "that defense counsel should speak so highly of the defendant. She is, after all, Ms. Royce's sister. I understand Mr. Bundy's mother said quite the same things when pleading for mercy in his case. But, as in that case, we are talking about coldblooded murder. The wife of one of the most prominent attorneys in our city is dead: a woman who was renowned for her good works, who was the beloved daughter of a retired U.S. senator. If this woman"—he pointed at Nora, and Amanda looked skyward, expecting fire and brimstone—"If this woman were let loose on the street, God knows what would happen in this volatile city of ours. Does Ms. Royce's education make her any less dangerous than any other murderer? Does Ms. Royce's—"

"Your Honor!" Amanda cried, but the judge was louder.

"Mr. District Attorney, your office seems to enjoy droning on about the evils of anyone in the box. I think we can skip the sermon." Judge Cotter had had a long day and an even longer career. He knew better than anyone that these emotional outbursts were nothing more than second-nature theatrics, easily dismissed and hardly entertaining. At least on Leo Riordon's part. Amanda's heartfelt plea was not recognized for what it was. "Perhaps Ms. Cross can talk you into a Livesay letter then you won't have to worry about a death penalty defendant being let loose on the street. That is if Ms. Cross is aware that a Livesay letter indicates a reduction of the sentence to life in prison from death?"

Amanda blushed, a hot miserable rise in temperature that started at her throat. She wasn't stupid. She wasn't ignorant. But she also wasn't ungrateful. With Cotter suggesting the Livesay, Riordon might just go for it.

"Thank you, Your Honor. I'll take it up with Mr. Riordon."

"I'm going to set bail in the amount of $750,000." The judge went on as if he hadn't heard her. "If you don't like it, Mr. Riordon, see the court of appeals."

"I'm not crazy about the bail, Your Honor," Amanda objected loudly.

"That's an outrageous pittance!" Leo cried.

Cotter, still standing, had no intention of sitting down or extending these proceedings one minute longer. Walking toward his chambers, he addressed Amanda.

"Ms. Cross, I've been sitting on this bench for fifteen years. In that time, I have never come close to making what your client made in one year as an associate for Dimsdale, Morris and Mott. I'm assuming your client is a smart woman, Ms. Cross. I doubt whether she squandered that kind of money in the course of her short, bright career. Bail is set, Ms. Cross, and court is adjourned. And Leo, stop being outraged."

The judge was gone.

Riordon was through the bar and out the door before Amanda could blink. The bail was excessive but the grand jury, that was outrageous. Without a backward glance toward Nora, Amanda followed, chasing Riordon down the hall, her short, thick heels sounding hollow and annoying as she half-ran, half-walked after him.

"Riordon! Riordon! You can't do this. There is absolutely no reason not to go to preliminary hearing. I can't believe this. The grand jury? Closed session? At best, if everything, every bit of evidence was true, the best you could hope for is a crime of passion. Murder two, Riordon. Maybe even voluntary manslaughter. Do you hear me, Riordon?"

Amanda's breath was coming in short, hot bursts. She damned the architect who decided the halls of justice had to be a mile long. "This is not the Hillside Strangler we're talking about. You go to a secret grand jury and you'll look like an idiot when they come back without an indictment. They'll never go for it, all this circumstantial crap. It's a waste of the taxpayers' money!"

Leo Riordon stopped so abruptly Amanda landed two steps ahead of him and had to come back to get in his face. Puffing was not flattering, she knew, and it ticked her off that he could probably see the thin trickle of sweat that was inching down the side of her cheek. Amanda had the uncontrollable urge to ask whether or not his hair had been manufactured or actually grew out of his head, just to put them on the same footing. Instead, she remained silent, trying to breathe normally.

"I seriously doubt I'll be the one with egg on my face, Ms. Cross." Leo clipped his words and swelled his chest. Peacocks had nothing on him. Then he surprised the heck out of her. "You know, you've always had this problem.

Never knew when you should take your toys and go home. Didn't you ever wonder why, when you were a deputy DA, you never, ever were assigned a trial of import? It was because you have no judgment, Ms. Cross. You actually do believe that everyone is innocent until proven guilty." He laughed a little, a staged, canned sound that grated.

"Well, the world doesn't work that way. There are budgets to meet and common-sense issues to pay attention to. Plead your client guilty and you'll save the government untold dollars while you save a bit of face for yourself."

"You're crazy," Amanda said. "You're a crazy, flicking, headline-grabbing politician. You're no lawyer."

"And you're outgunned," he retorted. Sticks and stones, as the old adage went, might mess up Leo's exterior but nothing Amanda could say would dent his ill-found hubris. He sighed as though all this was becoming quite tedious and the only thing really left to do was drop the dime once Nora was strapped into the chair. "Look, I've gone over all the paperwork and I've no intention of playing games with you. In fact, I left instructions for every bit of it to be forwarded to your office immediately. It's probably there right now."

"You couldn't have taken care of that little matter before the arraignment?"

Leo ignored her. "You won't find us holding back anything on discovery because there's nothing in the evidence that can hurt us. Nora Royce had means, she had opportunity, and that woman had motive. Now, you think you've got what it takes to pull this out of the fire, fine. Give it your best shot. But unless you have radically changed in the years since you left the county's employ, I'm here to tell you that this cause is lost. I'm committed. I'm prepared. I'm going to bury you. No one can do what

Nora Royce did and get away with it."

"Nora didn't murder Ruth Mallory."

Leo Riordon began to move down the hall once again. Amanda followed.

"Yes, she did. And in doing so she's brought shame on the legal community. She's aired a hell of a lot of dirty laundry just to save her own skin by insisting to anyone who would listen that Lucas Mallory was sleeping with her. We're beyond that, Ms. Cross. We're beyond sex as an excuse or a defense. We're not doctors. We don't protect our own for the sake of protecting the entire industry. We're lawyers. Nora Royce betrayed every confidence the legal community put in her and I have every intention of showing the community at large—"

"Don't you mean the voters?" Amanda challenged, skipping a little to keep up with him.

"This community, Ms. Cross. I intend to show them that we police our own. We do not coddle those who should be prosecuted to the full extent of the law. I will see Nora Royce behind bars because—" Leo was at the elevators. He pushed the button like a prize fighter delivering the knockout punch.

"Because a conviction will look good on your record whether she's guilty or not," Amanda finished for him, scooting around his bulk to look him in the eye.

He gazed upward, thoroughly engrossed in the little numbers lighting up as the elevator came to fetch him.

"Because it is right and just. That woman is guilty of murder and I intend to prove it. Now, I don't think we have anything more to say to one another until trial unless, of course, you would like to discuss a plea?"

"When hell freezes over, Riordon." Amanda retorted in a fabulous show of bravado.

Leo Riordon kindly allowed her the demonstration. It was the last he would allow. He had every intention of doing exactly what he promised, even though Amanda Cross was closer to the truth of his motives than he would admit even to himself. It was then the elevator arrived. Leo Riordon stepped in, leaving Amanda behind to consider defeat.

Chapter 5

Grand Jury. The very idea of that august body evoked fear, fed apprehension, and destroyed hope. Twelve ordinary men and women, beholden to no one, and imbued with a power so grave they could designate ruination or decree exoneration without benefit of a preliminary hearing. It hardly seemed that decisions like that should be made without benefit of legal argument from both sides. Normal people shouldn't have that kind of power. They scared Amanda Cross to death.

Her career was about drunk driving, petty theft, maybe an assault and battery thrown in for good measure. She took care of her cases with a glance at the police reports, an index of arguments she knew by heart, and case law that had been burned into her brain through overuse. But this! Someone had finally asked her to dance and she didn't even know the steps. Amanda might as well not have come to the party at all. Excluded from the grand jury proceedings, isolated while Leo Riordon freely presented his evidence, Amanda sat immobile on the bench outside Department 122, staring at the door of the grand jury room. With an ever-increasing sense of despair, she watched the subpoenaed witnesses parade by, starting with hotel personnel. In through the doors went a young woman of indeterminate origin, terrified and quaking. Out she came, still terrified, still quaking. In went a young, poorly dressed man but cocky, imbued with an importance he obviously relished. Out he came, a tamed stud but stud nonetheless. What in the hell was she supposed to do?

Leo Riordon poked his head out once to whisper to an assistant and throw Amanda a look of utter, imperious delight. He was enjoying himself, God dammit. Coffee was brought in just before a stream of exquisitely turned-out, fresh-faced young men and women began to trickle in. DM&M associates. Junior partners, associates, secretaries. Amanda could smell them a mile away.

This was not productive. Not in the least. There had to be something she could do—should do.

Her eyes locked onto the handle of the door to the grand jury room. They glazed over. She was trying to think and only coming up with a great big, blinding blank. It took her a while to shake herself out of her self-imposed trance. When she did, Amanda realized it had been a good long while since anyone had been called to testify. The door hadn't opened in—how long? Long enough. Shit. It was lunchtime. Courtrooms were locked, the crowds had thinned, and Amanda—by 12:09—was depressed as hell. There was only one thing to do.

~ ~ ~

Phillipe's was a place to eat. It was not a great place for an assignation, nor one in which deals could be made. It was too noisy for love talk and too cold and dark to read a proposal and nobody cared if you were the naked Queen of Sheba because they were too busy trying to work their way through the mass of bodies to the counter. There they could partake in the frenzied ritual of ordering and receiving food. People were as thick as flies on the honey pot and the pot just wasn't all that big. In short, Phillipe's was the perfect place to be depressed. You could be jostled and insulted and made to feel generally worse than you already did. Along with the biggest French dips in town and the best pickled eggs, Phillipe's served up the perfect, sadistic atmosphere for someone in Amanda's self-defeating state of mind.

"Next!" The guy behind the high counter hollered at her; the better-dressed woman behind her thunked Amanda's shoulder twice to get her attention. Chivalry was dead at Phillipe's. Amanda jumped and threw herself at the counter to protect her place in line.

"French dip, coleslaw and a pickled egg. Oh, and a bag of chips. Barbecue." She never said please. It wouldn't have been appreciated. Feeling better for having done something right, Amanda listened as male voices echoed her order, passing it down the line to the men in little paper hats who slapped mountains of roast beef onto hard rolls.

While she waited, Amanda dug in her purse and counted out the exact change before realizing she'd added the chips to her usual order. She grabbed another buck. The counter guy was back too quickly, demanded her money too gruffly, and shoved her food at her so rudely Amanda became flustered and ineffectual. He tossed her change. She threw it into her purse. No doubt she'd find it just when it was needed if the nickels and dimes hadn't managed to render themselves unusable by becoming attached to the only unwrapped stick of gum in there.

Hunching her shoulders, trying to make herself smaller, Amanda inched her way between the almost connecting queues of hopeful diners. Someone finally realized that Amanda, sucking in her stomach, could not make her orange tray narrower, so they moved over a step. Lemming-like, the rest followed. Frowning, glowering, Amanda finally broke through the crowd, only to see it close in on itself like a sea anemone being tickled on its tummy. Now the real challenge: finding a place to sit. Amanda eyed the long, dormitory-style tables crammed with bobbing, talking heads. Then, a savior. He called not from heaven but from the middle of the crowded mess hall.

"Amanda! Amanda! Over here!"

He was standing, waving his arms, and not a soul bothered to look his way. Amanda acknowledged him with a tip of her chin and navigated the tables with a renewed sense of worth. Someone had seen her. Someone wanted her company. Sandy Seeley, one-time suitor, had made a place for her, if not in his life, at least on his bench at Phillipe's. The commitment was almost as solemn.

"Sandy, my God, it looks like every attorney and clerk and secretary in LA is here." Amanda dropped her tray on the table and stepped over the bench, sitting down as though she'd worked her way through a minefield. "Damn. I forgot to get a drink! I can't believe I forgot a drink. This just isn't my day. What am I going to do now? All this food and nothing to drink. Aw, Christ. Boy, oh, boy. Can you believe it."

"Whoa, Amanda," Sandy laughed self-consciously, fully aware that he couldn't expect her to be charming considering what she was going through, "all I've got is half a cup of cold coffee. But you're welcome to it."

"No," Amanda said, really getting into it now. "Forget it. I'll get back in line. I'll—"

She was halfway up again when an arm reached across

the table. A paper cup was put in front of her. The hand attached to the arm flipped the straw out and snapped off the plastic no-spill top. Amanda watched, fascinated. That took a lot of coordination since the arm was attached to a man so intent on reading his newspaper he hadn't bothered to look at what he was doing. Beside her, as she sank back to the bench, Sandy chuckled before raising his voice for a formal introduction.

"Mark Fleming. Amanda Cross."

Amanda settled in, adjusting her jacket as she muttered "Thanks." Mark Fleming nodded, poking his head out from behind the newspaper long enough to give Amanda the impression that he was one hell of a good-looking guy. And not even a babe. A real, honest to goodness man who had to be at least her age if he was a day. She'd thought guys like that were extinct. Amanda would have sworn to high heaven that every man over thirty-five had lost his hair, settled down, and saddled himself with two point three children or alimony payments to multiple ex-wives, not to mention the just-had-no-interest-in-women sort but not this one. He definitely had that manly look. Nice dark hair. Dark blonde, actually, and a bit long, swept back from a forehead that was discriminatingly creased with lines of age but probably not worry. His nose was long and straight and a little narrow. His mouth was, perhaps, a tad wide, but it balanced eyes that were deep-set and sported the most definite imprint of crow's feet. She even thought she saw a bit of gray in his hair but that could have been a trick of the light—or lack of it. She congratulated herself. Pretty good in the observation tower if she did say so herself since he disappeared behind the newspaper again, allowing her only a split-second perusal. His hands, that was all there was left to analyze. Nice. Perfect. Square-tipped fingers, nails cut close but not manicured. He didn't wear a suit, so he probably wasn't an attorney. He didn't seem to care who came or went in this noisy place, and he sure didn't care one twit about Amanda Cross beyond putting a cork in her complaining.

"Thanks," she muttered again as she picked up her huge sandwich, hesitating just in case he was intrigued enough to give her a second look. She bit into the sandwich when it was clear he was riveted by the paper. Shifting on the bench, she ignored him back.

Men like this weren't in her karma anyway and never had been. Nora's maybe, but Nora would never go for this guy. He was actually tanned. Nora liked them pale from hours in the boardroom, furrowed brows and creased eyes a result of concentrating on their portfolios, calculating returns on investment. Nora liked other women's husbands....

Amanda shook her head. No way for the defense to think. Nora was innocent. Just because she thought nothing of adultery didn't mean she was capable of murder; just because that expression of hers never changed didn't mean it was masking a criminal mind. Nora couldn't do anything so horrible. Because if Nora could take a life then what, by virtue of genetics, was Amanda capable of? Given the fact that all their lives they had balanced the opposite ends of the spectrum, Amanda would have to assume she would be on the road to sainthood.

"So," Sandy pushed away his tray, his plate completely cleaned like the good boy he was. Amanda eyed him, let her gaze flicker to his plate, and remembered the few times she'd had him to the house. He'd cleaned out the fridge, then propped his feet on the coffee table and watched the television until the food heated. Nice guy. Just a bit focused on the wrong things.

"So," Amanda repeated, crunching on a chip. The manufacturer had been stingy with the flavoring. She pushed the rest of the bag aside. What good were they without the barbecue bite? Sandy drummed his fingers on the table, searching for something to say that had nothing to do with Nora or the impending trial. He finally hit on it. For Sandy, the topic was a major stroke of social genius. He launched into it with gusto.

"You seen Judge Rostencowski's new robes? " Amanda shook her head and tussled with a less-than-crisp wedge of garlic pickle. Sandy laughed heartily and shook his head as if to say 'Ain't life odd'. Amanda nodded to prove she was listening. "She's really something. Yep. That robe. It's got ruffles on it. Can you imagine?"

"Naw," was all Amanda could manage with a mouth full of food.

Sandy was on a roll. Her minimal encouragement satisfied him. "For real! I was in front of her the other day. Another bankruptcy—"

Amanda swallowed hard, took a sip of her drink, and interrupted him, "Since when are you doing bankruptcy?"

"Friend of mine. Just wanted to help out. I'm only charging him half my normal fee."

"That's rich. I've never known you to knock a penny off anything."

Amanda took another drink from the cup the newspaper person had shoved her way. The drink was Pepsi, cold but flat.

"What the hey? I'm a saint. Besides, his wife got hit by a city bus three months ago and it looks like we're going to settle quite nicely. Want to help me celebrate? I could take you out to that place you always liked. What was it?

The little French place on the Westside where they have that fixed-price menu?"

Amanda had to force herself to look Sandy in the eye. The guy behind the paper was turning the page and she could use a little pleasure. Looking him in the face might be the only satisfaction she was going to get for the rest of the year. Unfortunately, he kept reading, Sandy kept talking, and Amanda was disappointed.

"Yeah." She polished off her coleslaw. "Sure, Sandy, that sounds great. Have they made a settlement offer?"

"Not yet, but it's bound to be soon. I've made myself as obnoxious as I can."

Amanda laughed, truly amused and grateful for it. "Then I imagine they're cutting a check right now. Call me when you get it. I'm going to be pretty busy for a while—"

"Can you believe this shit?"

Amanda's wish was finally, if rudely, granted. Mark Fleming spread his newspaper over the table, covering what was left of Amanda's lunch, Sandy's tray, and elbowing the two people next to him.

"What?" Sandy was the first to respond. A little slow on the uptake, Amanda just drank in the glorious sight of the guy full frame.

"This stuff about Nora Royce. That woman is a piece of work. First she chases this guy, making a bid for partnership any way she can get it, and then she kills his wife, and then tells the court she can't possibly be guilty because she was sleeping with him. What kind of defense is that? Sometimes I just can't understand why they let women in this profession. You can't spread your legs and expect everyone to forgive—"

Sandy cringed. Another down-on-lawyers outburst; another down-on-women tantrum. Mark was carrying a ten-ton chip on his shoulder. Sandy Seeley understood it, given Mark's history but there was a limit and Mark Fleming had just reached it.

Beside Sandy, Amanda's face blanched with disbelief and outrage except for the blaze of scarlet just above the collar of her blouse. She held herself so still Sandy wasn't sure Amanda was still breathing. Sweat popped out on his upper lip. He kicked Mark with the tip of his shoe, grazing the other man but getting his attention.

"Ow!" Fleming yelped. "What was that for?"

"Sorry," Sandy muttered before giving Amanda a huge, uncomfortable, wish-I-was-dead grin. "Amanda, did I tell you that my mom got married again? She met this guy…"

Sandy stopped chattering. Attempting salvage was useless; lost causes were not his forte. Mark was talking again. Sandy cradled his head in his hand and waited for the inevitable.

"Look at this, Seeley." He poked at the photo. It was Nora at her arraignment looking serene and gorgeous, the shot filtered by the dock's glass. "If that woman actually got her law degree studying, I'll eat my hat. I still can't figure out how she could have passed the Bar without help. That would be an astounding trick, so she's got to have something on the ball, but I'll bet you she—"

"She nothing!"

Amanda sprang up with such force, called out with such righteousness that she stopped all conversation in their general vicinity. Eyes turned her way. The shock was catching and, for once, Phillipe's was almost quiet. Deliberately, Amanda reached for Mark's newspaper. She picked it up, shook it out and folded it neatly. For a long moment, she looked at the picture of her sister, amazed that this stranger's comments should drive her to emotional distraction when the entire legal community was whispering the same thing behind her back. But actually hearing the disdain, letting it sink into her psyche, had triggered the release Amanda had been seeking from the moment she sat facing Nora in prison.

Now her dark eyes eclipsed to blackness as she scowled at Mark Fleming. He knew he was desirable. He knew he was handsome. What he was about to find out was that he was also an ass. And he had the audacity to look at her as though she had offended him by interrupting his macho nonsense.

On the other hand, his nauseating comments had a strangely calming effect on Amanda. Listening to him, she realized how afraid she was: afraid of Nora's predicament, of failing, of the system, even of being alone with time to think. Amanda feared making the wrong move so she froze, scared she'd be chopped to pieces before the battle began. Now Amanda understood she'd never been asked to fight before, no one had ever insisted she stand up and be counted. Well, things had changed. Maybe Amanda Cross didn't have the slickest style but she had guts. Maybe she wasn't brilliant but she learned fast. Show her the way and she'd run down the road. This guy had shaken her out of her lethargy. This guy was dead meat.

Starting at the corner of the newspaper, she began to shred it. Meticulously, she worked her way in diagonals until it was tattered, protecting Nora by ripping her into an unrecognizable pile of cheap, inky newsprint. Slowly, she gathered the pile in both hands, leaned over the table and dumped it into Mark Fleming's lap. With equal care, Amanda took the drink he had given her and drizzled it over the mess.

"You, sir, are all wet. You have no firsthand knowledge

of the woman you are attacking and that makes your comments irrelevant and libelous. Your speculation is crude and insulting, not only to Nora Royce but to any woman who has managed to beat the system and put men like you in your place by succeeding.

"Don't you fret, she's going to beat it again, fair and square, and give you something else to talk about. She has more fortitude in her little finger than you'll ever have in that appendage in which, it would seem, your very small mind resides. I suggest you take that appendage, go do to yourself what this goddamn system would like to do to her, then keep your mouth shut until you know what in the hell you're talking about."

With that, Amanda turned, her legs tangling with the bench that pressed up against the back of her knees, stepped over it, grabbed her briefcase and headed back to the hallway in front of Department One twenty-two and the grand jury. Amanda Cross was fired up and pissed off and ready to work.

Chapter 6

——

"Ask yourself why Leo Riordon has opted to push this case through the grand jury instead of giving the defense a chance at a preliminary hearing? He'll say it's because he's got an airtight case. He'll say there's no need to spend the time or the money on a lengthy prelim, when he's got everything he needs to go directly to trial. Well, listen. That's just plain bullshit." Amanda moved closer, lowering her voice. "Change that word before you print it." She raised her voice again. "But that's exactly what it is. The case of *Nora Royce versus the People of the State of California* is in front of the grand jury for one reason and one reason only—Leo Riordon's ego." Amanda crossed her arms over her ample chest. She looked satisfied and happy. That she didn't feel these things didn't matter at this point.

"This whole fatal attraction thing is a bunch of bunk. It's a Hollywood ploy by an elected official who's beginning to believe his own press. I guarantee you, Leo is already thinking up titles for the screenplay on this one. He's a clown. A bit player with dreams of grandeur. This crap about Nora Royce running around hassling Lucas

Mallory is absolutely ridiculous and Riordon knows it. I say let's get real. Let's talk about the facts and I'll show you just how little he's got. But I can't do that, because he's taken the matter to a secret grand jury. There is your outrage. There is the injustice of it all. He has given this case a profile it doesn't deserve because he, Leo Riordon, needs to feather his career nest by more than a bit."

Amanda leaned over the reporter's notebook to see if she was being quoted properly. Seeing the shorthand, she felt disheartened and wondered if her assault on the available media was doing her any good. Probably not, since it appeared the reporter was getting bored. Amanda's circumstantial evidence spiel just wasn't as meaty as what Riordon was feeding them.

She didn't ask for this kind of pressure. She didn't want to listen to idiots like that guy in Phillipe's. She didn't want her life turned upside down and she sure as hell didn't want to agonize about whether what she was doing was the right thing. Self-doubt was shelved, the reporter forgotten. Someone else was coming out the door, finished with the grand jury, anxious to be away. Time for action again. Her strategy was simple—storm the fort, attack the troops.

"'Scuse me." Amanda pushed off, leaving the reporter hanging, skipping through the crowd and landing exactly where she intended—just to the right of and slightly behind the woman in the black suit. Nice suit. Expensive. A tap on the shoulder. The woman turned.

"Pardon me." She stuck out her hand. The woman kept moving, looking at that hand as if Amanda had offered her a dead fish. "I'm Amanda Cross, defense attorney for Nora Royce. Look, I was wondering, could you spare me a few minutes? I'd just like to ask you some questions that might help clarify my client's—"

"I know what you want. I'll have to think about it."

Amanda backed off. DM&M people had been in and out all afternoon and she'd talked to each one—or tried to. No more sitting on her butt waiting for the ax to fall. She touched their sleeves as they came through the cracked-ice doors; she tapped them on the shoulder when they bent down to get a drink of water. Amanda begged, she cajoled, she followed them down the hall shooting questions from the hip.

So far she didn't have much. A few corroborations that Nora had been seen exchanging words with Lucas Mallory fifteen minutes before Ruth Mallory did her danse macabre. A couple of nods but no verbal affirmation, when asked whether they thought Nora had an unhealthy fixation on Lucas Mallory. Amanda should have been disheartened. She wasn't.

What did these people know? They belonged to DM&M heart and soul. What were they going to say? Nora Royce is the sweetest thing since Twinkies and she's getting a bum rap? Her best bets were already gone and Amanda wanted to kick herself for missing the maids and bellboys from The Regency Hotel. They would have been easier to collar, easier to intimidate here, in the courthouse, if that's what she had to do. A business card would make them putty in her hands. One Latin term and they would have crumbled. Water under the bridge. Now she'd have to use what she had and what she had were a couple of reporters hanging around. She rushed back to the guy who had at least given her a shot. He'd been watching; he'd seen her fail to get what she wanted. Notebook at the ready, he smiled when she apologized and began again.

"Sorry," she muttered. "I was just making arrangements to meet her later. You know…"

"Yeah, I know." There was pity in his eyes.

Amanda cleared her throat. "Well, where were we? Oh, yes. I can't tell you how unfair all this is. I'd just like to be able to listen, to hear what the specifics of the case are. Why should I have to wait for discovery? Even the Beverly Hills Police Department wouldn't provide me with paperwork unless they checked with Leo Riordon and Leo Riordon is taking his own sweet time. Do you really think that's fair?"

"You're not going to change the system."

The reporter's statement was flat. Philosophy wasn't his forte. Okay. Regroup. He wanted to get detailed. He wanted to talk about sex.

"What about your defense? Crime of passion. Is she still hanging in there with the story she was sleeping with Lucas Mallory?"

"She was sleeping with Lucas Mallory and no, the defense won't be crime of passion. Nora Royce is innocent…"

Amanda was at a loss. She had no theory. But before she could contrive a full-blown statement of doublespeak her sixth sense kicked in. The reporter lifted his nose, sniffing the air like a spaniel, sensing the same thing she had. Something was happening. Something interesting? The reporter who had been so attentive left her and walked halfway down the hall only to be stopped by an invisible barrier, a line he couldn't cross.

Amanda focused on the end of the hall. She looked past the hovering journalist, past the human chaos in the halls of the criminal courts building. She looked past the deputies who peeked through doorways or lounged near ashtrays waiting to testify.

There they were, huddled at the end of the hall. The

train was in, the sheriff was out and they owned the town. Their suits were varying degrees of dark: navy, indigo, charcoal gray, and blue-black. Two appeared to be pinstriped, though it was hard to tell from such a distance. The rabble gave them space. They stood within a protective bubble of power and prestige and Amanda found herself drawn to them.

Here were the senior partners. Nora had told her about Oliver Hedding's wintry demeanor, his watery smile, and his old, hard eyes. Amanda remembered Nora's description of DM&M's answer to Rambo, Peter Sweeney. She moved slowly toward them.

They identified her, predators curious about a possible kill, unsure if she was even worth the effort of their fast, best moves. They stood still, the knot opening as she approached until they were queued horizontally, waiting for her. Now she saw Don Forrester, the sweet-tempered glad hander who eased the clients' hurt feelings when one or the other of the partners slashed through their fantasies with the cold, hard, legal facts of life. And there he was, Lucas Mallory. The widower. The man who swore beautiful, talented Nora Royce was obsessed with him. The man who was unable to fend her off, who found that he was not to be the only victim of her demented fixation. Poor man. Weak man. Lying man.

Amanda paused, her foot hovering in the air for a millisecond so that she could consider him before confronting him. Lucas Mallory was handsome the way men are handsome when they accept aging. His hair was thin but all there, his attire understated and beautiful. His face, Amanda imagined, could be considered compassionate, though she could see no hint of the sorrow he must feel at the loss of his wife, the horror he must have felt as she lay dead at his feet, the abstraction that goes hand in hand with grief. He must be a fine civil attorney to have the ability to hide so much with seeming ease so soon after his loss.

Their eyes met, and Amanda was electrified, filled with an awe that took her aback. He had communicated his superiority and she wanted the moment to be hers forever. Perhaps Nora had known this feeling. Perhaps it was she who didn't want to share with Ruth Mallory. But that gaze slid past her and she was nothing again. She would never be able to touch him. She wondered how Nora had; if, indeed, Nora had.

The moment of hesitation was gone. Amanda walked on, stalking the partners of DM&M not for attention but for the truth. If she waited a moment longer her courage would be gone. All Amanda had was her momentum, and she was about to test the force of it.

"Mr. Mallory." Amanda walked right up to him and stuck out her hand. "Amanda Cross, defense counsel for Nora Royce. I'd like to extend my sympathies on your loss."

The four men began to move away. Lucas Mallory did not take Amanda's hand nor did he acknowledge her presence. It was Oliver Hedding who, within the rhythm of their movement, spoke.

"Miss Cross." He exhaled his words with a shallow and dry breath. "We do apologize but we have been called here by the district attorney to appear before the grand jury. We do not find it appropriate to conduct an interview with you in the hallway of this building. Nor do we find it appropriate that you should be offering your condolences to Mr. Mallory. While I am sure they are sincerely felt by you personally, you do represent the woman who killed Mrs. Mallory."

"That is a false statement, Mr. Hedding."

Amanda hadn't followed them. She had to raise her voice to be heard. They had closed ranks, moving on in a pod, leaving Oliver behind. Amanda's heart pounded. He was better than her. They both knew it. So why did she want to convince him that she was worthy of a seat at the table? Her voice shook. The first syllable was out before Amanda was able to pull herself together.

"Mr. Hedding," she said then cleared her throat, "I have no desire to harass you or any of your associates. I want justice for my client and I'm at a loss. Because of DM&M's standing in the legal community, no one is willing to help. But you, Mr. Hedding, you and Mr. Sweeney and Mr. Forrester—even Mr. Mallory—you're lawyers and you understand I have to do my best. I have to do what is right. So do you." Oh joy. He hadn't stopped her. Amanda forged ahead, ignoring the glint in his eyes, refusing to interpret it for fear the translation would be amusement.

"You can't make a decision on guilt without a trial. You simply can't make blanket statements like that. The community at large will listen to you because of who you are." Amanda pleaded and she didn't give a shit what he thought of her groveling. She couldn't threaten him, she couldn't outfox him, but she could lower herself to him—just this once. "The people of this community want to believe you because you and yours have been dreadfully wronged. But there could be another explanation. There could be another person. There could be so many reasons—"

"It is hard to imagine, Miss Cross," Oliver answered quietly, almost kindly, "that you actually believe in Nora. Given the evidence, I would expect you to want to fight, but not to believe."

"You believed in her," Amanda contended and with that surprising statement, she saw Oliver Hedding close himself to her.

"At one time, Miss Cross, we all believed. Now we no longer do. We know. And we will tell the grand jury what we know. The district attorney will then tell you."

Oliver turned his back. Amanda was quick. She moved forward, put her hand on his arm. He looked at that hand but not at her.

"If I have questions, you can't refuse me. You can't hate her that much."

Breathlessly, Amanda waited. But there was nothing else for her. Oliver Hedding melted away like snow, leaving Amanda to wonder if she had touched him at all. The four men were joined once more. The reporters came forward, thought again, and stepped back gracefully, rebuffed not so much by word as by attitude. The senior partners of Dimsdale, Morris & Mott would remain solitary in their grief, appearing in public because that was required of them by law. They were such careful men, such private and successful men. They wanted to be forgotten by this unruly public so that they could, in turn, forget the horror of this murder, forget Nora Royce, and carry on with business as usual. Nora had been a mistake, a beautifully packaged, desirable mistake, of which they were ashamed.

Amanda had never come in contact with people like this and Nora was so like them. Long ago, in the gestation phase of her career, Amanda had imagined herself being like them. The things she would have—the power, the money, the respect that belonged to them would belong to her. In those years, women were unusual commodities in the legal field, and Amanda saw herself taking advantage of the confusion and the wariness of the industry. But reality slapped her in the face, and she woke up with a start. They didn't want her. Twelve years later, women were equals. Better than that, they were sought after. Affirmative action or die. Women could get where Oliver Hedding and Lucas Mallory were. Not many had and certainly not Amanda. Her time had come and gone.

Amanda cast one last lingering look at the men of DM&M. Oliver Hedding was being summoned into the grand jury chambers. Peter Sweeney and Don Forrester stood tightly, stoically together, hands in their pockets. Lucas Mallory remained apart, his hands by his side, his face composed and expressionless. He was a sleepwalker, resting in the course of his journey. It was dangerous to wake a sleepwalker, wasn't it? Then his head turned. He looked at, and into, Amanda before she realized he was actually looking through her.

Overwhelmed and unnerved, Amanda fled the building, grateful that Lucas Mallory was left behind, wishing she could leave her disquiet there, too.

Chapter 7

—

Amanda Cross could hear the miserable sounds of rush hour outside her office. It was a fitting ending to a day of equally miserable events: the morning's inactivity, the afternoon's affront at Phillipe's, and the late day impotence in the face of DM&M's partners. Damn and shucks. Amanda tossed a wadded-up piece of yellow legal paper toward the trash can just as a particularly obnoxious horn sounded, underscoring her misery.

"Idiots," she muttered and tossed another. She had the perfect solution to the mess down on the street. If Los Angeles wasn't going to give the nod to effective rapid transit, the city should make it illegal to own and operate a car that wasn't at least ten years old and needed body work. Nobody would care if they got hit. No horns needed. Big boy bumper cars. Fun and games.

She tossed another paper ball and missed—again. Putting her hand in the air, she checked her nails. They were looking better, almost healed after the fabulous fakes fiasco. Sitting back in her creaky old chair, she admired them. Short nails, still weak, but nice long fingers able to drum the desk as she considered the only victory in a week of disappointing defeats: the appraisal had finally come in on her house. Soon she could post bail. Funny how tough it was to come up with enough stuff to add up to $750,000 but she'd managed with the help of Nora's town house, Nora's bank accounts, and her own little piece of real estate. Amanda's damned, wonderful little house that meant the world to her was thrown in the pot.

Darn.

Another melancholy paper ball flew, another miss.

Sure the driveway was cracked. Sure the house hadn't been painted in ten—twelve—years. But it was hers and she'd poured everything she had into keeping it in working order. That house was the only good thing to come out of her marriage and the appraiser was telling her it wasn't worth spit. Nora's town house, on the other hand, was worth three times as much, thank God. Hopefully, the paperwork would be in on that one any day. So, between the two properties, Amanda would be able to post bail in the very—fingers tightly crossed—near future. Then what? Nora might be out only long enough to watch Amanda blow it, then back in the old slammer. Or worse.

Amanda grabbed her legal pad. There weren't any notes of consequence on it. A theory. That's what she needed. Every criminal defense began with a solid who did, how did, why did theory. Amanda laughed. She'd never become a poet. She wasn't even a very good attorney in the theory department. Every notation had a juvenile, first-year-of-law-school-ring to it. With uncontrolled frustration, she ripped three sheets off and tossed them—one, two, three—toward the overflowing can, missing every time. She needed help. She needed someone who could slam-dunk. She needed a white knight. She needed—

"Hello?"

A voice filtered in from the reception area. It was vaguely familiar, obscurely pleasurable. There was to it not quite a drawl but a tedious sound she recognized. There had been other sounds the last time she heard it. No, no. It had been noise—

Amanda was out of her chair. She opened the door of her office at exactly the same moment Consuelo Hernandez stuck her head out of hers. The two women looked at one another, then at the visitor. Consuelo threw her hip out, licked her freshly glossed lips, and tossed off:

"Yo, Amanda. If you don't want him, maybe I'll take a look."

"He's not mine." Amanda answered coolly ashamed that the sight of that ignorant, arrogant bastard from Phillipe's could ignite the warm fuzzies in the pit of her stomach. What was his name? Mark Fleming. Who was she kidding? The mental finger popping was a sham, so she cut it out. She wasn't kidding anybody. His name had been her first thought. Her first feeling was one of absolutely crazy delight. He was tall and Amanda loved tall men. That made her feel guilty. It also made her feel quite feminine. Guilt and femininity went hand in hand. A woman's lesson. Nora never learned it.

In an admittedly subconscious, terribly feminine gesture, Amanda left the door to her office open while she walked like a lawyer back to her desk. Mark Fleming moved in behind her. He stood just inside the doorway, checking things out: her office, her. Amanda reciprocated, positive that it was more pleasurable from her end. Mark Fleming was poised on the edge of the board that would plunge him into middle age. You knew that, even in the end, when the waters of life engulfed this guy, he'd go under in style.

"You're not very polite." He finished perusing the interior decoration and put Amanda in the spotlight.

"I don't recall you've given me any reason to be," Amanda answered evenly.

"Got a point."

Mark moved ahead like he owned the place. Amanda thanked the fading light and the landlord's electrical cheap streak for making both office and occupant look fresher and younger than they really were. Mark ignored the hunter green sofa with cream-colored flowers, preferring to stand in between the two rattan client chairs planted in front of Amanda's desk. In his hand was a brown paper bag. This he deposited in front of Amanda and then sat himself in the chair on the right. Leaning back, he rested his elbows on the arms and said, "I thought an apology was in order."

He didn't smile. Neither did she. Pretty cool on both sides. Amanda eyed the bag, its neat, three-turn top just waiting to be opened. She put it out of its misery.

"This is it? This is the way you apologize?"

Amanda pulled out her half-eaten French dip. He had wrapped the pickle in the same napkin and now there was a soggy, green-tinged, pickle-shaped indentation on top of the bread. Next came the partially eaten bag of chips. Thankfully, he hadn't tossed the coleslaw in for good measure. Then she remembered she'd managed to finish that before his appalling editorial about Nora. There was something else in the bottom. Fishing around, Amanda pulled out a brownie: a shrink-wrapped, iced piece of chocolate cake that was so heavy she doubted it had an ounce of flour in it. Just eggs and butter and a cup of sugar for good measure. Finally, Amanda smiled. He had proven himself to be exceptional. Mark Fleming hadn't even considered she might be on a diet. Bless him for ignoring the obvious.

"Thank you."

He shrugged and she liked the way his shoulders moved under his shirt almost as much as she liked the brownie. It was a dress shirt; expensive cotton; open at the neck. He had rolled the sleeves up to expose forearms covered with curling light brown hair. He didn't have a jacket or sweater though the March evening was chilly.

"You're welcome. It's the least I could do. Sandy told me I'd really put my foot in it."

"You don't seem the type who would be too distressed by that."

Amanda muttered as she unwrapped the brownie. Keeping her attention on that was preferable to watching him take her apart and put her back together with his icy eyes. She didn't want to see disappointment there when he finished. After the first bite, she couldn't resist a peek. He was still looking. Light blue eyes that looked as if he knew everything about her. That bothered Amanda somewhere deep inside, where she hadn't been bothered in a very long while. She broke off a piece of the sweet and held it up to him.

"It's all yours." He smiled nicely, not seeming to be disappointed in her at all. "Usually, I don't worry about someone being insulted by my opinion. This was different."

Amanda caught a crumb as it fell from her mouth and swallowed hard. If that was a compliment, she'd take it. "Well. Thanks again, then. I usually don't win that easily."

"Didn't know we were competing. Feeling a little out-gunned, are you?"

"Wouldn't you?"

Suddenly, the brownie didn't taste so good. Amanda

was out of her chair, feeling that insistent nesting urge to clean when an eligible male was about. She picked up the wayward paper balls that littered the floor and then realized he was watching. She smoothed her skirt over her hips, wishing she'd managed to whittle them down another inch before she'd bid adieu to the gym.

Sensing her discomfort, Mark rearranged his line of sight and laced his hands over his enviously flat midsection.

"Yeah, I guess I'd be feeling a little overwhelmed. I hear your sister's burned a few bridges by insisting the esteemed Lucas Mallory is a letch, instead of vice versa."

Amanda slipped back into her chair feeling better now that an effort had been made to straighten up. "She's yelling it from the rafters but it's not doing any good."

"Good for her. She can't get in any deeper with the legal beagles, so what have you got to lose?"

"Her life," Amanda drawled.

"Not if it's the truth," Mark countered.

"I didn't mean because of the affair allegations. I meant because I'm out of my league. I can't get a grip on something like this. Lord, first thing they teach you in law school is to formulate a theory. How do I get a theory when every piece of evidence is flashing guilt in neon? If he says she wasn't in that room with him and she says she was, all I've got is a standoff. What theory can I come up with? Lucas Mallory did it even though he was seen at the reception? A crazed maid? There was a jewel thief stalking the hotel? How about this one? I love this one. It was suicide."

Amanda whispered the last, winking conspiratorially, self-deprecatingly. He wasn't laughing. Neither was she.

"My goodness, we haven't been properly introduced, and already I feel the need to define myself in terms of failure to you. That's not what Cosmo would call a cool beginning. That's not the kind of attitude that would give Nora confidence, is it?" She stuck her hand out. "Amanda Cross."

He took her hand, and it felt wonderful. A man's hand.

"Mark Fleming. And you're right. Self-pity isn't exactly attractive. But sometimes you have to call a spade a spade. That's not self-pity. That's being realistic."

"Boy, you play hardball," Amanda said chuckling sadly under her breath. Good looking and a philosopher to boot.

"Call 'em like I see 'em. You do your best. When it isn't good enough, I say back off. No sense beating your head against a wall when you're not going to get through it. All you're going to get is a cracked head."

"Now there's a novel approach." Amanda glared at him but he returned the favor with such an utterly charming look of sympathy she decided throwing in the towel could actually be praiseworthy. "All right, I agree with you… to an extent," she added quickly, still slouched in her chair, her hand slipping from his and looking for the right place to rest. "I do think you ought to cut your losses when it's necessary. But I haven't even jumped into the fray yet. The grand jury's almost wrapped up. The way things are going we'll be in trial before I have Nora out on bail. It's taken me a week to get my ducks in a row on that one. I gotta tell you—do you mind me telling you?"

Mark smiled and shook his head. Amanda almost fell off her chair when he flashed those straight, beautiful teeth. Where in the hell was his flaw?

"I don't mind. I came to apologize, didn't I? I owe you."

Fleming liked that way she had of slapping herself around a little, then thanking herself for the lesson. Not to mention she was damned pretty. Not gorgeous. Not stunning. But damn pretty and that was great. Hadn't he had enough of gorgeous to last a lifetime?

"My pleasure," he mumbled surprised to find he was settling in for the long haul even though the plan had been to head straight home and watch the sun fall into the ocean, his only company a beer and a bag of peanuts in the salted shell.

"Okay, here goes. I don't know where to start, really." She shrugged, snapping the top button of her blouse open the way a guy loosens his tie when he's getting down to it. "You can probably tell I'm not exactly one of those boutique firms that handle special cases with a staff of five well-chosen assistants. It's me, myself, and I. I do indigent defense mostly, like a zillion other attorneys in this city. Handle some DUI, breaking and entering, assault. I do a lot of minority work so the bucks aren't good in private matters, but the court pays on time. I don't have a lot of money to spend on investigation and most of my cases don't require it. Get police reports, plea when I can, fight when I think it's right, and that's it. What in the hell do I know about a full-blown murder trial? What do I know about any of this? Hell, I don't even have a theory. Not even a theory!"

"What about when you were with the DA's office. You must have handled some pretty solid work there."

"Robbery, assault, drugs. Same stuff, different side of the argument. Leo kept the high-profile stuff for himself. That's why he's counsel on this case. Can't get any more high profile than Nora Royce, unfortunately. There were the favored few who took the real meat and potatoes stuff. Those of us who never made the social cut, those of us whose noses tended not to be permanently dulled by a brown tint, we handled everything else. If we needed help, we had it. There were investigators, a full library, secretaries. It never occurred to me back then that I'd be without resources."

Mark pulled the whole truth out of Amanda with a well-timed silence.

"Okay. Okay. Maybe I didn't wrap up my network real well when I was laying the groundwork to go out on my own." She laughed a little. "When I didn't get picked up by one of those respectable firms, I settled into rote stuff. I like it. Sometimes I even think I'm doing some good." She flung a glance around her little office, an almost proud smile on her lips. It disappeared faster than ice cream on a hot day. "Never occurred to me I'd be in the middle of something like this. I haven't been keeping up, so to speak. I don't have my finger on the pulse of the law. I don't read the latest journals. I don't go to seminars. I'm just a lawyer making ends meet and I'm up that proverbial creek on Nora's case, if you know what I mean."

"I do."

There was a minute of silence. Amanda weighed the situation. She had poured out her heart only to get back two words of solace. But they were nicely said, heartfelt. She leaned back in her chair and laced her fingers, letting them lay at waist level, deciding two heartfelt words were, in fact, very nice.

It seemed to get darker outside, and quieter. Rush hour was either over or there was a God, and he'd lowered the decibel level to give Amanda a chance to talk to this guy without yelling. She liked the fact that he just sat there and listened. She liked the fact that he wasn't one of those sensitive types who wanted to commiserate. Nor was he just being polite, waiting for her to finish so he could rush away. Mark Fleming seemed to genuinely hear what she was saying and even appreciate it.

"So, you a lawyer?" She puffed the words out. Sincere interest. No sexual tension whatsoever. Just-tell-me-about-yourself casualness. While you're at it, pull a defense strategy out of your hip pocket.

Mark shook his head. "Nope."

Amanda was disappointed.

"Clerk?" she asked incredulously.

"No way."

Too manly for that kind of thing.

"Are you going to make me guess?"

She almost blushed to hear herself flirt.

"Might be interesting to see what you come up with." That half-mocking tone of voice was back. Amanda liked his other voice better, the sincere one that made his eyes soften when he used it. But what the hey? She was hard to derail.

"Then I'd say you're either a gigolo or a political type. City hall? Press liaison?"

Mark Fleming's head fell back and he laughed a good, hearty laugh. Amanda could have sworn the lights brightened at the sound. When he looked at her again, those very pale blue eyes of his were richer in color, warmer.

"Hardly. I know a few people who would say I stuck it to them in one way or another but I'm not one to be kept. Not by a woman or a system."

"I was afraid of that," Amanda muttered. "So tell, then."

"I'm probably something you never heard of. I made it up."

"That sounds rich."

"I'm an investigator and a clerk and a process server and just about anything else any attorney who can't afford a staff might need. I'm the sole practitioner's dream. It would seem I'm the answer to your prayers and I didn't even know it."

He opened those strong arms, inviting her to step right in. Amanda had no reservations. She was ready to take the dive the minute he said, "Ms. Cross, I'm at your disposal."

"Lord above." Something good was happening. Amanda couldn't believe it. She never got exactly what she needed, exactly when she needed it, in exactly the right way. Never. She'd been planning for this day forever. Amanda knew just what to do.

"Thank you. I can't tell you how much this means to me. Thank you so much."

That was it. Gracious, without being overdone. Amanda had been practicing gracious since she was in fourth grade and her mother told her when someone complimented her she should offer a simple acknowledgment. She should lower her eyes demurely. Speak clearly and slowly. Amanda always assumed the day would come when she would have to go through those steps because someone was admiring her beauty. By the time she was twelve, she was a cute girl with a gorgeous baby sister. No one ever gave her a chance to be gracious until now.

"Hey, no problem. I've got time. I just wrapped up a case I was working on for a guy over on Fourth and Olive. I've worked my way around superior court for a few years. I think I can help." Mark leaned forward. Amanda did too. She caught a whiff of his aftershave. It was a really clean scent, something he'd probably been using for years because he wasn't the fussy type who liked to change. This guy was great. He was better than a white knight. He was flesh and blood. Amanda sighed, hanging on his every word.

"It sounds like you need it."

"I do." Amanda whispered in a perfect imitation of

Doris Day, perennially the virgin trying to give it away.

"Good, then it's settled." He extended his hand. She took it to seal the bargain. This time it felt softer, warmer, the handshake of a friend and savior, and she missed it when he let it slip back onto his lap. "I usually charge by the hour if it's something simple, but I'm assuming this is going to be full time for a few months, maybe longer. So let's say fifteen hundred a week plus expenses but only because you're a friend of Sandy's."

He grinned and his pretty eyes crinkled. Amanda's narrowed. Her pretty eyes looked pissed.

"I'll also need a permanent parking place in the building. If you want to do a monthly pass, it would be easier than having to worry about petty cash on a daily basis. I can hike to the criminal courts building as long as the weather holds. If it gets bad I'll do taxis but you'll always have a receipt."

Amanda's body gave out as he continued to talk. The anger was gone, replaced by utter incredulity.

"I can't believe this."

"What?" Mark curtailed his list making and cocked his head, waiting for a question, ready to clarify any point.

"I can't believe you just offered to help me. You told me you owed me, for God's sake. Now you're telling me you want me to pay you more in a week than I make in a three? You are an idiot! I knew it. You're a legal gigolo. You'd have to be. Nobody could afford your personal services if this is how you deal professionally. I can't afford that kind of fee. Look at this place. Look at me." Indignantly, Amanda sprang up. "Do I look like I've got a whole lot of disposable income? I own two really good suits. Three hundred bucks new, all wool. Great looking. But I got 'em at a hole in the wall in the garment district, wholesale. I've been wearing them five years. I've had my shoes resoled six times. I work in a raunchy, collective suite and use law books that are a hundred years old. Why don't you just take me for everything and be done with it? Take my car, my house, you're already asking for blood."

Slowly, Mark stood up, trying desperately not to laugh outright. Rounding her desk, he took one outstretched arm and turned her toward him. He took the other and crossed her hands, covering them with his own. Amanda would have thought she'd died and gone to heaven if she hadn't been so ticked off.

"I'm charging your client," he whispered cockily. "She's got it. The money, I mean. Don't worry. You, I'm not taking for anything but dinner. Come on. It will all work out, I promise. You need me, so don't waste your energy trying to tell me you don't."

It didn't take much to convince her. A tug. She searched for her purse. Another tug. Amanda went with him. He didn't have to tell her it would all work out. She only hoped it would be for the best. And if it didn't, at least she'd have a decent last meal. Dinner sounded nice.

Who was she kidding?

Dinner sounded heavenly.

Chapter 8

It turned out dinner wasn't heaven but it was close. The tables were small, which meant Amanda and Mark sat more intimately than they would have had he been a fast food freak. There were candles on the tables. Short, fat pieces of white wax nestled in little clear glass holders that were even shorter and fatter. This meant that Amanda was looking pretty good. Candlelight, after all, was her friend. It was Mark's friend, too, and she only hoped she looked half as good as he did.

The menu was marvelous, so Amanda would go home full and happy. The prices were reasonable. If Mark expected her to pick up half the tab, she would be able to handle it. They had ordered drinks immediately, as Amanda hoped they would. She worried for a minute, given Mark's physique, that he might be one of those men who scorned the finer things in life, like fat-marbled meat, alcohol, and dessert. He drank scotch. She assumed the marbled meat was a shoo-in and she'd let him slide on the desserts.

Their drinks were still half full forty minutes after they were delivered. They'd been talking since they arrived, and Amanda liked that most of all.

"…so she left."

Mark raised his glass. The ice cubes clinked against the side, and when he lowered it again Amanda saw there was a glistening line of icy water on his upper lip. She smiled despite her outrage at his story.

"I can hardly believe that. It seems so absurd." She was amazed at how Mark's woman had flown the coop and grateful that she had.

"I thought so. Then I asked myself, who am I to define loyalty and love and commitment? My ideas on the subject weren't any better than hers I suppose."

"Give me a break," Amanda scoffed. How could he give the bimbo the benefit of the doubt? "Look at the facts. You're working your butt off in law school. You're engaged to the woman you love. She swears she loves you back and, when you flunk the Bar exam, she takes off? Fleming, that is not a loving act by any stretch of the imagination."

"Might be interpreted that way," he countered matter-of-factly. In fact, it almost sounded like he wanted that interpretation. "Look at it from her standpoint. She wanted something out of life. My success as a professional was part of the whole package. It didn't work out. I wasn't going to be wearing suits and driving a BMW anytime soon, so part of the package collapsed. I think it's a loving thing to do. She could have felt guilty and stuck around, married me, and been miserable. Then I would have been miserable, too."

"Right. And she could have said go for it again, you know. It took me two times to pass the Bar. If I'd given up, I wouldn't be where I am today."

Mark let that little comment hang between them for a minute. Amanda blinked. Obviously, that wasn't as encouraging a footnote as she'd intended. She buried her nose in the bowl of her wine glass.

"Well," she said when she surfaced, "you seem to have survived."

"Oh, beautifully. I'm my own man. None of that pressure-cooker lawyer stuff for me. And I didn't waste the education or the connections. I've got all those guys I went to law school with keeping me in referrals. I'm still using the knowledge. It's a living. I cut back in the summer and play beach volleyball, gear up in the winter and give myself a Christmas present that my wife—if I had one—would never have understood."

"Family?" Amanda asked, intrigued that he could have let his dream go so easily, or rearranged it so neatly, at the very least. He may not know it but that's exactly what he had done. Nobody who went through the grind of law school did it because it was fun. They did it because they dreamed, the way she had at one time, of arguing that one stunning case, saving that innocent person, winning a settlement that would be one for the books.

Mark shook his head. "None to speak of. A brother in Ohio. You know how that can be."

"I know how that can be when your sister is down the street."

"Not close, you and the infamous associate?" This time Amanda shook her head. "Too bad in a way. Better, in some others."

"I don't know how it can be good that Nora and I aren't close."

"It'll make it easier if this doesn't come out the way you want it to," Mark answered. It was his turn to take a drink. But he didn't lower his eyes. He watched her every move. Amanda was getting warm and having second thoughts about working with him. She discarded them the moment they popped into her mind. She needed him, after all.

"I suppose." She heard the sadness in her voice. Mark didn't seem to. She let it go. "So, what are we going to do to make sure that doesn't happen?"

"Work hard. Work together. Are you smart?"

"I work hard. When I know what I have to do, I do it well. Yeah, I'm smart enough to get through this. If the question is, am I brilliant enough to win, then I might have to lie."

Mark laughed, "I'm about the same. Maybe together we can be brilliant."

"Hey, at your rate you better be," Amanda reminded him.

"I'll do my best. Now, what we've got to do first is go over all the paperwork. Did the DA send you the police reports, autopsy, all that info?" Amanda nodded. Mark looked pleased. "Okay. Then we've got to start asking questions. You told me you didn't get very far with the associates or the partners outside the grand jury room. That's understandable. Lot of pressure going in there. They don't want to be seen talking to you in the hallway, especially not with the press around. But we've got to try to get some firsthand interviews. Things happen when you're face to face with people."

"So what do I do, call up and ask Oliver Hedding for an appointment?"

"Sure." It made him happy to surprise her. He liked the way she tried to cover it up. Her lips turned down at the corners, her head cocked to one side but she blushed. She blushed when she was caught off guard.

"Oh, please," Amanda scoffed.

"I mean it. I want you to call and keep calling, write and

keep writing. I want you to wear them down with every argument you can think of to get in and sit down with each and every one of them and talk about that night. What we need to know is where they all were."

"You think one of them did it?" Amanda was aghast.

"Amanda," Mark explained carefully, "this isn't about finding out who killed Ruth Mallory. We're not detectives and this isn't an Agatha Christie novel. All we want to do is find a way to prove that Nora didn't kill Ruth Mallory. Or at least we've got to create enough questions in the jury's mind for a reasonable doubt stance. Got it?"

"Yes, thank you," Amanda answered icily. "I had actually figured that out on my own."

"Good. So you get to those guys. Just talk with them. Find out where they were. What they saw that night. When they were aware of Nora's movements and when they weren't. Why they think Nora was hot on Lucas Mallory without the feeling being reciprocated. Just let them talk and take notes. Go all the way back to when she was hired. Talk to any associate or partner who'll talk back. Get to the secretaries. Follow them down the street if you have to."

"And just where will you establish your cheering section?"

"Don't worry. I'll be earning my pay."

Just before their first fight, the waitress popped in to let them know forty-five minutes of considering the menu was the limit. They ordered without enthusiasm. The waitress disappeared. They were squaring off again.

"There's more to do than talk to the partners or the people at DM&M. That's the tip of the iceberg. So, while you do that, make your motions, do your legal research, et cetera, I will be handling everything else. In fact, scratch Lucas Mallory from the list. I want to talk to the bereaved widower myself. I think this might be a guy thing. I want to get some vibes from him. I'm also going to try and talk to people who knew Ruth Mallory. From what I hear, sainthood was imminent. I find it difficult to believe that one existed but if she did, I find it truly hard to believe she was married to a lawyer at Dimsdale, Morris and Mott. There's got to be more to this scenario. It's going to take some time to crack, though, because people don't like to talk about dead folk, if you know what I mean."

"True. Character assassination is a lot more fun when you can watch someone squirm."

The waitress was back with a salad. Bib lettuce. Amanda's favorite. Mark drained his glass and ignored his plate.

"Which brings us to the physical evidence. I want to get out to Nora's place and go over it with a fine-tooth comb. Maybe check out the blood samples if we can, get our own expert witnesses to talk about blood type, DNA testing, you know. With some luck, we can get into the sheriff's crime lab—this was Beverly Hills PD, right? They were the ones who investigated?" Amanda nodded since her mouth was full of buttery little green leaves. "Good. They use the sheriff's crime lab. I'll try to talk to them directly but it'll be tough. Leo will want us to have reports. I doubt he wants us to talk to the technicians directly."

"Sounds like you know what you're doing," Amanda said quietly, surprised to see excitement reflected in his eyes. Unfortunately, the moment he realized she'd tagged him, Mark Fleming hid it away and closed himself off. That was sad. Amanda needed someone to get her adrenaline flowing and he'd been doing a fine job. But he still smiled at her. He still liked her. She wondered if he liked himself.

~ ~ ~

"Kitty, that was marvelous, as usual."

Don Forrester carefully folded his napkin, placing it properly on the long table, patting his small, round paunch as though he were full to bursting. The Don Forrester grin was in place but there was an agitated light in his eyes that made Kitty Hedding uncomfortable and Oliver Hedding impatient. Min had been looking at it for days. It was even making her nervous. She didn't ask what the problem was, assuming it could be any number of things that wouldn't really interest her: work pressures, empathy for Lucas, his own receding hairline. So many things. Hopefully, though, it was nothing that might affect her or Marissa. She so preferred him to keep his work problems at work rather than upset the delicate balance of their personal harmony.

"Yes, Kitty, you must have your cook give me the recipe for that marvelous raspberry sauce. I think our cook could use a bit of a challenge."

"Of course, Min. My pleasure."

From the head of the table, Kitty murmured her answer, while she kept her eyes on her husband. He had been so quiet all evening. Detached was actually a better adjective. It was the way he'd been since well before Ruth died. It was as if he were dissecting a problem again and again only to remain dissatisfied, the solution eluding him.

At first, Kitty assumed it was the embarrassment of Nora Royce that had tamed him. But shame wasn't something Oliver felt—ever. Sometimes she wondered if his odd mood had to do with Ruth. A memory flashed through Kitty's head. Ruth's voice on the tape: *Everything is going my way, Kitty dear.* Kitty shook her head, not wanting to remember the glee in that beloved voice. Not wanting to think what it might have meant.

Then, quite suddenly, Kitty realized she was doing exactly what she'd promised herself she wouldn't. She was focusing on Oliver again, to the exclusion of all else. Tired of speculating, exhausted by the odd thoughts running through her head just before she fell asleep at night, bored of trying to figure him out, Kitty was, at times, quite simply, weary of being Kitty Hedding. When Peter Sweeney folded his napkin as if it were a revered flag, Kitty turned her attention away from her husband. She couldn't bear to look at Peter Sweeney, so she spoke to his wife.

"Peg? Have you had enough?"

Peg Sweeney started. Kitty saw again how poorly Peg was aging. She made a mental note to use candles during their next get-together. Peter's young wife, forty to his fifty-nine, had seemed to age five for every year of Peter's. Her neck was crepey; her eyes were deeply wrinkled at the edges. It was all that tennis, that sunbathing. Soon, she'd look older than Peter, because Peter looked ageless, with his smooth, tanned skin, the ring of hair around his tight, bald dome, the cocky grin and piercing eyes. Men like him never aged. Pity. Kitty smiled more broadly at Peg, encouraging her to hang in there.

"Plenty, Kitty, thanks."

"Lucas?"

Lucas Mallory raised his head. He was such a neutral man. Not a tragic man by any means, simply one who was there. He had recovered so well from the ordeal of the funeral. Now he sat in Kitty's home, quietly making a comment or two, as was standard. Lucas had never said much, even when Ruth was alive. Kitty would have preferred a scene, a sudden, unexpected breakdown. Anything to let her know what Lucas was truly feeling. Yet, in his oddly removed way, he was probably feeling just what she was and she was feeling lost and lonely.

The table seemed so odd. The chair Ruth usually occupied stood empty between Lucas and Don. Kitty tried
not to look at it. She should have had it removed. Next
time, she would remember. Now, Lucas was looking at
her curiously.

"Yes, Kitty?" he asked quietly.

She thought he had a lovely voice, so well modulated,
so reassuring. It went with his pallid visage, his air of
sanctity, and his perfectly put together person. She often
wondered if he ever was a happy person. Kitty's one wish
was to see Lucas truly happy, just to satisfy her curiosity.

"Is there anything I can get you?"

It was Oliver, not Lucas, who answered. Lucas moved
his head, turning it slightly toward Oliver, in deference to
the managing partner.

"No, Kitty. I think we've all finished. You can have
Terra clear the table."

"Would you like coffee here, Oliver, or in the living
room?"

"Neither. I think the gentlemen and I will have brandy
in my study. I'm afraid we can't end the evening on a high
social note. There's so much work these days."

Kitty inclined her head and inquired, "Would you like
a pot of coffee in there, too?"

"Thank you, no. Don? Peter? Lucas?"

They stood, their chairs sliding easily on the silk Iranian
rug upon which sat the beautifully restored Louis XIV
dining table. Peter Sweeney pulled his jacket together and
stuck out his chest as if waiting for everyone to admire it.
No one did. Peeved, he leaned over and kissed his wife
with a good deal more vigor than was called for. Don gave
Min a quick little peck on the neck. She moved her head,
to keep him from messing her hair then smiled up at him.

So blond and cute.

Don adored his wife. He wished she adored him back. His smile broadened, asking her to like him now. The frantic light in his eyes deepened, so Min gave his hand an extra pat. Lucas, having no one to kiss or touch, waited patiently until Oliver led them away. The women were left alone.

They sat in silence for a long while. Though Oliver's study was far from the dining room, it seemed as if all of them were waiting for the doors to close before they felt comfortable enough to speak.

Kitty spoke first. Perhaps her ears were better than the others.

"I think I'd like a drink. Anyone else?"

The other two shook their heads. Kitty made no attempt to rise and fetch the liqueurs. Terra bustled in, cleaned the table, and served coffee before disappearing into the back part of the house.

"It seems so odd without her." Min sighed.

Hers was a heartfelt lament. Min had envied Ruth her single-mindedness, wishing so to emulate it. Oliver called it outspokenness. Kitty called it courage, a sense of self-worth. Ruth always spoke out, had a thought, an opinion, a plan of action. Yet, Min was talented in other ways. Not overly intelligent, she was golden-hearted, sweet as the day was long, a perfectionist in the things she could control. It was sad that the one thing Min wanted, to be a woman of worth, escaped her. Ruth had made her feel as though she was just that.

"We're all missing her, Min. I kept looking over to that side of the table. It feels as if she's just been there. It was almost as if she'd only excused herself for a moment. I keep expecting her back."

Kitty spoke quietly, the nip and tuck of her Eastern upbringing still evident. So refined, people said when they heard her voice. Such a lady. Such a fake.

Kitty Hedding was an old debutante who'd realized too late that her life was worth spit in terms of her husband's. He was the one with power, the one who set the standards and the stages. She moved within his world and, lately, just lately, she'd begun to think about creating her own, because something just wasn't right in the one Oliver had made.

"I keep expecting the other shoe to fall." Peg Sweeney stood up so abruptly, spoke so curtly, poor Min jumped a foot.

Peg was strong. Min could see the muscles rippling up her arm. Tennis, swimming, boating. Min wished she could do that, too. Min wished she was more than a blond in an angora sweater but she was as afraid of failure as she was of success, so she just remained what she was. Everyone seemed to accept it; some even liked her that way. Someday, though, she would do something—dramatic. She felt it. She knew it. All she had to do was wait and watch for the right moment. Now, Min watched as Peg fairly attacked the whiskey decanter and poured herself three fingers straight up, then confronted the other two.

"Sometimes you two are very strange. Don't you feel it?" She demanded. "Something is really wrong here. Peter is crazed. He's obsessed with this whole murder thing. Sure, we all loved Ruth. But Peter barely gave her a second look, he only has eyes for the commandant." Peg snapped her hand to her forehead in salute, thought twice, then looked sheepishly at her hostess. "Sorry, Kitty." Kitty nodded her understanding. Peg wasn't finished. "Peter wants that woman to burn. I mean, he doesn't just want to see her put away. He wants her obliterated."

"Don't you think that's understandable, dear?" Kitty asked the newest member of their little group. Five years and still Peg didn't quite catch on that certain things weren't talked about.

"No, I don't." A hearty swig. Not even a blush from the burn of the whiskey. "I think it's natural to want to see justice done, but Peter, he's…" The cut crystal was held high. The light from the chandelier bounced off it, sending sparks of inspiration Peg's way. She was sneering now, disgusted with her husband's behavior. "He's almost gleeful. He watches this whole thing like it's a made-for-TV movie. We all know there was no real love lost between them. I didn't see him shed a tear at her funeral. Hell, he's probably happy she's gone. She was always sticking it to him, winning every debate, shoving her nose into the firm's affairs, offering DM&M's assistance for her charities. He didn't like that and he made no bones about it but he didn't talk about it night and day. Now Ruth's dead and Nora Royce is charged with her murder. He's obsessed with this Royce woman. He can't talk about anything other than how she's going down. Down hard. That's what he says. I think it's sick. I think the whole thing stinks."

Kitty heard the catch in Peg's voice. This was the closest she'd ever come to sharing her real feelings with them. There was no hysteria, just the hiccough of frustration and the tightness of fear. Kitty wanted to tell Peg she shouldn't worry about what these four men did and thought. It was masochistic, a waste of time and effort, because nothing they could ever do would change what the senior partners of DM&M were. But Kitty remained mute, sitting in her chair at the head of the table as Min went to Peg and put her arm around the other woman. It seemed to anger Peg that she appreciated Min's efforts.

"I liked Ruth a hell of a lot. I respected her," Peg muttered into her glass.

When she raised her head again, there were tears in her eyes. They were beginning to course down her wide cheeks past that mouth of hers that smiled so readily in victory—just like her husband's.

"What scares me is I feel the same way he does. I've never felt so hateful. I want to watch her the same way she watched Ruth die. But it's because I loved Ruth. Peter didn't love her." Peg turned to Kitty without leaving the confines of Min's arm. "Is that so wrong to hate someone I don't even know? Is it so wrong to hate the way Peter does? Without waiting for the trial? I mean I have good reason. Peter just enjoys it. Sometimes I think he got a thrill out of seeing Ruth like that, on the floor dying. Sometimes I wonder… am I becoming like him?"

"No," Kitty answered quietly, looking serenely at the other two. How odd human emotions were. She fully understood what Peg was saying. Peg feared for her soul. She had married him, therefore, she must be like him. Kitty understood that line of reasoning. They had all felt that way at one time or another and been horrified to find out they were close to becoming what their husbands were—clannish, forceful in the little world they ruled. For them, their tyranny translated into funds for charity. Their husbands? They controlled an even smaller, more tightly knit world. There was so much the wives didn't know. Nor did Kitty think they wanted to, really.

Kitty thought for a minute, wanting to tell them that Ruth had learned that lesson the hard way. She thought better of it. Ruth's last message had been cryptic at best. Certainly, there was a great deal that could have been read into that flippant, pleased communication. On the other hand, it could have meant exactly what it said. Ruth was a very happy woman only hours before her death. It was not up to Kitty to judge or to interpret, she would only cause greater grief, further discontent in their shrunken little sorority. The three of them had no one else but each other, after all. All Peg really needed was permission to hate and to mourn. Kitty would give it to her. Dead, after all, was dead. Changing the perspective on Ruth Mallory wouldn't help anyone, least of all Peg Sweeney. Nothing could help her. She was married to Peter.

Oliver Hedding pulled the carved pocket doors closed with the touch of a priest sealing the confessional. He loved the doors to his den. He and Kitty had found them in Italy. Doors that had been salvaged from a cathedral suited him. Oliver had learned early in life that people did their best work not for love, nor often for money, but because of their faith in an omnipotent being. Understanding this made Oliver extraordinarily successful. It was Oliver Hedding to whom people turned to solve their problems, make them rich, pull them out of the fire, elevate them to heavenly heights. They had such faith. It pleased Oliver never to have faltered, never to have disappointed anyone who came to him looking for a miracle. He was fair, he was wise and he thought clearly. He made hard decisions and lived with the consequences. Born without a conscience, Oliver considered himself blessed. The men gathered in his study were the only people he had ever met who came close to being his peers. None of them ever would be his equal, because their strengths were singular, their talents concentrated.

Peter, with his mental brawn, his swaggering street smarts, was useful often, but his heavy hand could never be tempered

Don, with his absolutely endearing features, his bright, optimistic outlook, could ease over even the most caustic of confrontations. Never ask him to make a life or death decision, though.

And Lucas, so dear to Oliver, came closest to becoming what a leader should be, failing and proving himself fallible only at this late date. Lucas made mistakes. That would have been acceptable, had Lucas controlled the consequences. Unfortunately, he didn't and that was so very, very sad. A terrible, almost fatal flaw. Yet, he seemed none the worse for wear because of it, settled as he was on the silk-covered sofa.

"Lucas." Oliver laid a hand on Lucas's shoulder before moving toward his desk. "If any of you would like a drink there is brandy on the sideboard."

Peter did the honors, pouring first for Oliver, then for himself. Oliver smiled, amused, as always, by Peter's arrogance. He was such a very small man with nothing to feel so terribly secure about. They were all expendable, after all. DM&M would go on even if they didn't.

"How can you do that?" Don demanded.

Peter laughed, feeling no need to immediately acknowledge the man by looking his way. When he finally did, Lucas and Oliver had already given Don their attention.

Gone was the open smile with its slight overbite that so endeared him to judges and juries, secretaries and clerks. His mouth, when not smiling, was unattractive. Small and without definition, it enhanced the slope of his weak chin, the broadness of his cheeks, the length of his face. He ran a hand over his forehead, which grew in prominence with each passing year, as his fine, blond hair receded.

"Do what? Wet your whistle? It's easy. Watch. Pour it out. Drink it down. Simple." Peter laughed, hating Don.

He was smart enough to know, though, that he could only toss barbs Don's way and never a killing, poisonous dart—especially now.

"I meant how can you sit there with your wives, at dinner, while this thing is going on?" Don addressed the men as a whole before taking Peter to task. "I'm not ashamed, Peter. I'm not ashamed that I was shaken by the grand jury. I don't want anything to do with this trial. Lucas, I'm sorry Ruth is gone. I really am. I'm sorry she had to go that way. It was dreadful. But this last week has been worse than dreadful and I don't want to be a part of this trial."

"You can't help but be a part of it. We all chose Nora Royce—remember that. We all bear the burden. So stop whining. I hate it when you whine."

Peter was disgusted. Don didn't care. He was distraught and expected support from someone in the room. Since Peter wasn't going to give it, he faced Oliver and Lucas.

"But when I think—oh, God—when I think it could have been any of us. Then I think about Min and Marissa. What would have happened to us—Marissa and me—if it had been Min? I couldn't imagine, Min…"

"But it wasn't, was it?" Oliver said calmly, coldly, from the depths of his huge leather chair. His old, fading dark eyes glittered. There was as much perverse pleasure in watching Don squirm as there was in holding out his hand in measured sympathy. Tonight though, Oliver had no desire to play games. The situation was under control; there was no basis for Don's proactive fear. It never would have been Min because it never would have been Don. He was too careful, too in love with his wife, and he followed rules far too precisely.

"I think it's kind of exciting myself." Peter was moving, talking again as he paced the room.

Lucas eyed him, thinking how odd it was that this man had become an attorney. He should have been, at best, a general. At worst, a high school coach abusing the big, strapping sons of mid-level managers in some bedroom community. He let his eyes flicker away, knowing he would have to listen to Peter's opinion no matter what.

"I don't know why I didn't take up criminal law. I think I would have been good at it. Kind of makes your blood boil, your adrenaline start pumping, when you've got all those people looking at you, when someone's life is held in the balance. I loved it, being in front of the grand jury. It's like hunting. That's exactly what it's like. And I think Riordon's good. I think he'll keep our involvement to a minimum. We'll each testify. Probably the whole damn office will testify, and that will be that. Sorry about Nora. She had a bright future. She was crazy to get involved like that. Not that our Lucas here isn't someone to lust after." The barking laugh again.

"That's enough, Peter," Oliver murmured smoothly. There was no need to be offensive. "I think we should all remember that whatever emotions we are feeling are grounded in the fact that Ruth is dead and that there was reason for her death. Those emotions are different for each of us. I suggest we temper our speech when we discuss this situation. We are lawyers, we are friends, but there are lines we shouldn't cross. Lucas"—Oliver let his eyes flick toward Lucas while his body language indicated clearly he was speaking to them all—"did you follow up with Riordon?"

"I did," Lucas answered evenly. "He's pushing to start within three months. He thinks no more than a week and a half once the jury is seated. He's got no problem with defense counsel."

"I know." Oliver agreed.

"I don't." Don stepped forward stopping abruptly before coming between Oliver and Lucas.

Oliver looked at him. "Miss Cross used to work under Leo. She was an assistant DA. Very little to recommend her. Leo doesn't expect any problems given her abilities. He suggests we cooperate with the defense and I tend to agree. I don't want any of us, or anyone on our staff, to be considered hostile witnesses." Oliver swiveled in his chair, the action of a contented man. "This matter shouldn't have a legal leg to stand on if it comes to appeal. Naturally, should the death penalty be indicated—"

Lucas sprang upright, stunning them all. Peter took a long swallow of his drink to cover his astonishment. Don uttered a startled "Oh, my Lord." Only Oliver appeared not to be startled. He watched Lucas walk quickly to the far end of the room, where he rifled the books on the shelves, choosing to examine a first edition of *The Grapes of Wrath*.

"I can't imagine that would happen, however," Lucas remarked tightly. "The evidence, though damning, is not definitive. I don't think there's a snowball's chance in hell Leo will get the death penalty on this."

"Forgive me, Lucas, but these things must be talked about. Nora Royce meant something to you, we're not denying that. How could she not? She was handpicked. You were her mentor. None of us could have foreseen any of this when she first joined the firm. A certain degree of ambiguous feelings is understandable, as is Don's nervousness."

Don fairly glowed with Oliver's assurance that he was not hysterical. Oliver raised the tips of his lips but refused to offer a full-blown smile. "We must all forgive Peter his idiosyncratic fascination. That is in character and cannot be changed."

"Fine, Oliver. Whatever." Lucas closed the book. He had never been much of a reader but he did appreciate the fine things money could buy. No. That wasn't true. He appreciated money as the end result of all their efforts.

"Oliver's right, Lucas. Don't get so hot. We've talked about unpleasant things before if you recall." Peter sauntered up behind him and put his hand on Lucas's shoulder. Lucas didn't pull away. Don turned away. He couldn't stand the thought of Peter being that close to him. "Hell, we've had to make some really tough decisions together."

"Peter, I've never shirked doing anything in the best interest of the firm. I think I've proven that. But I don't have to like the consequences. And, Peter, I'm not hot." Lucas turned around, his clear blue eyes meeting Peter's darker ones.

"No, I can't imagine you are. Funny that Nora could have gotten bothered over you, buddy. I would have thought you two were too much alike. I mean, if she'd wanted anyone, I would have figured it would be…" Peter looked around the room. He laughed once. "I guess it would have been me. Nice and physical."

"Peter, that's uncalled for," Don said.

"Excuse me, Don." Peter swept a bow, keeping his drink high and level. "I didn't realize your sensibilities could still be offended after all we've been through and seen. The real-life drama of it all. No accounting for what women will do, is there, Don?"

"Oh, stop." Oliver said. This nonsense was tedious. How like small children they were at times. Pointing fingers. All save for Lucas. Flawed Lucas. A man who proved to be irresistible. Funny thing this protective, forgiving feeling he had for Lucas. "I know it's not late but I don't wish to spend the rest of the evening discussing this issue, nor do I intend to spend it with you. I have work to do and the ladies should be finished with whatever it is they talk about when they're on their own."

"Always so gracious, Oliver," Lucas commented, smiling softly, so no offense was proffered.

Oliver offered a dry, sardonic, chuckle, "Lucas, Lucas. There is nothing more to talk about. We've covered all the bases. If the death penalty is called for, the appeal is automatic. I don't want there to be a possibility of a new trial. I believe we should all talk to Ms. Cross. Tell her what we know or what you deem relevant. This way, the case will be cleanly prosecuted, justice done, and DM&M, and our surprisingly dramatic problem, will be forgotten all the more quickly. Unless there are any objections or comments, I would like to suggest we all bid one another goodnight."

In the silence, they had the guarded looks of siblings afraid to challenge the father's decision. The patriarch was well pleased with his power. He smiled and opened his hands in a magnanimous gesture.

"I believe we are all of one mind, then. This is to be wrapped up as quietly and calmly as possible. Cooperate with the district attorney, gentlemen, and instruct your staff members in the same manner. Do the same with the defense attorney as best you can. I would only suggest that we do not talk to the press. We don't need a second trial on the tabloid pages running concurrently with the one in the courtroom if it should come to that."

The men nodded their accord without a second thought. It was wonderful how well they worked together, wonderful that they thought and acted as if with one mind, one body, perhaps even one soul—when Oliver Hedding pointed the way and jerked their chains.

Chapter 9

It had been exactly nine days and twelve hours since that first, frantic drive through downtown Los Angeles and up the hill to the Sybil Brand Correctional Facility for Women. In that time, Amanda had been back to confer with Nora every day but two. In a budget conservation effort, the authorities had chopped Monday from the attorney visitation schedule and Wednesday found Amanda in one of her wretched blue funks. Not exactly the right attitude for visiting. The cause of this condition was twofold: Tyrone Williams had decided to change his assault plea to not guilty, insisting that Amanda now mount a defense to clear his good name and, sadly, on Wednesday, she had come to her senses about Mark Fleming. The latter had been a far more disappointing turn of events than the former.

Charmed by him during dinner, it wasn't until three in the morning that her eyes popped open, her brain kicked in. How typical, she told herself. She'd fallen for a pretty face and a decent line. The brownie. God, the brownie! Wasn't that enough to just sweep her off her feet and make her hire him without even asking for so much as a reference?

Disgusted with herself, Amanda didn't sleep the rest of the night. By seven, she was on the phone and ready to prove she wasn't as dumb as Mr. Fleming thought. By noon, Amanda had found out all she needed to know. Mark Fleming was a dream: well regarded, highly respected, his slightly insolent attitude tolerated because his work was impeccable. A gun for hire. A private contractor. He'd do what you wanted and move on to the next job, whether it be serving a subpoena or running a background check. Simple. Amanda could count on him to do anything—except stick around. So what else was new?

Sitting now in the reception area of Sybil Brand, waiting for Nora to be processed out, Tyrone and Mark were both put in the proper perspective and left behind. But Nora's bail? That was a hard thing to put in its place. Amanda had cut off her right arm to free Nora. Not literally, of course, but she might as well have amputated her arms and legs since she'd torn out her heart the moment the trust deed for her house had been signed, promised to the courts for her sister's freedom. A sister she barely knew and wasn't even sure she liked. A sister with so much more. If Nora's bail hadn't been so high, her town house would have covered it. But no, it took Amanda's little bungalow to make up the difference. Mean spiritedly, Amanda mentally grumbled that Nora's town house was expendable. But her house? Hers!

Abruptly, Amanda stood up, tired of sitting in the molded plastic chair, eager to be on her way back to the office, where bad thoughts could be buried under a pile of work. Leo Riordon had pushed the grand jury forward at record speed, the indictment was down, thankfully, minus special circumstances, and Nora was officially charged with murder in the first degree.

Amanda wished she had a cigarette. She would have liked to have something to grind to a pulp other than her brain. She paced, unable to keep the muddle inside her head straight. Mark Fleming. Doing whatever it was he was doing. Part of the team of two. Her house. The house she loved. Nora. Leo. Failure. Nora. Amanda blinked and readjusted her focus. Through the small, rectangular window in the steel door that protected Amanda from the shift-clad prison population, she watched her sister come forward.

Rayon slacks, silk blouse, silk underwear, all the same elegant mole color. Amanda knew about the lingerie because she had dutifully retrieved the ensemble from her sister's posh home, pausing only long enough to acknowledge an incredible moment of overwhelming jealousy before dashing back to the car and heading out to Sybil Brand. Amanda had delivered the clothes and dealt with the envy during the forty-five minutes until Nora was processed out. Now, Nora came closer, flanked by two deputies, as was the policy with high profile prisoners. Amanda's covetousness disappeared in the face of Nora's need. She felt a momentary sympathy because Nora looked less than stunning.

She had lost weight and her face was pale, her eyes red-rimmed. She was silent, not sullen, perhaps, but beaten. Sad. Her heart almost empty of hope and confidence because, if Amanda failed, Nora knew she had lived her future in the last nine days and twelve hours. The steel door was opening, the stern-faced deputy holding it while Nora slipped past. She was out. Free at last and, perhaps, only for the moment.

"Hi." Nora's husky voice greeted her.

"Hi."

The two women went through the door that had no lock, one made of wood and clear glass. Neither of them wanted to see chicken-wire-laced glass again for as long as they lived.

Outside, their heels made hollow sounds on the concrete walk, muffling slightly when they stepped onto the asphalt parking lot. Amanda moved quickly, ahead of Nora by a foot. That she was unhappy was evident.

"Amanda?" Nora called.

Amanda stopped abruptly, only now realizing that she'd been storming through the visitor's parking, leaving Nora in her wake. She waited, muttering "Sorry" when Nora caught up.

"It's okay," Nora answered meekly in a timbre so atypical it grated on Amanda's ears.

Nora came alongside, moving automatically, falling in step with her sister, allowing the uncomfortable silence between them. Amanda tightened her lips, waiting for Nora to speak. She remained silent and that silence seemed to Amanda accusatory. She hated shit like that. She hated pouting. If Nora was pouting…

"What?" Amanda stopped again.

Nora shook her head. "I…" She seemed to be struggling. Her eyes darted past Amanda then back to the ground again. This was a far cry from the Nora of nine days and twelve hours ago. Poor baby. Life was hard. She was scared. Like she was the only one!

"Look," Amanda snapped, "I know you've been through a lot. I'm sorry for that. But don't lay it at my doorstep. If you want me to apologize for taking so long to come up with the bail, I won't. I did my best. This was as good as I could do so don't give me any crap."

"That's absurd." Amanda heard the confusion shading

Nora's voice but chose to dismiss it. "I don't blame you for anything. Why would you think that?"

"Because of the way you're acting." Amanda breathed out harshly in exasperation. God, it was as obvious as the nose on her face. "This lip-biting shit. Silence like I should know what you're thinking, like you're accusing me of something. Or maybe you're waiting for me to say or do something to make you feel like everything's going to be all right. Well I can't, Nora. I can't. I haven't got the words." Amanda dropped her hands. She felt like a fishwife, standing in this parking lot, giving her sister what-for. A half step to the left and she leaned forward as if to whisper but couldn't bring herself to get too close to Nora for fear of doing her bodily harm. "I don't know what to do and I'm not going to have you sulking around making me second guess myself, like there really is some way I'm letting you down even though I'm doing my best."

"Amanda." Nora was tentative, as though the effort of speaking was tiring. "That's not it at all. I just want to tell you that I realize I made a terrible mistake. I can't hold you to your promise to defend me."

"Big of you, after I just posted bail," Amanda drawled. She wanted to bite her tongue. But the bite was in her tone. Nora hadn't noticed. She talked on.

"I know it's bad timing. I've put you in a terrible position. We haven't meant much to each other over the years. I didn't look for you when times were good, I shouldn't be putting you on the spot when things are bad. If you don't honestly feel you can defend me properly, then I don't want you to feel you owe me anything. I mean you really don't—"

"Oh, for God's sake, Nora," Amanda said pushing her hands so deep into the pockets of her jacket she could feel the seams give.

"For God's sake, what?" Nora demanded without much force. Tired and frightened and not at all ready for a confrontation, Nora was baffled by Amanda's response. She had expected gratitude, a little soul searching, and a final, reluctant acceptance of the offer. Anger hadn't been one of the options.

Amanda looked at her sister. She was sorry she had. There were tears—goddamn tears—in her sister's eyes. Darn. Darn. Darn it all. Amanda walked a few steps away.

A group of young men hovered near an old blue Chevy. Their baseball caps were worn backwards, their clothes five sizes too big, as if their mothers were hedging against a growth spurt. But they'd never be big men. Even Amanda could see that.

Behind her was the prison. A typically unattractive county building, a temple erected to the god of mediocre architecture and bureaucratic ineptitude.

The hill on which the prison sat was silent, solitary, pretty. Amanda wanted to sit down and look at the trees, feel the cool air, forget that the blackened heart of LA was a short ride down the road. Instead, she started to walk. Slowly, the cadence not dictated by her anger. Nora was only a step behind.

"Christ." Amanda muttered. "All you think about is yourself. This martyr thing doesn't suit you."

"Amanda, please." Nora had never needed words like this before. They came with difficulty.

Amanda picked up the pace, moving fast as if they were playing ditch 'em. Then there were second thoughts. She stopped, twirling as if to reason with Nora, starting forward again, arms flapping, shoulder purse slipping and being flipped into position once more to cover her own loss of words. No. She was afraid to say the ones that came to mind. Thirty-eight years of loneliness, of trying hard, of working her ass off, to end up needed, then discarded once again. There were thoughts of Mark Fleming, of her house, of Leo Riordon, of a system that would chew her up and spit her out. Amanda was going to burst with frustration.

"What do you want me to do, Nora? What?" Amanda was talking loudly almost yelling, her voice rising to assault the hills and trees, the late-day sunshine, and the surprisingly clean air. This was her special brand of pollution. Already she was feeling better. Anxiety completely out of control was therapeutic. "Do you pull this kind of crap so people will fall at your feet? I mean, is it a reassurance thing? Test the commitment time? Christ, I'm glad all I have to do is defend you; I sure as hell would hate to date you."

Stop. Start. Amanda's face flushed. It was enough said but she couldn't help herself. The floodgates were open.

"Nora, you're just not that special. You are not that smart. Don't try to wrap me around your little finger. I've already wound myself around it and I'm not too thrilled about that. Guilty or not, I'm not going to turn my back on you. I keep my promises."

Amanda stopped to get her bearings. They were almost at the car. To slip inside now, together, was dangerous. She and Nora were a combustible mix. Better to finish this in the open, where they could keep their distance, where Amanda could breathe fire and not burn herself in the process. More calmly now, Amanda spoke to her sister, keeping her eyes trained on the horizon, locking them anywhere but on Nora.

"Listen. In the grand scheme of things what really matters is that we're in the middle of this mess and we'd better do the best we can to rectify it. I would have preferred that neither of us found ourselves here. But all we can do is hang together. I'll do my best. I don't know…"

Another group of visitors to the jail had just rolled up. Amanda indicated to Nora that they should move closer to the car, then turned on her heel, forcing her sister to follow like a child fallen out of favor.

"I'm not happy about putting my house up as bond. I'm not happy about that at all. I've worked years to get that place and I could lose it in the blink of an eye if you get hinky. Now, I know it probably doesn't look like much to you," Amanda threw up her hands, surprised at her own stupidity. "I forgot you've never been to my house. Gosh, guess you've just been too busy. But I can tell you that after seeing your place, mine would make you cringe. No high ceilings, no recessed lighting. I've got a little booth in the kitchen that's upholstered in green Naugahyde instead of a fancy glass table."

Amanda skipped around the rear of a pickup, her damn purse slipping off her shoulder again. She gathered it up, pulled it close to her, and never missed a beat. She was on a roll. Maybe all these years she had been ticked off at Nora for being better. Maybe she was just pissed because she, Amanda, wasn't good enough.

"You wouldn't like it at all but it's mine. I love that house and I've put it in jeopardy because you let your hormones run wild and decided you couldn't live without Lucas Mallory. You left half your body in that suite. Hair and blood. And what about your accessories? How am I supposed to defend you with the kind of evidence they've got? Why didn't you just leave the poor man alone? Why couldn't you just be happy having almost everything?"

"Whoa! Wait!"

Nora skirted to the left, circumventing a BMW, half skipping to cut Amanda off before she reached her Toyota. So much for pity. Nora obviously hadn't been as adversely affected by her stint in Sybil Brand as Amanda had imagined. They faced off over the shining hood of the little German car. It was red, the same color as the flush of indignation staining Nora's cheeks.

"You are a misery, Amanda. How you love to wallow in all this self-destructive nonsense. Nobody ever handed you anything. Nobody ever gave you a break. Nobody loved poor old, plain Amanda. Well, drop it, Amanda, because it's not flying with me. I'm sorry about your house but I didn't ask you to put it up for me. As I recall, I suggested you might want to think twice about it. Or have you conveniently forgotten that?"

"What else was I supposed to do?" Amanda muttered. "Leave you here?"

"You should have had the guts to do what you *wanted* to do." Nora's nostrils flared, making her thin face look animated and beautiful once more. "But you know what I think? I think you are doing exactly what you want. You like the fact that I'm dependent on you. You're strong; I'm not. You're in control; I'm losing it. I think you like that, playing the lawyer, the savior. Or at least you did until reality set in. Now you've got to face the music. Or—what would be a typical Amanda Cross to-hell-with-convention adage?—how about 'Shit or get off the pot'? Is that appropriately crude?"

Amanda could barely mask her humiliation. Considering their estrangement, Nora had a surprisingly clear idea of who Amanda was. Amanda only wished the situation could be reversed. She moved forward, not wanting to hear anymore, but Nora wouldn't let her go so easily.

"You know, Amanda, now that we're getting down to it, I think I understand what's going on. You're trying to make me feel responsible for your decision. You're mad at yourself, have been for years, but you're taking it out on me so you won't get hurt. God, that's rich but it has nothing to do with what needs to be done. Work out your problems with self-esteem on your own time. I'm paying you and this is my dime so we'll make this business only, okay? Here goes, one more time: business only."

Nora looked frail despite the strength of her words. Her vanity was faltering, she was desperate to hold on to the last vestige of her arrogance—not to mention her only hope for a sympathetic defense. She spoke slowly, forming her words with lips that had lost all color.

"I did not pursue Lucas Mallory. We were having an affair. Two adults who knew exactly what they were doing. It was a regular, run-of-the-mill affair. That—is—the—truth."

Nora stopped talking. Amanda didn't respond. Nora still had the ball. She decided to take it down court on her own.

"I offered to release you from your obligation to me because it has become obvious in the last week that you don't think I'm innocent. I thought you would respect that offer and make a professional decision, or a personal one if it boils down to that, based on what you feel is best. But don't you dare turn this thing around and try to make me responsible for the ineptitude of my own defense. Christ, you're setting me up. You're telling me exactly why you think I'm guilty so I can't blame you when you fail to do your job. What a scam, Amanda. What a miserable, mean little scam."

Amanda didn't want to hear any more. It was a trick

with mirrors. Nora was turning everything around. She was clever. Amanda didn't know what to think. The hill on which they stood seemed less a refuge now than the natural barrier to freedom it was meant to be. Behind her was a prison. Beside her was a woman who frightened her with her insight. Amanda needed time to think.

"Let's go, Nora. This isn't the place," she muttered, making halfhearted motions toward the ever-growing crowd of visitors that was wending its way through the parking lot, visiting hours ending for the day. It would be so easy to stop this if Nora cooperated. She didn't.

Nora rounded the BMW's hood, still keeping her distance, standing off as if she were ready to fight if necessary. The color in her cheeks had become near neon, making the rest of her complexion appear ghostly pale. Amanda watched with fascination. That Nora could become so angry, so ready to physically underscore that anger, amazed her. *Ruth Mallory.* Amanda shook her head, dispelling the images of the bloody body seen in the pictures Leo had provided. Amanda really didn't believe it possible, even now, that Nora could have done that. Not really. But Nora was snarling, demanding Amanda pay attention. Had she demanded the same of Ruth?

"I don't care if the Pope is passing. I want us to understand each other. Now, I'm not a criminal lawyer but it's easy to see that the evidence is pretty damning. I just don't think it's enough." Nora's arched brows pulled together— the outraged queen finding out Snow White still lived. Her fingers trailed along the hood of the BMW as though the touch of it kept her grounded. When she spoke again, the outrage was laced with apprehension and frantic fear and her voice was quieter. "I thought you, at least, believed I was sleeping with the man. You won't even take my word for that one thing? That one, most important thing? You won't even give me the benefit of the doubt, will you? And why? Because you feel inept. Because you want me to be guilty. You want me to be dreadfully flawed so that your own faults don't look so awful."

Amanda met her sister's eyes.

So passionate.

She tried to ignore the questions and accusations.

So correct.

She opened her heart.

So difficult.

"Get in the car."

Nora remained where she was. Knuckles white, tendons cording along the top of her slender hands.

So strong.

Surprise.

Her lips were dry. Amanda licked them before she spoke.

"Look, I didn't mean to do that—set you up like that. I was venting. I have no intention of taking off. And I don't think you can fault me for being afraid for both of us." Amanda conveniently sidestepped the question of her ineptitude, moving right along to the heart of the matter. "Nor do I think you can fault me for wondering about you and Lucas Mallory. Stuff like that doesn't happen in my life. Casual affairs don't happen in most people's lives. Usually there are feelings involved, emotions, desires. You and Lucas Mallory and everybody at DM&M, you're all just different from the rest of us. You have objectives and that's where you head come hell or high water. We mere mortals aren't sure how to react when you fall into the middle of our lives. So I accept I might have acted badly. But, Nora, hey," Amanda shrugged, still managing to keep her purse close. "I'm at a real loss here. Facts are facts. A law firm, no matter how big, is an intimate place. People see things."

Amanda let Nora think about that while she unlocked her Toyota. The driver's door creaked when Amanda pulled it open. She used it to lean on. Behind her, a young child shrieked, a woman railed, a slap was heard. Neither Amanda nor Nora turned to watch. Everybody was getting beaten up in this parking lot one way or another. Quieter now, Amanda put forth her case.

"Eyes are everywhere in a place like Dimsdale, Morris and Mott, Nora. People want to know what's going on especially with the higher-ups or the fast trackers like you. It's just human nature. Secretaries talk. Associates talk. Hell, the janitors talk. So why is it that nobody—not one single, solitary soul—has bothered to come forward and back you up regarding Lucas Mallory? Why hasn't anyone I questioned corroborated your story?"

Nora opened her mouth. Her full bottom lip quivered beneath a light sheen of clear gloss. Her direct gaze wavered slightly, then reestablished its focus. She remained silent. Amanda dug deeper.

"Think about it. You tell the world that this thing between you and Lucas was real and what happens? Anyone who's anyone in the legal community in Los Angeles turns their back on you. They point the finger. They want you taken down. They commiserate with Lucas Mallory. They side with DM&M. They…" Amanda kicked at the ground, and then looked down to see if she'd done any damage. This wasn't new information, she needn't waste her breath. "If just one person, just one"—Amanda held up a finger and shook it heavenward. Her voice was rising, not in anger now but in frustration—"Find me one person to support your story and I'd be much more inclined to give it some credence. But how am I going to prove it if you can't? If even the guy you were supposedly sleeping with denies it?"

Amanda ended on a note of despair. A woman hollering affair and a guy calmly insisting she harbored an unhealthy fascination was no contest. Bottom line: nobody was going to believe a woman like Nora was a victim, even if Lucas Mallory was the fastest talking, most libido-driven, power-wielding guy about town. Nora was too pulled together, too smart to be a victim. And from what Amanda knew of Lucas Mallory, he was a gentleman, unexciting, and hardly a sex object.

"Amanda. *I'm* giving the story credence," Nora insisted any hint of dread well hidden or completely banished. Nora was a chameleon and Amanda needed a plain, garden-variety client if she was going to keep up. "You don't know a lot about me and I don't know much about you but one thing you must know is that Mom and Dad didn't raise a liar. You're not. Neither am I. The best that's in you is in me, too. Not better. Just the same. Different circumstances, same right stuff."

"Then why isn't there anyone who'll back you up?"

"Because Lucas was a smart man, and," Nora added miserably, "I was a smart woman. I wasn't in love so I didn't do stupid things."

Nora splayed her hands on the beautiful red BMW, needing it to support her, now that the time had come to be completely honest. A female Atlas, stoic with the weight of the world on her shoulders.

"Amanda, I didn't want Lucas Mallory for the rest of my life. He was a senior partner in one of the largest law firms in the California. He's attractive and attentive. Lucas could even be a bit of fun. But more than that, I could learn from him. Things I never could have found out in the course of a professional, office relationship. The politics of it all, the subtleties of this legal life. We discussed our strange commitment to the business of law, over and above the commitment to another person. It was a game, a challenge, and the affair was interesting for both of us."

Nora pushed herself away from the car as if to prove she could stand alone. Her hands were in the pockets of her trousers. She looked like a Ralph Lauren model; she sounded wounded.

"I wanted to be where he was. He, I think, wanted to be back where I was. You know, starting over, clean slate, seeing things he could have done differently. Maybe he was looking for the excitement again. Some of his choices had been bad. He admitted that. Sometimes I got the idea that maybe Ruth was one of those bad choices but I didn't question it. She didn't interest me."

Amanda watched closely. Here was the crux of the matter. Nora looked perfect. More importantly, she sounded perfectly candid.

"So it was really good for both of us. This affair was meant to be terminal. I don't need a man to validate me, for God's sake. I only needed one of those men to mentor me. I got that and a lot more. Lucas got a lot back."

"I'm sure he did," Amanda muttered, still wary. "But why didn't anyone else know about your relationship?"

Nora's head fell back, long hair cascading down her back, gold highlighted and silky. Her unending neck arched elegantly toward the sky. Slowly, she pulled in a deep breath, righted herself, and tried to explain with not-quite-defeated, not-quite-shamed patience:

"Lucas is an extremely careful man. If he makes

a mistake, he rectifies it and learns from it. Mostly, he doesn't make mistakes. We had rules for everything and I was happy to follow them. I didn't want any ties and I didn't want to ever have it be said that I slept my way to partnership. I worked my butt off for that firm and I was going to earn the partnership when it was offered. I would be the first woman to do so. I was just as happy as he was to keep our relationship quiet.

"The only place we were ever affectionate or intimate was in my home. It's secluded. My neighbors are all professional, private people. We ordered food in or I cooked. Sometimes he tried to make something but he'd been married to Ruth for thirty-two years."

"Ruth was the perfect partner's wife. She stood by him when he was struggling and enjoyed the rewards when he was at the top. Her life was the house, entertaining, charities. His was the law. That's what we shared. Everything else of Lucas's belonged to Ruth. Lucas respected her and he would have died before hurting her. He really is that kind of man."

"I thought you said that he'd made a mistake marrying her."

Nora flashed a look of impatience her sister's way. "I said I thought he felt that. We didn't discuss it. It was a feeling I had. That didn't keep him from not wanting to rock the boat. Ruth made his life very easy. He didn't want to leave her. I didn't want him to. Ergo, I had no reason to want Ruth Mallory dead."

Nora moved toward the Toyota, then opened the passenger door. Amanda wondered what memories she was reliving at that moment.

"That sounds reasonable. But, Nora, you're not fooling me. I asked a question. I want a specific answer. Why can't anyone else corroborate your story?"

Nora seemed startled as if she'd forgotten Amanda was even there.

"That's easy enough to explain. I told you before, we had rules—times he would leave the office, times he would arrive at my house, leave my house. In the office I was assigned to his supervisory group well before we began to sleep together so there were no changes in our office habits."

Nora wasn't looking at Amanda anymore. Not quite as forthcoming. Lying? Fudging? Who knew?

"Sure, I might go to his office for a minute or two to play those stupid games people in situations like that do but the point is it wasn't unusual for me to be in there behind closed doors. My walking into Lucas's office couldn't be construed as anything more than an associate checking in with a senior partner who has supervised her work since day one. End of story. There aren't hidden cameras, no recording devices. What was anyone to know?"

"Is there someone you confided in?" Nora shook her head. Amanda reiterated in disbelief, "No one?"

Nora shook her head harder, refusing to look Amanda in the eye. "I'm not much of a woman's woman if you know what I mean."

Amanda sighed.

"Somehow I could have guessed that. At least we have something in common." Amanda tried a smile. Nora's return grin was weak or possibly uninterested. "Any guys he might have told?"

"The rest of the senior partners. Don. Oliver. I doubt he would have said anything to Peter. He doesn't like Peter very much. Lucas is such a gentleman and Peter Sweeney is gutter bully made good."

"Great. So, all I have to do is get an interview with these guys and beg them to tell the truth about what they say in the senior partners' john."

Amanda shook her head as if to say this was not going to be an easy thing, this was not going to be a fun thing. No wonder the god of legal snafus had never tapped her for anything more complicated than indigent defense. This was downright ulcer-generating stuff.

Amanda was suddenly tired. She wanted away from the jail, she wanted a burger, and she wanted to get to work. Memories of Nora's pained, enigmatic expression as she came out of jail, the sad, clinical recitation of Nora's love life, had left Amanda feeling lucky in a way and for that, she felt guilty.

"Okay," Amanda muttered. "Okay. Don't worry, we'll figure something out. Get in. I'm hungry and I'm tired. There's a lot of work to do, and the day is almost over."

Nora nodded. She did as she was told. Inside the car, their seat belts firmly fastened, Nora and Amanda sat side by side without saying a word. Finally, Amanda inserted the key into the ignition and started the car. She sat back once more, as if too weary to drive. Finally, she reached for the emergency brake. Amanda was about to set the world in motion when Nora's hand covered hers.

It was a cool and lovely hand. Amanda looked at it and figured out something very important. Lucas Mallory, being at the core of all things only a man, would have had a difficult time running away or ignoring or spurning that hand if it reached out for him. Wasn't it much more likely that any man, even Lucas Mallory, would have been flattered and desirous of Nora Royce's attention? In fact, couldn't it even be said that any man, even Lucas Mallory, might kill for Nora's affection?

Amazed at such a thought, shamed that she had refused to believe Nora and accept that which was natural, Amanda turned toward her sister. Nora was already looking at her, tears swimming in her eyes, her beautiful face twisted with a terrible, undefined emotion.

"I'm so afraid." Nora whispered. It was her secret.

Amanda needed to hear no more. Her arms wrapped around her sister. Her little sister. She held tight, not wanting to admit that now, believing Nora, Amanda herself was more terrified of what lay ahead than she had been the day this nightmare started.

Nora, safely comforted in Amanda's arms, stared dry-eyed at the Sybil Brand Correctional Facility for Women.

Chapter 10

"I want you to make a list of all the assignations you had with Lucas. Every meeting, no matter how insignificant. If you saw him at the Laundromat and shared a load I want to know about it. Names of friends he mentioned. Addresses of anyone you know about in his life who isn't affiliated with DM&M. His jeweler. His dentist. Where he has his car washed. Everything. We need to start thinking in terms of hard data. All this mooning about, swearing to ourselves that a jury is going to take your word over his is ludicrous. I don't know what's the matter with me but I seem to be procrastinating like a pro. If I don't stop running in circles we're going to have a hell of a mess on our hands once this thing goes to trial. The way Leo's pushing, you'd think he was a defender of the Constitution. Fair and speedy trial. Hah! This thing is going faster than the speed of light. The grand jury handed down that indictment like it was a hot potato."

Nora laughed quietly and without amusement, in a nod to Amanda's attempt at humor. A few hours ago, in her sister's arms, she had finally cried. It was a new experience, crying for emotional release, and one equally uncomfortable for Amanda. Thankfully, she was not a needy person, so she put those uncomfortable moments behind her, answering Amanda in a steady voice.

"That's not a problem. I don't believe it will do much good. Lucas hasn't—"

Amanda cut her off quickly, her hands over her ears. "I don't want to hear it. Your job is not to point out how futile my efforts are, Nora."

"Sorry."

Amanda dismissed the apology, abandoning the hear-no-evil stance.

"We don't care what he does. The strategy isn't to *prove* anything with this exercise. Listen," Amanda used her hands to punctuate her speech. "I had a guy once who swore up and down that he'd been with the same woman every Saturday night for the past year so he couldn't possibly have robbed a liquor store on Saturday night. Jim L. Beanerd." Amanda chuckled and shook her head. "Name sounded just like it was spelled, poor guy. The court reporter broke out laughing every time she had to type that name.

"Well, the woman was on the stand, and the prosecutor kept asking her date by date what she'd been doing every Saturday night starting the first of January. She got so confused by the tactic that even though she actually had been with this guy on each occasion, the jury didn't believe she could be telling the truth because she couldn't remember exact times, what she was wearing, you know, the details. It worked great, that strategy was a stroke of genius. I lost the case. Felt awful because Mr. Beanerd wasn't guilty. But I learned something, too."

"Amanda." Nora interrupted peevishly. "Lucas Mallory isn't some woman who has a standing date. He's not going to get confused. I've seen him handle witnesses without as much as a note on a scrap of paper. The question, after the prosecution gets finished, will be how he could screw around on Ruth, no matter what we prove. Ruth was one of those well-loved society types, I'm a..." Nora's smile was wry as she leaned her chin on her upturned palm. Amanda could have sworn she swaggered, even though she was seated. Her eyes were bright and very pretty. Amanda realized they got that way when Nora was about to be terribly honest. "I'm a bitch on wheels, determined to rise to the top of the legal ladder. I don't bow to propriety. I don't believe sensuality has to be put on the back burner so I can perform mental gymnastics in the courtroom. I know what I am and I know people hate that. They could forgive me for being myself if they thought I honestly didn't have a clue about the effect I have on people. But I know everything about how I affect the people I work with. If I edited a fashion magazine they would not only accept me, they would admire me. This affair would be imbued with panache, making it not only acceptable but chic." The smile was gone. "But I don't edit a fashion magazine. I write briefs. I argue cases. I win and that makes me feel great while it disturbs everyone else. Sometimes it even makes them angry. They're jealous, the women and the men. They never stood up to me They're not going to stand up for me. If I'm gone so is the competition so is the need to examine their poor, miserable little lives in comparison to mine."

Lounging in her chair with the languid look of a film star, Nora toyed with a button on her sleeve. She picked at it, positive she was better, that she was a threat. Forsaking the button, Nora let her arms lay on the chair rests.

"We also must mention the fact that Lucas taking me

to bed is considered highly unethical in certain circles."

Amanda, feeling the need to move in order to escape the dreamy spell Nora was casting, switched on the desk lamp against the gathering gloom. Nora's eyes seemed brittle in the artificial illumination and they were on Amanda. She turned away from the desk and opened a file drawer.

Passively, Nora complimented her. "I think you're awfully courageous to do this."

Amanda laughed roughly and slammed the drawer shut harder than she intended. She'd found what she wanted. Notes from an article on the process of discovery in criminal cases. It was a long article that said little much like Nora's uninformative transgression.

"It would be courageous if I had something to lose. I'm a nobody. That makes me stupid, not courageous." Nora shifted in her chair as Amanda slid into hers, ready to turn the tables and set the mood herself. "So who do you think killed Ruth Mallory?"

Nora started ever so slightly, life coming back into those glassy eyes. "How would I know?"

"Come on, Nora, you were sleeping with the lady's husband," Amanda reminded her, legal pad set up for notes, eyes forward. "I've got to assume you didn't discuss issue-in-fact, screw, then move right on to a lively debate on bilateral contracts along with the post-coital cigarette. There had to be pillow talk. There had to be some inkling that he was unhappy with his wife. Maybe her dog hated her or the mailman was making advances to the little woman. Something. Anything. Maybe she was skimming the charity take and we're looking in the wrong direction completely. People who sleep together don't just do it and depart. If that was the case, then you wouldn't be colleagues. You'd be on call and he'd have to change his name to John."

"That's crude, Amanda."

"I practice."

Nora was miffed and she looked tired.

"Amanda, I've been trying to explain what kind of relationship Lucas and I had but you seem to be resisting understanding it. We're not the same, you and I. You just keep charging ahead chasing after things. I sit and wait for whatever. So, doesn't it follow that I'm not going to involve myself with someone who wears his heart on his sleeve or expends a lot of energy doing something that is actually a simple physical release? I never expected to see stars, you know? I never expected love the way you do."

"How would you know what I expect?" Amanda challenged.

"Oh, come on. I saw a lot when you popped home for a visit. You always had a plan and four contingencies. When none of them worked out, you charged after the next option. You just never gave up. Dad thought that was a good quality. Mom worried."

"And you?"

"I thought it was a shame you wasted so much energy. I never could figure out why you didn't get exactly what you wanted. You were pretty, you worked hard, you were intelligent." Nora laid her assessment in front of her sister.

Amanda sighed. She was older. She was wiser. She knew the answer to Nora's question.

"And you're beautiful, worked for what you want, and are brilliant. Things come differently to different people. Fate. That's all it is. Let's shelve the reminiscing and philosophizing and get back to work."

Amanda shut her mouth, tired of this conversation and unwilling to spend anymore time on it. The fact that

Nora had such memories of her was unnerving. The fact that there was a shade of pity in her voice was appalling. Amanda picked up the file but the door opened before she could refer to it.

Peeved, Amanda looked up. Nora glanced over her shoulder. Amanda felt the beginnings of a smile. Fully expecting the visitor to be Mark, Amanda found herself staring at an unfamiliar man. It was Nora who rose to greet him, a surprisingly warm smile on her lips.

"Edward! Edward!" She was in his arms. Nora kissed his cheek, held him by the shoulders as though he were a long-lost brother.

As sisters, they had never touched in happiness, only briefly in grief at their parents' funeral.

"Nora, I wasn't expecting to find you here." The voice went with the bearing. Both were ill at ease.

He was no taller than Nora, compact, and beautifully proportioned. A clothes kind of guy. He eyed Amanda, who eyed him right back. She was disappointed in Nora's choice of friends but not surprised.

Edward's hair was slicked back from a low, sharp brow giving his pretty face a hard edge. His skin was smooth. Small ears rode low and were neatly pinned back against his skull, his ultra-cool razor cut showing them to their best advantage. His nose was slightly hawked, the way a good Italian stud's should be, and it shadowed lips that Botticelli's angels would have killed for. Pink and comely, the bottom one was full, the top bowed. Black, hungry-looking eyes took a chunk out of everything in the office. His appetite was hard to satisfy, because the eyes kept moving, glistening under full, straight brows. Amanda was losing interest. She did a quick take on the rest of him: teal-colored silk turtleneck, multicolored scarf knit with a fine needle, corduroy trousers of such delicate weave they fell in perfect soft pleats. Expensive.

Wordlessly, peevishly, Nora stepped away.

"No, Nora, I didn't mean I wasn't happy to see you."

Edward took her hand, pulling her back into his personal space easily as if that was proof enough she'd been mistaken.

"You must have been looking for me then." Amanda stood up, offering her hand as she came around the desk, ready to get this show on the road and head it out the door. Nora could do whatever it was she did with this guy on her own time. "You don't look like the type that needs a nanny."

Edward looked puzzled. Amanda let it slide. It would take too much energy to explain and lose whatever pithy flavor it possessed in the translation.

"If you're Amanda Cross, yes, I was looking for you."

Nora took over. Old habits died hard.

"Amanda. Edward Ramsey. We worked at Dimsdale, Morris and Mott together. Well, not really together…"

"No, not really." Edward released Nora and moved away from her.

Amanda watched. Satisfied that he was only nervous and not malevolent in Nora's presence, Amanda gave him her attention. They all sat as if for tea. Amanda waited for Edward to ask her for Nora's hand. He was on the edge of his seat, ill at ease. He did the only thing he could. He explained.

"I was fairly new, not exactly in the same league as Nora. I must admit I envied you your court time." With a small laugh, he apologized for that character flaw. Nora remained silent. There wasn't much to say. She was a better attorney than he. "Anyhow, I, uh, feel awful about what's happening to Nora." He was talking to Amanda now in low, dismayed tones. "It's unconscionable that DM&M has abandoned her. That she spent even a minute in Sybil Brand is beyond me. This is a nightmare. The prosecution would be happy with a lynching."

When Edward shook his head, not a hair on it moved. Edward could play the role of Barbie's perennial date, Ken or one of Don Corleone's overenthusiastic henchmen. It was surprising DM&M had found a role for him. Perhaps the Anglicized name helped pave the way. Whatever his story, Amanda wanted the condensed version. There wasn't time to sit and listen to his very hip condolences.

"Mr. Ramsey, I don't mean to be rude. Perhaps you'd like to talk with Nora alone. I have an awful lot of work to do. There's a coffee shop two blocks down—"

"No. Oh, no. I really meant it when I said I didn't expect to find Nora here. I came to see you. You're her attorney of record, aren't you?"

"I have that distinction," Amanda concurred, the opulent word sounding ridiculous in the context of her third-rate office. Edward didn't seem to notice the contrast.

"Good. Then we can talk about this case."

Amanda laughed. "Mr. Ramsey. Do I look stupid or is it just you?"

"Amanda," Nora objected only to be brushed aside.

"Nora, I'm busy, okay?" Amanda snapped pressing against her desk as if it were the only thing keeping her from throwing herself at him. "I seem to remember some professor in law school telling me that it would be a really idiotic thing to do—talk about my case with anyone before I presented it. In this instance an employee of Dimsdale, Morris and Mott is the last person I would choose to bare my soul to. I'd love to take your statement but I have no intention of entering into a discussion with you even about the weather."

Edward blushed. Amanda thought it was, perhaps, with youthful embarrassment at his ridiculous faux pas; a moment later, she realized he was reddening with annoyance. The physical manifestations of his irritation disappeared so quickly Amanda wondered if she had imagined them. When he spoke again, she realized that something had changed. Gone was the anxious young lawyer. In his place was a man with a mission.

"Amanda."

She bridled at the use of her given name but the guy was into what he had to say and suavely ignored her.

"If you won't discuss Nora's case with me, then I'm afraid I've done something I'll regret for the rest of my life. You see, I no longer work for Dimsdale, Morris and Mott. I came to ask if I could work with you. I want to help Nora because, in fact, I know she's not guilty."

Chapter 11

Amanda and Nora stared at Edward Ramsey. The silence was so acute they could hear Consuelo in the office next door reaming someone out in a rush of piercingly pitched Spanish. The minute she slammed the phone down, the spell was broken. Nora picked up the slack.

"Are you out of your mind? Your partnership…" Edward's small, heavily lashed eyes widened, proving them even more beautiful than Amanda had originally thought. Funny that Nora should worry about the kid's partnership problems before his incredible statement exonerating her.

He stuttered his reply. It was a charming effect. "No. I—I actually thought I was doing something quite heroic. What's happening to you isn't right, Nora. If it can happen to you, then what chance do the rest of us have? I mean—"

"Wait just a goddamn minute, you little twit!"

Amanda was up and around her desk. Roughly, she pulled the client chair toward the couch. It caught on a small tear in the rug. She jerked it upright, slammed it down, and plopped herself in the seat. Edward popped up. She motioned him back down. He complied and their knees almost touched. Sadly, his were skinnier. She leaned forward and got in his face, simultaneously warning Nora into silence with a glance as the younger woman perched herself on the arm of the sofa beside Edward.

"What's going on here?" she demanded. "You walk into this office almost two weeks after Nora's arrest and announce you know she's not guilty. You let her go through hell and then you want us to believe you've got the key to this mess? Now you're very kindly offering to help us put it into the keyhole? Well, shit, where were you on day one, Bucko? Somebody have you hog-tied in the associate's john at DM&M?"

"I was doing what I thought was right for me then," he shot back, undaunted by Amanda's ire. "Now I'm doing what's right. Period." When Amanda didn't gather him gratefully to her bosom, Edward got defensive. "Hey, I'm not a saint. I had to think about the consequences. It took me a while."

"Ain't that just sweet."

"Amanda," Nora broke in, her husky voice dragging Amanda's attention toward her. "He's here to help. Maybe we should listen to him." To Edward, she said, "I can't believe you quit. That job meant the world to you. It was your life."

"No. No, no, no. This is screwed. Nora, you're acting like this guy is really worried about your butt. He's not. I tell you there's more to this," Amanda said flatly. Angrily, she turned back toward Edward. "Did you get fired or something?"

"I did not," Edward flashed back but the ensuing silence was almost transparent. As much as Amanda wanted to see through it, only Nora could manage to do it. Thoughtfully, she offered an explanation.

"The Marilee merger."

Edward's face reddened, "I don't unders—"

"I think you do," Nora responded cutting him off easily, impressed that Amanda had caught on before she did. "Just before"—Nora lowered her eyes, twirled her finger in the air—"all this, Lucas mentioned that account was in trouble because someone misworded a guarantee clause that cost the client millions." Silence. "You were working on that merger, weren't you?"

"Yes. And I admit I was the one who messed up but I wasn't fired for it. Sure, Sweeney wasn't happy." Nora snorted at the understatement. More firmly, Edward reiterated, "All right, he wasn't happy at all. But my being here has nothing to do with Marilee. I know there was a possibility that the Marilee problem might affect my partnership status at DM&M but that was years down the road. It would have been forgotten. But—"

"But you were up shit creek nonetheless and you weren't sure a few years were enough to ingratiate yourself to those fellows." Amanda finished losing interest in him. He was a hustler. She needed help, not someone walking off with the store in the middle of the night.

"All right, I'll admit it," Edward held up his hand like a wayward Boy Scout. It was an unconvincing gesture but Amanda gave him an *A* for effort. "That was a sticky situation. But Nora's right, too. That firm was my life. I'd made a commitment to it. I was going to ride my wave to the end and I would have despite the Marilee screw up."

"Except for?" Amanda prodded.

"Except, I realized what was happening to Nora had larger implications. The firm wasn't standing up for her. At first I could understand it, given the evidence. But then it got kind of creepy because everybody was just sort of going on with their business as if Nora had never existed. Then I thought what if I was in a mess? I couldn't count on jack shit from them—any of them."

"And you think you should be able to rely on them?"

"Yeah," Edward's chin jutted out in momentary defiance. "I think I should be able to. I give them fifteen hours a day, sometimes more. I live there on the weekends. My billings are my life and it's my billings that make the partners rich. I would have given them years and they could still keep a partnership from me. Now, I'll admit I was never as good as Nora."

He shot her a look that was at once unreadable, yet somehow telling. Amanda didn't have time to decipher the underlying meaning because he was talking at her again.

"And if they're going to throw the best of us to the wolves the minute they're at the door, then I say screw 'em. I can do better on my own."

"Mr. Ramsey, I think you're wasting our time," Amanda commented coolly, "and I resent it. I think you're on the rebound because, if you weren't fired, DM&M made it pretty clear that your future with them was limited. Which brings us to the next point you made. If you can do better on your own, if you're so damned independent, what are you doing here?"

"Excellent question." Edward perked up, black eyes dancing.

He blossomed as he launched into his pitch. The kid should have been a used car salesman, Amanda thought. He would have made a fortune. "I'm here because I'm not that good. I mean, I don't want to spend the next ten years scrounging around, hoping for a good case to come along so I can make a name for myself. I like to eat. I have a certain standard of living I'd prefer to maintain, if you know what I mean."

"I wouldn't know," Amanda rejoined hoping she wouldn't have to point out the obvious. Edward's eyes flicked over her, then over her digs. It was a minor fumble. He recovered nicely.

"Anyway, I need to jump-start my practice, get out there with a bang. Nora's case is going to get a lot of attention. I think there's major notoriety potential here. If I'm part of the team and we win, I look like a goddamn crusader. You know, I quit the big time to fight for right. You can get a whole lot of mileage out of something like that."

"And if we lose?" Amanda drawled.

"I'm still part of the publicity chain. We put on a good fight and then I look good. People will say the evidence was overwhelming so there was no way we could win. They'll forgive me for it, they'll say I was part of a heroic effort, and they won't forget my name." Edward grinned. He was pleased with himself to no end. "But I don't think that's going to happen. I don't think you're going to lose."

"What makes you so sure?" Nora asked, leaning forward, almost animated with curiosity.

She watched him closely, her arms crossed in such a way that her blouse ballooned up and fell open, revealing a beautiful swell of breast. Edward didn't even notice. No sexual preoccupation, no divine fixation on Nora. That was a good sign as far as Amanda was concerned. If she let this guy in she didn't want his libido riding along with him.

"Because Lucas Mallory wasn't your victim, Nora. I'm sure you can prove that, no matter what the rest of them say."

The women fell silent until Nora asked, her eyes narrowed as though that would make the truth clearer to see, "You believe me? You believe he and I were having an affair?"

"Sure." No hesitation on Edward's part. He was positive.

Amanda pushed her chair so that it tottered on its back legs. She wanted to jump out of it and into his arms, kiss his face, have him spill his golden guts with the proof they needed that, indeed, Lucas Mallory was a liar. Instead, she plucked a pencil off the desk, flicking the tip of the eraser with her tongue. She thought it would be cool, a demonstration of literate composure. But all she'd done was condemn her tongue to the taste of rubber. The pencil was discarded. She crossed her hands in her lap.

"You're the only one, besides Nora, who has suggested Lucas Mallory, or any of the senior partners, for that matter, are lying about this particular issue. So far we don't—" Amanda stopped herself just in time. To admit to anything, even defeat, would be to tip her hand improperly. "Would you testify that she and Lucas Mallory had a personal relationship, one that was intimate?"

"Be kind of tough, if I'm second seat."

"If I take you on, you'll assist, nothing more. I'm the attorney of record. Would you take that?"

Edward didn't like the idea but he burned his bridges.

"I could live with it."

"Then you could take the stand." Amanda reminded him. "So, I'm asking. Would you testify that Nora and Lucas were an item?"

"Sure. No problem."

"And what proof would you offer? Did you know Lucas Mallory well enough for him to confide in you?" Edward shook his head. "Nora?" He glanced at her almost with regret and shook his head again. "Then what, Mr. Ramsey, have you got?"

"Myself. I have a talent for reading people that is unequaled. Almost a sixth sense, if you will. Believe me, there was never any doubt in my mind that Lucas and Nora had a thing going. There was energy, electricity, between them. It was a quiet kind of business. They were the best I've ever seen. Never a wrong look or word. But it was there. If you're attuned to what people do with one another, it's easy to pick up. But it doesn't surprise me everyone else missed it. For the most part, the people at DM&M are soulless twits."

"But not you? Not Nora?" Amanda prodded.

Edward shook his head, those black eyes of his impudent and cold under his luxurious lashes.

"No," he answered flatly. "There is a method in all my madness and a poetry in all I do and think. As far as Nora is concerned, I don't think romance had anything to do with it. Did it, Nora?"

From the corner of her eye, Amanda saw her sister stiffen. There was affirmation without words, admiration without confirmation, for his deduction.

He smiled contentedly and almost cruelly. "But that didn't keep her from having style. Style and romance are often the same thing—both require a great deal of individual attention to be affective."

With that their triangle pulled taut. Edward was smart. Knowing when to cut the gab, he sat back comfortably on the couch, waiting for the two women to reach a decision. Amanda looked at Nora, Nora at Edward, and Edward at Amanda. He saw the tightening of her jaw. She could have sworn she saw him smile.

Nora turned her head so she could look out the window. The office building across the way was deserted, lit up like a Christmas tree for the benefit of the cleaning crew. The brightness seemed to help her mind work. She commented:

"I can't pay everyone: first you, then that guy you hired—Fleming. I don't think I can afford anyone else. I don't know what you think I can shoulder, Edward."

"Did I ask for money? Our salaries at the firm were comparable," Edward snapped, then, more quietly, "I can last for a while if that's what you're worried about."

Both women looked at him quizzically as if he should have known they'd heard enough from him and now must talk between themselves. His anger surprised them and gave them momentary pause. Edward saw that and took the offensive.

"Christ, is there some problem with you two? I'm offering you help. Legal, Harvard-educated, Bar-sanctioned help. Whatever kind you want. I'm not trying to scam you. We all want something. If I'm part of this, I'll get what I want and you'll get what you want. No shit. No hassles. I know you run the show," he deferred to Amanda, "but I might know things you don't. In fact"—here he smiled broadly and curiously—"I'm sure I do."

More silence now and deeper than before. It was the kind of female quiet that so unnerved men. Women thinking: Caution. Finally, Amanda, matriarchal and capable, addressed him.

"Look, I appreciate you coming here and letting us know that you're on Nora's side, Mr. Ramsey. Personally, I think you've got to be a nut case to take such a drastic step before you talked to us. I'm afraid I'm going to have to say thanks but no thanks. Stick with civil litigation. I really think that's your forte. Deal making and such." Amanda shrugged as if to say she was sorry to have to point out his shortcomings in this matter, but the meeting was over.

Edward didn't see it that way. He was on her, a touchy-feely kind of guy. His fingers dug into her wrist.

Amanda didn't like it. It only took one look to get her point across. He let her go.

"Hey, sorry I don't make the cut."

There was a belligerent undertone in his voice that surprised Amanda, frightening her just a bit. He apologized for it in the next round by keeping his hands to himself and lowering his voice.

"You're right. I don't know a hell of a lot about criminal law. But I've been straight with you and I think that counts for something, here." He was excited, moving back so that he became the focal point of the room. "Think about it. You're in the same position I am. You're alone just like me, and you're on DM&M's shit list. It's not a happy place to be. But together we might actually be able to accomplish something. At least I'd be another voice. Bounce stuff off me. Let me play devil's advocate. Let me do grunt work. Use this with the press. You know, a defection story. Come on! It's cold out in the big bad world. The experience I've had at DM&M isn't going to mean a thing to the kind of clients I'll have coming to my door. But it will mean something to you"—he faced Nora briefly—"and especially to you. We worked there. We know who came and went. We'll put our heads together and try and figure out why everybody's hanging back. I could be valuable. You know I could be."

Nora only stood accused, so, knowing it was Amanda who would make the decision, she bore the brunt of his argument. It was becoming more forceful by the moment. Amanda felt as if she was being seduced, his voice was syrupy and soft.

"Look, Leo Riordon isn't going to stop with getting an indictment in record time, he's going to push this trial to completion as fast as he can. Think about it. He's up for election, and his chances don't look good, given the number of times he's screwed up recently. He'll need some place to settle down after he loses or bows out before the going gets rough. He wants to make friends at DM&M. The senior partners want this thing cleared up posthaste. Nora's very existence makes them look like fools because they hired a woman who used sex to get what she wanted and she screwed—figuratively and possibly literally—one of the most highly regarded attorneys in the city. Whether it was a fatal attraction or an affair, the spotlight you've put on that firm is just about the most offensive you can imagine. They just want her to be put away and Leo is anxious to do it."

"Thanks, Edward," Nora drawled.

"It's the truth," he answered. Then back to Amanda.

No more take-me-I'm-sincere looks, no more fast talking. Edward came close to Amanda. He smelled like some designer fragrance distilled from an endangered species. Leaning close, he looked at her with a determination that bordered on domination.

"They have resources. You have none. It's that simple. I'm offering you some. With me on the team, you'll at least have a leg up. It's that simple. I don't care for people's problems unless I can get something for myself by solving them. That's up front. That's all you'll ever get from me. Let me in. I'll do my best. I'll use what comes of it then I'm gone. Earlier if you say the word. But I don't think you will."

Edward reared back slowly, meeting Amanda's eyes with a level gaze. She wanted to shower, feeling somehow violated. In the depths of those black, shameless eyes, Edward Ramsey managed to make her feel as though every decision, any decision, had been taken out of her hands. She was released from her suspension of responsibility the minute he lowered his lids. Enviously thick lashes. When he looked at her again, he was waiting for her blessing. Good game.

Amanda turned away, walked to the window, and pressed a hand against the pane. Family sacrifice was one thing, especially when one of the family had nothing to lose. But him? Edward said all the right words, yet there was something ... something not quite simpatico.

Amanda pushed herself away from the glass. The view was lousy anyway. Her head remained bowed as she walked around and settled herself on the side of her desk, more comfortable being close to Nora than Edward. She had to tell him no. But Nora changed her mind before she could speak.

"We need help. Amanda." Simple as that. "I deserve the best shot I can get."

Then why was Amanda hesitating? Because she wanted to be the decision maker, the knowledgeable one. big sister taking care of the kidlet? Let Amanda make or break the future. She wanted to beg, *Let me try, for God's sake*, but Nora gave her no choice. Nora opened the door for Edward Ramsey and Amanda could do no less than invite him in.

Amanda offered him her hand, sans smile.

"I hope you know what you're doing," she muttered. "I hope I do, too."

Edward took her hand, dropping it before they really connected, his attention diverted by the opening door. The room became smaller. Mark walked in as if he owned the place.

"Amanda, I—"

He looked at Edward with surprise and caution before giving Nora the expected, appreciative once-over. Perfectly natural for their first face-to-face. Nora looked back at him, barely a flicker of appreciation for the fine figure he cut. Finally, Mark looked in Amanda's direction. Thankfully, selfishly, triumphantly, she rejoiced. Score one for the old broad—Mark Fleming's smile was reserved for her.

"Looks like the party's almost over."

Amanda smiled back.

Nora watched, unmoved.

Edward Ramsey relaxed.

Chapter 12

———

Mark stacked the grand jury transcripts on Amanda's desk. The four of them stared in silence. They were all tired and no closer to answers a week later than when they'd first come together in this office. Amanda's chin was buried in her upturned palms. Edward, dressed today in jeans and an Armani jacket, crossed his arms over his chest. Nora looked miserable, almost afraid of the stack of foreboding documents, a distressing physical representation of the seriousness of her plight. Between the cover sheets, every condemning word had been recorded. Listed in the pages were the comments of associates, partners, and senior partners of DM&M, the employees of the Regency Hotel, the guests occupying the concierge floor, the coroner's testimony, Leo Riordon's sanctimonious statements and presumptive questions. They had all commented - talking about the relationship between Nora Royce and Lucas Mallory—as if they knew anything.

Amanda slid the top bound transcript off the pile, pulling it toward her as though she expected to open it and find a hairy creature inside. Mark took the next. Edward the last. Thankfully, there was none for Nora. Amanda didn't want her reading the verbatim testimony of her peers and employers. She and Edward would encapsulate their comments, condense their accusations, and question Nora when Amanda was more prepared.

Mark flopped on the couch, legal pad on his lap, pen flipping between two fingers. Amanda swiveled in her chair and propped her feet on an open desk drawer. Edward hunched over the desk, devouring his document, Evelyn Wood's prized student. Nora was put to work compiling files, labeling boxes that would hold interview data, court records and such. Amanda would have preferred that Nora go home. Her second choice was a busy Nora.

Minutes earlier, Consuelo had poked her head in, insisting she just wanted to say goodnight to Amanda. In reality, she hoped to get a rise out of either Mark or Edward. When none was forthcoming, she muttered something sharp and quick in an undefined language and disappeared, on her way out bumping into the pizza guy Mark had summoned. The pizza was cold, the delivery man crazy, and Mark made Amanda pay. It was a normal end to a normal day. The night was on them and there was silence as they read until one or the other called out to Nora to clarify a point.

Mark: "Why did you fight that night so publicly?"

Nora (intent on centering the file label just so): "He'd changed the rules. So careful for six months then he wants to sleep in his hotel room with the entire firm wandering around downstairs, not to mention his wife."

Amanda: "Why then? Why not fight when he suggested getting together?"

Nora (label-centered, still not looking up): "It was exciting then. I didn't give it much thought. It wasn't the sleeping together anyway. The more I thought about it, the more it became a matter of principle. He changed the rules. He made a fool of me. Manipulated me."

Edward: "Did he give you a reason?"

Nora: "He wanted to see if we could get away with it. He knew I liked risks. Maybe he thought I was getting bored."

Amanda (snapping): "Don't give us maybes. What did he say?"

Nora (firmly, eyes up now, angry eyes): "He said he wanted to screw me and everyone else in the process. He was giddy, anxious. Hard to believe? He was really mean and playful all at the same time. It was exciting at that moment. Quote, unquote."

Mark: "Where was his wife?"

Nora: "The tea for all the better halves."

Amanda (muttering): "Sounds like fun."

Mark (thoughtfully, the tip of his pen between his lips): "How'd he know how much time you had?"

Nora (labeling the next folder): "The tea was scheduled. Three hours. Ruth was the perfect firm wife. She wouldn't step foot outside the room until it was over. Even I knew that."

Edward: "Did he say anything about Ruth?"

Nora (smirk): "We weren't doing a lot of talking. Certainly not about Ruth."

Mark: "What kind of sex did you have?"

Amanda: "Mark!"

Mark (half lifting his head, grinning at her): "Hey, it's my question."

Edward (all business): "Relevant?"

Mark (smiling): "Maybe not but admit it, it's an interesting question."

Nora: "I like a curious mind." (a look too long, too

mocking) "Hard sex. Games. The usual. He actually was quite imaginative for an attorney."

Mark (no nonsense, no more fun): "How hard?"

Nora: "Hard enough. He liked the scarf. This encounter was more physical than most. I told you he was wound up. Maybe that made me mad, too. Like he was trying to prove something. I felt used for the first time."

They all got tired. The questions became comments and the night wore on. Every once in a while one of them would move. Amanda had been pacing and was now exhausted.

"The physical evidence still bothers me," Amanda muttered, collapsing in her chair, rubbing her eyes.

Nora picked up a pen and ran it between her fingers. She had tired of playing secretary hours ago. Edward watched her. Mark watched Amanda.

"I understand the hair found at the scene. That's not a problem. But your blood was found at the scene and on your scarf. Mark? Have you got that dupe photo the cops sent?" She reached for it. He was quick. It was in her hands, a photo of a bloody room. Lots of blood just outside the bedroom door. Beneath it another photo. Blood, a very small amount, by the bed. Another few drops by the door. "We've got to explain the blood."

"It was hard sex, Amanda. There was some bloodletting." Amanda stared. Edward looked up. Mark closed his eyes to listen. He'd heard it before.

Nora held up her hand. "Here. He bit me. He was really into it that afternoon. He liked very physical sex but this was different. He'd never done anything like that before. See, you can still make out the mark. Broke the skin in a few places and that's why I bled. I pulled back when he did it so I guess some blood could have gone over there. It hurt like hell."

"Did you see a doctor?" Edward was up looking closely at the remnant of the wound.

"You like that stuff, Nora?" Mark interrupted, asking his question as if commenting on the weather. Nora answered as if the weather wasn't her concern.

"I have an open mind." Bad vibes. He wasn't enjoying the tour of her sexual landscape. "It wasn't bad enough to see a doctor. I didn't even put a Band-Aid on it. I wrapped the scarf around it. It stopped bleeding after a bit."

"Anybody seen a report on the scarf? A photo?" Amanda asked. Mark said he hadn't, Edward hadn't had time to see anything since he was working on a motion to petition DM&M attorney records. "Shit. They aren't giving us everything. That would explain how the blood got on the scarf but we haven't seen the scarf. I want to see how much blood was on it. I mean if Nora just wrapped her hand then the blood stains would be localized. If it was used to strangle Ruth Mallory and was then discarded while she was being stabbed the blood would have gotten all over the thing, right? And there should have been some strain on the fibers. Mark can you call the lab again?"

"No problem." Mark made a note.

Edward swung his head toward Amanda. "I was thinking. What if we could prove her scar was the result of an injury made by teeth? We might be able to match it up with Lucas Mallory and—"

"And then prove that she and Lucas were having an affair," Amanda finished for him. "I mean, if he got close enough to bite her we've got to assume he wasn't mad that she'd messed up a case. They obviously weren't talking law."

Edward responded, "It will prove that Lucas Mallory is lying about a really big thing. He's on record saying Nora was chasing him. We could start people really thinking about what went on between them and make a better case for her being in that suite. With that kind of stuff, it's not her word against his anymore. Leo's got to prove her guilt beyond that reasonable doubt and so far all he has is circumstantial evidence. If we can prove there's a reason for those things being in that room, we're way ahead. Lucas Mallory's teeth marks in Nora's hand is a real fine start."

Nora's fingers twitched. Her form of an electrified reaction. Edward smiled. Mark didn't move.

"Won't prove Nora didn't kill Ruth Mallory," Mark muttered.

"Thank you for that comment, Mark. I mean, don't get too excited. All we have here is a goddamn breakthrough," Amanda drawled peeved that he was relishing his role as devil's advocate. It was as if he wanted her to be wrong. "Edward, can you find someone—what do they call those dentists?—a forensic odontologist, that's it." Amanda snapped her fingers as it dawned on her. She felt good having recalled such an obscure thing. "I don't know where to start looking."

"ADA. American Dental Association. I'll work from there. Civil does have its uses. If there's one thing I know it's how to research." Edward grabbed a piece of cold pizza, suddenly hungry. "Shouldn't be a problem to find a doctor but that injury is pretty faint. And who's going to ask Lucas if we can make a mold of his teeth?"

Amanda laughed despite herself. Mark joined in. He still wasn't off her shit list but the laugh helped. Amanda was, at heart, the forgiving kind.

"We'll cross that bridge when we come to it, Edward. Do what you can. If we can prove that scar is the result of a bite and not a knife slipping in Nora's hand while she

stabbed Ruth Mallory, we're well on our way. I'll talk us
through it without a plaster mold, if I have to. But we'll
request a court order for the mold. We have cause."

"What about attacking the affair thing head on, without
proof?" Mark asked, interested once more. "From what I
read here, Nora, the senior partners insist they were all
aware you were a problem child for Lucas Mallory. This
one, Peter Sweeney, thinks you're a cross between Medusa
and a siren. He really has it in for you. According to him,
you were lurking outside Mallory's office on an hourly
basis, scooting yourself in whenever there was an opening.
He has you trying every trick in the book except planting
yourself on Mallory's desk and spreading your legs."

"Peter has a vivid imagination," Nora commented
seeming indifferent. "Would you expect them to say anything less? I mean, this kind of thing is sort of like a priest
sleeping with the altar girl."

Mark raised a brow. "Don Forrester seems to have the
same sort of imagination. He's a bit more of a gentleman
but says basically the same thing Sweeney does. Oliver
Hedding, too. Mallory is your best friend in the grand jury.
He says he thought your obsessive behavior toward him
personally was a reaction to your excessive need to be
mentored professionally. He thought the problem would
rectify itself, that you'd settle down. What a guy."

"He was. He is. Lucas Mallory was incredibly loyal
to his wife. He had no desire to hurt her or break up a
marriage that worked," Nora objected.

Mark fell silent. She had slept with the man. Maybe
there was an emotional tie somewhere inside that majorly
gorgeous body of hers. He still wasn't crazy about her.
Good-looking, ambitious women were not high on his list.

"So." Mark slid himself up to a sitting position, his

lazy gaze enough to tell Nora that she didn't affect him the way she did ninety-nine-point-nine percent of the male population. He let it float toward Amanda. She was another matter. He liked her, the way she looked, the way she smelled, the way she thought. He liked the way she kept plugging away, a Mutt to the world's Jeffs. Nora was the focal point of this discussion so he snapped back toward her. "What's his excuse now? His wife is dead, therefore, we can discount the hurt the little woman theory. Is he feeding you to the sharks to protect his own lily-white reputation? If he is, I'd think twice about defending him even to yourself and I say we just pound on him until he tells us the truth."

Nora moved—not far, not quickly—but definitely as if she was regrouping for defense. Amanda could see she was wary of Mark. He didn't walk and talk like the men she knew, the men she admired. From Mark Fleming, there came sharp little vibes of distaste and distrust. Nora didn't want to fight him; she knew enough to want him on her side. When this was all over, she wanted him gone. Smiling thinly, acquiescing, Nora responded.

"Of course. You're right. I have no answer. I don't know what he's protecting now. It's always possible that Lucas does actually think I killed Ruth. Many people do. But we had a six-month personal relationship and we worked together for nine. Lucas knew me as well as anyone in this world. It would take a great intellectual leap for him to imagine me capable of a crime of passion."

Nora had turned, offering Mark her profile. Her hand in her pockets, she cut a fluid figure, stylized for the utmost impact. She looked through lowered lashes. She looked at him.

"I didn't fall into this affair. Bed was one thing. It was

pleasurable and convenient and I enjoyed it. I admit that. But, my Lord, to say the sex was so great I wanted to get rid of the man's wife is ludicrous. In his heart, Lucas knows that, ergo, he knows I'm innocent. Unfortunately, the rather brutal strategy of 'pounding him' would result in nothing more than Amanda tiring in court. Lucas Mallory doesn't respond to brute force. He will simply keep his own counsel."

"But why? God, what an incredibly simple—utterly complex—question! Why won't he talk?" Mark was up, pacing. He sideswiped Nora and braked beside Amanda. While he thought, he touched her shoulder, mumbling aloud, piecing the puzzle together. "Because the partners don't want him to? Because they don't want this to be more complicated than it already is? More sensational? More hurtful? Because he's a guy who simply wouldn't want it known he was an adulterer? Weird, in this day and age. Or is it because the firm and the DA want an easy way out? Edward? You have a thought on that?"

Edward leaned back. The client chair was exactly the right size for him. He looked comfortable. Mark would have filled it to overflowing.

"I don't know. I was an associate, like Nora. Peter Sweeney was my mentor. A tough guy. He scared a lot of people because of his overwhelming commitment to the firm. Maybe he scared Lucas into thinking he should just be quiet. To us that might seem immoral; to them that's second nature."

Edward fell mute. He spoke in the next heartbeat. "Not that I really know, of course, but from what I've observed I'd say the senior partners are very protective of the firm and each other."

"Is Lucas that easily swayed?" Amanda queried.

Nora answered, "Absolutely not."

Edward shot her a glance before confirming. "Nora knows better than I, but I'd tend to agree. I never could get a real handle on Mallory."

"He's a lawyer," Nora answered. That seemed enough explanation for everyone in the room.

"Yeah. Well." Mark slid his hand off Amanda's shoulder. She leaned back and put her own over the warm spot. He bothered her in the worst and best of ways. But there was something else that bothered her more and it had nothing to do with Mark Fleming. Amanda stood up. Believing they were progressing if someone in the room was active, she paced.

"Nora? Why do you think Lucas choose that day, that really public situation, to break all those rules he'd set up? I still can't get a handle on that kind of behavior." She twirled, a little pirouette, into the corner near the filing cabinets. She and Nora were so close Amanda could almost whisper. Instead, she made her question public. "I sure as heck can't figure out why you went along with it. I'm sorry. I just have a really hard time believing you were that pliable."

Anticipatory silence cluttered up the lines of communication. Either Nora was lost in assessing the intricacies of the filing cabinet construction or she was accessing the mental bits and bytes that would generate an appropriate, helpful answer to her sister's question. Amanda looked at the floor, preferring not to make herself crazy by trying to second-guess Nora.

"Lucas could be spontaneous." The beginning was cautious. No one breathed. "There were moments when he could be funny, insightful, even"—here she paused, as though to say the next word would implicate her shamefully in the corresponding behavior—"he could even be tender. And that weekend, those days we were at the Regency, was particularly heady. The firm had been doing extremely well. I had completed a series of terribly intricate depositions and formulated a fantastic defense for a client who, until that point, had required Lucas's—and only Lucas's—attention. Oliver had been particularly attentive to me. Don Forrester, even Peter Sweeney seemed to have spare moments for me. I mentioned it to Lucas. He said it was because they were so impressed with my work."

Nora turned and put her cheek against her hand. Dreamily, images of that weekend slipped through her mind like slides through a stereopticon. Silent. So vivid.

"At the partners' retreat, I felt marvelous and so did Lucas. There was a sense of something momentous about to happen. It was in the air, yet only he and I seemed to feel it. Even the month or so before the retreat, Lucas had seemed more animated. We were seeing each other more often. There was a frantic quality about him that actually was exciting. He wouldn't tell me why, but, after hearing Oliver during that retreat, I'm assuming it was the health of the firm and the possible signing of a new client that gave him such a thrill, such energy. He'd been telling me how much I meant to him. That since we'd been sleeping together, he felt as though his life was back on track. Things sort of came to a head that day."

"So he was feeling good, feeling his oats?" Mark broke the spell.

Nora looked askance at him, "I suppose you could put it that way. I would prefer to think he was on a professional high."

"And you?" Amanda asked.

"Me? I was definitely along for the ride. The euphoria was catching. He asked me to be indiscreet. I was because I didn't think there would be any consequences. There never had been any consequences since the affair began. If anything, the sort of naughtiness of it all heightened the experience of working at DM&M. It was as if the energy we had professionally was transferred to our personal relationship. Lucas and I thought so much alike, we felt the same way about so many things. Damn!" Nora looked toward the door, then got up and walked forward only to realize there was nowhere to go. The office was small, every space occupied, and there was nothing beyond the door for her.

These people were the only ones in the world willing to help but they made her feel ineffective, less than worthy, because she couldn't explain about Lucas and herself. It had never occurred to Nora that an explanation would ever become necessary. She and Lucas... they just were. "Why won't he just tell the truth?"

She hadn't meant to speak aloud. The sound of her voice surprised even her. She raised her head to cover the mortification she felt, the weakness she heard in it. She was the only one responsible for her situation, no one else. Lucas could have his mouth surgically sealed, never breathing a word of what went on between them and still, Nora couldn't blame him for this predicament. She was a big girl, a smart woman, ready to take all the pleasure. Now she was about to find out if she could bear the pain. She supposed it was about time. She answered herself.

"I don't know why Lucas is suggesting I was obsessed but let's not rely on his change of heart nor on the possibility that he might crumble under, what I'm sure, will be stunning cross examination by Amanda."

She sat down, her testimony given. Amanda bridled

against her sister's sarcasm but said nothing.

Edward filled the silence with what seemed to Mark an idiotic comment. "It would seem obvious to me that Nora couldn't be the murderer just because of who she is."

"Explain," Amanda snapped. Mark rolled his eyes dramatically enough for Edward to notice and stumble before picking up stride.

"Too much of her is in that room. Not just one hair, not just a partial fingerprint but hair near the bed, in Lucas's brush, on the terry robe. And fingerprints everywhere. All things that would lead us to believe a woman was in that room for pleasure not with an intent to kill. A smart woman whose purpose was to kill wouldn't leave behind a trail of clues like that. She even admits that she knew the maid saw her go in so you've got to put all this in context. Nora is a smart woman. These are not the actions of a smart woman trying to do a really dumb thing."

"That sounds so nice, Edward." Mark was back on the sofa, prone and drawling. "Why don't we just have Amanda stand up in front of the jury and say, 'Excuse me, but my sister is really smart so she couldn't have done this terrible thing."

"It's worth a try, Fleming," Edward responded, with little indication, other than a cold undercurrent in his tone, that Mark's barbs had hit anything but his shield.

"It's also just as easy to believe that Nora had access to the room and, in a bizarre mental state, in a fantasy world, touched his things, used his things, wore his things, and was surprised by Mrs. Mallory. Equally plausible."

"Anyone who knows Nora—"

"And who in the hell does?" Mark shot back. "She can't even find someone who knows her well enough to say she was sleeping with her boss."

"Boys!" Amanda stepped forward. "I don't think it's going to be quite that simple. Let's look at it another way. We've talked about what we have to do, we just haven't made a commitment to do it. Face it. We have no theory. We haven't got an inkling of what went on in that room after Nora left it. The only thing we can do is create doubt. And I have a feeling it's got to go far beyond reasonable. That's our goal. Let's show the jury that things are not always what they seem."

"It will implicate Lucas," Nora reminded her.

Amanda turned a cold eye, "Like we give a hot damn?" Nora opened her mouth but seemed to think better of making a comment. Amanda thought that was a wise decision. She continued. "Let's attack the physical evidence from all angles. I need to find out anything we can about the blood spatters. Where Nora's blood was found. How much of it was on the knife. I want to know everything there is to know about blood, even if we have to call Dracula as a material witness. The hair we can deal with as long as they don't do a DNA match. You haven't by any chance given them permission to DNA your blood or hair, have you?"

Nora shook her head emphatically.

"They're going to ask for a court order and they'll get it," Mark reminded her.

"We'll cross that bridge when we come to it. Meantime, we've got a lot of work to do. It's the end of March. Riordon is pushing for this thing to come to trial the first of June. That's less than three months. Good grief." Amanda swiped at her brow. "We're going to have to scramble. Even if we can show that the evidence is circumstantial, Riordon is going to come in with all the dramatic clout he can muster. More than likely, he's going to be using computer-assisted design. I hear his office has the capability.

Can you imagine if he animates the crime on computer? That's going to kill us so we're going to have to be on top of all the forensic stuff. Mark, can you get into the lab at all? Any contacts?"

"I'll do my best but no real close contacts."

"Try." Amanda turned to Edward. "Edward, I want you to go over Nora's story with a fine-tooth comb, prepare her as a witness and contact anyone at DM&M you think will talk to you more freely than they will me. We'll work on questions and see if we can't get some kind of consensus that will help our side. Also, let's take a look at Mallory back—like the beginning of his career, his marriage. Let's look for enemies. Even hit the law school if you have to. Do the same with Ruth Mallory. Mark will help you if he has time but at least get a start."

"No problem. Nora and I can also work on keeping the files straight, drafting motions for you, making those phone calls. I'm assuming we don't have a travel budget?"

"You assume correctly." Amanda almost smiled but was on to the next thought, and it was a serious one. "Let's look into everything about Lucas Mallory's daily activities, too. Where he takes his dry cleaning, buys his flowers, has his car washed. Maybe we can come up with someone who saw Nora and him together, saw him with another woman, saw him fighting with his wife. Anything we can use like that. Mark?"

"I'll fit it in."

"Good, earn your keep." They smiled at one another. "Thanks."

Mark said, "What about the other guys? The senior partners? The other partners?"

"That's going to be impossible," Edward interjected verbally throwing up of his hands. "Nobody's going to say anything bad about them. We're not private investigators. I'm an attorney. He's a—"

"Edward?" Amanda put her weight on one foot. "Mark is an investigator. He's a little bit of everything that we're not. Let's not worry about our credentials. Let's worry about getting the info any way we can."

Edward grinned looking quite charming when caught off guard, "Sorry. My nature, I suppose. Always been a little pessimistic. What are we trying to prove by looking into their lives anyway?"

Amanda answered suddenly animated and ready to work, "How many times do I have to say it? I don't want to prove anything. Even I know I can't do that. The physical evidence points toward Nora being there so I want to stand up and say, 'Sure, she was there, and why not? She was invited.' Nobody is going to corroborate that. We're not even going to prove the affair unless we get really lucky. We'll doublespeak. I want to confuse the hell out of that jury. I want to make them wonder if these guys are hanging together because they knew what was going on and if they are protecting one of their own or someone in the firm." Amanda threw her arms up as though the acquittal was in the can. Her audience didn't seem convinced. "Come on, you guys, get behind me. Maybe we can find out that Oliver Hedding lies about his bowling score, then we can ask if he told the truth about Nora and make it sound impossible that he did. Right? Right?"

The others murmured in unison and Amanda grinned. She assumed they were in agreement.

"Great! Great! We'll stick to a simple game plan. How hard can it be to confuse a jury? I've done it before. Hell, I've confused judges." She was settled behind the desk again, pencil in hand, trying to convince herself that she was good. "I can do this. We can do this. We'll annoy the heck out of them. Let's find enough to really make 'em wonder who's telling the truth—Nora, or the incredibly closemouthed Lucas Mallory and his cohorts."

Amanda began to scribble, the adrenalin was flowing, hope was damn well springing eternal, and it felt good to command. Deserter, quitter, exile; faceless though they may be, this team would, if nothing else, fight hard. Amanda would see to that. She'd show Los Angeles. She'd show Lucas Mallory and the demigods at Dimsdale, Morris and Mott. She'd show Nora that her desperate act of hiring her sister was actually an inspired one. But, more than anything, she'd show herself—so many things.

Chapter 13

———

Mark parked in a driveway as big as the southbound sweep of the San Diego freeway where it struck off the 10. The garage to his left was bigger than ten mobile homes huddled side by side at a rest stop. There were five doors and he would bet money there was a car behind each that got less than twenty miles to the gallon. Thanking his lucky stars he wasn't the envious type, Mark sat in his '78 Z, dismissed the garage, and considered the house. It was a fortress. Aggressive, almost ominous, it suited its owner.

Chateau de Conspicuous Consumption was obviously Peter Sweeney's pride and joy. It was a shame he insisted on slapping passing motorists in the face with his poor taste. The house boasted the tallest gates, the longest, widest drive, the thickest oak doors, and probably the tackiest facade Mark had ever seen. The architect—and he used that term lightly—was obviously the indecisive type. The final structure was a schizoid mix of styles that resembled at its core either an Irish castle or the south wing of the Vatican. Mark opened the car door, swung out, and let his tall, still-lean body follow naturally. He loved this car of his. Small and sleek, compact yet roomy enough for a big guy to feel relaxed at the end of a long drive. He wouldn't trade his car for all the Irish castles/Vaticans in the world—or even the car behind Door Number Three.

Ducking his head, he rummaged in the back well, came up with a leather portfolio in which he carried a never-been-doodled-on legal pad and a pen that didn't have the name of a bank stamped on it in gold. Finally, he grabbed his jacket, brought at Amanda's insistence. He drew the line at a tie, court appearances excepted.

With a flourish, he closed the door of the car and locked it. The LA city limits didn't stop at Sweeney's gate; crime knew no bounds. He took a hike across the drive, shot up the tiled steps, stood under the conical chandelier that the Sweeneys hung out for a nightlight, and rang the bell. Mark listened, waiting to hear the bell chime Danny Boy or the Alleluia only to be disappointed by the silence. The chime was evidently hooked up somewhere in the bowels of the house because he didn't hear whatever it was that called the cute little maid to the door.

Her eyes were bovine, all black and brown and big. They should have been nifty to look at but they were glassy with lack of interest. Mark couldn't be tricked. Smarter than she, he could see what was behind the blankness: grudging acceptance of her situation, reluctant gratitude for her position, and a healthy disdain for her employer and his friends. Her dark hair was pulled back in a bun; her gray uniform had obviously not been custom-made for her. Perhaps the Sweeneys just kept a closetful, allowing the servant of the hour to choose the one that was a close fit.

"Mark Fleming. Here to see Mrs. Sweeney." No response. "I have a two o'clock appointment."

Stepping back, the woman was hidden behind the huge

hunter green painted door with the knocker that cried out
for a pithy comment. Unable to think of one, sure the maid
wouldn't care even if he did, Mark stepped inside. Noting
that the interior designer was probably the architect's
sister, he followed his silent guide through a seemingly
endless maze of rooms.

First, his heels clicked on the black-and-white entry
marble, only to be muffled in the wainscoted yellow and
white dining room by an exquisite Oriental rug, its tiny
flowers intricately woven in silk. His progress sounded
hollow on the superbly maintained peg-and-groove floor
of—what Mark assumed—was a living room. He'd felt
cozier in stadiums.

The maid seemed to glide through each room, almost
skating on the hardwood floor in her soft, slipper-like
shoes. The better not to disturb the master if you could
ever find him in this cavern. Mark was about to request a
rest stop when the black bun he focused on bobbed and
took a sharp left. He was led through a narrow hall that
opened into a beautiful and intimate breakfast room. It was
here Mark wanted to linger but his friend kept going until
they were outside again, this time standing on a terrace as
long as the house and half as wide. The raised and tiled
veranda was surrounded by a white plaster balustrade and
the reflection nearly blinded him in the afternoon sunlight.
He hesitated, figuring they'd arrived. He was wrong. The
lady forged ahead. At this rate, Mark figured she clocked
about ten miles a day without ever leaving the house. Not
wanting to be left behind, he caught up with her. Down
the sweep of broad stairs he went, to the rectangular pool,
and on until he finally saw them.

The woman leading Mark sensed him slowing and
looked over her shoulder. There was a twinkle of triumph

in her eyes as if to say she knew the mistress wasn't alone but had decided not to tell him. A small joke. A little bit of power. He was no better than she. That made her day. When he smiled as if to say he understood, she waited until he caught up. They walked toward the gazebo together, now in a companionable silence. He was almost sorry when she melted away and left him on his own. He hoped he was up to this. Women in groups had ceased to scare him in his sophomore year in high school. But with this group, regression was a definite possibility. None of them smiled. Thankfully, one came to greet him. He assumed it was the woman he'd come to see, the woman who was supposed to be alone.

"Mr. Fleming. I'm Peg Sweeney." He shook her hand. She made it brief.

She was an attractive woman, the kind who looked as if she'd be athletic in bed if you got her in the mood. She'd have to watch the sun, though. Five years tops before even all the salons in Beverly Hills couldn't put Mrs. Sweeney together again. There was already that telltale creping of skin on her neck as it ran down toward the ample cleavage she showed off so matter-of-factly.

"Nice to meet you. Mrs. Sweeney."

She inclined her head, smiling a little. Pretty white teeth.

"I know you must be surprised," she said verbally drawing him into the gazebo, motioning him to a seat. He stood until he was sure he was meant to sit. It was a good move. There were more hands to shake. "I know you called to meet with me but I asked the other ladies to be here. I assumed you would want to talk to them."

Peg's arm swung out in a well-honed backhand, indicating the other women. Her words faded into the gesture, so he followed the lob, nodding as Peg introduced the other two.

"This is Min Forrester, Don's wife."

The little blond with the ends of her hair upturned a la Mary Tyler Moore, circa 1968, nodded. Her apricot-colored lips smiled prettily. Her eyes, shadowed in an almost tasteful shade of blue, should have twinkled with good humor but were flat with seriousness.

"And here," Peg swung again. An exquisite forehand. The ball was moving one more time. "This is Kitty Hedding."

She was close to Mark, only a lattice-backed chair between them. Mark held out his hand. She took it over the top of the chair. They looked at one another. He was immediately intrigued. There was something about this woman that crackled out at him like a downed low-voltage wire popping around on a front lawn. Let loose, that kind of thing could be dangerous. But Kitty Hedding wasn't the type to let go. She kept to herself. That was exactly the kind of woman Mark wanted to talk to. Silent, watchful, intelligent, and possibly explosive. Unfortunately, it was Peg Sweeney who called the match.

"Sit down, please, Mr. Fleming."

Mark did.

"Coffee? Tea?"

"Coffee," he said, unbuttoning his coat and taking note that neither of these women looked at him with hungry eyes. Dissatisfied they were, that was apparent, but it had nothing to do with sex. They wanted something more. What was it? Understanding? Security? Out?

A delicate cup of very aromatic coffee was put in front of him. Min Forrester's little hands waved toward a sugar bowl, a crystal plate stacked with blue-and-pink packages of sweetener, and a creamer that matched the sugar bowl. Mark thought of an aging Vanna White, retired from letter turning, finding old habits died hard. Kitty Hedding remained exactly where she was, waiting almost warily.

"Well." He managed this heartily, smiling at each of them individually before widening his grin to include them collectively as though he could endear himself to them. They were making him nervous so he talked while he unzipped his portfolio, taking out the pad and pen. "I suppose Mrs. Sweeney filled you in on why I'm here but let me go over it again. My name is Mark Fleming and I'm working in association with Amanda Cross, who is the attorney for Nora Royce, the woman accused of murdering Ruth Mallory during the DM&M partners' retreat." It was time to take a breath. He did so, looking about him once more. Their expressions hadn't changed. Polite, but that was it. He might as well have murdered Ruth Mallory for all the warmth here. "Yeah. Well, I want to assure you right now that I am not a private investigator. I am a paralegal of sorts. Responsible for interviewing people who might have information regarding the crime Ms. Royce is charged with. You don't have any obligation to speak with me. This is absolutely voluntary on your part. I want to make that clear."

Mark looked from one well-kept face to the other, pleading with them individually not to challenge that. When his gaze fell on Kitty Hedding, it lingered long enough to compel her to speak.

"We are more than willing to speak to you, Mr. Fleming. Our husbands have advised us that, to their knowledge, this is a normal course of events in a criminal investigation. We have nothing to hide but we have nothing to say that will help you, either. Ruth Mallory was our friend. We loved her dearly and we miss her horribly. We cannot fathom why this terrible thing has happened."

"I understand, Mrs. Hedding. I have no desire to harass you, nor do I expect to find anything specific here that will build a case for or against my client. I'm only attempting to fill in the background, to sort of paint a bigger picture for the attorney of record. Naturally, she is working closely with her client yet one point of view is seldom sufficient, especially when that point of view sees innocence where everyone else sees guilt."

Mark let his statement hang, inviting response by his sudden silence. He would have made a great lawyer. Min Forrester jumped right in. He wasn't surprised. She wasn't the type who liked thoughtful silences.

"We don't know that she's guilty." It was sad how hard she tried to sound oh-so-fair and intelligent. Min couldn't pull it off. "She has to go to trial and all that." Mark lowered his chin just a bit, urging her on. Her eyes became a little frantic. She was lost. "I mean, I suppose all of us have assumed she's guilty. There's the evidence and such. I've read about it in the paper."

Min was flailing, unsure of herself. Peg looked away almost immediately and Mark thought he saw Kitty Hedding smile affectionately.

"Have you given any consideration to Ms. Royce's story that she and Lucas Mallory were having an affair and did, during the afternoon of that day, have relations in the Mallory's suite?"

Peg snorted her opinion that Mark was probably a very stupid man. She made a grab for an embroidered case, missed it, grabbed again, and angrily opened it to retrieve a long, slim, cigarette.

"That's absurd," she muttered, the cigarette already

bobbing between her lips.

Mark saw now that there were fine lines surrounding those lips. No wonder she didn't use lipstick; it would bleed most unbecomingly.

She lit the thing, slipped into a chair, and sat back, looking at the other two women quizzically. "You don't agree with me?"

"Of course we do, Peg," Min insisted. "I know Lucas would never do anything like that. He was devoted to Ruth. Absolutely devoted. Besides, the idea that he would"— here she paused, giving Mark a moment to wonder if she undressed in the closet at night—"that he would make love to an associate is just beyond me." Like a partner would be okay? Mark jotted on his legal pad while Min objected to the question in her tiny voice.

"Lucas is such a professional. He just exudes confidence. You could trust him in any matter, I'm sure. He's a man of honor. Terribly loyal."

The last left a question. Who was he loyal too? His wife? Nora? Himself? And would she trust her husband? Or Peter Sweeney? Or Oliver Hedding? Was Lucas Mallory a saint, whose very deportment was such it didn't permit a character flaw, a moment of madness, a sense of lustfulness? Had the guy been loving law so long he'd forgotten how to use what God gave him? Good questions, no answers—yet. Peg was talking. Mark listened closely.

"I agree. The idea that Lucas would even look at that woman is beyond me. He had a lot of taste and Ruth had a lot of class. They were the perfect couple. She was always impeccably dressed. Everything she did was for the good of others. She was the one who made that firm human. Heaven knows the men couldn't do it but when Ruth walked in, people knew they were appreciated and that was because Ruth knew that everybody in that place made it possible for her to live the way she did. Lucas knew that, too. Lucas knew what a prize he had in Ruth. They were an incredible team."

"Mrs. Mallory was at the office quite a bit?" Mark queried looking directly at Kitty Hedding for an answer. But Peg had the floor and didn't want to relinquish it.

"Oh, definitely. She was a philanthropist, you know, always into one charity or another. She used the offices sometimes to make copies of things for her projects, sometimes borrowed the conference room. She ran an intern program for college students who thought they might want to go into law. Yes, I'd say Ruth was at the office quite a lot and I never heard her breathe one word about any misgivings over Lucas's behavior with Ms. Royce. I just don't see that happening. Lucas was too focused on work; Ruth was too good a thing to screw up."

"I agree," Min reiterated coming to the defense of their dead friend. "They were a perfect couple. Absolutely perfect. What possible reason would he have had to do anything so vile?"

Mark had the overwhelming urge to ask if marital bliss was unusual among this group.

"What about Ms. Royce's attitude toward Mr. Mallory?" Kitty's turn. "Mrs. Hedding?"

"Yes?" She wasn't going to make it easy. Her refined, thin brows rose delicately in question. Her voice was pretty because it was well modulated, the way it must be in an educated woman married to a powerful man.

"I was wondering if Mrs. Mallory had voiced any opinion regarding Ms. Royce?"

"Not a personal one. Ruth was a terribly secure woman."

"A professional opinion, perhaps?"

"I don't remember any indication that Ruth thought about Ms. Royce one way or another. And she would never venture to offer an opinion regarding the professional status of anyone at the firm. She was not a partner."

Mark was uncomfortable on the chair but he didn't move. Far be it from him to give them any reason to believe he was squirming. "And your read on the Mallory marriage? Is it the same as Mrs. Sweeney's and Mrs. Forrester's?"

Kitty laid her hands, one over the other, atop the lattice-backed chair as though determined to keep it between them. Then, without apology for her reticence, she said simply, "They had a marriage like any long-term marriage where children are not involved. Her interests were varied. He was more centered. His work was his life." She thought for a moment before adding, "I suppose that can be said of any of our marriages."

"But I have a child," Min objected.

"Yes, I know," was all Kitty said.

Peg Sweeney studied her nails. Min looked hurt. Obviously, Kitty had hit one nail right on the head. Too bad it wasn't the same one Mark wanted to pound. A very smooth sidestep. Ruth and Lucas's perfect marriage? Were any of them happily married?

"That answers my next question. No children." He made a check mark on his pad. It meant nothing but kept him looking busy. "Any close relatives?"

Min shook her head, her pretty golden hair tickling her chin, "No. Ruth's parents are dead. No brothers or sisters. Lucas never spoke about his family but Ruth told us once he and his parents were estranged. I believe his mother died some time ago. I think his father is in a home. He had a brother who was killed in a car accident and a sister he doesn't communicate with. A very sad situation, but, in a way, it was a good thing. We're all so close we didn't have to worry about them running off to family every holiday. I always loved it when we were all together."

Mark found himself staring at Min Forrester. Every response ended on an up note, like the final punctuation of a pom-pom after the last cheer faded away.

"Min is our social director," Peg drawled but with enough inflection to indicate to Mark that there was a sincere underlying affection. "We have to rely on Min for Christmas cookies and caroling every year."

"I love doing that kind of thing." For a second, Min forgot why they were gathered. There was someone new in their midst, and she glowed under the challenge of painting a rosy picture for him.

"I'm sure you do it very well." Mark was rewarded with a grateful and frankly beautiful smile. It disappeared just as quickly with his next comment. "I'm equally sure Ruth Mallory will be missed dearly by this group. But one thing I don't understand."

Mark tapped his pen against his nicely sculpted lips. He narrowed his eyes, the fine lines around them fanned out, making him look to Kitty like a television lawyer on cross. But they weren't in a courtroom, this wasn't television, and he wasn't a lawyer. Kitty had to remember that. She had to remember she didn't have to answer or offer, anything.

"I don't understand why, if Mrs. Mallory spent all afternoon with the husbands and wives of associates and partners at an afternoon tea, and if she had already made an appearance that evening at the partners' reception, and it's been established that she was dedicated to her duties as hostess, why would she leave the party? How on earth could anyone know—much less Nora Royce, who was an employee of the firm and not a friend of Mrs. Mallory—that Ruth Mallory was going to her room? It doesn't make sense. The way she was attacked, the person had to be in the room waiting, for her. That would lead me to believe it was someone who had no interest in the party downstairs. Perhaps a burglar, perhaps an employee of the hotel who wasn't quite right in the head and was surprised doing something in Mrs. Mallory's room." Mark looked expectantly around the room, praying one of them would corroborate his theory. Kitty surprised him, seeming almost eager to answer. "That's easily answered, Mr. Fleming." Mark tried to appear casual

"Please, go on."

"It's quite simple. Ruth Mallory was a diabetic. Dinner was to be served exactly at eight. If there is anything Oliver insists upon, it is punctuality. Ruth knew that. After all these years of Lucas and Oliver working together, it was as natural as the sun rising and setting. So if Ruth understood that dinner would be served promptly at eight, she would naturally have gone back to her room at seven-thirty for her insulin. Ruth gave herself a shot exactly one-half hour before eating dinner or breakfast. Anyone who knew about Ruth's condition was aware of the time she would be in her room. I don't think her situation was secret, though I would doubt if every associate and partner knew about it. Yet..."

Mark sat back. She didn't have to finish. He could fill in the blanks. If Nora Royce were stalking Lucas Mallory, it wouldn't be a difficult thing to find out about Ruth's condition. An innocent question to her mentor about his wife, a conversation overheard regarding Ruth's doctor's appointment, a scribbled message left by a secretary asking Lucas to pick up a package of test strips on the way home. So very simple. A smart girl like Nora could figure out exactly when and how insulin was taken.

Yet, if the affair was real, one could extrapolate very different information. Suppose Lucas told Nora his wife was insulin dependent. Over an intimate little dinner, he might have commented how lovely it was to just sit down and eat, rather than watch the clock and time the needle. Stroking Nora's beautiful, taut stomach, her sleek derriere. Lucas might kiss her, sighing that it was heaven to look at skin that wasn't black-and-blue with puncture wounds. There were so many ways Nora Royce could have known that Ruth Mallory was going to be in her suite at seven-thirty and, if she knew, she could possibly have been lying in wait. Nora actually could have done the deed. Then again, it could have been anyone who knew about Ruth's condition.

"I see. That's very interesting. Well, thank you."

Mark jotted a note and asked one last question, though he had many others. But they would have to wait. He needed time to think and the wives needed time to talk. He would call on them again, of that he was sure, somehow corralling all into a one-on-one. Women who loved one another, respected their husbands, said good things about their deceased comrade, didn't treat him with hostility, and gave him a perfect answer as to why Nora could be waiting at a specific time, in a specific place, for Ruth Mallory, were just a wee bit difficult to believe.

"Did Mrs. Mallory have any enemies?" he asked deciding to go out with a bang.

Kitty shook her head. Min and Peg followed suit, adding a murmured "no" and "you've got to be kidding." respectively. Mark probed.

"She didn't have a fight with the maid at the hotel?"

"Ruth hadn't been there long enough," Peg answered.

"She only arrived that day for the luncheon and reception."

"Lucas was at the Regency alone for two days?" Mark shifted. The wrought iron back of the chair was getting uncomfortable.

"For the first two days, yes. Ruth had…" Min furrowed her brow. "How did we find out that Ruth wasn't going to be there?"

"I think she called Kitty," Peggy said.

"Yes, she did," Kitty answered quietly. Mark was now more interested in what wasn't being said. She added, "Ruth had tried to get me at home. She left a message but I'd already left, so she called the hotel. I hadn't arrived yet. She left another message there telling me she had a meeting to attend. Something rather important. Something of a personal nature."

"A doctor?" Mark asked hopefully.

Terminal illness would be a good thing. Might throw a different light on the matter. That theory was instantly discarded. Even if Ruth Mallory was terminally ill, strangling herself with a scarf, stabbing herself with a hotel knife, and hiding the whole mess a few floors down before seeking help from her husband at a formal reception was not exactly a smooth scenario.

"No, I don't believe so. She didn't actually tell me who she was seeing that day."

There had been emphasis on the word that. Mark let it pass.

"Want to guess, Mrs. Hedding?"

Kitty's eyes were hard, the look of the privileged facing off against the working man. "I don't think so, Mr. Fleming. Now, if there's nothing else, I'm afraid I must make a phone call. I hope you'll excuse me."

Mark half stood, smoothed his jacket, and looked at

the other two women. He was ready to wrap it up. Min probably didn't know anything more and Peg would rather have her tongue pulled out before she'd jeopardize her position with these women.

He listened politely as Min and Peg reiterated that Ruth hadn't an enemy in the world and was a woman of perfect virtue, a woman to be admired and mourned. They continued to do both over their coffee after Mark excused himself, thanked them and walked across the lawn, past the pool, up the stairs, across the balcony, and almost out the door, detouring only when he caught sight of Kitty Hedding standing near a delicate little desk in the corner of the huge living room. He hesitated, thought about approaching her, and then did it. What was she going to do? Glare him to death?

"Mrs. Hedding?"

Moving toward the doorway, the kind that was big enough to shelter seven or eight people under the mistletoe during the annual Christmas party, Mark abandoned any pretense of deference. He wanted to talk to her, she didn't want to talk to him, and that told him a lot.

"Mr. Fleming. I'm sorry, I do have a few calls to make, and I really have nothing more to tell you."

"I don't believe you."

"I'm not sure that truly makes a difference," Kitty replied. Her lips tilted up in an odd, wry smile as if to say he had no idea how tenacious she could be. Mark watched her, appreciating the beauty she once had and the cleverness she still possessed but now kept subtly hidden.

Mark felt like hanging his head and stubbing his toe against the hardwood floor. Instead, he decided to get personal.

"You're right. I doubt you care what anyone thinks

about you. And what I want has never been handed to me on a silver platter. I'm not a man like your husband, Mrs. Hedding. Once there was a woman who thought I would be but I'm afraid I disappointed her."

"That's a pity, Mr. Fleming, but it's not surprising. Men often disappoint women."

"So I've heard. Sometimes women disappoint men, too." She closed her eyes briefly in agreement. Mark asked, "Do you think Lucas Mallory disappointed Ruth Mallory or vice versa?"

"That's an odd question. Why on earth would you ask that?"

"I don't know. I just don't think any relationship could be as perfect as you all would like me to believe that one was. You make it sound as if the world revolved around the Mallorys."

Kitty Hedding's face closed, clearly signaling the end of the conversation. Mark wasn't ready. He wanted to bound into the room, take her thin, silk-clad arm in his strong, big hand and make her talk to him. But the effort was too much and the space between them too large. Such a heroic move would have lost its effect. Kitty Hedding would have laughed and Nora would not have been helped. If Kitty was going to say or do anything useful, she would do it in her own time.

"I don't think any relationship is perfect, Mr. Fleming, even our dear Ruth's. Now, if you'll forgive me."

She turned away. Mark saw her back stiffen as she listened to the sound his heels made on the floor when he walked toward her. Her fingers were on the buttons of the telephone, ready to dial, but they weren't moving. Mark crowded her. She watched him cautiously. He could have sworn she was holding her breath. Carefully, reaching around her slender, aging body, he laid his card on top of the dainty desk with the gilt legs.

"I have no intention of being disrespectful to the Mallorys. I'm just doing a job, trying to make sure an innocent woman doesn't lose a whole lot here. She might not have done it. I'm not sure any of you have really thought about that. If you know anything, suspect anything, have even the slightest bit of information that could help me, I'd appreciate hearing it. I may not be a big shot like your husband but I'm sure he and I believe in the same thing."

Kitty said nothing. Mark gave her credit. Not even the flicker of an eyelash. She wasn't easily moved. He tried again, not knowing how far off base he was.

"I believe in justice, Mrs. Hedding. If Nora Royce is innocent, you should help set the record straight no matter how much you loved Ruth Mallory, no matter what Nora Royce was to Lucas Mallory, no matter what your husband has told you not to talk about for fear of a scandal. I'd really like us to discuss this privately, if possible."

Kitty had turned away from Mark, showing him only the exquisite profile of her face and a body of indiscernible proportion hidden under the columnar cut of her simple, elegant dress. There was a moment between them when Mark felt her thoughts. She was warring with herself. Her eyes lowered for an instant and glanced at his card. She had made a decision.

Facing him, with no indication that he had said anything of import, Kitty looked into his eyes. He felt something happening; he believed something meaningful was transpiring in her heart. She was good, though. Well trained to be the face she showed the public. He had lost.

"I'm so sorry, Mr. Fleming. I'm sorry for you and for Miss Royce. I'm especially sorry for my dear Ruth. You have no idea what she meant to me. And I'm sorry that I don't know anything that would clarify this situation for you."

That was the end. Mark nodded. He thanked her. He left Kitty Hedding with her hands folded low in front of her body, watching him through the leaded windows until he had driven through the electric gates and disappeared. He left her thinking about Ruth and that last short message left on the tape of her personal machine. Perhaps she would ask Lucas about that message someday. Perhaps he could clarify it for her. Then again, she might just let that young man listen to it. He might know exactly what it meant. She picked up the card he had left. Yes, she might just share that little message with Mark Fleming—someday.

~ ~ ~

"The reception began at exactly six that evening. Black tie had been suggested. We didn't expect the associates to be in dinner dress but a surprising number were. I must say, this year it was wonderful to see such a solid group of young people in our firm. We have a fine balance of partners and associates, our clients are quite content. All this makes me feel as if I have steered this ship properly, as if the Dimsdale, Morris and Mott of today is living up to the charter of yesteryear, so to speak."

Oliver Hedding rasped a satisfied chuckle, tapping his small, narrow lips with tented fingers. The office seemed overly bright, considering the grim force of his personality.

"You know, when this firm was founded one hundred years ago, there was a specific dictate to conduct its affairs with decorum and discretion, to choose those who represent this firm wisely, so all actions were calculated, the outcomes predictable. We have done that, year in and year out. We have nurtured those we've taken into the fold and created a rare atmosphere, where restrained creativity is encouraged."

The hands lowered. He seemed to remember Amanda was there, listening.

"You realize there is a delicate balance between those two adjectives. Flamboyance was never tolerated here—until Ms. Royce. Such a pity, for everyone concerned, that we were blinded by our appreciation of her—shall we say—style?"

The question was rhetorical. Oliver Hedding didn't care what anyone had to say, really, so he went right on talking.

"It is, more than likely, the first personnel problem we've had." A thoughtful swivel in the chair. A dry sigh filtered through his teeth. "Other than that unfortunate young man who had difficulties with alcohol five years ago, of course. Nora, though, was a sad case. She needed so much. Constant input. Unending admiration. Contemplation and research never brought her the same degree of satisfaction as arguing her case in the partners' meeting or the courtroom. That alone should have been enough to warn us off her. Yet, I admit to the same fascination that afflicted everyone in this firm. Nora is so lovely. So unusual. A sharp legal mind encased in such a woman. I'm afraid she was just a bit too thrilling even for us levelheaded old lawyers to pass up."

Another sigh. Oliver Hedding was making an important transition.

"But she brought discontent because we were not what she wanted us to be. She pushed us, she pushed Lucas, to become"—a skeletal hand waved in small circles before picking the word out of the air—"more. A sad situation. Young lawyers these days—Nintendo attorneys. They want action, upward movement. They covet what we, who have worked so hard, have—our cases, our homes, our bank accounts, and, in a rare instance, they want us. That is what happened to Nora.

"She wanted everything, including Lucas Mallory, and, when she couldn't have him, she demanded him. Following him. Insisting he pay attention to her. A most embarrassing situation for the firm and a tragic situation for your—do I refer to her as your sister or your client, Ms. Cross?"

Amanda was so taken aback at being addressed directly she almost dropped her pen. Oliver Hedding's whispers, his odd speech peppered with clauses and commas, had a cadence that lulled her with a hypnotic effect. The huge office was so bright, warmed by a wall of windows that acted like a magnifying glass, it was uncomfortable. Amanda had an odd vision of Oliver Hedding bursting into flames. Spontaneous combustion.

Tired to begin with, she knew Oliver Hedding was testing her stamina. He was the last in her line of interviews that day. She had drifted along with his stream of consciousness, garnering minimal information, half thinking about the other men she'd seen.

Don Forrester, glad-handing, gentleman extraordinaire, soft-spoken, soft-jawed, baby-haired big man that he was, had answered her directly, his brows knitted together in a forty-five-minute demonstration of concern. She wrapped up the interview in forty-six, afraid his forehead would stay furrowed forever if he held the pose much longer.

She survived an offensive attack from Peter Sweeney. Pacing through the interview, he answered each question perfunctorily before clasping his hands behind his back, challenging her to ask another, even more difficult, one. He would have been happy if Amanda had whipped out a gun and challenged him to catch a bullet between his teeth. She would have been happy if he put her out of her misery with one in the head.

Finally, she faced Lucas Mallory. Mark had been unable to follow up, so Amanda gladly stepped in. During their time together, Amanda proved her professionalism. Instead of clawing his eyes out and demanding to know why he was putting Nora through the wringer, she sat quietly, listened and watched.

His office was oddly impersonal, as if a decorator had come in one day, ordered everything the next, and put it in place by the third. Amanda commented, surprising Lucas, but he offered no explanation for the lack of golfing trophies, the missing ash tray brought from home, a clean corner of his desk where a picture of his recently deceased wife would most likely have resided. Lucas Mallory was obviously not one for warming touches—or small talk. Hard as she tried, Amanda couldn't imagine him having a rough roll in the hay with Nora.

So Amanda had asked him questions. She jotted down notes. There was no evidence of deep emotional conflict as Lucas Mallory sat facing her—the attorney for, and sister of, the woman who had supposedly stalked him and was accused of murdering his rather perfect spouse. An odd man. A serene man. A deep-thinking man, yet not terribly thoughtful. He answered every question Amanda put to him, taking her hand and shaking it when the interview concluded. She stood outside his door for the longest while, before being urged to move toward Oliver Hedding's corner office by an impatient secretary.

Charmed by one partner, verbally assaulted by another, completely confused by the third, Amanda was finally ushered into the managing partner's office. When the door closed behind her, Amanda was sure her name was Dorothy and she was facing the altar of Oz. But, as in the movie, the headman had been proved only human and not a very likable human at that. Instead of a curtain and levers, he rested in a beautiful chair behind an elegant desk, commanding his universe with a stroke of his pen or a rustling remark. Exhausted, Amanda sat down, murmuring a rote thanks before questioning him in the same manner she had the others. Instantly, Oliver Hedding had changed the rules. He would speak; Amanda would listen. They had both done their jobs beautifully. Now he was winding down and she was fading fast.

"Ms. Cross?"

"Yes, Mr. Hedding. I'm sorry. It's been a very long day."

"I'm sure it's been a very long few months." Oliver offered his condolences. To Amanda that seemed a bit strange, considering the situation.

"Yes. Yes, it has." Amanda referred to her notes. Oliver Hedding had talked for a very long while without saying anything specific. "Mr. Hedding, you indicate that Ms. Royce's attitude toward Mr. Mallory was unseemly and you further indicate that everyone was aware of her odd behavior. But my associate, Mr. Fleming, has been able to speak with many of your employees. We're not putting together a picture of a crazed woman harassing a senior partner. Could you clarify this, please?"

Oliver frowned. That expression made him look cruel rather than simply nasty. Seeing her reaction, he consciously turned up the corners of his linear mouth. The resulting smile was less than reassuring.

"I believe I answered that, Ms. Cross." Had he a switch he would have rapped her knuckles. "However, if clarification is needed, I will do my best to oblige. We—the other senior partners and I—knew exactly what was going on. Lucas had been quite perturbed by Nora's attention. I would be remiss if I didn't admit that there were some jokes, some laughter, regarding Lucas's problem. That he could turn down, or be disturbed by, such a marvelous invitation was almost laughable. But Lucas is not a passionate man. He is cool and levelheaded, not swayed by physical attraction to the degree many men are. He is also an amazingly loyal man. That is a virtue I have admired in Lucas since the day I met him—loyalty. A virtue your sister seems to have difficulty understanding. She was relentless in her pursuit of Lucas and she was careful."

Oliver's eyes narrowed to steely pinpoints of darkness. He spoke to her in his jury voice, the one that indicated it was not wise to question the validity of what he was about to say.

"Nora decided Lucas Mallory was her key to complete fulfillment. Very much like a girl who falls in love with the first boy who kisses her. Lucas admired her ability. She adored his legal mind. Lucas could appreciate her beauty, she his power. Yet Nora wanted more than that. She would walk into his office with a brief, looking as if she was intent upon discussion. There was nothing unusual about that. It was the length of these conferences that came into question."

"That isn't unusual, given the types of clients you have and the intricacies of their problems," Amanda interrupted.

"Ms. Cross," Oliver snapped. Amanda's mouth closed instantly but she stopped herself before she apologized. If he could cow her here, alone, what on earth would he do to her when she had him on the stand? "I myself walked in on one of these conferences in time to hear Lucas reprimand her for her impudence. There wasn't an ounce of remorse from Nora when she realized what I had witnessed. She actually seemed amused by the situation. I believe she felt above even us. We discussed letting her go. We didn't because of the difficulties that would pose."

"I'm not quite sure I understand," Amanda interjected. She reached a new low with that one. Oliver gave her a pitying look, the kind one would give to the runt of the litter. She could almost hear him questioning her genetic makeup. He explained slowly.

"Think for a moment, Ms. Cross. Had we done that, there was nothing to stop Nora from twisting the facts and suing this firm for sexual discrimination. Even you must know that would have been a most difficult situation to deal with in this day and age. The year of the woman and all that. Dimsdale, Morris and Mott did not need that kind of publicity, just as we do not need the publicity we are receiving now. Although now we see that would have been the wiser course of action. I must say it was a lesson we heeded. That is why we all agreed to see you for an interview."

Oliver leaned closer. Though the desk was still between them, Amanda felt pinned down, closed in. There wasn't going to be much to say after this. She needed some fresh air.

"That is why we have opened our offices to you. We want this unsavory matter finished as quickly as possible and we would like Lucas to be able to mourn privately, without this glare of publicity."

Finished with his lecture, satisfied that Amanda understood her place, Oliver sat back, visibly relaxed. He wound up with an epilogue.

"Sadly, in the last month before Ruth's untimely demise, Nora's behavior had become more insistent regarding Lucas. She had been taken off a major case on which he was head counsel. We couldn't take a chance that Nora might be indiscreet. She was angry about her removal from that case. Perhaps that is what pushed her over the edge. She was a very, very angry young woman."

"That's an interesting assessment," Amanda murmured, realizing it was he who was angry—furious, in fact. She could tell by the set of his jaw and the flare of his nostrils. Strange yet oh-so-interesting.

"Her removal meant she had little need for personal contact on a daily basis with Lucas. Peter saw Nora lurking in the parking structure on the nights Lucas worked late. Don, as I'm sure he told you, saw her shaking the knob to his office when she found the door locked. Nothing overt. She was very smart, extremely subtle. Yet because we, the senior partners, were aware of the situation, we saw more than any of the other associates or partners would. We understood that which might have been construed as normal, was not."

Aware that he had perhaps become a bit too impassioned, Oliver offered a studied chuckle. Amanda jotted down a note.

"I must say, we keep our employees rather busy, so it would surprise me if any of them were truly tuned in to Nora's sexual game playing. Certainly, they understood the sexual nature of their colleague. That was difficult to ignore."

"I see." Amanda continued to write, wishing she had paid more attention in her shorthand class. Things had definitely perked up here at the end of the interview, just when Oliver was cutting her off.

"If there are no other questions, Ms. Cross, it is getting

late, and I'm due to meet my wife."

"I don't think so, Mr. Hedding. If I have any further questions I assume you'll do me the courtesy of taking my call?"

Whoa, tight and controlled Amanda. She impressed herself but probably not him.

"Of course." Oliver's hands widened magnanimously just before his expression became serious and his voice somber. "Ms. Cross, may I speak frankly?"

Amanda dropped her pen in her purse. She knew off the record when she heard it.

"Certainly. I would appreciate it."

"Thank you." He smiled.

Amanda assumed it was meant to be pleasing. He missed the mark.

"I wish to ask you to consider pleading your sister guilty, Ms. Cross. If not to murder one, perhaps plead to a lesser charge if Mr. Riordon is amenable. Please, imagine yourself, Ms. Cross, standing in front of the lab boys trying to find a way to ask a question that will prove that blood was not your sister's, prove those fingerprints weren't hers. It is impossible, Ms. Cross. Even if you were Clarence Darrow, you would be unable to completely exonerate your client. And, because you are not Clarence Darrow, because, indeed, you have a highly emotional stake in the outcome of this trial, it is actually impossible to imagine that you will do nothing more than make Nora's situation worse."

Oliver hadn't moved, only lowered his voice, yet it seemed to Amanda he was moving closer. She didn't like the feeling.

"Think about it, Ms. Cross, does Nora seem to be reacting normally to this situation? Does she sit in front of you looking quite beautiful and terribly concerned, offering gems of wisdom from her very well-trained legal mind? She is not frantic. She is not emotionally crippled by all this, is she? I would venture to guess that she seems quite calm and collected, and, I imagine, I have described her behavior rather well because that is exactly how she pursued poor Lucas. Calmly, she would ponder her situation, choose the proper time, then gleefully offer herself to Mr. Mallory, follow Mr. Mallory, basically abuse Mr. Mallory's good and serene nature.

"I would put it to you, Ms. Cross, that your sister should be pitied and helped. It is a shame we here at Dimsdale, Morris and Mott did not have the courage to help her before Ruth Mallory..."

Oliver let his thought trail off. He seemed wrapped up in memories of Ruth Mallory. They were obviously succinct because he was back in a blink.

"Think about it, Ms. Cross. Please. Do us that favor. Look into your soul. Look at your resources. Now that I've spoken with you, I know that you're not an imprudent person. How could you be if you are Nora's sister? Don't be so now when your sister's life and mental health are at stake."

Oliver leaned back, slowly, the lesson completed, satisfied with the student's attentiveness. His warnings, his condolences, his suggestions were filling Amanda's head, pushing against her skull. She hadn't fooled him. He knew she wasn't up to the trial. He could smell her uncertainty, her fear. Awful thing was she could, too. So she moved fast, muttering all the while. If she didn't, Amanda knew she might just take the easy way out.

"I appreciate the advice, Mr. Hedding. I'll think about it."

"I know you will. It would be best for everyone concerned. It would be best for Nora in the long run. Don't you think, Amanda?"

Amanda shivered. She didn't like him using her given name. Oliver Hedding didn't shake her hand when she left him. Amanda was grateful for small favors.

Chapter 14

___

"Anybody ever tell you, you look nice in green?"

Amanda kept her head down, afraid if she looked directly at Mark she might do something really ridiculous. Grin from ear to ear. Blush. Ask him home to dinner. Give him her class ring. He was gorgeous. He was nice. He liked her or at least he liked her better than Nora, which was understandable given his history with the bimbo that skipped out on him. Most surprising of all, the mystery of Mark Fleming was that he appeared—dare she hope—to be unattached.

A guy like him should be dating a twenty-year-old who looked great in a thong, maneuvered better on rollerblades than high heels, and had no idea what one did with a mind. Try as she might, though, in the last two and half months, Amanda couldn't find a stray blond hair on his jacket or the lingering scent of teeny-bopper perfume when he leaned close to check her notes or offer an opinion. So here she was, listening to his compliment, faced with a situation of extreme delicacy. This could possibly affect their working situation, might even affect the outcome of the trial, if she did the wrong thing and ran Mark off. If she did the right thing, it might ruin her concentration and she might run off. It was a tough call. Amanda did the only thing she could do. She ignored him.

"I'm just not happy with the interviews from those guys. Something isn't jiving." She entertained mental mug shots of DM&M's senior partners, letting her lack of comment speak for itself. She flipped a page of notes and buried her chin deeper into her upturned palms.

Mark swung his legs off the couch. It had become his place. Amanda thought of having a plaque made. No one, not even Nora, when she managed to drag her depressed person into the office, tried to usurp his right to lounge there.

Amanda felt him looking at her. That crooked little closed-lipped smile of his was probably plastered on his face. His eyes were beautiful and blue and, dammit, shining. Mark Fleming could sparkle if he wanted to, when he wanted to. But he could be dour and short-tempered just as easily. Not erratically, not selfishly, but there were times when things set him off. Sumptuous surroundings, law talk that excluded him, men in suits, high-powered offices, the trappings of success and wealth, Edward, and Nora—all made Mark edgy.

Times like this, though, when he lowered his voice, teasing her as if they were close—those times were pretty amazing. Amanda couldn't concentrate. He was coming nearer, his aura kind of reaching out, tickling her the way a kid would touch a kitten in the hopes it would roll over and beg for more.

"You do look pretty in green."

Tease.

"Thanks."

Cool.

She leaned back in her chair, pencil to lips, hair limp after her long day, eyes red. Mark smiled, as if he found her attractive, and walked across the room. That did it. Amanda wasn't in the mood for games.

"I appreciate the compliment. I appreciate you noticing I'm wearing green. I appreciate you throwing me a bone. I know you have a charitable streak in you when it comes to me. You've proven it many times over. But listen, Fleming." The pencil was flipped onto the desk. She covered her face with her hands and massaged it. "This exchange serves absolutely no purpose. I am not overly concerned with my status as a single working lady who goes home alone at night. You needn't be either. Now, do you mind? There are more pressing matters to attend to than my ego. When the trial is over, if you still feel the need to pump me up with your flirtations, I might be willing to do my part and act properly impressed. But for now, could we get on with it?"

Mark lolled, crossing one leg over the other at the ankle while he leaned against the file cabinet. He looked fine and knew it. His shirt was just the palest blue, a shade lighter than his eyes. He needed a haircut. Amanda liked the way his hair was a little shaggy over his ears. He smiled at her and nodded. God, why did he give up so easily?

"You're right. I won't mention that a simple thank you would have taken less time than that lecture. I verbalized thoughts on a subject other than People versus Nora Royce. Happy thoughts. Self-serving thoughts. Sorry, I must have been out of my mind."

Mark gestured, an amused defeat. Amanda almost laughed. So did he and that was when she realized what was happening between them, a really nice something that she would sure as heck label attraction: deep, delightful, absolutely time-inappropriate enchantment. Or maybe it was happening only in her mind.

"I'd tend to agree with that," Amanda answered softly, suddenly sobered by the realization that he might be right and she might be the one who was wrong. Locked in this little office with her day in and day out as they pored over interview notes and labored mightily to build witness port-folios that had an ounce of meaning, Mark had probably forgotten what it was like to hang out at the beach with a tall blond or two. Why else would he turn his attention to a passably decent-looking, just-the-wrong-side-of-svelte, thirty-eight-year-old attorney?

"You didn't have to agree so quickly," he complained.

"I'm made of snap judgments." Amanda crossed her feet under her chair, pulling herself closer to the desk, suddenly self-conscious. "Come on, let's take a look at this stuff one more time. We have Oliver Hedding indicating in interview that he was meeting with Don Forrester and Peter Sweeney at the same time Nora had her little tiff with Lucas and headed out to the balcony. Some of DM&M's associates seem to think those three men weren't in the room at the time Nora entered. Actually, most of them think that. But there were others who wouldn't swear to it. They were not seen on the concierge floor where their individual suites were located. That's been corroborated?"

Mark's turn.

"Far as I can tell. Your motion to subpoena the hotel records and track down the guests on those floors helped. There was a woman who was checked into the suite two doors down from the Mallory suite. She swears she poked her head out to check for room service and saw a gen-tleman in the doorway of the Mallory suite. She doesn't identify him as Lucas. She thinks it might have been Don Forrester but can't swear to it. In fact, she's not even sure it was exactly the right door. Had her hair in rollers and didn't want a man in a tux to see her. Guess it would have been okay if he was in a sweater, huh?" Mark waited for a chuckle. Amanda manufactured one. He laughed back, thoroughly amused.

"What time does she say?" Amanda inched ahead.

"Approximately 7:20, 7:25. Ruth Mallory hadn't even left the reception yet to get her insulin. Anyway, this lady can't be sure what she saw. She wasn't paying attention and her memory isn't that great."

"Did you check room service?"

"Her call went in at seven, so, if she was checking, the time seems about right. Her meal was delivered at 7:47."

"Remind me never to order room service at the Regency," Amanda commented. "I'm too impatient."

"Most women are like that." He was peeved again. Amanda had learned to ignore the little flares of ire he indulged in whenever women's fashionable tastes were alluded to.

She said, "So the guy with the tray probably missed Ruth Mallory by seconds. She actually made her entrance, such as it was, a little after 7:55, as I recall. Remember, Oliver Hedding likes dinner to be punctual. They were opening the doors to the dining room when she stumbled in. But the guy with the tray on the concierge level, he didn't notice anything because he's inside that woman's room a good four minutes. Taking off the little silver dome thing, pouring her coffee, waiting while she digs in her purse for a tip. So Ruth Mallory's stumbling across the hall, the elevator comes quickly for once, and she stumbles in. The room service guy finishes up and bows out of the room. I wonder how come he didn't notice the blood in the hall? The elevator? Somewhere?"

Mark had been working the kink out of his back with butterfly stretches. Now he laced his hands behind his head and leaned to the side with an "oof." Not as young as he seemed. He was upright again, abandoning the calisthenics.

"Amanda," Mark was the teacher, ready with an overly patient explanation. "The guy came up the employee elevator and approached from the south. When he came out again, he went north. He never went as far as the Mallory suite. Unless the waiter was looking for something, he wouldn't have noticed a thing. Ruth Mallory crawled out of her room and went straight for the guest elevators. Those are only a few feet away from her door."

Amanda doodled a caterpillar, then poked the end of her pencil into the paper, jabbing eyeballs through the creature's head. She poked another hole. The head was gone.

"Okay. Nothing there. Still, we might call that woman again. If she saw a man in evening dress near that door at 7:20 and not a tall young woman in an electric blue dress, then we've got something really confusing going on here. It was a man in that room—coming or going—and it wasn't Lucas Mallory, because we have witnesses who see him downstairs arguing with Nora at 7:30."

"Time's going to be a problem. We've got all these times within minutes of each other and nobody can pinpoint the exact moment of the attack or the exact time between death and attack, so we can't point the finger at anyone for being anywhere at any time," Mark reminded her.

"Confusion is our strategy and I think you just managed to create it for me. I'm thoroughly puzzled."

"All I'm saying is we're talking about minutes during

which this crime could have taken place. It's easier to point a finger if you have an hour or more in your time frame. We just don't have that."

"I don't want to point a finger unless I'm sure. I only want people to question where all the main players were and to come to the conclusion that Nora is no more likely to have murdered Ruth Mallory than anyone else," she reminded him. Satisfied, he picked up the ball again.

"According to your notes, Peter Sweeney waffles about his whereabouts during that time, give or take five minutes. He absolutely swears he was with Oliver Hedding but he says they were together from 7:20 to 7:45. Oliver Hedding says his meeting with these two men went from approximately 7:15 to 7:40. Since Hedding's such a stickler for time, I'd go with his statement. Five minutes is plenty of time to kill someone. Ruth Mallory could have been strangled, stabbed, and left for dead all in the space of a few minutes.

"Did you confirm that?"

"A forensic pathologist I know tells me it's thirty seconds to pass out when someone's got you by the neck. If they know what they're doing, or are strong enough, death isn't far behind. But Ruth Mallory didn't die by strangulation. She was just rendered senseless."

"How does your doctor know?" Amanda asked.

"I showed him the coroner's report. No petechial hemorrhage." Mark waited, anxious for her to make a comment. "Aren't you impressed?"

"Not by a twenty-five-cent word. If you know what it means, I'll consider it," Amanda drawled.

"Petechial hemorrhage—pin-point capillary breaks that are always present after death by strangulation. You can see them around the eyes." Mark's fingers traced a

Batman-mask pattern and Amanda shivered.

"Neat. I'm impressed. So she's just out cold, bleeding like a pig. and—whoever—leaves her for dead."

"That's about it. The stab wounds didn't do it right off. Heart didn't stop until she was downstairs. The wound was aggravated when she moved, trying to reach her husband. It allowed more blood into the heart, and that as they say, was that." Mark swiveled and put his hands on the filing cabinet. Amanda had had enough.

"If you do push-ups off that thing you're fired." He laughed and abandoned the cabinet. "Okay, so you're smart about how she died. We're trying to figure out what time she was attacked and who had opportunity. I think you're wrong. Go back to a meeting with Oliver and Peter. They aren't off by five minutes. My calculations say ten. See, right here."

Amanda poked at the notes. She'd typed them herself, a far cry from the meticulous witness files she had seen stacked in tidy boxes at DM&M weeks ago. Hell, everything she had was a far cry from the perfection of that office. Mark was leaning over her smelling like the ocean as if summer came lovingly early to him even though it was the end of April. They had spent six weeks together, close but not close enough.

One of his hands was on the back of her chair; the other was splayed on the side of the desk. He had nice hands—wide and just rough enough. Amanda moved as she tried to diffuse that hard, tight feeling concentrated in a part of her body that shouldn't even be thought of until satisfaction was imminent. She suspected hers was a one-sided heat. Mark was thoughtfully scanning the page in front of her. A surreptitious glance upward confirmed he had forgotten she looked great in green. Amanda focused on the notes.

"Peter has only a five-minute differential that we're interested in. We don't care what happened before 7:30, because Ruth was pinpointed at the reception. She left there on, or just before, that time. Now, Lucas Mallory says he's with Oliver Hedding and Peter Sweeney from seven to approximately 7:20. He indicates they all were at the reception earlier in the evening but excused themselves to meet on some business matter. Yet, Mallory is the only one anyone can remember seeing until Oliver began his speech. Forrester says he stopped off in his room after his meeting with Oliver and the rest of them and before he went downstairs for the second time. Lucas indicates he left the meeting early by a few minutes and that's why he was in the reception room and fighting with Nora while the rest of them were still out of sight. Where was it they were supposed to be meeting?"

"Hedding's room," Amanda murmured, "at the far end of the hall and around the corner from the Mallory suite." She shifted, seriously into this now. "And from your notes we find that Mrs. Hedding was already at the reception. She'd gone early to oversee the dinner arrangements then she acted as hostess along with the other wives. The room filled up pretty quickly. There were a lot of people. I suppose the rank and file wouldn't have noticed when the higher-ups came and went but it is likely they would remember a peon fighting with the overlord."

Mark straightened. Amanda heard a bone crack. Age did that. "I don't buy the crowd bit. Minions always know when the boss is around. Maybe we just haven't talked to the right ones yet. It's tough to go through a hundred and seventy-five people plus in a few months. I wish Leo would lighten up on this thing. He's pushing too hard."

"His case is ready, why not push?" Amanda sounded

flippant but she was far from feeling good about the court date. What did she have? Nothing. Nada. Zip. Where in the hell was she going to take it once she got into court? "Forget Leo. Make a note for Edward to look at the time discrepancies and write up some questions that will put the partners and some of Nora's peers on the spot regarding their whereabouts."

"You got it." Mark didn't make a move for his notebook. Amanda thought of harping but changed her mind. He had an amazing memory. That made her jealous.

"What have you got on Nora?" Amanda asked instead.

"Alone in her room. Trying to decide whether or not to confront Lucas. Makes up her mind. She's on the lower floor, so she takes the elevator up, not down, like the partners would. I did find a guy who remembers seeing her in the elevator."

"How'd you do that?"

"Put an ad in the *Times*." Mark shrugged. Common knowledge stuff. "He doesn't want to testify but I've got an affidavit."

"What time?"

"Won't do us much good," Mark said, setting her up for a fall. "He says after 7:15. He was on his way up to change for dinner and he was late. Could have been ten minutes earlier or later." Mark moved away, hands now clasped behind his back. While Amanda spoke, he thought.

"Nora got into it with Lucas a little after 7:30. Ruth was already gone. Nora was on that patio from approximately 7:40 to 7:55 according to both Nora and Edward. Granted, that's to the best of their recollection and it's tough to remember exact times. And Edward was gone a solid ten minutes, maybe more. God, I hate these minute-by-minute things. But that's pretty weird, because the reception started at seven and the associates and partners I was able to interview all say that they tend to remember Lucas being at the festivities when they began. They can't swear he didn't leave the room but they certainly are sure he wasn't forty minutes late. He couldn't have been. Nora confronted him and fought with him about 7:30. We've got a dozen people that will swear to that."

"What about Don Forrester?" Amanda mumbled, knowing full well that Don had said very little about anything.

"Says he was with his wife, who was having trouble getting her hair to do just the right thing. He was in the living room of the suite, she in the bathroom. It's fair to assume he didn't leave the room, as he said. Then again, I don't know."

Mark shrugged, stood up, and then settled himself on the edge of the desk as casually as you please.

"I don't see him as a possible suspect. He certainly could have zipped down the hall and murdered Ruth Mallory but if he did I'll eat my hat. He adores his wife. He's not the kind to covet someone else's, unless it's from afar and, most importantly, he just isn't a man who could commit a violent act like that and wander back to help his wife zip up her dress."

"Think you could check this out with his wife? Just a few questions about his general state of mind. Or with any of the people who were at the reception? Maybe he said something unusual or did something that would change your assessment."

"I doubt if Min Forrester is going to talk to me without the other 'wives'." Mark hung quotation marks in the air above his head.

"That's weird. Three women who don't do anything without the others' permission." Amanda sighed. The thought gave her the creeps. Mark shoved off again and paced slowly around the small office. He was antsy.

"I don't think that's it. I think they actually like one another. They probably have a real deep affection for each other because they know they're different from other women."

"Yeah, they're rich." Amanda laughed.

"Naw, it's more than that. They know they're weak."

Amanda sat back, watching. Mark fascinated her. His sixth sense about people was uncanny. If he hadn't given up so easily, he would have made a good lawyer. Someday she would ask him why he didn't try again. But she knew the answer. He'd lost faith, in himself or the system. When his lady labeled him a loser, he accepted it. Now that he was working on instinct instead of faith, though, he was in his element. He was even excited.

"These women are smart, mind you. Smart enough to have married well. They live in homes the size of a decent office building. They spend more on their gardeners than I have in my entire life on food, clothing, and lodging. They order servants about, they run charities, they manage budgets—"

"I'm waiting for the weakness factor here," Amanda interrupted. "What is it? Men? Booze? Drugs?"

"Nothing that exotic. They're simply afraid, unhappy. You can feel it when you're with them. They've lost themselves. Min's cute as a button but the cuteness is rote. And then there's the newest member of the club. Peg Sweeney?"

Amanda nodded, a picture of the tennis wife, as Mark called her, flashing through her brain.

"She's smart, a trophy wife, only onboard the last five years. She's already figured it out. She married an asshole who happened to have made good. He blinded her with money but now she doesn't like what she sees. Neither do Kitty or Min. Not one of them can walk away because they aren't twenty, they aren't sexy, they aren't smart in the way the world wants women to be smart these days, and they haven't got the guts to stand on their own. It's sad."

Mark stopped pacing and Amanda knew he was thinking about another woman who had made the wrong choice. His fiancée had thrown in with him because she was sure he was going to be the next Oliver Hedding. When it was clear he wasn't going to cut the mustard, she walked. Amanda couldn't help but think that babe had made the wrong decision. Maybe if she'd stuck around, offered a bit of encouragement, Mark wouldn't be selling himself out by the day. Water under the bridge. There were other women to worry about.

"What about Ruth Mallory? Do you think she was one of those kind of women?"

Mark started. He was clearly still thinking about the past. Amanda wondered why he didn't just get as far away from the practice of law as he could. Working the way he did was like pouring salt on a wound. Not Amanda's style. She had a funny feeling it wasn't Mark's, either, way down deep.

"Ruth Mallory," he muttered, pushing himself off the desk. He sat down again and looked at Amanda. It was four in the afternoon and she looked great.

No fussy hair, no fussy clothes. All business, Amanda Cross, with her tough shell. She didn't fool him. There were those vulnerable moments when he just wanted to gather her up, see how she fit, hang in there with her awhile. But Amanda didn't want to hear what he thought of her. She wanted to hear about Ruth Mallory.

"I think Ruth Mallory was the odd man out, in a way. She was naturally classy. Didn't have to work at it like Min or fail at it like Peg Sweeney. She was a lot like Kitty in that way. Younger, but still the same natural instinct for graciousness. She and Kitty were very close. When Mrs. Hedding talked about Mrs. Mallory, there was a deep and heartfelt sadness, not just shock or fear. She really will miss Ruth Mallory. But she was different from Kitty, too. Ruth Mallory was outgoing, some say outspoken."

"Who says outspoken and about what?" Amanda asked.

"Nothing, really. When I talked to some of her Junior League sisters, they indicated Ruth could bring discussions to a head. You know the one they turned to when all the little women of the club couldn't come to a consensus. She was also a liberal. Not flaming, you understand but it seemed she was kind of a feminist non-feminist. I don't know any other way to put it."

"How about she was her own person?" Amanda suggested dryly. "I know it's an outrageous concept, but what the heck, this is the nineties."

"Okay. I'll stop labeling. It just seems she was different from the others."

"Different enough to have caused someone trouble?"

"Maybe."

"Different enough to have moved out of her circle, into one that wasn't exactly kosher?"

"No. That I doubt," Mark answered, thinking hard, too lazy to get up and get his notes. "I don't think she was into anything fringe. No extra men, nothing like that. I talked to the cleaning lady and the cook at the Mallory house even though they would have preferred to talk to the devil. I think they had the impression that they had to talk to me."

"Can't imagine where they got that idea." Amanda

abandoned all pretense of work. The exchange of ideas was far more stimulating. She opened her mind and tried to understand the whole picture.

"Doesn't matter. They talked. Nobody came to the house that shouldn't have been there. Men or women. The house was a busy place—Ruth's kind of busy. Club meetings, teas, luncheons, charity stuff. Lucas was usually at work. According to the help, there was never a cross word between those two. Not perfect. Not lovey-dovey. Just a couple who've been married a long, long time. She'd been married before, by the way."

Amanda shifted, sitting up straighter. This was good.

"Really? That's interesting. Do you know who he is? Where we can find him?"

"Relax. I got my heart pumping, too, when I heard it. The guy's dead. She was a widow by the time she was thirty-five. He was a lot older. A statesman. Peer of her father's. He dropped dead on the senate floor. No kids. Big estate. She met Lucas when she was forty. They've been married, as happily as anyone can be, for eighteen years. No children. Even the trash man thought she was okay. She used to leave him a lemon cake at Christmas. If she had a fault, it was that she was a thinking woman in a group who had given up their right to function independently of their husbands. Ruth was the only one who probably didn't ask her husband if every move she made was all right or checked out the itinerary so nothing would reflect badly on the firm."

"That's kind of interesting, Fleming."

"That's what I'd call it. Nothing earth shattering. Just interesting that Ruth Mallory could survive in that atmosphere."

"Naw." Amanda waved her hand. "That's the least

interesting part. If Ruth Mallory liked those women—the partners' wives—then she would adapt. This woman was a politician's daughter. Now we find she was a politician's wife. She could probably adapt to anything. That was her job. But put it together with a really well-grounded personality. That's kind of unusual. She was outspoken, huh? Had her own ideas?"

"Right, but not obnoxious. No major campaigns against anything. Didn't chain herself to the docks in order to save the whales or anything. Just said what was on her mind. If she didn't like something, people heard about it. If she did, they heard about that, too. You could call her involved—passionate, I suppose."

"I would like to have met her," Amanda muttered not expecting a reply. Her mind was going a mile a minute. She was charged. "So, let's take this really way out. Maybe we shouldn't be worrying about where the four men were when Ruth Mallory was wiped out. Maybe we should be wondering where those wives were?"

Mark barked a laugh. That was the last thing he expected.

"Give me a break, Amanda. You think those ladies could do anything like what was done to Ruth Mallory? I can just see it. Min Forrester, those teeny little hands of hers holding onto that knife, kneeling beside Ruth Mallory while Peg Sweeney held Ruth's arms and Kitty held her legs. Then Min would say 'Excuse us Ruth, but you've really gotten out of hand. We just can't have you as part of the group anymore.' Bam, good old Min blasts Ruth with the knife. And what about the strangulation? Who on earth would have been able to carry that off? Kitty? Then they go downstairs looking cool as cucumbers and hobnob with the rabble? Oh, please!"

"Come on. Stranger things have happened," Amanda objected. "Women are strong. When are you guys going to get that through your heads? Min Forrester could use those teeny little hands of hers to break your neck if she really wanted to. I mean, where do you get off? Now, I take your point about them being at the reception looking cool and collected. They were all dressed formally, right? The men too?"

Mark nodded.

"That's a tough one, but, hey, they lived half their lives dressed like that. They could probably roller skate in formal dress. Somehow they would have had to make allowances for the blood but it could happen." Amanda saw the set of skepticism on Mark's brow and insisted, "It could. Not to mention there would be easy access to Ruth's suite. She's going to open the door without a second thought when one of them knocks."

"She would have done the same thing for Nora. Face it. Nora identifies herself as one of the associates on an errand for Lucas. Or she even says she's looking for Lucas. Ruth Mallory's going to at least open the door."

Amanda shot him a peevish glance. "Why is it you always have to be so damned pessimistic?"

"I'm not." He laughed defensively. "I'm doing what you pay me to do. I'm being a devil's advocate. Man, Amanda, you are so touchy."

"Sorry," Amanda apologized knowing he was right. Unfortunately, Mark was using that throw-in-the-towel tone of voice and that ticked her off to no end. Forgiveness was at hand, though. She had learned to be magnanimous. Alone, with Edward, the team effort would be lacking, to say the least.

"No offense taken. But you've got to have a point. Then

there's the question of why. Why on earth would they want to murder a woman who was so much a part of the group?"

"Maybe it was because she was the group. You know what I mean? Maybe Ruth, by force of personality, had sort of taken things over. Her way the right way. Do-what-I-want-to-do kind of thing. Maybe it just became too much for those little ladies. Women are funny creatures, Mark."

Amanda sat back, happy to talk about a subject she knew so intimately. "What if Ruth Mallory took their last vestige of self-esteem away from them and outdid them on the social thing or the charity thing? Maybe it would be enough to kill for. Or maybe one of them just cracked up, was really tired of Ruth being perfect or of her telling them what to do. They all went to see Ruth in her room." Amanda's voice was quickening, she was weaving a scenario that was plausible but highly unlikely. "They went to talk about something, then Ruth pulls rank and one of them goes nuts."

"No," Mark thought again. "No way. Not even plausible. I've been with those women, watched them and listened to them. They just couldn't do it and still have tea with me while I asked them questions. One of them would have given me a hint. I've been around enough liars to know there aren't many good ones—"

"Probably Peg Sweeney. Didn't you tell me she's the real athletic type?" Amanda shot a glance Mark's way but it was one of those unseeing looks. She wasn't asking for corroboration, just an audience.

"No," Mark said simply.

"She's not the athletic type?" That stopped Amanda for a minute. He had her attention. "But I thought you said…"

"I did say she was the athletic type. What I'm saying no to is this entire line of thinking. Amanda, we've got enough trouble just trying to prove that Nora just might not have killed Ruth Mallory. Why are you trying to figure out who did? And why are you sticking so close to home? If you want to paint Mrs. Mallory officious and obnoxious, then she would have left a trail of offenses. People would have talked."

Amanda puffed herself up, ready for a fight. Never give up, do or die—that was Amanda. Let it go, it's not right, it's useless to pursue it—that was Mark. This time he won.

"I guess I was wrong. I thought I could live with the reasonable doubt strategy but I can't. I want to know who did it so I can be sure Nora didn't."

Here was a confession. A heartfelt truth. A painful realization. Mark wanted to beat it across the room and grab her. Instead, he asked, "Think she did?"

Frustrated, Amanda confessed, "I don't know. Sometimes yes, sometimes no. After all this, I guess she's going to have to fit into my life somehow. I just know that I don't want that if I'm wondering about her innocence all the time. Could you do that? Could you just walk away from a trial with an acquittal or see your sister sent off to jail and not have a definite answer?"

"I don't know. I don't have a sister." Mark's eyes were soft, taking the edge off his wisecrack.

"That was a rhetorical inquiry."

"Yeah, well. Here's a theoretical question for you. Are you going to walk into that courtroom and spin some tale about crazy rich, middle-aged ladies or are you going to go in there and talk about the issues? The issues being: why are there discrepancies in the time frame of the partners the night of the reception? Why is it that nobody I've talked to got the feeling that Nora was a raving maniac when it came to Lucas Mallory? Why is it that nobody wants

to look at the physical evidence from the standpoint of a
woman having an affair but they are perfectly willing to
accept that Nora walked into that suite, or waited in it, and,
with premeditation, violently attacked Ruth Mallory? And
make no mistake—it was violent. So, either your sister is a
first-class wacko who can turn off and on some deep-seated
flaky emotions or she's innocent but unwilling to act like a
shrinking violet to make us believe it. Now, which are you
going to believe? Which Nora are you going to talk about
when you walk into that courtroom, Amanda?"

Such a silence. It sat between them like a big fat cat.
Nobody needed to point out that Mark made sense. Work
had to be done. But Amanda couldn't shake the feeling.
She needed to know positively that Nora was innocent.
Not that it would change Nora's defense. This was personal. Amanda needed one shred of evidence that her sister
wasn't lying to her. Amanda wanted to know that Nora
wasn't a psycho. The only way she could prove anything
was to prove one thing; that Nora and Lucas were sleeping
together. In short, Amanda had to make a jury believe that
four of the most powerful attorneys in Los Angeles were
liars. Then again, that might be easier than she imagined.

"Okay. You're right and there isn't much time. Prosecution starts its case in four weeks. On cross-examination, I'll pick apart the time discrepancies and the rest
of it. Did you find out anything at the town house? Any
background on Lucas Mallory that we can use to show
he was a womanizer?"

"That's the last line of questioning you can use. It seems
Lucas Mallory was one of the most faithful husbands in
Los Angeles. Sorry."

"Don't worry. I'll work it out. I hate to ask you but I'm
going to send you out again. Somebody had to have seen

them together and remember. Do you mind trying to talk to the secretaries at DM&M? I know we had decided we only had time for the attorneys but I think this is important."

"No problem. I'll plant myself outside the office and grab them when they come by. It's a big place. There's got to be one who has eyes and ears. I just haven't hit the magic combination."

"What's that?"

Mark stood up and grabbed his jacket. He slipped into it, flipped his shirt collar up, and shot his cuffs. "The secretary who uses one properly and doesn't mind shooting off the other." He was already at the door, his hand on the knob. He had one more thing to say. Amanda waited expectantly. But the door was open and the phone was ringing before he could speak.

She picked up one and watched the other.

"Amanda Cross."

Heavy breathing for a split second. Then: "It's Edward. She's gone. Nora's gone to find Lucas."

"When?" Amanda was up, the phone cradled between her head and shoulders as she grabbed for her purse and screamed, "Mark!" into the hall, hoping he hadn't already caught the notoriously slow elevator. She screamed for him once more. Consuelo came rushing in, babbling in English, swearing in Spanish, with Mark hot on her heels.

"Edward's going to meet us at Dimsdale. We've got to go now."

Mark didn't think twice. He went after Amanda like a trooper blindly following his general.

He still thought she looked great in green.

Chapter 15

"Anything?"

Amanda skidded around the corner of the elevator banks, her shoes slipping on the black marble. Two huge lobbies flanked the elevators, each so large it was impossible to keep an eye on both at one time but Mark was standing in the middle of the corridor between the gleaming doors trying his best to do just that. He shook his head, his face clouded with concern.

"Nothing. I haven't seen hide nor hair of her. Edward was sure she was headed this way?"

Amanda pushed closer to Mark. The end of the day was almost upon them and people were beginning to pour out of the building. They were, in Amanda's mind, parallel people, moving the same, looking the same, eyes forward, business suits, briefcases. A sea of black and navy and gray. Jackets and ties. Women as preoccupied as the men; men as exhausted as the women.

Amanda's lip found its way between her teeth. Her eyes darted here and there, landing on any form and figure that resembled Nora in the least. How wonderful it would be if Nora could do her magic once more, bursting onto the scene so uniquely, so overwhelmingly divine she would be as noticeable as the fireworks on the Fourth of July. In her heart, Amanda knew that wouldn't be the case because Nora had fizzled in the past few months, a dud unable to ignite the outrage she'd once felt at her predicament, the exquisite arrogance she'd felt in face of the world that had abandoned her. She had faded to a shadow of herself and, if she became invisible, all was lost.

"Edward swore," Amanda whispered jostling closer to Mark. Instinctively, his hand came around her waist. He pulled her to him protectively as they moved back a step, never suspending their vigil. "I dropped the phone before I got all the specifics but I gather he was watching her pull out of her garage while he was talking to me. It takes about twenty-five minutes to drive from her town house to downtown. Maybe another ten to park and get up the elevators this time of day. We made it over in fifteen running. We've been here another-" Amanda tipped her wrist to check her watch "-say ten, so we beat her. We had to. If she makes good and does get a hold of Lucas Mallory we might as well throw in the towel before this trial even starts. Obsessive stalker? This will look like Nora fits the bill."

"No kidding—"

"Amanda! Mark!"

Both of them twirled toward the sound of their names. Edward Ramsey hurried toward them, jogging around the masses of people like a salmon heading upstream. His expression was one of concern or absolute terror, Amanda wasn't sure which. She stepped away from Mark, going to meet him. Edward stepped between them trying to talk while he caught his breath.

"Jesus, Ramsey." Mark took the lead obviously not thinking much of Edward's distress. "You can't keep an eye on a woman who's depressed? Who hasn't gotten out of bed in weeks? I wouldn't hire you to watch a two-year-old."

"Yo, wait a minute, Fleming." Edward's finger was raised pointing directly at Mark's chest. He squared off like a prizefighter, bantamweight challenging the champ. "I'm not your lackey and I'm no damned babysitter. I think you better take a look around and rethink things. I'm the attorney here; you're just hired on for the shit work."

Mark pulled in tight, his hands balled into fists. Amanda moved closer but Edward dodged, closing in on Mark. They'd been coming to this for a while. He wasn't going to give an inch.

"I was going over her testimony and a hundred other stories, looking for inconsistencies, formulating strategy, looking for police records among hotel employees. I was working my butt off coming up with a decent cross-examination for Amanda and I needed Nora's help for that. Do you know how tough it is to get her to do anything but sit on the damn couch and look out the window? That is if she even bothers to get up in the morning."

"You're right." Mark laughed cruelly. "You're no match for a woman in that condition."

"I was doing all right. She was beginning to open up. She was walking back through the entire night Ruth Mallory was killed and the affair. I was getting a solid, cohesive story that was going to be tough to break. I go to the john and she disappears, leaving me a note like a kid running away from home. So sue me. Would you have preferred I drugged her, then hit the john when she was out cold?"

"Edward. Mark." Amanda had heard enough. This

wasn't the time or place. The longer Nora was out of sight, the more frantic Amanda was becoming. "Forget it. We've got to find Nora. Even if she's calm as can be, I don't want her having any contact with Lucas Mallory. Edward. You worked here. Is there any way she could get past us?"

"Naw, this is the only bank of elevators that runs to the thirties floors. There's no other—" Edward stopped, looked this way and that. "Wait. She could go through the hotel. Go through the hotel and across the walkway that connects the two buildings. There's a stop on the mezzanine that will take her on express to thirty."

"Shit," Mark muttered leaping toward the button and hitting it instead of Edward. "How long did she leave before you?"

"Two minutes. Maybe three. I was on the freeway fast as I could. If she has five minutes on me I'd be surprised."

"Five minutes can make a lot of difference," Amanda spoke. A rock the size of Gibraltar was sitting in her stomach and it felt like there were bats on the wing upstairs. Everything she was, everything this mess represented, had coagulated in the pressure points of her body. She was scared because maybe Nora had lost her mind. If that happened, Nora would destroy Amanda's chance to prove she was a good lawyer. A selfish fright, but real, nonetheless. On top of everything else, Amanda was horrified that Nora might be exactly what Oliver Hedding said she was. What if, instead of discovering a confrontation, they found Lucas Mallory dead by the time they got upstairs? An elevator opened. Mark was passing people out as if he were counting heads at a class field trip. The minute the elevator was empty he was in, Edward and Amanda dashing after him. Mark punched the button for the thirtieth floor.

Amanda flashed back, "I met Lucas Mallory on the

thirty-second floor."

"Right. That's where his office is. Thirty is general lobby." Edward's fingers were beating a tune on the soft-sided wall.

"We'll stop there anyway, just in case she decided to prowl," Mark ordered saving face, recovering his sense of worth. Edward and Amanda let him have it. Everybody was on edge. No need to pick a fight until they could see it through.

The elevator vibrated as it went up. When it slowed at the twenty-eighth floor, it seemed to shudder before coming to a disappointingly ordinary stop on thirty. Mark and Amanda were out first, darting around to see if Nora was about. Edward headed toward the receptionist.

"Mr. Ramsey, we haven't seen you—"

"Have you seen Nora Royce?" Edward screamed cutting her off midsentence.

Amanda pivoted, turning in surprise to watch. Mark, poised at the head of a bowed staircase that connected the general reception area with the offices above, was stunned into inaction. The receptionist's face fell, mortified, angry, she remained silent. That stillness seemed to anger Edward even more. He was shouting at the woman, leaning over the high wooden desk.

"I'm asking you. Have you seen Nora Royce?"

"Mr. Ramsey, I…" Her gaze darted to Mark then Amanda. A look that asked what she'd done to deserve this.

"Have you or haven't you?" Edward reached out, thought twice and jerked his arm back. Had he wanted to touch the woman? Pull her toward him? Abuse her to get the information he needed?

Fascinated, Amanda moved forward a step or two, eager to see this new side of DM&M's little bad boy. She cocked her head, peering around his shoulders. He was whispering to the woman now, asking hard and insistent questions that left her with no recourse but to shake her head and hope he would go away. When it was clear she was useless, Edward backed off. The tendons in his neck tightened in rigid cords, his jaw was clenched, as were his hands. Amanda moved closer to him.

"Edward?"

His head snapped toward her and they stared at one another through a long, swelling moment. Perspiration dotted his forehead. Amanda realized she was unrecognizable to him in his fevered state. The neighborhood pup had changed. Had she thought too little about Edward all this time? Quietly going about his work, burrowing into Nora's life when she should have bonded with her sister. Edward Ramsey had been out of sight so often, out of mind more often than that, that Amanda had not given him his due.

Amanda waited an instant longer not knowing what to say. Then her fingers lightly touched the sleeve of his jacket and Edward relaxed. Vertebra by vertebra, he let his body fall back into place Hands open, he flexed his fingers, looking at them as if surprised to find he still had ten, until, not knowing what else to do, those hands were in his hair, pushing it away even though the razor cut kept it well off his face. His pretty lips, his full lips, puckered up and pushed out the bad air.

"Sorry," he muttered half turning toward the receptionist, including Amanda in his stance.

Who the apology was directed at was unclear. Crazily, Amanda wondered if he were apologizing to himself for letting things get out of hand. But his hand was on her arm, turning her toward the stairs and conjecture was left behind. The receptionist could entertain it. They joined a cautious Mark and were bounding up the stairs, Edward talking that fast, nice talk he did so well.

"I don't need to have a receptionist tell me I haven't been here for a while. Stupid thing for her to say. Everybody knows I left on less than friendly terms. I hate it when people do that. Try to make happy… nothing happy about it… had to be done. Let's find Nora. I want to get out of here."

With that, he took the last two steps in one leap, skirting the receptionist and heading for the individual offices. Not knowing the layout, Mark and Amanda had no choice but to follow. Amanda fell behind for a moment, trying to get her bearings. It was impossible. She couldn't remember anything from the short time she'd spent there. She hurried on. Edward was just ahead, poking his nose into an office as if he owned it.

"This was hers," he called back to them. Amanda had just enough time to look through the open door and see it had been completely stripped. Not one file, not a picture, not one indication that Nora Royce had ever sat confidently behind the large desk. Unfortunately, Amanda also had time to see the beauty of the desk, the breathtaking view of Los Angeles and the Hollywood Hills, the privilege that Nora had enjoyed all these years, while Amanda worked less than a mile away—a world away. Mark was on her, his fingers lacing through hers. He held her hand, understanding. Two of a kind.

"We're going to lose him," he whispered. It was enough. Amanda forged ahead.

Edward was disappearing up the next flight of stairs. She and Mark picked up the pace. The top. Thirty-second floor. End of game.

Amanda shot onto the wide, deserted landing. Behind

closed doors, attorneys labored over the paperwork of leveraged buyouts, mezzanine financing, real property acquisition; they created corporations, helped license technology, divorced corporate entities. They worked hard, leafing through their files, scribbling their notes, never lifting their heads, letting the sun rise and set before they thought of food or sex or breathing. Past these offices, Mark and Amanda walked, slowing their pace, trying to look as if they belonged. They didn't do a very good job. Fish out of water, they swam right by the few overworked secretaries who still mauled their computers in a desperate attempt to get their work done.

Walking on, lulled into thinking that nothing untoward would be found in a place as obviously contained and content as DM&M, they proved themselves wrong before they reached the end of the hall. There stood Edward, his back to them, visible through the half-open doorway of a small room just past the fourth secretarial station. They approached cautiously, senses alert for any interruption. Mark handed Amanda through the door and followed, closing it quietly after him. Nora was found.

She sat in a metal chair with her knees pulled tightly together, her hands cupping them. Her eyes were belt-level, unwavering, as she rocked back and forth. Her body trembled and her face was pale with an anger that surprised Amanda. Nora, frightened, mad, and human, was a sight to behold.

Edward stood above her, one hand braced against the wall, the other slapped onto a slim hip, glaring at a spot above Nora's head. They were locked in a cocoon of vibrating fury, neither able to speak or move. Mark took Edward's forearm and tried to move him and Edward tried to jerk away. Wordlessly, Mark insisted, with a twisting clutch to the younger man's upper arm. Edward moved, pulling away from Mark in the process and heading toward one of the little round tables by a Coke machine. Petulantly, he flopped onto the seat, crossed his legs and buried his chin in his upturned hand.

Amanda had slipped to the floor and was crouching at her sister's feet. Amanda's warm hands covered Nora's icy ones, fingers quivering at odd but consistent intervals. She clutched tighter at those fingers, trying to calm them, knowing how painful this must be for Nora, this lack of control.

"Nora," Amanda whispered, "what on earth were you going to do here? What were you trying to prove?"

Nora's fingers jumped, she rocked forward, then back again, hitting the chair so that it danced away an inch or two. Amanda held on tight. Nora's fingers fluttered once more before her head fell back, hair cascading over her shoulders. Her eyes were closed, long lashes lying on her high cheekbones. She looked like one of those prayer cards the Catholics hand out to the faithful. Every saint was beautiful and every damn one was innocent. Just like Nora.

"I—wanted—to—confront—him," she muttered in staccato, making it sound as if her diaphragm wasn't pumping right. She pulled in a deep breath, feeding the bellows with oxygen to make sure her voice wouldn't fail her. Her head fell forward until her chin rested on her chest, her eyes almost but not quite hidden by a curtain of hair.

"I wanted to confront Lucas and make him tell the truth. I am not a liar but he's making me look like one because he's not telling the truth. Him, not me." Her body pulled up fast and tight.

Amanda wanted to look away, understanding the degradation, the pain of being brought to this level of impotence.

"I'm not a murderer. Murder. I couldn't do that. I couldn't. Why would I want to? I didn't give a shit about Ruth Mallory. She could have him. Stupid, stupid, stupid! He didn't want to hurt her. What about me, Amanda? Why does he want to hurt me? Why do they all want to hurt me?"

Nora leaned close, the heat of her breath touching Amanda's cheek. Amanda wondered if this was it for Nora. She was talking fast now, her hands bouncing up and down beneath Amanda's for emphasis, her lament a whisper, then a wail.

"What does he have to protect now? What? We're so close to trial and I know there isn't any defense. I know that. I watch you and Edward and I look at your notes when you don't know that I do. I'm going back to prison, Amanda. Don't let that happen. I had to do something so that wouldn't happen."

Suddenly, Nora was looking right at her sister, their faces inches apart. Amanda was angered and frightened by her pain and fear. It was her job, after all, to ease this misery, to soothe the fear. It was her job to wake Nora from this nightmare and she was failing.

"Ruth is dead, Amanda," Nora whispered frantically. "Who could he hurt by letting people know that we were sleeping together? He should tell people that I left the room right after we did it. He might be embarrassed, Amanda, he might feel bad. But what's that in the greater scheme of things? This is my life, Amanda. He's going to take away my life because he won't tell the truth and all his friends are telling lies, too. They are all lies, Amanda. You've got to believe that. I'll make him tell you. Come with me. I'll make him tell you the truth. I'm the only one who tells it, Amanda."

Nora's feet were moving, pounding the floor lightly.
A powerless little girl trying to express herself when
words failed.

"I know, Nora," Amanda soothed instinctively reaching
out and cupping Nora's head, releasing it as if she'd been
burned when Nora stiffened at her touch. Comforting
murmurs seemed the only acceptable solace. "I know.
But he's not going to tell the truth. He's going to protect
his butt. When we get him on the stand, that's the time to
confront him and prove he perjured himself. Not now."
Amanda fingered the ends of Nora's hair, baby hair, so
soft and long. "If you try to see him you'll look just like
they want you to look. Do you understand? Do you see
how they could turn it around and point the finger? And
what jury wouldn't believe them? You come down here
dressed like this."

Amanda leaned away, taking her Nora's arms and
spreading them wide. It was an impetuous action that
served its purpose. Nora blinked at her torn jeans, the
old sandals, her faded sweatshirt. Slowly, she slipped her
hands from Amanda's. Those pretty, long-fingered hands
that hadn't been tended by a manicurist in so long hovered
in the air about her head as though afraid to touch. They
fluttered to the front of her face before she lowered them
to her lap, ashamed and oddly calm.

Clearly, she was making an effort to hold steady, to
transform herself and become what she had been before
this horror began. Nora's strength was in appearances;
now, even that failed her. Hope had been overcome by
apprehension, been beaten down by fear. Nora was being
destroyed by Lucas Mallory, the man with whom she'd
shared her ambitions and her body, and by the firm to
which she had pledged her loyalty. Nora had been aban-

doned, completely and without remorse. The effort to retrieve her self-esteem was an exercise in futility. Nora buried her face in her hands. She began to cry.

"Shhh," Amanda whispered taking her sister awkwardly in her arms. They had never touched like this, not in greeting nor happiness nor grief. Now, with Nora broken and needy, Amanda gained strength, her reserve swept away. Ineptly, with the best of intentions, Amanda whispered "Shhhh" again, still not daring to stroke that long, silky hair. When she thought the time was right, when it was clear this would never be comfortable for either of them, she spoke quietly and stood slowly.

"We have to go now, Nora. We have to—"

The moment—their moment—was shattered in one swift stroke. Nora shook Amanda off with a sudden burst of energy and a strangled, "Not until I've seen him."

Amanda, the stronger of the two, grabbed her again and pinned her to the chair.

"You won't see Lucas Mallory unless it's in the courtroom," Amanda commanded her voice soft. "Nora, don't be a fool. Don't ruin what little chance you have—we have. Please," Amanda said. "Don't make me look like a goddamn idiot." Nora froze, her face hardening. It was as if Amanda had slapped her. Behind her, Amanda could feel Mark and Edward tense unsure whether they should step between the two women. Amanda's words hung shamefully in the silence that followed.

Don't make me look like a fool. Don't stand up for yourself. Don't make a scene. Don't do anything except wait.

That was Nora's punishment for years of getting everything she wanted when she wanted it. This was Nora's hell—to be useless and powerless—and Amanda was taking advantage of it. Mark, jack-of-all-trades, took charge,

REBECCA FORSTER

plucking them out of the lick of flames in the nick of time.

Amanda stood up, feeling heavy and tired. Mark almost had the broken Nora on her feet when Amanda found the energy to help. She reached out, affection drained from her touch. She was Nora's lawyer. It was time to remember that and forget the rest.

Mark opened the door. Word of Edward's outburst, Nora's appearance, and Mark and Amanda's presence had spread. But, like the professionals they were, the staff of DM&M kept their distance. A few secretaries had gathered into a knot and were watching the lunchroom, waiting for something to happen. Two attorneys lolled in the doorways of their offices. Mark scanned the hall. Security hadn't been called. Thankfully, neither had any of the senior partners. Their little band was in the clear—for now. Without a backward look, Mark called for Edward.

"Come on. Edward. I think we're done here." By the time they reached the elevators, Edward was ahead of them, pushing the button and trying to ignore what had grown to be a group of curious onlookers who followed them out to the lobby. A weeping Nora Royce was probably something everyone needed to see for themselves. Amanda, Edward, Nora, and Mark entered the elevator and stoically waited for it to take them away from what could have been a most disastrous confrontation.

"I'll leave my car," Edward mumbled as they reached Nora's in the subterranean garage. "I'll drive her home."

Amanda settled her sister in the front seat while Mark took Edward aside.

"Don't be stupid again, Ramsey."

"You may want to think hard before you use a word like that again, Fleming. Don't forget who passed the Bar." Edward brought a finger to his chin, tapping it thoughtfully. With an exaggerated sigh, an embellished concern, he said, "Come to think of it, maybe we've been doing this all wrong, you and I. Why don't I go interviewing and you stay home and babysit? It's actually a kind of mindless task. You don't need to pass a test to do it." Edward's tone was friendly, utterly reasonable. Coupled with the sneer on his lips, it turned Edward into a thoroughly unlikable sort.

"Sorry. I didn't make myself clear," Mark said. "I meant to say we appreciate you keeping an eye on Nora. But to run into DM&M screaming at some poor little receptionist is unacceptable. You're not helping Nora. You're not helping yourself. Don't you agree?"

Thunderheads of anger darkened Edward's eyes. The sneer faded, his face became hard and cold.

"Great advice from a guy on the fringe. I know what I'm doing, so don't you worry about me. No harm, no foul, Mark. I think we can agree on that."

"I don't know that we can agree on anything, Ramsey."

"Sure we can. We're men. We know there are times you gotta play a little rough if you want to get results. Long as you're not caught, there's no problem. I don't see anybody hot on our tails because I got excited and hurt a little girl's feelings. Now, get off my case. Nora needs me. We've been doing fine. This was an exception, an emergency. It's taken care of. It won't happen again."

"I hope not."

"I don't think you have anything to say about it. Last I heard Amanda was running the show."

"I—"

"Mark. That's enough," Amanda called. He backed off. She joined them, curious and demanding. "How did you know she'd head here, Edward?"

"Wouldn't take a genius to figure that one out." His

bad attitude transferred smoothly toward Amanda. "She's been talking about Lucas all week. You'd know that if you bothered to check in with her once in a while."

Amanda accepted the reprimand like a trooper. Disgusted, Edward took off before she could apologize. He rounded the car, opened the door, and got in. Mark stood back and touched Amanda's arm, silently suggesting she should do the same. They watched Edward brush back a strand of Nora's hair and loop it behind her ear. She didn't move but Edward's lips did. Behind the sealed windows, the conversation was kept completely private. Nora nodded, tired and weak and beaten. She leaned her head against the window as Edward drove out of the parking garage. He pointedly ignored Mark and threw Amanda a perfunctory wave as he spirited Nora away.

"I hate that kid," Mark muttered.

Amanda couldn't exactly come to Edward's defense; her feelings about him were so ambivalent. Helpful, he was, forthcoming, he wasn't. She had no more idea who Edward Ramsey was today than she had when he first walked into her office. That was fine as long as he did what he'd promised to do, but Mark, unfortunately, couldn't be quite that uninterested.

Edward was a thorn in Mark's side. He was everything Mark Fleming was supposed to have been, should have been, and Edward didn't deserve to be. Even Amanda knew that. There was something about Edward Ramsey, something itchy deep down inside that young man that rubbed them both the wrong way.

Amanda took Mark's arm. Gently, she pointed him toward the bank of elevators. In silence, they rode up to the building lobby, joined the exodus, and found themselves swept out the door along with the rest of the working stiffs. Simultaneously, they stopped at the top of the long, graceful sweep of shallow marble steps. Below them was Figueroa. Silently, they surveyed the teeming street. It was time to go home, regroup, and recharge. Tomorrow wasn't that far away. It would be no worse or better than today.

Mark squeezed Amanda's hand against the side of his body. He smiled at her. She was a damned handsome woman and the lure of his trailer in Malibu was minimal. It was lonely there, sometimes.

"How about a drink, Ms. Cross?" There was a trace of sadness in his voice that wasn't directed at Nora's situation or at Amanda. It was for himself, a small and easily discarded sadness.

"I'd like that," she said softly. Neither of them moved. When Amanda's sigh was almost swallowed up by the noise of the city, Mark asked:

"Is that the sound of regret or defeat?"

"Neither, specifically." She laughed wearily. "It was one of those all-purpose sounds. Sad. Content. Worried. Miserable. Confused."

"Surprised I didn't recognize it. I make sounds like that all the time. I just don't admit to it."

"Maybe you should. It's therapeutic. You might smile more."

"Gosh, I thought I'd been doing a lot of that lately. Must not be doing it right if you didn't notice." His hand slipped over hers, keeping it tucked safely under his arm.

Someone else would have put two and two together and figured something kind of nice was going on here. Amanda put two and two together and figured Mark was buttering her up to get her to pay for the drinks. Optimism had its limits, after all.

She started down the steps, slipping her hand out of

its wonderful, warm nest. She wasn't going to let Mark Fleming's great eyes tell her lies, or affectionate words convince her she was anything but what she was—a nice lady attorney with a very big problem. If she were more than that to him, she would have been in his arms instead of walking side by side talking about Nora.

"So, do you think Nora screwed us up here?"

"Naw." Mark stuck his hands in his pockets.

"I could always plead insanity."

"It's an option to consider." He put his hand out stopping her as the light turned yellow. When it changed again, Amanda Cross and Mark Fleming were swallowed up by Los Angeles. They were faces in a crowd, two people walking along, trying to figure out how to admit they actually liked each other.

~ ~ ~

Edward wheeled into his own garage a few minutes after nine. It was pitch black, the bulb burned out in the electric door opener. He was dog-tired but there was still work to do. Extra work that he knew would pay off nicely in the end. This was going to be a heck of a trial and he wanted to make sure every single conversation, every nuance of this case, was noted and communicated.

Inside, Edward carefully hung up his jacket, surveying the tasteful, if somewhat uninspired, gray, white, and black living room to make sure the cleaning lady had done her job properly. Satisfied, he went to the back bedroom, which had been converted into a home office. There he fired up the computer, punched in the proper codes, and began to type. It was just before ten when he finished. With a keystroke, he concluded his business, headed for the shower, and went to bed. It had been a very, very long day.

~ ~ ~

Lucas Mallory hated going home. He hadn't been able to bring himself to sleep in his own bed since Ruth died. As long as he didn't look at the bedroom or go into Ruth's study, Lucas was able to function quite nicely. The house-keeper managed to ease the transition from married man to widower by picking up the laundry and secreting away all of Ruth's newly cleaned suits and blouses. She went through the mail and returned all of Ruth's correspondence. She did such a good job it was almost as if Ruth had never existed. Instead, he worked, effectively and efficiently as always, doing what needed to be done, especially when it came to the case against Nora Royce.

Alone in the office, with only the cleaning people for company, Lucas Mallory stared at his computer screen wondering how long he'd been reading the same informa-tion. Finally, he rubbed his eyes while he scrolled. Tired, he read on. And as he read, he wondered what had hap-pened to his life. When had he stopped living? Was it when Ruth died or when Nora Royce was arrested? Perhaps it was the day he sold his soul to Dimsdale, Morris & Mott.

Chapter 16

———

Leo started quietly, almost jovially, as he built his case. His opening statement was the foundation of his pyramid of evidence against Nora Royce. Secretaries and paralegals from DM&M who testified regarding their observances of the goings on between Nora Royce and Lucas Mallory, along with the hotel staff, were the bricks and mortar. The minions were easily led down the primrose path. Even Edward was pressed into service as a hostile witness for the prosecution. Even the most innocent of answers were given a lascivious spin that left the jury enthralled and Amanda depressed.

"Mr. Ramsey," Leo cooed. "Did you see Nora Royce between seven thirty and eight on the night in question?"

"I did."

"Mr. Ramsey, can you attest to Ms. Royce's whereabouts during that time?"

"I can. Ms. Royce was on the patio just outside the reception room."

"And how do you know that?" Leo was grinning.

"I was with her."

"The entire time? From seven thirty to eight o'clock?"

"Yes."

"Mr. Ramsey?" Leo offered a verbal finger wag.

"I was with her a good deal of that time. I watched her leave the reception and I followed approximately five minutes later, after Mr. Hedding began to speak."

"And?" Leo urged.

"And I remained with her until Mrs. Mallory came into the reception."

"I beg to differ, Mr. Ramsey."

"I'm sorry?" Edward could have been apologizing for stepping on Leo's foot. He wasn't afraid. If anything, he seemed bored.

"I believe you were not with Ms. Royce the entire time."

"I'm sorry. You're right. I left her for approximately five to ten minutes. She seemed upset. She wanted to go home. I offered to get her suitcase. She gave me her key. I went down to her room and gathered her things. I was back pretty quickly."

"Then you didn't see her during that time?"

"Well, no. But I wasn't gone long enough to—"

"Thank you, Mr. Ramsey."

"But I was only gone for a few minutes—"

"No further questions, Your Honor."

Leo's back was to Edward. Amanda could see his face. He offered the jury an expression that said, "Ten minutes can be a very long time" before he sat down. Edward was back at the defense table. Leo kept building his pyramid.

Don Forrester was next.

"And how would you describe Mrs. Mallory's relationship with her husband?"

"I believed it to be excellent."

"Did you discuss with Lucas Mallory his relationship with Nora Royce?"

Don started. He knew the question was coming but seemed ill prepared for it. Amanda sat up straighter, watching his every move. His eye, the right one, twitched slightly. He looked out onto the group of spectators as though searching for support. He found it somewhere out there. Without further hesitation he said:

"Yes. Lucas, reticent though he was, did discuss Nora with all of us."

"In what capacity?" Leo asked.

"I don't understand the question."

"Did he discuss Nora as a professional, regarding her future with the firm?"

"At one time, he did."

"Recently, in what light did he discuss Miss Royce?"

"He talked about his unwillingness to continue his professional association with her. He was…"

"Yes, Mr. Forrester?"

"He was afraid of her. Nora had made it clear that she wanted more from him than his help as a mentor."

"Could you be more specific, Mr. Forrester?" Leo leaned forward, leering as though with one fell swoop he could wrap this case up and prove himself a lawyer's lawyer.

"I believe Lucas Mallory actually feared Nora Royce. She had become obsessive about his attentions. He indicated that she was becoming quite lewd behind closed doors, when—"

"Objection! Objection!" Amanda fairly screamed the word as she bounded to her feet. By her side, Nora's head hung just a centimeter lower, as if getting ready for the guillotine to fall. "This is all hearsay, your honor. I can't believe you would allow this."

"Miss Cross." Judge Petty turned a cool eye her way.

She shut her mouth. She waited. He spoke. "Overruled. Continue."

The judge had just picked the tune and Leo was happily dancing to it.

It was three when court was adjourned on day four. Amanda was exhausted and Nora clearly disheartened. Thankfully, Edward had moved away, busying himself with the clerk. Amanda tried to cover her gloom while she packed her trial box.

"Not to worry, Nora. You wouldn't know this but it takes me a while to warm up. Then, watch out. Leo won't know what hit him. We'll discredit those jerks if it's the last thing we do. Go on home. Why don't you get Edward to pop for dinner? He wasn't much help today on the stand. It's the least he can do."

"I won't worry," Nora answered and Amanda believed her. Nora was beyond worrying. Resignation had set in like a Thule fog. Nora turned away. Amanda turned the other way, afraid that hopelessness might be catching. She managed to bump right into Leo Riordon.

"Amanda." Smoothly sincere, that no-nonsense, I-have-only-your-best-interests-at-heart voice of his assaulted her. "It was a rough day. I apologize. It had to be done."

"Right."

Knowing there was nothing to do but face him, Amanda did. Her smile was engaging. He faltered. She took advantage of the moment.

"Don't you have anything better to do than stand here staring at me?" she demanded, proud that she had just the right amount of chutzpah.

"I was thinking, Miss Cross." He recovered beautifully by the time her personal kudos were nothing more than a memory. "Thinking that I really have no reason to want to publicly crucify you this way. I do have better things to do than go through the motions of a trial to bring this open-and-shut case to its natural conclusion. Perhaps I should be more generous and attempt to come to an agreement."

Amanda's eyes narrowed. Leo offering a deal was like Jaws passing on an invitation to the municipal plunge. Leo liked blood and he liked the press to watch him spill it.

Warily, she encouraged him, "I'm listening."

"Good. It's a simple, straightforward deal. Best I can do." God, he was clipping his words. It wasn't going to be generous and it sure as hell wasn't going to be gracious. "Fifteen years to life, parole in twelve to seventeen."

"That's it?" Amazed, Amanda rested her weight on her back foot, leaning away from him, her mouth slack with disbelief. She had an overwhelming urge to ask, "You talkin' to me?" Instead, she gave him a piece of her mind. "Leo, did anyone ever tell you that when you're going to behead a person you should move their hair out of the way so the ax goes through smoothly? Executioners did that because they were humanitarians. Get a clue. You're suggesting we lock Nora away because we're too busy to get on with this trial? Because you worry about my profes-sional standing? That offer was bullshit and you know it." Amanda clucked her tongue, playing her ladylike outrage to the hilt. "I wasn't all that impressed today. I mean, what did you put up there? A bunch of people who had an opinion. Period. You made it sound like real evidence, but when I get a hold of them during defense, their testimony won't mean—"

"But Amanda, they are the words of such respectable members of our community. What the jury heard, what they've been told, is relevant as to motive. Judge Petty understood that. I think the jury will, too." Leo sighed, a heartfelt and put-upon sound, as he realized she was going to cut off her nose to spite her face. "This plea bargain was just a thought, Amanda. A professional courtesy." Leo shrugged to show there were no hard feelings because she didn't think as much of his offer as he did. "If today is any indication of how things are going to go, your sister will end up with life and no possibility of parole. Your bravado is one thing, your actual talent as a lawyer quite another. If I were you, I'd think twice before I threw away a chance."

"For what?"

"Life, Amanda. I won't go for the maximum. Your sister is beautiful now. By the time she gets out, maybe she'll have a little humility to go along with that pretty face. Might not be so bad for someone like her, someone who thinks she can do what she wants and get what she wants without consequence. I'll hold the offer open for forty-eight hours. Let me know, Amanda. Just call me anytime. You've got the number."

Leo was gone, moving fast for a guy with a gut. Then Mark was there, blessedly making no comment. He and Amanda stood side by side, the bar between them, literally as it had been for so long figuratively. Together, they watched Leo Riordon go, hearing a politician's greeting before the sound of his voice disappeared completely. Amanda hated that silver aura he left behind, all gray hair, gray suits, and pearly ties. He'd been living in LA too long, he was a silver screen lawyer. Unfortunately, Leo was good, too, and that made Amanda feel sick. If she was going to be trounced, why did it have to be Leo who wore the stomping boots?

Feeling alone, Amanda pushed open the crotch-high swinging door and crossed to the wrong side of the bar. Mark fell into step beside her and she was alone no more.

In silence, they walked past the empty pews, through the deserted courtroom, and out into the hall teeming with the oppressed and the evil. Outside walking away from the courthouse, Mark put his arm around Amanda's shoulder. She sank into it, grateful before realizing this was not simply a display of solidarity. This was something—personal. So personal that Amanda couldn't look him in the eye for fear she'd see laughter when he said:

"I know someplace that will make it better."

"I've got to prepare for trial tomorrow."

"You've got to come with me." His arm tightened. What could she say? He was a commanding kind of guy. Amanda closed her eyes briefly, letting him lead her without a word of protest. When her eyes were open again, Amanda hitched her briefcase to the other side and let her free arm wind itself around his marvelous waist.

~ ~ ~

"I like it. Really." Amanda said it once more with feeling. "I like it. It's you."

"I'm not sure what that means." Mark laughed obviously pleased that Amanda's spirits had picked up.

"I mean, it's kind of gnarly on the outside, but sort of…" Amanda paused before the last word. She looked over her shoulder—and would have died if she knew Mark thought there was a bit of the temptress about her—and grinned. "Kind of perfect on the inside."

"Really?" Mark handed her a scotch and soda. She took a sip and wandered around the trailer's living room. He sat to watch. Comfortable and content in a heavily stuffed tub of a chair, Mark saw his home through her eyes and decided he liked it, too.

"Yeah. Not a lot of furniture but good stuff. Nice little

touches, you know?" Amanda stooped and picked up a knickknack. "I like this. What is it?

"A box."

Close enough. Mark leaned forward and slipped it from her hands, replacing it on the rosewood coffee table. She missed the peevishness in his voice and chattered on. It was prom night.

"This is neat. I like the bookends. Crystal, no less!" Amanda pulled a la-de-da face and the bad part of the day was pushed tidily into the nether regions of her head.

Mark crossed his legs, looking indifferent, sounding brittle. "And I've got a full set of china, too, no thanks to my good taste. My fiancée, before she decided I wasn't the man for her, picked all this for our perfect home. Now it sits in my perfect little trailer. Curious about anything else?"

"Nope." Open mouth, insert foot. Amanda bounced on the balls of her feet just to make sure they were still where they were supposed to be. She wanted to drop through the floor, or, better, gracefully leave. Then he took her hand and led her away from the other woman, into the world he loved. She left behind the embarrassment; he the anger. They were outside.

Sitting in a folding chair, incongruently gay with its stripes of yellow and purple, under a bamboo shade, Amanda dug her feet into the sand outside Mark's trailer and admired his beautiful place. Not the trailer, that was on the same par with her house, but the real estate on which he parked it, away from the world, on a hill above the beach in Malibu; that was beautiful.

Amanda breathed deeply, her eyes sweeping over the hill, dry in a drought year, but pretty still because it was rugged and solitary. Like him. Burying the romanticism in a long sip from her drink, Amanda guided her attention away from Mark, who stood at the barbecue. Fat oozed out of the huge slab of meat he was tending, dripping onto the hot coals and sending billows of white smoke upward to engulf him. The fire smelled good, a scent made all the more powerful because it was almost, but not quite, summer. Below them, rush-hour traffic inched along on Pacific Coast Highway, and, beyond that, the Pacific Ocean.

It was hard to see the water since the light was fading fast but Amanda could hear it and smell it and feel it. Nature at its best. No neighborhood sounds, no moms screaming for children, or dads screaming at moms. No dogs barking. No doors slamming. No trial. No Nora. Almost. Then Amanda felt that Mark was looking at her and the almost disappeared, too.

She took her time returning his notice. A drink first. The liquor tasted great, cool and biting. The ice against her teeth felt sexy. Amanda raised her head toward a breeze before looking Mark fully in the face. They weren't kids and that suited both of them just fine. Nice this wasn't a charity thing. Mark Fleming liked her. She liked him. Amanda had known that for some time. If true love came tagging along, all the better. Amanda had given up worrying about hearts and flowers ages ago, yet she was more than ready for some good, honest affection. She smiled. From that first meeting at Phillipe's to this very moment, Amanda had wanted him. Now the feeling was mutual. Nice.

"Steak's almost done." Mark waved a two-tined fork toward the sizzling meat. Amanda tried to imagine him in a chef's hat and an apron that said, Kiss the Cook. It didn't wash. The suburbs would never be his style.

"It's so quiet out here."

The time of day, the place, the man, and the feelings

gave the situation a 3-D quality. Amanda envisioned a cartoon bubble over her head: *He's going to kiss me. Should I kiss him back?* It popped when Mark turned back toward the grill.

"I think that's it." The meat was flipped onto a plate. He walked toward her. He was walking past her. His expression hadn't changed, not a glimmer of desire sparked in those sea-blue eyes. Wrong again, Amanda. Damn.

But as he passed, as he drew alongside her yellow-and-purple striped chair, Mark's hand slipped into hers. He pulled her up. She stood easily, resistance was never a consideration. Mark paused and their eyes met long enough for Amanda to see the softening behind him. He leaned into her. Kissed her. She murmured against his lips.

"Nothing I like better than cold steak sandwiches."

He kissed her again. "I haven't got any bread."

"Nothing I like better than cold steak," she assured him, reaching up, touching him. On the neck. Behind the ear. Gently. Tenderly. Amanda Cross as giver. Amanda Cross at her best.

"Good." He pulled back just enough to look her square in the eye. He was either searching for something or trying to reassure himself. Whichever it was, Mark obviously found what he was looking for.

"Good," he said again, tugging on her hand. He pulled her through the pretty living room, leaving the steak to cool on the beautiful coffee table next to the crystal bookends, and into the back of the trailer, where a queen size mattress lay on the floor. The sheets were clean but rumpled, clothes were strewn about. Evidently, this hadn't been a planned seduction. Obviously, too, Mark's ex-fiancée had preferred the bedroom furniture to the living room and had cleaned him out.

Mark's fingers were on her cheek, turning her face toward him. His other hand slid behind her head, pulling her close to him.

"No more lawyer thinking. Stop trying to figure it out."

Amanda smiled a smile he had never seen before. One that made her seem younger than she was, guileless, and so desirable. Amanda, for all her tough talk, all her take-care-of-business attitude, was a woman easily loved.

"How do you know me so well?"

"I know me. We're alike, Amanda. We…" he was nearer now, body and lips "are…" he pressed up against her and he felt good "…two of a kind." His lips were on hers. He was on her. That felt good, too. Mark had a thing for pillows. Three were behind Amanda, three behind him. Two had rolled off the mattress and Mark and Amanda had come precariously close to tumbling after them. Amanda loved all those pillows; toppling over them, lying on top of them, burrowing under them. She adored what had gone on in that pillow-laden bed.

With the flush of lovemaking dwindling, sleepiness warred with hunger and Amanda was ready to let her mind work again. She started slow. No sense jumping into anything.

"How come you have so many pillows?" Nice, basic question. She twirled a pattern on his chest with one finger and snuggled closer. Mark indulged himself with one of those male sighs. What it lacked in romance it made up for in satisfaction. He kissed the top of her head.

"I don't get laid that often. Gotta have something to hold on to these cold nights," he drawled. Amanda hit him lightly. He recanted, laughing.

"Okay, okay. I get laid a lot." Amanda hit him again, giggling like a schoolgirl as she wound her arm over his marvelous chest. Lord, the man was aging well.

"Okay, I hate getting laid." He was chuckling now, and Amanda laughed a little louder, rolling atop him.

"It has nothing to do with getting laid and you know it," she teased thoroughly enjoying the moment.

"You're right." Mark closed his eyes, his hands content to lie quietly on the small of her back. "Pillows. That was the topic, I believe." Amanda nodded even though he couldn't see her. "Easy one. I like pillows. What can I say?"

"Nothing you need to say. I was just curious if you had some deep-seated fixation for soft things. "

"Oh, absolutely. I have an overwhelming need for soft things. Some warm, soft things I doubt I'll ever get enough of."

Mark grinned and made rutting noises that only those in the throes of lust find amusing. He ran his hands up her back and straight down to her derriere at which point she rued the day she had chucked the diet. The next squeeze exonerated her. Amanda sighed and laid her head on his chest. He caught the mood and wrapped her in his arms and the sheets, respectively. It had been too long since there'd been a man in Amanda's life.

~ ~ ~

"I can't believe this," she whispered in a deeper, ever-more-satisfied voice.

Glad she wasn't looking at him, Amanda preferred to imagine that the contentment on his face matched her own. Then he hugged her and she almost looked. Then he kissed the top of her head tenderly and she knew desire was coming on strong again. She fought it back, wanting words now. Amanda, alone so often, liked words of love and fondness and caring. That's what she wanted from Mark, so she prodded, fishing shamelessly, "I really can't believe this."

Mark laughed, a clear and beautiful sound, nothing like the derisive one he threw at Edward—or at himself—every now and again.

"Come on, Amanda. It was inevitable and you know it." That peck on the head again, those wandering hands. Heaven.

"Really?" Amanda lifted her head, trying to remain alert and remember every detail, for instant replay.

What little makeup Amanda had worn was long gone, leaving her skin ruddy and handsome. Her hair was tousled and he could see a faint light through it so that it seemed she wore a golden halo. He reached up and ran his hands through all that dark, dark hair and let it fall, watching it instead of her.

"Really," he murmured. "Did anyone ever tell you, you have great hair? It's so damn thick."

"Hardly poetic, Fleming, but I'll take what I can get." He fanned it again and let it fall over her shoulders. Amanda dipped her head. "Come on. Be more specific. Tell me why this was inevitable."

"First define this," he challenged.

"This." Amanda blushed, waving a hand in no specific direction. She wasn't going to beg for sweet words. He kissed her neck. He kissed her shoulder. He slipped his hands down low, between their bodies.

"You mean this?"

Amanda clamped her lips shut. Panting was not on the agenda. Her eyes closed, the lids fluttering. She tried to stop those telltale signs of need but it was friggin tough. She made a sound somewhere between a moan and a real word and nodded like crazy.

"I thought that's what you meant." His hands slid out again, much to her dismay, but tenderness seemed to be the order of the moment. He smoothed back her hair, a look of actual marvel on his face, as though she was just a little bit of a miracle. "It was inevitable because we're two of a kind. Amanda. We look right, we talk right, we have—or, in my case, had—ambition, but we just never quite make it. People like us." He paused as if there were many, many others to consider and he didn't want to leave anyone out. "We're meant to be average but we talk and act like we really believe we might just be better than that. I knew it the minute I saw you, that you were going to be special to me. I've waited a long time for a soul mate. I'm content with what I have, now that I know what kind of hand I've been dealt. I never dreamed I would find someone who felt the same about her life."

Amanda watched him. His dreamy eyes were just a glitter in the darkened room, his body a warm haven in a world that had been damned cold of late. Yet, as he spoke and she listened, Amanda felt herself losing everything she'd gained in the last two hours. All that affection she felt for Mark, all that confidence he gave her, dried up like LA under the cruel, hot Santa Anna wind. Ever hopeful, Amanda rallied, giving him one more chance. She chuckled but it was an uncomfortable and disillusioned sound.

"I don't know what you mean, people like us. You make it sound like we're losers."

"Naw, that's not what I meant." Mark rolled her over. She was on her back. Now she was beneath him, pinned and wishing she wasn't. "*Losers* is such a miserable word, babe. We're…" he had to think. No doubt he couldn't come up with a synonym. "You know what I mean. We're just people who are smart enough to realize when we're out of our league. I gave up on passing the Bar because it was pretty clear I wasn't going to make it as an attorney. You made it by the skin of your teeth, but, hey, you're not Dimsdale, Morris and Mott material. You've done your best for Nora. It's not going to be a fairy-tale ending but you still plug away like you think it will." Mark smiled like a diffident devil apologizing for the heat of hell. "I give you a lot of credit. It's a shame she's going to get convicted. It hurts when you fail. I've been there. You've been there. We'll be there again. This time, though, we've got each other. I can't tell you how much you mean to me. I can't begin…"

Mark lowered his head. Amanda could feel the warmth of his breath on her neck. He was going to kiss her and suddenly she couldn't stand the thought. Her hands reacted before she even realized a conscious decision had been made. They were on his chest, staying his forward movement. He pulled back an inch, enough to look her in the eye. He was surprised; she more numbed than angered. Then numb wore off and angry filled the void. With a grunt, Amanda pushed Mark away and rolled right off the mattress.

She was quick; he not quick enough to stop her. Lying on his side, pulling the sheet around his hips, Mark watched Amanda's frenzied activity with a smile on his face, assuming he was supposed to smile. Wrong again. Amanda banged her leg on the chair by the closet and cursed. Mark winced. She ripped a white thing off the floor only to find it was his T-shirt, not her blouse. She tossed it away, spinning around the room like a whirlwind, muttering and cursing and flailing until she was half dressed: a bra, a skirt, stockings. The blouse proved elusive.

Finally, Mark got a clue. He was on a downhill slide. "So why don't you just let it out?"

Amanda stopped mid-expletive, one shoe in hand, the other on her foot. Amazed, appalled, she looked at him as she tried to decide whether he was worth an explanation. He wasn't but she'd never sleep if she didn't give it a whirl.

"You know, I used to feel sorry for you because of the way your fiancée treated you. I mean, walking out on a guy just because he doesn't make the grade first time out is one of the most rotten things I've ever heard. But you know what, Fleming? You know what? You know what?" Amanda was so heated she couldn't get the words out. Mentally, she gave herself a kick. Stupid she wasn't and stupid she wouldn't look. Indignant, mad, ticked, and downright pissed she was.

"Damn! I didn't even give that woman credit for having a brain. Did I ever ask myself was she smart? Was she right? Naw. I just dumped on her because I… because I…" Amanda waved her shoe at him but would have preferred rattling a chain.

"I fell for you like a ton of bricks, Fleming, because you were good looking, because you were nice to me, and because I goddamn believed that she was the one who took away your self-confidence. But she didn't. Hell, you threw it away. You gave it away. You probably never had it in the first place and she saw that. She boogied because there was all the reason in the world to do it."

Realizing she was losing the grip on her shoe, Amanda raised her foot, faltered, reached for the dresser, steadied herself, and slipped it on. She couldn't look at him anymore but she sure wasn't finished with him.

"Now, you listen to me, you idiot. You may be a quitter but I'm not. I'm a damned good lawyer and I've been hanging under your cloud too long. I've been working like I intend to lose. Talk, talk, talk. We were talking things to death and not doing anything. We're pussyfooting around interviews. We're limiting our investigational scope because we're afraid to think, much less do anything. My brain is working in slow motion. Yours must have ground to a halt a hundred years ago. Well, no more. No more, buddy. I'm out of here and I'm going to come out smelling like a rose on this one. I may not save my sister. She may end up in prison, but people are going to say, 'Amanda Cross never gave up.' Never!"

Amanda leaned down and Mark could see the shadow of her breasts as they rose and fell, full above the half cups of her bra. Incredible things ran through his mind. Lust and surprise. Shock that there was even more to his feelings than that. He didn't want her to go. He didn't want to be alone again because Amanda was worth holding on to. But she didn't give him time to think, much less react. Amanda snatched her jacket off the floor and threw it over her bare torso, buttoned it as best she could, then held the lapels together. She shook her hair back, braced her shoulders and put him in his place.

"Don't you ever lump me in the same category with you, mister. Don't you ever call me a loser. Ever."

Amanda turned away from him and shot through the door, stamping around the living room, only to reappear a minute later, purse in hand.

"I'm not going to bother firing you, Fleming. I wouldn't give you the satisfaction. I don't want to be another woman who dumped on you. Besides, you'd probably rather quit. That seems to be something you do extremely well. Thanks for everything—the cold steak, the roll in the hay and the slap in the face."

She was out the door and Mark was out of bed. Naked, he stood at the window of the trailer looking out into the black night. The dim porch light radiated a weak, yellow glow. Amanda stood under it, her dark hair glimmering, her cheeks chalk-white against the matte night colors. He almost smiled to see how sexy she looked, half naked under her well-cut navy blazer. Mumbling, gesturing, she searched her purse and found the keys to her car. She dropped them, retrieved them, and then twisted her ankle on the step. Mark was just about to go out when she righted herself and stormed toward her car. The old thing was fired up a few seconds later and Amanda was out of there.

~ ~ ~

Mark Fleming opened the trailer window and leaned against it. There was a cool breeze coming from the ocean and he could hear the waves washing the beach way down the hill. He'd spent a lot of time in this trailer alone. When he wasn't alone, he was bedding women half his age: women who lay on the beach all day, pretty women who would marry guys with great bank accounts someday. Now, he knew that had been a mistake. Amanda made him feel that way. Now that she was gone, he was just beginning to realize how much he liked her. He hadn't felt like that with his fiancée—the woman whose name he couldn't remember at the moment.

Mark abandoned the window and lay naked on the mattress. The sheets were cold, but he could still smell Amanda: the scent of her happy and lost in lovemaking and the other scent, of righteousness and anger. Maybe she was right. Maybe what he interpreted as being realistic was only his way of denying he was a loser, a quitter. It was hard to think about himself in those terms—in any terms. It had been too long, too many years of feeling at odds with the world.

Throwing one arm over his eyes, he let the other slide off the mattress. There, beside the bed, was her shirt. Without thinking, Mark Fleming pulled it into bed with him. He wouldn't be sleeping that night. Amanda Cross had walked out on him and he just now realized that it might be time to stop throwing in the towel.

Chapter 17

"Yo there, Consuelo."

Mark slipped into the corporate headquarters of Maid
For You and caught the CEO off guard. She was holding a
mirror in her hands and pursing her lips. Today they were
magenta and appeared larger than they'd seemed a few
days before. She was mumbling to her incredibly desirable
reflection and did a fair imitation of a peeved Betty Boop
when he walked in unannounced.

"Hey, you don' knock?" The mirror was slammed back
into a drawer, the drawer slammed back into the desk.

"Lot more interesting when I don't," Mark didn't smile
outright. Though he may have been born again, he wasn't
about to start running around with a grin plastered to his
face. "Lookin good though, lady."

"Yeah?" She threw back her mane of hair, her boobs
pressing forward as a matter of course "You're not doin'
too bad yourself, muchacha. Wha' happened? You look
downright happy. You get laid?"

"I wouldn't call it that." Now he smiled.

"Love?" Consuelo drew out the word like taffy and

batted her lashes.

"Not sure I'd call it that, either." This time he grinned just a little so she could see he actually had teeth. She'd been wondering about that.

"Whatever." Consuelo was wearing violet, some shiny fabric that winked at Mark the way her words did. "Did you some good. You got a nice smile. It's not goin' help you, though." Consuelo threw her thumb toward the wall she shared with Amanda's office. "She's pissed bad at somethin'."

"I know." Mark came close to sheepishness.

"You? Oh, Christ. You two?" Consuelo clapped. She used the heel of her hands for fear of damaging her drag-on-lady nails and raised her eyebrows the way guys did when they were discussing the same subject in a locker room. "You don' mean the dance of the dirty frog?"

"Consuelo, do you have to?"

"Naw, I can be a lady." She popped her gum and lowered her lashes. Mark wasn't sure which gesture was supposed to underscore the comment about her status. Then those flashing bright eyes were on him and she was giggling, having a darn good time at his expense. "But you're no gentleman, so what the hell, heh?"

"But Amanda's a lady," Mark said, surprising himself with how serious he sounded. Consuelo threw her hair over the other shoulder. She would wring her neck doing that one day.

"Yeah. Okay. I'll buy that." Consuelo gave the gum another twirl with her tongue. "You need advice? You wanna talk 'bout what you did?"

"Nope. Just want to know if you think this will help."

Mark pulled a rose from behind his back. It was red. The tips were a little brown so Consuelo knew he'd picked it up from the guy on the corner, who stole what he could from the flower mart on Maple.

"Lame," Consuelo decreed.

"Then what?"

"Nothin'. I say nothin'. She's so ticked I don' know if you can even go in there without gettin' burned."

"I gotta try."

"So, go try. Be yourself. The nice stuff just doesn' work too good if you know what I mean. You're cuter the other way. Not so much like a puppy."

"That bad?" Mark rubbed his chin. Even Consuelo could feel a bit of a flutter for him. If only he had bucks.

"Naw, just potential. You have real potential for wimpin', got it?" Consuelo was tired of the conversation since it was clear she wasn't going to be the center of it.

"Got it. Here." He tossed the rose. She caught it, smelled it, and smiled.

"Gracias." She held up the rose but he was gone. She called, "Good luck," but he didn't hear. He was in Amanda's office, wishing he'd brought an overcoat.

Amanda's head was bent over her work, the rest of her body hunched over her desk. She raised her eyes when he came in and that was it. She didn't even break stride but continued to scribble on the legal pad in front of her. He went for coffee, tossing a plain brown bag on the desk just to the side of her. It wasn't cute anymore and Amanda wasn't in the mood for brownies. She pushed it away but not so far she couldn't get to it if she wanted. Cup in hand, he flopped onto his back in his usual place. The sofa seemed to welcome him. She scribbled. He sipped and stared at the ceiling.

"The scarf bothers me," he said after a while as if she weren't sitting on the other side of the room with smoke coming out of her ears. Amanda scribbled faster. Mark put one hand behind his head and talked to a particular dot in the acoustic tile. "It doesn't really bother me so much as it intrigues me, because it's the only piece of physical evidence that can actually be checked out. Know what I mean?"

Silence, save for the scratching of the pencil.

"Granted, I should have thought about it before but now that I have, I should get on it. I want to talk to Nora about it. Where the scarf came from, for instance. We've got a picture of it but I've never even seen the real thing. Held it. There was blood on it. I mean Nora's blood, not Ruth Mallory's."

Scribble and scratch, faster and faster.

"I do know I should have been looking at this before but, hey, water under the bridge. Let's find out what other kind of stuff he gave her. If Lucas gave Nora a lot of things, we're bound to come across some evidence that he actually bought it then…"

Scribble. Scratch. Slam. The pencil was down and Amanda was swinging her head back and forth trying not to look at him. He could tell she was sneaking a glance.

"For God's sake, Fleming," she said wearily, "what are you doing here?"

He looked at her with such appeal that Amanda had to stand up and head toward the coffee pot to explain away the sudden heat flush.

"My job, of course. I'm still on the payroll. Did you forget you left that decision up to me?"

"No, I didn't forget," she answered quietly staring into the pot of black liquid as if it might change into tea leaves and predict the future. Knowing when to cut her losses, she poured herself a cup. Coffee was coffee. Miracles didn't happen. There wasn't going to be an easy way out. "I haven't forgotten anything about last night."

Mark made a sound that was vaguely like a rumble but really was more a settling of his body and mind as he readied himself for one of those despised heart-to-hearts. The phone rang and he was saved from sensitivity. From the way Amanda fell on the receiver, it was pretty clear she wasn't looking forward to the encounter, either.

"Amanda Cross." A beat while she listened. Her expression didn't change. She put her hand over the mouthpiece and whispered, "Edward." Mark slid into a sitting position, paused a second, then stood up to wait his turn.

"I want to talk to Nora," Mark whispered.

Amanda ignored him, a look of concern coloring her face.

"Has she showered today? Dressed?" Amanda listened some more. "She hasn't even gotten out of bed? Come on, Edward, we're due in court at three tomorrow afternoon. She can't look like something the cat dragged in. She knows that." Edward was obviously talking again. "Oh, for God's sake. Remind her she's an attorney. Tell her to start thinking like one not like some beaten puppy."

Mark eased the phone out of her hands, knowing full well the residue of her nocturnal anger—righteous though it was—was not going to serve any purpose if she lashed out at Nora or Edward.

"Maybe a ray of hope might make a difference," Mark whispered moving her out of the way. Resisting, but not well, Mark had the urge to dig his fingers into her shoulders, looking for the woman who had been in his bed last night. "Edward. Fleming. Get Nora on the phone. I don't care if she's in bed. You've never been in a woman's bedroom?" Mark winked but didn't smile so Amanda did for him. The ice was cracked but not quite broken.

Mark turned toward her, half sitting on the desk. They watched one another, communicating without words. Then Nora was on the phone. Mark turned away, afraid that Amanda might see the shock on his face. It'd been a while since he'd talked to Nora. She sounded like an old woman, a mental patient, a slow child. This was going to be tough.

"Nora, how're you doing?" Mark held the phone against his shoulder and reached for a pad of paper. He wasn't really interested in her response but he thought if she practiced moving her lips she might get on a roll and tell him what he needed to know. "Good. Yeah, I'm glad you're hanging in there. Listen, I've got something I need to clear up with you. That scarf. Where'd that come from? When did Mallory give it to you?"

Mark slid one leg onto the desk and jotted a note. Amanda waited across the room. Had he been true to cynical form, he would have found that amusing, now it wasn't so funny. He wished he had enough magnetism to drag her back to him. Plain-talking, deep-loving, undemanding Amanda had punched him in the gut and Mark appreciated that, probably even loved her for it.

"Okay. Okay. What else? I mean, what else did he give you and do you have any idea where he got it so I can start checking for receipts and things? No. Hey, Nora, this could be really important. Look, we show that he gave you an expensive gift and we've got the sucker. He's lying when he says you were just an employee. Why would he give a woman who is stalking him and turning into a sex maniac behind closed doors an expensive, personal gift? Got it? Yeah. Yeah. Okay. So think about it. You just think about it and try and figure out something else I can move on. I'll do the legwork. You just sit there in court beside Amanda and look innocent. Right? Right. Now, don't give Edward any problems. Poor guy can't take stress. Okay. Okay. Bye."

When Mark didn't move, Amanda did. She came up behind him, didn't touch him but stood close enough so he could smell that perfume she wore. It wasn't anything fancy but he liked it. She moved to the side of the desk and studied his profile.

"So?"

Mark swung his head her way. His hair waved charmingly over his forehead. Amanda had paid good money once to try to get her hair to do that.

"So she needed something to hang on to and if you'd stayed on the phone you would have put the final nail into the coffin with that nasty little lecture of yours."

"Come on. She's no Camille. She made it through law school, tough cases. She can handle this if I can."

"And you're still ticked off at me so you're taking it out on her. Don't do that, Amanda. Even if nothing works out for us. Even if I am a quitter. Even if I walk away and you never see me again, you shouldn't ever be mad at anyone but me. I'm the one that deserves it."

"Are you going to walk?" That was a quiet question and it surprised both of them that she didn't have another harsh word in her. There was a lot of fear in it and childish hope.

Looking for a sign that would help him make up his mind, Mark stared hard at Amanda and paused—almost too long.

"I don't know. I don't think so."

That was the right answer. She didn't want him to go.

"So what about the scarf?" she asked gently.

"Interesting." Thoughtfully, Mark moved away from the desk, knowing they would work out the personal details later now that business was at hand. As he passed her, he brushed his hand across hers. She clasped it between her fingers, releasing it as she moved back toward the desk and sat down to listen. "The scarf itself is very expensive. An Anni. He gave it to her the first night they made love so obviously this was not quite the spontaneous thing."

Amanda made a questioning noise. Mark needed no more encouragement.

"He wouldn't be carrying an expensive gift around on the off chance he was going to get laid." Amanda nodded. "The way we can prove that he was planning this is to prove he actually bought the scarf and gave it to her. Nora says it was really special. Lucas told her it was ordered from Italy and he couldn't get it in this country. That means he had a good long time to figure out what he was going to do with it." Mark thought of something and raised his finger as he sat back on the couch. "Got a phone book?"

"Yep."

"Good. See if there's an Anni store in LA."

"Boy, are you sheltered! Beverly Hills." Amanda flipped through the yellow pages, muttering all the while. "Camden or Rodeo. Got to be Rodeo. Ah-ha. Rodeo." She noted the address and put it on the desk, right at the edge.

"Okay. So there's a store. That's where I'm going to start. But the other interesting thing is that scarf is the only thing he ever gave her."

"Really?" Amanda sat back, twirling a pencil against her lips. "What? Nora felt funny about taking presents?"

"Nope. According to Nora, Lucas just never gave her anything else. Made a real big deal over this gift, then that was it. She didn't even think it was weird until I asked her about it. I think it's weird, don't you?"

"Very. Yes, very," Amanda answered thoughtfully.

"Why would he plan and prepare for that first night, having an expensive gift in his hip pocket because he was so excited at the prospect of bedding Nora, then suddenly turn all businesslike? I mean, that sounds awfully calculating. Yeah, yeah. Mr. Mallory did some thinking here. But why?"

Amanda raised surprisingly clear, dark eyes toward Mark. There was life in them, excitement. He took that from her and tried to believe they were actually going to do something wonderful. Amanda grinned, bounce coming back into her voice.

"I think there might be something here. Run with it. Check it out because I start our case Monday and I don't have jack shit. That jury is so impressed with the trail of witnesses Riordon's been parading around that they're predisposed toward the prosecution. With what I've got, they're going to be twiddling their thumbs and thinking the case is sewn up within the first hour. If you think you can find something, find it."

"You want me to be kind of like a white knight?"

Amanda pulled a face. "I want you to kind of do what you were hired to do and should have done earlier," Amanda shot back instantly sorry she'd resorted to peevishness and pulling rank.

"Yeah." Mark took a deep, rough breath, drawing way down in his gut for it. He slapped his thighs and pushed off the couch. Disappointment spread over him like a rash. "Yeah."

There was nothing else to say. She'd called him down; he'd decided to prove her wrong. Now it was time to strut his stuff. Problem was it had been a long time since he had wanted to give a hundred percent. Maybe he didn't have it to give anymore. Without another word, he let himself out of the office.

Amanda watched him go, feeling sad for herself and him and them together. She wanted to go back to the way things were, to a darkened bedroom in a trailer, on a mattress without box springs. She wanted to be held and loved like she had been only hours ago. But things had been said. Life went on. Amanda was lonely and she didn't think Mark was the one who was going to ease that. Not that she was giving up. Amanda was just getting on.

To that end, Amanda pulled her work toward her, knocking the bag off the desk. The cheap brown paper crackled under her fingers when she picked it up and set it on her lap. Opening it, Amanda barked a laugh, clamped her mouth shut, and then started to laugh again in earnest. Inside the bag was her shirt, discarded in the heat of passion and left on the trailer floor in a fit of passionate anger. It had been washed. It had been ironed. Mark had done a horrible job of both, not that it mattered. She was just buttoning it up when Consuelo poked her head in.

"What are you doing?"

"Changing my clothes." Amanda winked. "I've got to be in court at one on Johnson's plea bargain. Thought I'd look my best."

~ ~ ~

Mark wasn't oblivious to the appreciative female glances sliding his way. Lately, though, his preferences had been redefined, so it seemed pointless to look back. The anorexic, leather-clad, jewel-laden women of the Beverly Hills big hair crowd didn't seem to have the same allure as a lady in a blue suit laboring in a small office downtown. But, when it happened one more time, Mark realized he wasn't exactly dead and offered a twitch of the lips to the next platinum blond before ducking into the tastefully turned-out Anni boutique.

That was where Mark Fleming met his match.

Instantly, he was deep into an experience. Mark Fleming, who eschewed the materialistic trappings of Los Angeles and all its sprawling suburbs, was suddenly dying to touch and feel and buy. Weird. Especially since the stock seemed meager. There was a cashmere coat on a mannequin more attractive than half the women walking by the window, a silk blouse draped over a handbag that some cow had given its all for, and buttery-soft shoes designed to be worn only by a lady whose legs started at her neck. Fully aware that his khaki slacks were a blend that erred on the side of some manmade fiber, Mark rolled up the sleeves of his shirt, trying to draw attention to the all-cotton, well-tailored garment. He had taken two steps into the deathly silent boutique when he saw her.

She was dressed in black. So slim in profile as to barely dent the atmosphere. And, on that exquisitely gaunt frame, she carried the most marvelous set of knockers Mark Fleming had ever seen. Her face was attractive but so contrived it was hard to tell if she was actually beautiful or simply put together in a way that convinced you she was. Her hair was pulled tightly away from her face, giving her skin a lift she didn't need—yet. Her lips were full but so defined by plum lipstick they looked like a detachable accessory. Her eyes were deep set, gray, and lacking any discernable intensity. She didn't even seem particularly interested in him as he approached the glass display case behind which she stood. This, Mark felt, was understandable. A woman like her knew a guy like him couldn't put a down payment on a toothpick in this place. Much to her credit, however, she addressed him as if he could.

"Good afternoon, sir." A selling voice. Nice, but Mark assumed it would have had the same inflection whether she was in the throes of an orgasm or showing an evening gown. Of course, it was possible those two activities might be interchangeable.

"Good afternoon." Mark deepened his own voice an octave and tried to sound debonair. "Quiet in here today."

The saleswoman inclined her head. That went without saying, she seemed to indicate. Failing miserably in the debonair department, Mark tried charm. But he had too much of the beach about him, not enough of the big board. She wasn't moved.

"Listen. I came in to find out about something but I can see my trip was wasted."

"Never a waste, when you come to Beverly Hills," she murmured. "What was it you were looking for?" Rote. She was too polite to just let him walk out. Probably had a quota system for how long she was supposed to talk to people. Mark helped her fill it.

"Well, I was coming to find out about a scarf a friend of mine ordered from Italy. She said if I was interested I should check in here. But"—Mark spread his arms while that fetching half-smile of his spread over his face—"I can see I don't even have to ask about it. It's not as unusual as I was led to believe."

The woman cast a silvery eye about the boutique, surveying the obvious. Gold and navy, with only a touch of burgundy slinking through the freeform pattern, the scarf in question had been used to drape a mannequin standing gloriously and unabashedly in the middle of the store, only her most private parts hidden by the silk. There was just enough of her showing for the display to be provocative. The sales associate slipped from behind the counter, showing off long, black-sheathed legs and unending fingers that played delicately with the hem of one of the scarves.

"This is the one that interests you?" She tugged at it and off it came. Mark almost blushed. He felt a little sorry for the plaster lady, so easily and heartlessly exposed, so utterly helpless.

"Yes. That's the one."

Mark took it, pulling it through his fingers, imagining it pulled between two bodies in the midst of hard sex, or wrapped around a neck in the act of killing. Either way, Mr. Lucas Mallory's gift had obviously heightened the experience.

"Beautiful," he murmured. "I'm just surprised to see so many available. I thought this was sort of a one-of-a-kind thing. Really special."

"But of course." The detachable lips moved, the elongated fingers plucked at the edge of the scarf in Mark's hand as if to say 'You don't know much if you can't tell how special this is'. She smiled as if he were just one of the rich boys anyway. There wasn't a speck of lipstick on her perfect teeth. "But if you're looking for something more unique perhaps you'd like to look at our one-of-a-kind scarves?"

Mark shook his head. He pulled the fabric through his hands once more then handed it back to her. Gracefully, reaching up to show just a bit more of her very thin thighs, she expertly covered the mannequin while Mark spoke.

"Actually, I understood this scarf wasn't available in the States. I was told it had to be ordered from Italy."

"Oh, your friend must have had one of the very first ones. Certainly, at the beginning of the season we would have had to order this item."

"The beginning of the season?" Mark asked

"Six or eight months ago." A loving pat on the mannequin's derriere. A final, critical look before her attention
was all his again. "I believe we had a few orders. We often
order directly after the couturier showings for our more
fashion-conscious clients. Well before the ready-to-wear
lines are available."

"I see," Mark felt his pulse quickening. Nice warm-up.
The pitch was coming. "Oh, that makes sense. Listen, I was
wondering, could you tell me who might have ordered one
of these before you got them in for general sale?"

Suddenly, the saleswoman became more than sister to
her naked-plaster double. She was alert, her eyes narrowed,
lips pulled together, her jaw tightened. Even her body reacted adversely. Those glorious breasts of hers seemed to
shrink under her fine wool dress. And Mark? He was no
longer worthy of her attention. He was a fraud, not a simple
customer with limited potential. He embodied everything
management had warned her about. He was an ex-husband,
an ex-boyfriend, an ex-pool boy out for revenge. He was
a private eye hired by a rich and powerful wife. He was
something, but he wasn't in her store to spend money.

"I'm sorry." Icy. She wasn't sorry at all. "But I couldn't
tell you who made those requests."

She was turning away and Mark did what came naturally. He reached out and stopped her. She looked, to put
it mildly, horrified. He had touched her person. Not with
a smooth hand that did little more than lift a telephone
to conduct business but a man's hand that was intent on
stopping her from brushing him off.

"You have to give me that information," Mark said quietly, nicely, and firmly. "This is a matter of life or death for
a woman who looks very much like you. She's a beautiful
woman and she's in court right this minute because some

guy is swearing he didn't sleep with her. So she's going to take a dive for a crime she didn't commit. If I could help prove that he was sleeping with her or just that he gave her a present, like that scarf, then the jury might have reason to question everything else about this mess. Do you understand? Do you understand that a woman, just like you, so beautiful and used to the finer things in life, could be put in jail, where there isn't anything much to look impressive for, except maybe other inmates?"

"Sir, I have no doubt that you—"

"Please." It was a new approach, one that Mark couldn't remember using before when he needed something. "Please," he said again and it sounded good. "It's a small piece of information that may help. My client's attorney could call you into court, could subpoena those files." More apologetic. "But I don't want to call you into court. I don't think you want to be involved in a murder investigation or have the cops come down on this establishment. But…"

Mark shrugged as if to say, what could he do? She didn't need to know he couldn't ask the cops anything but the time of day. Happily, the lady with the lips was easily intimidated. She didn't want to schlep into court to testify to anything. The thought of leaving Beverly Hills probably gave her the heebie-jeebies and downtown was more than likely akin to a trip to Hades.

Taking a second to think, she turned on her heel and disappeared through a door behind the glass counter. Three minutes later, she was back carrying a small, yet tasteful, black box. This was opened, and Mark watched as the sales associate flicked through a neat stack of pearl-gray three-by-five cards.

Without a preamble, she announced, "Mrs. Samuel Jenkins ordered a scarf. Mr. Samuel Fitzwater ordered a scarf. Ms. Holly Daniels. Ms. Eve Patriarcha. Mr. Lucas Mallory. Ms. Heather…"

"That's it. That's it." Mark held out his hand, sticking his finger between Lucas Mallory's card and Ms. Heather-whatever-her-name-was. He could smell victory and it was sweet.

"Do you have an order from a woman named Nora Royce?"

Flick. Flick. Flick. The woman shook her head.

"Anybody other than these people who would have been able to order a scarf in Los Angeles?"

Shake.

"That's great. Do you mind?" Mark held his hand out, wanting to see Lucas Mallory's order, wanting to check the address, the phone number the signature. Finally, something hard, something real. They could prove Lucas had bought the scarves and now they could certainly create a good dose of reasonable doubt about his situation with Nora. If Lucas had lied about his affair, what else had he lied about? What other miserable, skuzzy things was he hiding? The saleswoman hesitated, holding the information to her marvelous chest for a minute before handing it over. Mark held his breath. He looked at it and whistled. If he had been wearing a hat he would have tipped it back and rubbed his jaw while offering her a golly gee. "Twelve hundred dollars for a scarf?"

Mark was just lucid enough to realize her *tsk* was one of disgust for the uneducated eye. A long nail pushed under his nose, pointing to the left-hand column of the very proper receipt.

"That is a receipt for two scarves, sir." She sniffed. "Anni offers our customers both style and value."

Mark's very nice blue eyes lifted. He wanted to kiss her

but thought twice. Instead, he asked for a copy of the receipt. When she refused, he only smiled. There was always a subpoena. He might yet see her and her pretty legs and her detachable lips in Hades if Amanda wanted her there. Now, all he wanted was to get back where he belonged and share the news. All he wanted was to talk to Amanda.

~ ~ ~

"Marissa! Marissa!"

Min Forrester stood at the top of the sweep of stairs that led to the upper floor of their Hancock Park mansion. Her tiny voice bounced off the tiled entry, the Spanish arches, the overstuffed, ecru-colored furniture in the living room, and stopped before penetrating the state-of-the-art, country-chic kitchen, where her daughter was halfway out the door. On dainty feet, her blond flip bobbing, Min hurried down the stairs, calling for her daughter, only to find Marissa sauntering into the entryway as though she hadn't a care in the world. Min pulled up short, clutching the curve of the wrought-iron banister, her mouth pulled into a tight rosebud of pink lipstick and tiny age lines. Marissa had seen that peeved look before. She found it laughable.

"Marissa, you scared me half to death! I've been calling and calling. Why didn't you let me know you heard me?"

"I'm not supposed to yell in the house, remember?" Marissa hitched her backpack higher on one shoulder, her prettiness hidden by her insolence. She had her mother's soft, round face. Her hair would one day be bleached blond, like her mother's. But the set of her mouth showed she would be tougher than mom, smarter, too. "What do you want?"

"I need you to do me a favor. I want you to drop your father's tuxedo off at the cleaners on the way to school."

"Mom." The whine was well rehearsed. "I'm already late."

"Am I supposed to believe that worries you? I'm sorry but it has to be done. Your father forgot to tell me about this dinner. Now the cleaner will have to have it done tomorrow. I hate it when your father forgets to tell me these things." Min started back up the stairs, having delivered the closest thing to a disciplinary lecture that she could. "Wait right there. I've just got to check the pockets." She was running up the stairs now, still clucking about her husband's common sense. Marissa watched until Min disappeared, then leaned over the banister and waited, thinking of absolutely nothing.

In the opulent peach-and-mint bedroom she shared with her husband, Min grabbed Don's tuxedo and rapidly searched the outside pockets, unsure of whether her daughter would wait or not. *One can never tell with teenagers.* Min's hand dug into the right pocket. *Teenagers have no respect for anyone, it seems.* She poked into the left. *Especially their parents.* Nothing in the breast pocket. *There must be some way to make Marissa understand...* Her hand was in the cigarette pocket. *Understand that there is a level of...* Her fingers closed around something. Something in the pocket. Respect. That was the word she was searching for. *Marissa had to understand...* about...respect.

Slowly, Min pulled her hand out of the pocket not really wanting to see what she had found. Tossing the jacket on the bed, Min stared at her booty. Soft and silky, something hard wadded up inside. She knew exactly what it was but Min steadfastly refused to process the information. In true Min form, she stared without thinking, thought without formulating a conclusion.

"Mom!" Marissa insisted from the bottom of the stairs.

"Hurry up." Min did exactly as her daughter ordered.

She moved faster than the speed of light, leaving the tuxedo pants on the bed, jacket on the floor. Purse in hand, she dashed down the stairs as if the devil himself were after her. At the bottom, Min pushed her daughter out of the way and. to the strains of Marissa's indignant cries, flung herself out the door and into her car. The Mercedes choked. Min pushed down on the accelerator, fumbled with the key once more. A grating sound tore through the quiet neighborhood. The car had been running all along.

She was almost out of the drive when Marissa hit the front door, hollering her anger at being ignored while watching with concern as her mother tore down the street. For the first time in her life, Marissa realized she loved her mother. Given the way Min was driving, Marissa wondered if she would see her again for long enough to fill her in.

Chapter 18

"Okay. Okay. We've finally got something. Damn, Mark, this is great!" Amanda was crumpling all her notes, tossing them toward the trashcan, and making every shot. "I didn't have a thing. You know that. I didn't have one goddamn thing except for the blood spatter patterns showing Nora could have been in the bed."

"And the five-minute differentials in the partners' stories," Mark reminded her.

"That was nothing and you know it."

"It looked pretty good yesterday."

Amanda ignored him. She was jazzed.

"In two days we're set to present and you come up with this. This is great. It would have been greater if you'd thought of it earlier but it's great. Two scarves. Neat." She made an arcing shot. It swished right in. Amanda grinned. "But, what does it mean? Let's think."

"I have been thinking!" Mark objected thoroughly delighted with himself and trying not to show it. "I can only come up with two possibilities. One, Mallory bought a scarf for Nora and for his wife."

"Why?"

It was Edward who asked the question. Amanda stopped crumpling and pulled a clean pad of paper her way. She looked toward the black-haired man. She'd almost forgotten he was there. He had spent the afternoon quietly going over crime scene photos and statements from the entire membership of the Junior League regarding Ruth Mallory's character. The office, he claimed, was the only place he could think. It was, Edward said, impossible to work in the depressed atmosphere of Nora's townhouse.

"Why?" Mark repeated, his eyebrows shooting up. "Why not? How about he felt guilty because he bought one for Nora? Or it was Ruth's birthday and it was an easy present? He was in the store anyway, so he just ordered two."

"Not likely. Ruth Mallory's birthday is—"

"Was," Amanda piped up.

Edward blinked. He hated to be interrupted and at times made that abundantly clear to Amanda. His attitude usually grated on Amanda's nerves but today she let it slide. Edward wiped his brow and Amanda saw there was perspiration dotting it. He wasn't looking well at all and just when she needed him.

"You're right." he mumbled. "Her birthday was in… I can't remember."

"That's okay. Edward," Mark drawled, "I don't think we need the exact date. But you're the expert on Lucas Mallory. You worked with the guy. What do you think? Was he the kind to just pick up a present for the old lady?"

Edward shook his head. Paying little attention to Mark's patronizing tone, he answered the question succinctly. "I didn't work directly with him. He was the most reserved of the partners. I have no way of knowing if he'd buy his wife a gift on the spur of the moment."

"While he was buying his mistress one," Amanda reminded him.

"And, if you want my opinion, I'd venture to guess he wasn't the type to buy anyone anything without thinking it through. He's a really methodical guy, really low-key. It's almost as if someone had suggested to him that he do something nice for a woman. I just don't believe he'd be that spontaneous. I would have actually expected Peter Sweeney to be the one fooling around on his wife. Lucas Mallory would have been last on my list."

"Could you imagine Nora with Peter Sweeney?" Mark asked half laughing. It was a sick joke, a disgusting thought.

"No, you're right. Physically it doesn't work, does it?" Amanda buried her chin in her upturned palm. "It sure would have made all this easier, though. If she was sleeping with Sweeney and Mallory's wife got killed, we wouldn't be here."

"There's a downside to that, too. To not being here, never having to work on this case, I mean," Mark said.

Amanda graced him with a smile. Things were better. It was getting easier to forgive him.

"Yeah, well, we can debate that some other time. So, we've got two scarves. One is Nora's, the other we're going to assume is Ruth Mallory's.

Whose scarf was used to strangle the woman? If it was Nora's, then Ruth's should still be in her house. Let's see if we can get a court order for access, Mark."

"You got it. But that might prove what we don't want it to prove."

"Won't prove a thing. We can talk around it without a problem and really get those jurors thinking. We can bring up the question of whose scarf it was and why Lucas Mallory bought one for his wife and one for Nora. We've at least proved that Lucas Mallory bought a very unusual item. Nora wore it on a daily basis. Everyone knew it had become her trademark. Quite a few of them can pinpoint when she began to wear it. Oh, oh," Amanda was cookin' now, each piece of information leading to another theory. "Listen, Mark. Go back to the boutique and get a listing the names of the other people who purchased the scarves before they were stocked in Beverly Hills."

"Why don't you just have me walk over hot coals," Mark complained. "That woman didn't want to give me the time of day."

"Dress nicer," Amanda suggested. "We need that information. Let's rule out any connection of the other people with Lucas or Ruth Mallory. Wouldn't that be too cool if we found out someone else had a connection with them or her specifically? Then we could really start playing games with the prosecution."

"That would make your case more interesting. Might even keep the jury awake."

Amanda laughed. Edward watched. Mark continued.

"We should also consider the other alternative. Maybe Lucas Mallory wasn't fooling around just with Nora."

"What do you mean?" Edward asked looking downright gray. Amanda would have to send him home soon. Better he get a bit of rest in the next few days so he'd be ready for the assault. She was sure he wouldn't want to miss the fireworks in court.

"What if Mallory had two mistresses?" Mark began to pace. He was grinning, looking gorgeous now that his mind was working. "Picture this. Lucas Mallory is a real efficient guy. He has two women on the side and he's in one store. He figures they'll never see each other, so why not buy them the same thing?"

Amanda laughed and tossed her pencil onto the desk, thoroughly amused. "Mark, give us a break."

"What? It's possible. It's as possible as anything else we've come up with."

"The guy was a lawyer, successful. Men get anesthetized when they get that big. Sex isn't that big a deal, not that high a priority."

"Look who's talking," Mark countered. "How many senior partners have you slept with?"

"None," Amanda snapped. "But I know enough to know these guys work too long and hard to have the time for more than one lady on the side and a wife. They just don't have that kind of stamina."

"Remind me to thank my lucky stars I flunked the Bar exam."

Amanda eyed him, waiting for that telltale chip to settle on his shoulder. When it didn't, she assured him:

"Never." She gave him her best, warmest smile.

"Listen, guys." Edward was up, out of his chair, hurriedly pulling together his files. "I'm sorry to break this up. But I really don't feel all that great. Do you mind if I cut out tonight? I'll take the files home and see if I can come up with any discrepancies between the police reports and the photos. I'll work in the new information for questioning, Amanda, but I've got to get to bed."

"Sure, of course." Amanda was all concern now. He moved as if he couldn't stand to be in the tiny office another minute. It was hard to blame him. The place was stuffy. "Anything we can do?"

"No. No, thanks. I just want to get some rest."

"Yeah, okay," Amanda said. She and Mark exchanged a glance and then busied themselves—Amanda with paperwork, Mark with the crease in his slacks.

In silence, Edward packed everything up, muttered something that sounded like "See you in the morning," and left. Mark didn't speak for a few minutes, and when he did, his comment was an interesting one.

"Kind of odd he wanted to cut out just when things were looking up. The bubonic plague wouldn't keep me away from this office now."

"Edward doesn't have what it takes. He's a quitter. What can I say?"

Mark looked at her fondly.

"I never did like quitters," he said before he stood up, went right to her and kissed her cheek. He was off. Unlike Edward, Mark was feeling fit. There were things to do, places to go, people to see.

~ ~ ~

Mark had rung the bell but there was no answer. He'd stood beneath her window and called and still, Nora didn't open her shades. That wasn't really important, though. He'd been given the cold shoulder by many a babe. The important thing was that no one else looked out, either. He was making enough noise to wake the dead, yet there wasn't a soul in this very nifty development who bothered to find out what in the hell he wanted. Okay. Apathetic neighbors. Maybe just well traveled.

The place sat on a hill surrounded by trees. Pretty. Really nice from a privacy point of view, bad news for nosy neighbors. Nora's end unit shared one wall, with the guy on the right. No Curious Georges on the left. The guy on the right was a pilot. International flights. Big birds. Lousy schedule. He wasn't home often and had, according to Nora, tested the waters with her long ago only to find they were frigid and had retreated. Nora had a two-car garage and only one car. Lucas Mallory could easily have parked his beside hers and closed the door. Nobody would have been any the wiser. The house was a wash. Nora's housekeeper did an exquisite job of cleaning. Even Nora's fingerprints were hard to find.

So, what next?

Mark kicked at a stone, pushed his hands deep in the pockets of his pants, and sauntered into the sunshine. He swung his head left. Nothing but a tree-break that divided Nora's development from the one down the hill. He admired the roofline of the less-ritzy complex, but that was all there was to see. Except… Mark squinted, looking closer at the something else that caught his eye. There it was again. The glint of glass. A corner of a window or maybe a sliding glass door. Just above the treetops. But glass didn't glint like that.

Mark traversed the drive, stepped into Nora's flower beds and over to the other side. His shoes sank into the soft dirt and bed of decaying eucalyptus leaves. He ducked, crouching low to see if there was a clear view at that angle. Nothing. Cautiously, Mark backed up the hill, keeping his eyes on the glint. Now it was coming into view. Yeah. Yeah. He was right. Glass didn't look like that but metal did. Through the trees, pointed his way, Mark saw the one thing that made him happier than hell.

In seconds, he was in his car, careening out of Nora's complex and into the one below. Like a bloodhound on the scent, he made a beeline for the end unit just below the tree line, the one that faced Nora's unit on the other side.

The place wasn't quite as classy as the one he'd just left but it still must have cost the owner a pretty penny. Mark hit the bell. He admired the hand-painted number tiles. He rang again, leaving his finger on the bell, only to be disappointed when being obnoxious didn't bring results. He was about to leave when a voice shot through the door. It was male, it was confident and Mark knew he was being watched through the little peephole. That made him feel vulnerable. He backed away so the guy could get a better look. He'd also have a clear shot if he had to run.

"Who are you?"

"Name's Mark Fleming," he called back knowing now how the Fuller Brush man felt. Mark pulled out Amanda's card and held it up, knowing there was no way on God's green earth the guy could read it. "I work with Amanda Cross, an attorney. I'd like to ask you a few questions."

"I don't know anything about lawyers, and I don't want to."

"Come on, man. Give me a break. Don't make me do this the hard way. You know something about at least one lawyer. She lives behind you. I want to talk to you about her the lawyer you peep at through your telescope."

Mark held his breath. His counterpart was probably doing the same while he tried to decide what to do. Finally, the door opened. Mark smiled brilliantly and walked inside.

~ ~ ~

"What a day! What a day!" Amanda would have kissed him if he'd been there but Mark on the phone brought her almost as much pleasure. One thing did lead to another. Good things come to those who wait. There was a goddess. Fate had intervened. Silver linings. She was headed back to Kansas and Toto was along for the ride.

"I know. It's almost too good to be true. The couple of times I went out to Nora's, I guess I wasn't thinking about anything but her immediate universe. I didn't give that tree line a second thought. And I sure as heck didn't look over it. Anyway, when I climbed up that hill and saw that his patio was parallel to her bedroom window, I knew I had something.

"So I get over there and this guy was so nervous I was going to turn him in for being a Peeping Tom that he told me everything. Not that there's much to tell but it's enough. Lucas was definitely having contact with Nora. Our guy saw a Mercedes. Dark blue with vanity plates. Easy enough to remember: CNTRCTS. My contact at DMV confirms it's registered to Lucas Mallory."

"Great. I'll work it into questioning. He's going to try and cover but there's no way to explain this."

Mark rolled around so that his back was to the glass of the phone booth. He never thought Mulholland was all that pretty a street until today. Now it looked absolutely spectacular and Amanda's voice sounded like an angel's.

"Mallory's no dummy, Amanda. There are a million ways to counter. My Peeping Tom couldn't swear that he'd seen the car more than two or three times. So Mallory can say he went there trying to talk Nora into letting him off the hook. Something like that. Trying to convince her that her obsession wasn't healthy for her career."

"No problem," Amanda responded. "I'll just hit him with the scarf and the receipt. I know we can't prove he handed it to her and we can't show home movies of them hitting the sack but we've got enough to get the jurors thinking. They might even start to wonder if he could have been in two places at once. Maybe they'll start figuring he did it."

"Give me a break. The most physical thing Mallory ever did was climb into your sister's bed." Mark laughed.

"Suppose you're right. Still, it would be a nice way to

wrap this up. You know, the evil twin or something."

"Listen, I don't really care who did it. Let's just get that sister of yours out of this mess and back to normal. She wouldn't even open the door for me and I'm the good guy."

"I know. I've got to go see her. It's been way too long. I suppose it's the same feeling you get when someone's got a terminal disease. You don't have anything to say so you stay away. But now, I've got a ton of things to tell her. She'll pop back to her old self-absorbed idiocy real fast." Mark heard the phone crackle as Amanda held the receiver between her cheek and shoulder. "Listen, I've got something else. Kitty Hedding called and wants to talk to you."

Mark whistled. "When you're hot, you're hot."

"Right. No information, though. I asked if she wanted to leave a message or if I could help her but she was pretty insistent. She wants to talk to you."

"I can handle that. I always had a feeling there was something more she wanted to tell me. Do you have her number?"

"Nope. She wants you to…" The phone clattered to the desk then, from the sound of it, to the floor. "Sorry. I've got it now. She wants you to meet her at LA Trattoria. It's on Third Street, near Beverly."

"I know it. No problem."

"You never cease to amaze me," Amanda muttered. "Noon tomorrow. She was pretty insistent you be there."

"Is that okay with you?"

"You're joking, aren't you?" Amanda drawled. "Edward and I can manage fine. You meet with the lady and bring me something more to play with in court. We're down to the wire, Fleming. I gotta have as much as I can when my case begins. Heaven knows I haven't been stunning crossing the prosecution's witnesses."

"You'll do fine." His voice was lower, the kind of voice he'd used in a dark room when their heads were together on a pillow. Amanda's matched it.

"I'm almost more scared now," she said softly.

Mark held the phone closer to his ear.

"It's because you know something. When you didn't know anything, you could face failure. When you know something, or think you do, failure is harder to take. It's because you think if only you knew just a little more, or thought a little harder, you could lick the problem."

"That's experience talking," Amanda whispered.

"Yeah. But experience is a great teacher. I've learned, Amanda. Want to hear how much?"

"I wouldn't mind. I might learn something, too."

"Meet me at the trailer?"

There was a heartbeat of silence. "I'll be there at nine." One connection was broken as Amanda hung up and another had just been rewired.

Happily, Mark replaced his receiver and went in search of a grocery store. This time he was going to keep things simple. He'd stock up on cold cuts for dinner.

~ ~ ~

"Amanda, this is Leo."

Amanda wanted to ask Leo who but he hadn't said knock, knock. Needless to say, she was surprised.

"Leo, what can I do for you?" She knew she sounded downright chirpy but couldn't help herself.

"Listen, Amanda. I'm wrapping up my case day after tomorrow and my conscience is bothering me. I want to help you. I watched you sweating through the cross-examinations. You know, and I know, and the jury knows, you can't dent the testimony that's been given. So I'm going to make one last offer. It's the best I can do but I think it's enough to put this thing to rest."

Amanda envisioned him checking his manicure. She wanted to laugh. If he only knew.

"I'll go down to voluntary manslaughter. Eleven years. Out in seven. It's the best I can do. For old times' sake, so to speak."

Amanda sat back, twirling her chair thoughtfully, posturing only for the sheer pleasure of doing it.

"Leo," she said, "that's amazing you should call today. Amazing you should think of me just now because this case is all I've been thinking about lately. And you know what I've been thinking?" Amanda considered this a rhetorical question. By his silence, she assumed he did, too. "I've been thinking I never did get enough trial experience when I worked for you. Now I'm primed. I've been watching you work; I've been getting hyped and I think I'm ready to give the defense a whirl. Try my wings, so to speak." She attempted to imitate him and thought she'd done a pretty good job.

"I've got a lot invested here. I want to go ahead with this trial. What's the worst that can happen? Leo? Nora ends up in jail. At least she's not strapped into a chair, waiting for an undignified end. No, Leo. Thanks for the offer but I think I'll pass. See you in a few days. And hang in there, you're doing great."

~ ~ ~

Amanda had hung up and Leo was left worried, rubbing his jaw as if the massage might get his brain working again. He sat back in his chair and considered the day. It was weak and blustery, much like his initial assessment of Amanda.

Now he wasn't so sure that evaluation was correct. But he sure wasn't going to tell that to the four men seated in front of him.

"I gather Ms. Cross was not receptive to your offer?" Oliver Hedding asked lowering the temperature in the office a good ten degrees.

"Well, I don't know. I think if we give her a little bit of time, say two or three days to think about it, at least a couple of days with her own case, seeing it's going no-where"—Leo raised his hands, pleading now, swiveling in his chair as if he couldn't wait for them to call a bathroom break—"she'll see there just isn't much of a chance. You know, come around."

"Jesus Christ." Peter Sweeney erupted. "I cannot believe you couldn't convince that little twit to take the offer. She's dying out there and she knows it. What is she, some feminist freak who thinks—?"

"That's enough, Peter." Oliver raised his hand less than an inch. The gesture silenced his partner. "I don't think railing at Leo is going to do us any good. We came here in good faith, concerned with the disruption this was causing in our lives, not to mention our business."

"Damn straight." Peter glared at Leo.

Don added his two cents: "One of our largest clients has refused to have Lucas handle their business until this thing is wrapped up. They're worried his mind won't be on their problems. Lucas was head counsel. We can't have this."

His voice caught a bit as it often did these days. He looked drawn and pale. Oliver was quite sure Don had egged on the client in question. There wasn't a day that went by when Don didn't make a comment about Min, how he couldn't possibly imagine life if it had been Min, how she was beginning to show the strain. Wouldn't say much at home. He wanted this whole thing put behind them and was sick of opening his paper only to be reminded of Ruth Mallory's untimely demise. Oliver's concern, if the truth be known, was more for Don's peace of mind than their client's interest in the case of People vs. Nora Royce. Oliver was not at all comfortable with Don's continued and escalating distress. It made him so careless.

"I'm a bit surprised," Lucas commented thoughtfully. He stood, his exquisitely tailored suit making him look taller than he actually was. "Can you imagine anything that you might have missed, Leo? We've not had the time to follow the trial on a daily basis. Is there something that happened recently that might perhaps give Ms. Cross a different perspective on this matter?"

Leo shook his head, his lovely silver hair catching in the late afternoon light. The waves were in place, his clothes looked as though he hadn't done anything more than sit in his chair for the last twelve hours but Leo Riordon's face looked worn, like that of the tired public servant he was.

"No, Lucas. I can't see that anything has changed. She's been unable to rebut the testimony of any of our witnesses and those witnesses, including yourselves, have all been straightforward. The physical evidence is irrefutable. There is nothing—nothing that I can think of or ever imagine—that would make Amanda Cross think she's got a snowball's chance in hell of coming out of this clean." Leo shook his head in dismay and bewilderment. He looked at the four men. "Can you?"

Oliver Hedding stared back as did Peter Sweeney and Lucas Mallory. Only Don Forrester declined to participate in the silent indictment of the DA. He turned and walked out the door. It was late. He was tired of talking about Ruth Mallory's murder. He was so tired of it all.

Chapter 19

Amanda didn't bother to knock or ring since Edward made it clear Nora wouldn't bother to get up. In a mental fetal position, Nora was giving up and waiting it out. Naturally, Amanda didn't believe any of it—until she walked through the door of Nora's townhouse. Then there was no choice. She was a believer.

Heavy and stale, the air was that of a home closed up too long, unused and unappreciated. An apathetic place. Without thinking, Amanda went to the French doors that led to the patio off the L-shaped living room. Throwing them open, she breathed in. Fresh air and eucalyptus. Nice. But there wasn't a hint of a breeze to blow the scent her way, nature declining Amanda's invitation to sweeten this house of doom. Amanda wasn't too crazy about being there, either. Depression, she well knew, was contagious. But, then again, so was hope. Taking a deep breath, throwing the drapery back even farther though there was precious little light left in the sky, she called to her sister.

"Nora! Hey, it's me."

Her voice was that of a contrite mother apologizing to a child left too long alone. From the bedroom, she heard a sound, weak but discernible. It was Nora's voice. She called, "Edward?" without interest or excitement.

Amanda froze, gathering her thoughts, rearranging her reactions. How things had turned around. Amanda the mundane was suddenly the strong; Nora the bright star, had burned out. Amanda should be gloating but this situation gave her precious little pleasure.

How many times had she dreamed of walking up to powerful and confident Nora? In those fleeting visions, just before she woke, Amanda would open her mouth to speak, would reach out a hand and the dream would fade. She would be left to wonder if she had been gracious or vindictive once she was Nora's better.

She wasn't dreaming now and, with a typical Amanda response, she was left disappointed by reality's lack of drama. She walked into the bedroom. The shock of seeing Nora made words tumble out, one right over the other, to keep Amanda from crying out in dismay.

"Nora! My God! What's been going on here? Come on now. You can't do this."

Amanda was across the room in a flash. The drapes parted. Another set of French doors opened. This time a breeze kicked up, the eucalyptus fluttered, their pungent smell filled the bedroom. Nora moaned and rolled over, trying to escape both the fresh air and the light Amanda turned on at her bedside.

"Go away," she groaned. "Where's Edward?"

"Edward isn't feeling well. He's sick, Nora, and he looks better than you do. Come on." Amanda reached for her sister's shoulder. Nora pulled away, burying her face in the pillows. Amanda knelt on the bed and grabbed her. A double fist of sister. Nora didn't have the strength to resist; she was dead weight and skinny as a rail to boot. Amanda had a good twenty pounds on her. "Come on, Nora, that's it. Time to wake up. Time to figure out that life ain't always a bowl of cherries. I know it's tough."

Yank.

"I know it's not fun."

Pull.

"But what the hey. You would have had to face it some-day. No lying down on the job."

With a great tug, Nora was at the edge of the bed. Her eyes were deeper set than Amanda remembered. They weren't as bright nor were they as beautiful. She wasn't as beautiful anymore.

"I don't want to get up," Nora whined. "Leave me alone. I'll be ready for trial but leave me alone now."

She tried to roll back into the warmth of her bed but Amanda was too quick. Both of Nora's thin arms were firmly in her grasp. It was easy to pull her to a sitting position. Her pretty little panties peeked out, as her T-shirt rode high. Red lace. Amanda wondered if Mark would like her in a T-shirt then discarded the notion. She may never make it to Mark's in time to see him awake. If nine o'clock came and went, Amanda's world wouldn't end if her sister didn't come back to the land of the living, Nora's might. Amanda touched Nora's face tentatively. There was no resistance. She whispered:

"I'm not going to leave you alone. You're the one that came to me, remember? You're the one that said, 'Help me out, sis,' and I said, 'Sure, no problem.' That's what I'm doing. Helping you out. Now, I didn't worry about payment back then but I damn well want it now. You're going to settle your debt by doing exactly what I say. Do you hear me, Nora?" Amanda leaned down and got lov-ingly in Nora's face. Nora turned her head away. Amanda breathed deeply, gathering patience and strength. "You're going to cooperate with me if it's the last thing you do, babe. Now, up!"

Amanda grunted. Nora was all muscle and for a tall, thin woman, she was damned heavy when Amanda didn't have the bed for leverage.

"That's it!" Amanda cried with delight, willing to accept any victory. "Now we're cooking!"

Sleepily Nora protested, "Amanda, no. I want to go to sleep. It's late."

"Bullshit." Amanda laughed. "It's early and things are looking up. Now move it."

Nora pulled back but Amanda had gained momentum. She pushed forward. That beautiful black marble bathroom Amanda had coveted was up ahead and to the right. Now it held no allure. All Nora really had was a fantasy, easily destroyed. What Amanda had was real, flawed, and far preferable to perfection. She murmured just to hear herself talk, just to keep Nora interested.

"It really isn't late and I've got a couple of things to talk to you about. Good things, Nora. Really good. We can prove that Lucas Mallory was sleeping with you or had at least come awfully close. Do you hear me?"

Amanda pulled up short to see if the info had sunk in. She looked into her sister's face half expecting to see it transformed with gratitude. But Nora wasn't the excitable type.

"How?" she asked, her voice slightly stronger.

"The scarf. We can prove Lucas bought it. And there's more." Amanda smiled. She felt needed. She felt good. She wanted to brush back Nora's hair and hold her face between her hands. She wanted to shed a tear and forget they had ever been so distant. Instead, she gave Nora a little tug of encouragement. "First a shower. I want to talk to a lucid human being, not a slug. Get in there." Amanda pushed her forward but didn't immediately let go just in case Nora was as fragile as she looked. "Do you need any help?"

Nora looked over her shoulder and shook her head. Amanda thought she saw embarrassment in those eyes. Then Nora was away and Amanda waited until she heard the water running before she went about her business. Gone was the attorney Amanda Cross, in came the housekeeper.

She threw back the sheets and comforter on Nora's low, big bed to air it, switching on the other bedside light as well as the one on Nora's art deco dressing table. The room looked cheerier for her efforts but Amanda didn't take time to admire the cream-colored walls and carpet, the lacquer furniture. Confident that Nora was okay on her own, Amanda scooped up the clothes scattered on the floor as she left the room, found the washer, and dumped them inside. The machine was agitating a second later. There weren't many dishes but the ones that littered the sink were caked with food. They were left to soak in hot, soapy water. The dining room table was next.

Edward had left his paperwork neatly stacked on one end; the other was a mess. Mail had been piled high, toppled over, picked up, probably by Edward, and thrown back on the table. Amanda guessed there were probably two months' worth of ignored letters and bills. After illuminating the living and dining room, plumping a few pillows, and examining a unique and incredibly heavy piece of metal sculpture, Amanda started sifting through the mound of paper. Ten minutes later there were three neat stacks: bills, junk mail, and letters. The letters were interesting, two from overseas. She was dying to open them, but those were personal and none of her business. Amanda put them aside. Maybe someday they would sit over a glass of wine and giggle about Nora's international admirers but today wasn't it. Bills had to be paid. Don't give Leo one chance in a million to revoke bail.

Amanda ripped open the top one and smirked. Nora's Neiman Marcus bill was in arrears to the tune of Amanda's mortgage payment. Impressive. Amanda set it aside.

Next, the gas bill. Recent. Easily dealt with.

Cable television.

Telephone.

Carpet cleaning.

MasterCard.

Next. Next? Amanda didn't go on to the next. Her hands lay atop the stack of paper. She was thinking, trying to identify the source of her discontent. That something eluded her. She sensed, rather than saw, what was out of sorts. But what was it? She had flipped through the MasterCard invoice. Force of habit. She did it with her own to make sure no one had charged anything to her number. Nora's seemed extravagant but in order. Carpet cleaning. Nothing unusual there.

Amanda raised her hands. Her fingers hovered, itching like a divining rod waiting to tremble at the first sight of water. There was only one other bill she'd paged through. One other…

The telephone. Digging in, she located it, looked at it, got up from the table, and still couldn't quite figure it out. Then it was there, plain as day. Like a hidden picture game, it smacked her right between the eyes once she focused. In her mind, she drew a clumsy circle around the number that made her blood run cold. Her head snapped to the left and the right, searching for the phone. Locking onto it,

Amanda ignored all the beautiful things Nora possessed because the only thing Amanda could see was the bright-red lightning bolt of anger as it crackled through her brain, consuming her.

She lifted the receiver, took a deep breath, and then dialed the number that appeared over and over again on Nora's bill. Afternoon calls, evening calls, calls that succeeded the start of the trial. Calls that proved Amanda had been stupid, stupid, stupid.

The phone was ringing. One, two, three times before it stopped, curtailed by a machine and a mechanical greeting. Amanda could hardly breathe. She heard what she dreaded. Lucas Mallory's voice. Calm, cool, collected as he asked that the caller leave a message on this, his personal machine, or kindly call the switchboard and speak to his secretary. Lucas Mallory, for God's sake! Lucas Mallory!

Nora had lied.

Nora had made a fool of Amanda.

Nora needed help but not the legal kind.

Nora had used Amanda in her sick little game.

Nora was crazy. Crazy. Crazy.

Amanda let the phone fall, a white-hot light exploding behind her eyes, pain searing through her head. She had no memory of moving, though she obviously had. Her leg ached. She had hit it somewhere as she stalked through Nora's perfect place. Amanda was in the bedroom when cognizance returned. The bedroom with its airing sheets, its luxurious bed, its indirect lighting. The bedroom, with all the trappings of Nora's privileged, disgusting life. Enraged, Amanda ripped at the covers, throwing them to the ground, kicking at them, flailing with her fists at every object of beauty that surrounded Nora.

Soon there was nothing else to throw. There was only

Nora, still showering, standing under the hot, steaming water, laughing at Amanda as she had all along. Sweet Amanda. Stupid Amanda. Gullible Amanda.

Amanda was in the bathroom, throwing open the door of the huge glass shower. Nora clasped her arms to her chest, hiding her body, turning her face, the water streaming over her, making her look like one of Neptune's favorites. That's what she was. But insanity wouldn't save her. That was no defense in Amanda's court.

Amanda reached under the pulsing water mindless of her clothes. Nora screeched, a sound of question and dread and surprise. Amanda's hands slipped and Nora fell back against the wall. Her hip smacked hard against the tile. She sputtered as the water poured into her open mouth, then scrambled up only to slip again as Amanda dived for her.

"Amanda! Amanda!" Nora was full of life now, ducking under Amanda's flailing arms and crawling onto the tile floor. Amanda caught her ankle. Wet, Nora shook her off easily. Amanda followed her sister, drenched and slipping.

"You idiot! You stupid, stupid idiot! How could you do this to me? How could you do this? You liar!"

Half standing, half crawling, Nora dashed for the bedroom, stopping only a second to survey the damage Amanda had wreaked. Behind her, she heard her sister's heels skid on the wet tile. Without a second thought, Nora ripped open the door of the closet, grabbed her robe, threw it over her nakedness, and backed out of the room. Tying the robe, breathing in hard little puffs, she shivered with cold and fear as she watched Amanda come.

"Don't you dare try to get away from me," Amanda said. "You never will. You are a manipulative, blood-sucking, miserable excuse for a human being. I can't believe this. I can't believe what you've done. What is it you really wanted, Nora? How long have you been planning this? Did you get a chuckle watching us all run around trying to save your butt?"

Nora backed into a chair. Familiar with the room, she skirted it without taking her eyes off her sister.

"I don't know what you're talking about," Nora whispered, careful with her words and oh-so vigilant. "Really, Amanda, I don't." Frantically, she darted behind an overstuffed chair. They faced each other: one terrified and defensive, the other enraged and anguished.

"Don't say that. Don't say that! I know everything now. I know how you've played me for a sucker. The only thing I don't know is why you even bothered to go through this damned charade. Cripes, Nora, why didn't you just plead guilty and save us all a hell of a lot of trouble?"

"I am not guilty." Nora pushed the words through set teeth, her eyes glittering hard and cold, daring Amanda to disregard her objection.

Amanda did. Easily and with relish. "You are. You are guilty. You are everything—"

"I am not!" Nora screamed, backing away, cradling herself with crossed arms, since no one else wanted to give her comfort. Her lids closed and the hard eyes were hidden. Amanda could almost believe her agony. Almost. Except now she knew the truth.

"You are everything"—Amanda took a deep breath. She had to work at it. Her voice was shaking, her gut closed off—"everything they said you were. You killed. You killed Ruth Mallory and you're still doing it to him."

"Who?"

"Lucas Mallory."

Amanda ran her hand through her hair, pushing it back, away from her face. It was wet and clung to her cheeks in black tendrils. Amanda took a step away, a step back.

"You are cool, Nora. I can't tell you how I admire that. You are incredibly cool and calm and collected. What an amazing attorney you must have been. I'll bet you didn't give an inch in trial, the same way you didn't give Lucas Mallory any space to maneuver. The same way you didn't give Ruth Mallory a chance."

Amanda's laugh was derisive. She stood up straight and looked toward the high ceiling, her hands on the small of her back as though that part of her anatomy pained her. When she looked back to earth she saw her proof lying just where she had dropped it. With no regard for Nora, she walked toward the kitchen. Nora skittered, raising her hands defensively as Amanda passed. Amanda didn't give her a second look. Amanda figured a knife in the back might be preferable to the pain she was feeling now. Slowly, she bent down, picked up the phone bill, and turned to face her sister.

"What did you do, Nora, when he came to beg you to stop stalking him?"

"He didn't come here to ask that," Nora answered her voice quiet and guarded.

"He did," Amanda insisted flatly. "I know he came here. The guy across the tree line has a telescope. He knows Lucas Mallory was here."

"I know he was here, too, you fool," Nora spat back. "I've told you that a hundred times. He was here to sleep with me. To beg me to sleep with him."

Amanda ignored her. "I still can't figure out the scarf. I can't figure out why he gave you the scarf. Was it just a mentor kind of thing, something nice for the new kid on the block?" Amanda felt drained so tired it was hard for her to remain standing.

"He gave me the scarf because he wanted me, because he liked to play silly little games with it while… we… were… screwing." Nora moved cautiously into the center of the room, closer to Amanda but not close enough to touch. The light from the kitchen fell on Amanda, making her look like an avenging spirit, larger than life, haloed by the fluorescent light.

Nora's voice was dangerously calm, so restful to listen to. She used it like a warm hand to lull Amanda into believing. "Do you understand that? Amanda? I haven't lied to you. I haven't kept anything from you. I came to you for help. Why would I make it difficult for you to help me?"

"I don't know," Amanda said all the fight gone from her, tears welling and brimming, threatening to fall any moment and make her the weak one again. "I don't know why you do the things you do. When you were a kid I remember Mom saying you never kissed her. You hugged her, you talked to her, but you never kissed her. Finally, she asked you why. You said if you didn't kiss her, then she'd have to keep asking. That's weird, Nora. As weird as you stalking this poor man."

"I didn't. I didn't. How many times do I have to tell you?"

Now Nora was near tears. Her face, animated, was interesting. Not quite as beautiful as it was in repose. Her mouth was large, her widened eyes looked naked, her pupils small and unprotected. Her body was gangly and skinny rather than fashionably slim. It had all been an illusion—the beauty, the mystery, the honesty.

"You don't have to tell me that because I don't care anymore. I quit. I quit as your attorney, I quit as your sister. We were never close, let's never try to be again. You scare me. I don't like liars, Nora, and you're the best. But this tripped you up."

Amanda laughed, and it was a hollow sound. She toyed with the telephone bill.

"Good old Amanda. Always willing to go the extra mile. I thought I'd help sort out your mail, get your bills together. I felt so sorry for you." Amanda let the words drip from her mouth as though they were distasteful. She held out the bill. "And there it was. The black-and-white proof that everything you've told me is a lie. Look at this. Lucas Mallory's private number has been dialed—what?" She referred to the bill without really looking at it. "Ten times? Fifteen in the last month. That means all the while Mark and Edward and I were working our tails off trying to figure out how to keep your pretty little neck out of the noose, all the while the prosecution was putting on their case, you were still calling Lucas Mallory.

Amanda moved closer, Nora stepped back.

"Tell me. Did he talk to you? Did he beg you not to call him? Was he afraid of you? Did he conjure up images of his dead wife in the hopes of playing on your sympathies? Didn't he know by now you have no sympathies? The only agenda you have is your own and I'm not going to buy into it anymore. I've had it, Nora. You pumped me up, got me all ready to go. I was going to pull this thing out of the fire. This was my chance to shine, my chance to create a bond with my only living relative. Christ. I was so wrong. All this was a last, desperate effort on your part to get away with murder—literally. Bet you never thought all your highly placed friends would desert you, did you? Bet you never in a million years thought you'd be counting on me, good old dumpy Amanda, to save you. No wonder you were depressed. No wonder, Nora."

Amanda let the phone bill flutter to the floor. She considered it for a moment, walked to the dining room table, slowly put the strap of her purse over her shoulder, then went to the front door. Nora hadn't moved. There wasn't a sound inside the town house. It wasn't until Amanda's hand was on the knob that Nora spoke, making sense Amanda didn't want to hear.

"Why didn't Lucas say something on the stand, Amanda? Why didn't he tell the prosecutor that I was still calling? Why didn't they subpoena phone records? Nobody did anything because I haven't called Lucas Mallory. I haven't spoken to him. I didn't, Amanda. I didn't."

Amanda stopped. She looked over her shoulder, coldly refusing to be pulled into Nora's net once again. "It's your phone, it's your house, and it's your mess. You fix it."

The door was open; Amanda was out. The door was almost closed behind her. Nora called. "Amanda," and at that moment Amanda understood. She knew what was wrong with this picture.

Back inside, slamming the door behind her, she fell all over herself apologizing. Nora was telling the truth.

Chapter 20

———

"Couldn't wait, huh?"

Mark had changed into shorts. It was chilly for shorts but he didn't seem to be adversely affected by the ocean wind skimming his hill and perforating his trailer. His body-glove T-shirt had seen better days and he was shoeless. But, damn, did he look good.

Amanda admired him then abandoned him in one swift mental current.

"Don't flatter yourself." She grinned, sweeping past him into the trailer. "Or go ahead and flatter yourself but don't let it get in the way right now. We've got work to do. When that's finished, we'll spend all our time calling to order a perpetual meeting of the Mark Fleming admiration society."

Amanda was peeling off her jacket before the door was shut. Mark went to help, first noting her shivers, then feeling her jacket. He weighed it on the tip of one finger.

"You stopped for a swim before you got here?"

Amanda shook her head; she was unbuttoning her blouse, "Don't get excited, Fleming. I'm not here on a social call. I hope you've got something warm to wrap me in, 'cause I can't think while my teeth are chattering like this."

Without a word, Mark disappeared into the bedroom. When he came back he tossed her a gray sweatshirt and a pair of navy sweatpants. She was in them before he could even think lecherous thoughts.

"Damn," she muttered.

"What?" Picking up her damp clothes, he hung them on the first available protrusion.

"They fit." Mark laughed, stopped long enough to kiss her, then let her get on with it as she slipped onto one of his red vinyl kitchen chairs. "Listen, we've got some stuff I just can't believe. Look at this."

Mark took the phone bill Amanda had spirited away from Nora. He shrugged, not too quick on the uptake. That suited Amanda just fine. She felt so exceptional.

"That"—she poked at the offensive paper—"is Nora's phone bill and, that"—she poked lower, her voice rising with excitement—"is Lucas Mallory's private number."

"Holy shit." Mark whistled. "She was—"

"No! She wasn't anything. That's what I thought, too." Amanda moved in her chair, almost bouncing with excitement. "I thought she'd pulled the wool over my eyes. I almost killed her for it. You should have seen me. I was crazy. Pulled her out of the shower—" Amanda stopped talking, coloring. It was hardly a story that would impress a new lover. "Well, that's neither here nor there. The point is who else, if not Nora, had access to Nora's phone?"

"You," Mark answered quickly.

"Get real." Amanda rolled her eyes. "I hadn't been there in a month. When I saw her, she came to the office. Make sense of this, Mark. Nora and…" She waved her hands in two tight circles. Legal charades.

"You and... Oh, Lord." The light dawned, illuminating Mark's gorgeous face so that Amanda couldn't resist some contact. She placed her hands on either side of his cheeks and kissed him square on the mouth. When she let him up for air, Mark was on the right track. "Edward. That little prick was a plant. I knew it. I knew it all along. He didn't quit Dimsdale. He wasn't even fired. He's a spy. He's trying to make Brownie points with Mallory. Oh, God. Can you believe this?"

"It was so obvious. Edward's been dancing attendance on Nora like there's no tomorrow. I thought he had the hots for her at first but even I figured out it wasn't like that between them. I didn't think farther than that because he was helping out and he was keeping an eye on her and I was scared stiff and desperate. Not to mention it was easy to see how he could get himself in a tight spot with DM&M. I bought his story hook, line, and sinker because I believed he was an arrogant screw-up. But this! God, when I figured it out, it was just too cool to believe!"

Amanda was bouncing around in the chair as if she were sitting on hot coals. Mark grinned. He wanted to holler but somebody had to keep it together.

"Okay. Okay. Wait. Keep talking while I fix sandwiches. A drink. Want a drink?"

"Yes. Yes. I want a drink and I want someone's head in that order. Then, Fleming, I want you to..."

Mark leaned over and kissed her cheek. "You got it.

"I never was good on the first pass but I'm a real quick learner the second time around, no problem."

"Then I guess you were right all along. We are two of a kind. It takes me a while to get things right, too."

That was it. Sentiment be damned. Mark managed the

drinks, completely forgetting the sandwiches, but setting a plate of cold cuts between them for munching. Together they drew charts, they made doodles, they threw out ideas, and, as the night grew older, hope grew bolder. By two in the morning, they'd run out of scotch and the adrenaline flow had ebbed, leaving their minds still reeling but their bodies exhausted. At some point, Mark and Amanda found their way to the mattress on the floor. They talked quietly, lying side by side, not touching.

"So, this is what we've got." Amanda's voice was subdued but strong in the small room. "We can argue a good case for Lucas Mallory screwing around with Nora, given the scarf and your eyewitness with the telescope. We can make a good case for Lucas Mallory being so worried that this would sully his reputation that he alone or with the knowledge of the other partners, put Edward in our camp to keep an eye on us. Because of the affair, we can certainly explain away the physical evidence in that room. We can even get the jury to accept that Nora's blood was in the Mallory suite because Lucas bit her."

Wearily, Amanda held up her hand.

"I know the doctor couldn't swear the wound was made by teeth but I think we'll talk it through and get them wondering. We also have to emphasize that Nora was on that patio. The fact that Edward was with her part of the time will give that a lot of weight. He's on the other side now so he'll be considered a hostile witness. If he doesn't tell the truth he'll perjure himself. He's screwed either way."

They fell silent once again. Amanda yawned and stretched a bit, mumbling, "What else?"

"One of us should go back to the hotel and try to find anyone who remembers seeing Lucas and Nora together. Since Ruth didn't arrive until the reception, there might be someone on a different shift who saw the two of them."

"That's good. I can do it." Amanda was almost out now, fighting sleep because she was thinking of so many things. "And you'll meet with Kitty Hedding tomorrow?"

"Right. No kid gloves this time. That woman has something to say and this time she'd better say it."

"I couldn't agree more." Amanda yawned again. Mark slipped his arm around her. It wouldn't be long before she couldn't think at all. She turned into him, nestling on his shoulder. "I'm going to ask for a delay. I need another couple of days before Leo gets Mallory on the stand. I don't think they'll be laughing at the cross-examination this time."

Mark chuckled at her small joke. It was a gentle, lulling sound.

Silence once more but sleep wouldn't come. They were both thinking the same thing. Amanda gave the question voice.

"I wonder who killed Ruth Mallory."

"Do you care now?"

Amanda moved her head against him. Mark's free hand stroked her hair. He cared, too.

"Lucas?" she mumbled.

"I don't see how," Mark whispered back. "I don't even know why he would have. Not for Nora, certainly."

"No, not for Nora."

Silence. Longer than the last. It was deep night, almost morning. Amanda's last question was slipping off her tongue.

"Why did the partners lie?"

But she was asleep before Mark could answer. It was just as well. All he could think to say was, "Why not?"

Mark tightened his hold, running his hand down Amanda's shoulder. She curled into him, murmuring something sweet and unintelligible. Just as he was trying to figure it out, just when he decided to take a look at some public records in the a.m., Mark Fleming got sidetracked.

Slipping his arm from beneath Amanda's head, he took a moment to look at her. In his eyes she was beautiful, her dark hair spread out over a pillow, his clothes just big enough to make her look kind of small. He thought of waking her, of peeling off those clothes and making love to her until the sun came up. Instead, he turned on his side, took her hand in his, and closed his eyes. It was nice that he was going to sleep well, too. It was nice to feel excited about life again, about someone again. Even about himself.

Chapter 21

Amanda had called Edward first thing. He was still under the weather. She commiserated, insisting he shouldn't think of coming to the office. He was to stay right where he was. What she didn't say was that it would be healthier for him if he stayed away from the law offices of Amanda Cross altogether. If she saw his pretty little face she just might push it in.

The conversation with Edward had taken less than two minutes but the anger she felt toward him consumed her. Luckily, the sweetness of her night with Mark and the excitement of the trial had slowly overshadowed the black thoughts of Edward Ramsey.

Now, though, Amanda was cooling her heels, waiting to find out if Judge Petty was going to grant her motion for a continuance. Amanda wanted a few days to fine-tune her strategy, Mark needed time to talk to Kitty Hedding, scour the public records, and find out anything he could about Ruth and Lucas Mallory. Her hopes were up only to be dashed when the judge's clerk resurfaced and the news wasn't good. No continuance. That was that. So what else was new? Amanda had been flying by the seat of her pants for so long she wouldn't know what to do if someone offered a helping hand. But then, she wasn't really alone. There was Mark and there was Nora and Amanda found there was a spring in her step as she headed down the humanity-choked streets of LA to her office. There, she dumped her briefcase, grabbed her keys, called greetings and goodbyes to Consuelo, and hopped in her car. She was lunching at the Regency Hotel in Beverly Hills. After that, Amanda Cross had an appointment with a maid on the concierge floor.

"Are you finding everything you need?"

Mark was startled, as much to find himself addressed by someone at the Clerk's office as he was to find so much time had gone by. He'd spent so much time with the Plaintiff/Defendant Index it was beginning to feel like a marriage. For all his effort, the only thing Mark had found was that Ruth Mallory was not a drunkard given to driving under the influence, nor was she the litigious type, getting kicks by suing everyone from the green grocery to the president of the United States.

Mark smiled. The girl was half his age and a cutie to boot. He shook his head.

"Fraid not. But I'm not finished yet."

"I might have some time to help you in a little while. I'm supposed to go on a break but I wouldn't mind." A flash of thigh and a couple of bats of false eyelashes left Mark amused.

He shook his head again, harder this time.

"Thanks, no. I can manage. I'd hate to see you waste your time."

"Oh, it wouldn't be a waste of time at all," she cooed quietly, moving closer. She smelled of Opium. Expensive tastes for a little girl.

"Believe me, this would be the biggest waste of time in your life," he assured her. Her eyes widened. Message received loud and clear. There was a moment of regret when she walked away and her hips swayed prettily under a hand-span waist. With a sigh, he tackled the index alone. Turning the pages, Mark experienced a moment of utter, mind-expanding lucidity. He'd found what he was looking for. He smoothed the pages down as carefully as a lover caressing his beloved.

"Yes," he murmured. "Yes."

There it was. Spelled out clear as day. Ruth Mallory had filed for divorce from Lucas Mallory on the sixth day of April in the year of our Lord 1992. And lordy, lordy, what a bit of marvelous news that was. Lucas Mallory had no need to protect his wife from knowledge of his affair. Lucas could have been sleeping with the Rockettes for all Ruth cared.

Now what?

A simple divorce is no reason to kill your wife, unless... Was it Lucas who was obsessive? Lucas who was vindictive? Lucas who actually might have twisted the scarf and plunged the knife? Maybe beneath that implausibly calm exterior lay a man enraged when betrayed but calculating enough to kill, attend a party, and allow his mistress to take the fall. If that were the case, Lucas Mallory wasn't just sick, he was downright evil. Perhaps Ruth wanted Lucas back but she had a lover. Yes, a lover, one who wanted her so badly he would kill before he let anyone else have her. The lover did Ruth in with the scarf Lucas gave her. Then what happened to Nora's scarf? Too many questions. Too little time. Too bizarre to even speculate. Okay. That was it. He was off.

Mark allowed himself an indulgent chill of disgust,

closed the Plaintiff/Defendant Index, hauled it back to the counter, and thanked the pert little clerk before dashing out the door. Kitty was waiting. Kitty, who knew more than she was telling. He didn't want to take a chance on scaring her away. He'd lunch at LA Trattoria on Third with a handsome woman who he hoped had seen the light. Kitty Hedding knew exactly what was going on. Of that he was sure.

Two down, one to go. Amanda had managed to talk to the room service waiter, the day maids, and the concierge at the Regency, none of whom could provide her with additional information regarding the night Ruth Mallory died. Last on her list was the evening maid, that servile young woman who moved like a ghost through the lovely halls of this prestigious hotel laying chocolates on pristine pillows. No one took notice of her; with luck, she took notice of everything.

The maid was found on the sixth floor and Amanda was ashamed to admit it took a good minute for her to really look at the woman. There was something about the uniform—gray and white, the thick-soled shoes, the expression of utter exhaustion—that erased the stamp of individuality.

"Yes, ma'am?" The maid stopped what she was doing, politely awaiting Amanda's pleasure.

"My name's Amanda Cross and I'm interested in what happened here a few months ago. A woman was killed. Do you remember? Were you on duty that day?"

"Si, I remember," the woman said quietly. Amanda got the feeling she would like to cross herself. Instead, she hid her hands under a towel. "It was very bad. Very bad."

"I know," Amanda said sweetly. "I was saddened to hear about it, too. She was a fine lady. Did you see her the day she died?"

The maid shook her head.

"Not at all?"

She shook her head harder.

"But you told the police you saw a woman go into the room, the suite that Mrs. Mallory used."

"Yes. A woman. I did see a woman. But I don't know it was Mrs. Mallory. They say it was the other one. The one that killed her."

"Okay," Amanda went slowly. "You saw a woman. Would you recognize her if you saw her again?"

"Si."

"Did the police show you a picture of the woman who killed Mrs. Mallory?" Once again the head was shaking, her short hair bouncing. "Could I show you a picture?"

"Si."

"Thank you. Thank you." Amanda fumbled with her purse, hitched it higher to rest it on her hip, and pulled out the photo of Nora. "Is this the woman?"

The maid leaned over the picture as if she were afraid it might come to life and do her in. Leaning back, she nodded.

"Good. That's good. What time did you see this woman go into the suite?"

"About lunchtime. Everyone was gone. I came to my shift. So I cleaned the last rooms. I came out for towels and I saw her go in."

Amanda smiled. That was about right. Ruth Mallory at lunch with the associates' better halves, Lucas Mallory with time on his hands, eager for a little nooky on the side. Just as Nora said.

"And—Rosa," Amanda glanced at the plastic name tag. "Did you see this woman again at night, around seven or so?"

Rosa shook her head.

"Okay. Okay. That's good. Then, when did you see the man go into the room? This man."

Amanda pulled out a picture of Lucas Mallory. She'd come prepared, armed to the teeth, to get what she wanted. But Amanda didn't get it. The nod wasn't forthcoming. That cropped hair was bouncing the wrong way. Rosa was shaking her head.

"What?" Amanda demanded.

Rosa was apologetic. "I didn't see him go in the room, ma'am. Not afternoon or night."

"But you must have. He was with her," Amanda insisted, her voice breaking with disappointment.

"No, ma'am. I'm sorry. I didn't see no man go in the room," Rosa reiterated, her expression never changing. One answer was much like another to her. She wanted to be truthful, not involved. "Is that all, ma'am? I don't know nothing else, ma'am."

"Yes, thank you. Yes."

But Amanda knew that wasn't all. Her gut told her so. Rosa disappeared into Room 225 with her towels. Still, Amanda didn't leave. Instead, she leaned against the wall, a hand to her forehead. No way was she going to believe Nora let herself into that room, stayed there alone, and waited for Ruth Mallory to come back after the reception. Nora would have had to hide herself from both Ruth and Lucas while they dressed. It was impossible. Nora was not guilty. Lucas Mallory had to be with her.

"Ma'am?" Rosa had stuck her head back out and was reaching for the toilet paper. Two rolls, one in each hand. She carried them as if they were gold, not wanting to soil them before they reached their destination.

"Yes, Rosa."

"Did you want to know about that man when he opened the door of the room, ma'am, or just someone who went in with the lady?"

Amanda stared. She didn't move. Then Amanda began to laugh and Rosa was sorry she had even mentioned it.

~ ~ ~

There was some traffic on Third Street and Rossmore was a mess but Mark single-mindedly wove his way through it all. He'd cooled his heels for three hours at LA Trattoria, doing exactly what an anxious and impatient person might do. He ordered coffee. Pastry. He apologized to the waitress. She let him keep his table when the place got crowded at around two. He'd called Kitty Hedding's house. The maid answered. The answering machine answered. Kitty Hedding never did. Mark dialed Amanda, left a message, and had another cup of coffee. Then he got mad. Jerk-around time was over.

Mark phoned Amanda again. This time he got the real thing. They babbled at each other until they made themselves heard. Mark was impressed with Amanda's news, she not quite so thrilled with his. When she ordered him to stay away from the Hedding house, their connection was suddenly broken. Pay phones weren't what they used to be.

Mark found the house without a problem, parked the car, and took a minute to applaud the Heddings' taste. He slammed the car door, hitched his jacket, squared his shoulders, and walked to the door. There he reached a decision and put his finger on the doorbell.

He knew someone was there, cowering against the heavy oak door, listening to the incessant ringing. His finger tired. He took a break and then hit it again. Another minute and whoever was behind the door would scream for mercy.

Wrong.

No time to continue the torture. His arm was unceremoniously ripped away from the wall, curtailing his plan. He whirled, ready to do battle, only to find it would have to be done with Amanda Cross.

"What are you doing here, Fleming?" She was furious but the fury was controlled. Someday he'd tell her she looked beautiful when she was mad but not today. He didn't like her messing with his plan.

"Leave me alone, Amanda."

"Like hell. I specifically told you to stay away from Kitty Hedding. Do you think I have nothing better to do than chase you down and make sure you don't do something stupid?"

"She called me, Amanda. I'm just checking to see if she's okay."

"Right. And I'm the Tooth Fairy. The lady made it pretty clear she changed her mind. That's it. She could call the cops and holler harassment, you know?"

"But she knows what happened. We need to talk to her."

"Great. We'll deal with it in court. Court, Fleming. It's the place with the big rooms, the guy in the black dress refereeing. Remember? Kitty Hedding doesn't want…"

Mark's finger was on the bell again, his jaw set. He had to listen but he didn't have to look at her and he sure wasn't going to be stopped. Both Amanda's hands cuffed his wrist. She tugged. Her face flushed scarlet with the exertion of trying to pull his hand away.

"Mark." A word drawn out to a warning.

"Shut up, Amanda." He leaned into the bell. They could actually hear the chimes echoing inside and the sound was unnerving. "You've been harping at me because I'm a quitter. Okay. I've turned over a new leaf. I'm not leaving here until—"

Mark's tirade was cut short as surely as if Amanda had zipped his lip. But she had nothing to do with his sudden silence. The door was opening. Mark's head snapped toward the movement, Amanda's eyes followed the door as it swung in a little farther. Dracula's castle ominously beckoning them. Amanda's clutch of anger turned to a clinging need for reassurance. Sure, it was sunny and bright outside, but, from what they could see, the only thing that would feel comfortable inside would be mushrooms. It was dark. It was quiet. It was just kind of scary.

The door stopped moving. A face materialized. Big, black eyes blinked at them. A woman's eyes. Mark shook Amanda off. She stepped behind him. Silly. Nervous Nell and her mounty. They waited, the two of them peering closer. Those Bambi eyes were red-rimmed and more frightened than they.

"Please, go 'way, senor. *Por favor.*" The maid begged. Amanda let out a long breath. Mark did the same. Egor was nothing more than a frightened little girl.

"I can't go away." He put his hand on the door, pushing lightly, pleading gently, but close to insistent. "Let me in."

The little woman tried to push back but she was no match even for Mark's restrained effort. The door was opening wider, she was babbling, a stream of prayers and entreaties that made Amanda feel a bit like a Roman pulverizing a nest of Christians. Added to this were Mark's muttered, terse admonitions. Amanda wasn't sure, in the mess of words, if he was trying to assure the woman that they had no intention of raping and pillaging or if he was attempting to explain exactly who they were. It didn't matter. They were almost in. One more step. They were picking up momentum and the minute Mark pulled up short, Amanda plowed right into him. The prayers stopped and all eyes were on the staircase.

It took Mark about a second to react, Amanda a bit longer. By the time she did, Mark was headed up the staircase, ticked off as hell at the woman who watched so passively from the landing above.

"This is it, lady. We know part of it and you're going to fill us in on the rest. I'm sick and tired of these stupid games. I've had it with…"

He was puffing pretty good. He was a strong man suffering a minor indignation of age. Amanda was tapping up those stairs right after him, admiring the oriental runner as she went. She slowed when he did and stopped of her own accord beside him. Amanda gasped. It was a rude, though apropos, expression.

"Oh my God." Amanda muttered.

Mark's disgust was expressed in an eloquent silence. To her credit, Kitty Hedding did nothing, not even offer an explanation. She simply stood and let them look. Below them, rooted to the parquet floor, the maid wept. That face of Kitty Hedding's, delicate and heart-shaped, was swollen and many-colored: blue, black, purple.

"Mrs. Hedding." Amanda pushed past Mark, hands out, reaching to help a woman in need. But they were different women. A flicker of the eye stalled Amanda. Her arms dropped. Flatly, put off, she said, "Do you need help?"

Kitty tried to smile politely but abandoned the effort in deference to her swollen jaw and lack of interest.

"No. Thank you," she answered, perfectly and passively cordial. Her eyes locked back on Mark. "Mr. Fleming. I'm sorry I missed our appointment. Initially, I had concluded a meeting would not be beneficial to either of us then I realized it might not be wise."

"I can see how you could come to that conclusion," Mark answered and you could hear the sympathy in his voice.

"I'm sure you can." Cool. What a woman. Weird. "However, since you're here, perhaps it is time we talk. I shouldn't have listened to my vanity. I should have managed our engagement—somehow."

She saved Mark from mumbling ineffective apologies by calling down the stairs. "Luna, would you bring tea and coffee to the sitting room, please."

In a wave of stifled sobs and acknowledgments, the maid departed, moving silently through the still, dark, and impressive house.

"Mr. Fleming. Ms. Cross—"

Kitty led them regally to their destination. Amanda relaxed. She wasn't quite sure what Kitty Hedding's story was but one thing was sure, the lady wasn't a victim. Not anymore.

Chapter 22

The sitting room was nifty, just the kind of place Amanda would have loved to call her own. Fortunately, she understood her limitations. Any attempt on her part to emulate this place would result in a cross between Hansel and Gretel's gingerbread house of horrors and Martha Stewart's worst nightmare. Luckily, Kitty Hedding's decorator had no such weakness.

There were pretty chairs in chintz and checks, creating an old-money, Palm-Beach kind of effect. There were slipcovers and tablecloths, their hems dragging on the hardwood floor. There were brass lamps and silver picture frames, textured and properly tarnished. Tassels and good wood. Real oil paintings. Eighteen-karat gilt. And there was a scarf on the table nearest the place where Kitty Hedding settled.

It took every ounce of self-control Amanda possessed to keep from throwing herself on that jumble of silk and pressing it to her cheek in miraculous awe. The second Anni scarf. The end. The light at the end of the proverbial tunnel. But Amanda behaved herself. The three of them sat silently until Luna slipped in with a silver tray.

Coffee all around. Alone again, they waited upon Kitty Hedding's pleasure.

"I apologize to both of you. I behaved rudely. But I suppose manners are of little concern at this point."

"We won't tell Amy Vanderbilt there's been a lapse," Amanda drawled. A hard look from the rich lady. Not a good start.

Mark was kinder and it irked Amanda for some reason.

"We understand this whole situation is touchy. But, Mrs. Hedding, you know something and you might as well tell us. We'll find out anyway and the result of having to dig for the truth in court might be more embarrassing than filling in the blanks now."

Kitty's coffee was untouched. Carefully, she set the cup on the table beside her, using the moment to collect her thoughts. It proved to be an unnecessary hesitancy. Kitty, sure of what she wanted to say, was plainspoken.

"All right. Let's begin. I believe Lucas Mallory did, indeed, kill Ruth. I believe my husband knew about it. Before or after the fact, I'm not sure, nor do I think it really matters. I believe that Don Forrester helped Lucas to cover up his crime and I must assume Peter Sweeney was also cognizant of what was going on."

Amanda threw her arms in the air, her hands slapping her thighs when gravity brought them down.

"Wow! Really nice. Thanks for letting us know. That clears everything up."

Kitty ignored the sarcasm.

"Amanda," Mark snapped.

They stared at one another, her mouth set in the same angry, controlled line of disapproval as his. When they finally broke the connection, he leaned toward Kitty with a look of absolute respect in his eyes. Kitty Hedding softened. Amanda wanted to throw up. Why make it easy? Instead of voicing her opinion, Amanda listened.

"Mrs. Hedding."

"Yes, Mr. Fleming?"

"I know this is going to be hard. What you've just told us is damned serious. Made even more so because we're halfway through this trial. We can't take what you believe into court. We've got to have something to back up these allegations."

"I understand."

"Good." A quick, triumphant glance went Amanda's way. "I asked you once who screwed up the Mallory marriage. Now I know it had to be Lucas because Ruth Mallory filed for divorce months ago. Was it because of Lucas's affair with Nora Royce? Was Ruth Mallory jealous enough to chuck the marriage?"

The question amused Kitty. She laughed sadly, her lips tight, and raised a long-fingered hand to the injured side of her face. Shaking her head, she whispered, "Oh my, no. Ruth didn't even know about it. Nor would she have cared." She pushed out of her chair with swan-like grace, lessons from finishing school never forgotten. "I'd like you to listen to something."

Neither Mark nor Amanda moved as she inserted a small cassette into a recorder and pushed a button. Kitty Hedding raised the dead.

"Kitty? Ruth." Pause. Half a beat. "Darling, pick up if you're there. Oh, well, no harm. Here's the delightful news. Bound to get a rise out of Lucas now. Fred has checked out everything and we are legally in the clear. I can't wait to see the look on Lucas's face when I tell him. What a marvelous joke. See you at the hotel, ready to perform my last duties as a DM&M slave. Ta."

A click.

Ruth Mallory was dead again.

Mark glanced at Amanda. She looked back.

Kitty stood fingering the machine.

"My husband hit me, Mr. Fleming. He heard me calling Ms. Cross's office and he hit me without waiting to hear an explanation. He didn't care that I was about to cancel our appointment. And, just like in the movies, when he struck me, I came to my senses and saw things very clearly, indeed. I realized, Mr. Fleming, that I've forgiven Oliver many things over the years, but this I cannot forgive."

She flipped the tape out of the machine and walked back to her chair, handing the cassette to Amanda as she went. Amanda slipped it into her purse while Kitty reseated herself.

"I am married to a horrible man who has no feelings for anyone, even himself. I have known this for many years, sidestepping the issues and the truths because it was convenient. I rationalized that I wasn't hurt, that everything Oliver did was acceptable, reasonable, and best for our life as we wished to live it. By the time I fully understood Oliver's failings, as well as my own, and the ramifications of his actions and my inaction, it seemed too late to do anything about our situation. Nothing would be gained; we would be no happier. We would only experience a great deal of emotional discomfort."

Even this small speech seemed tiring to Kitty. Once again, she touched her bruises. She couldn't keep her hands off the injury but was too much a lady to make a scene.

"You know, when Oliver hit me, when he realized that I probably knew things I shouldn't, he wasn't afraid. I was a nonentity. I was nothing to him any longer. A servant was more useful and interesting than I. So he struck me because it pleased him and to keep me in my place. He had such faith that I would stay there. Truthfully, I almost did."

Silence blanketed them. Kitty was an invalid miraculously cured, a sick woman clinging to life. Her strength was minimal, yet she wanted to talk about the great white light, the revelations of a near-death experience. But she was dazed and needed help to continue.

"And Fred is… Ruth's lover?"

Amanda was impatient with Mark's coddling. She would have shaken the lady crazy until the answers spilled right out of her mouth and fell at Amanda's feet.

"No. Ruth was finished with things like that. Men are a problem, Mr. Fleming. I've yet to meet one who isn't." She gave him a look that included him in her assessment. "Fred was Ruth's lawyer."

"Do you know what information he had for her?"

"You're an impatient young man, you know?" Men might be a problem but Kitty liked this one.

"I am. A woman's life is at stake. A woman's freedom and integrity."

"You're absolutely right, Mr. Fleming, but you must understand this is difficult. Urgency has seldom played a part in my life."

"It does now," Mark reminded her sympathizing with her. Now Amanda got it. Mark was so taken with Mrs. Hedding because she was the ultimate quitter. He recognized it, understood it, and would let her quit for good after he got what he wanted.

"Yes. Of course. You're right." Finally, the sigh Amanda had been waiting for. It worked like a valve on her body. The figure Mark had once thought so fashionably slim seemed shopworn as Kitty let it cave in around her defeated heart. "Well, where shall we start? Perhaps at Ruth's beginning." Kitty laced her hands, ready to recite. "Ruth had been married before, to a man much like Lucas: a subdued man who made few demands on her physically, if I may say, but one who challenged her intellectually and admired her brightness, her joie de vivre. She was very sad when he died. Not devastated, you understand, but sad. Ruth's life never revolved around any one person, therefore none had the ability to crush her. She was a forward mover and true grief would have demanded she remain in one emotional place. He was a politician. He appreciated Ruth for her theatrics, her mature beauty, and her sophistication."

Kitty suddenly fidgeted as if she couldn't remember the thread of her story. She found her place once more and the tale continued.

"When Ruth met Lucas, she thought he was yet another perfect mate. Lucas was so much like her late husband in demeanor, the match seemed destined. What Ruth didn't take into account were the basic differences in her two husbands' lives. Specifically, their professions and the geography of her unions. L.A. is not Washington, DC and a politician's lot is not that of an attorney."

"I don't get it."

Kitty cast a sidelong glance Amanda's way. Indifferently she deigned to explain.

"A political life in Washington is quite exciting, very glamorous, full of drama. Drama." Kitty's sat back in the chair. Yesterday was more interesting than the here and now. "How Ruth loved drama. The balls, the lights and music, the gossip, who was bedding whom. She lived for the intrigue. Having a husband who was somewhat moderate gave her a counterpoint in a city that demanded both reserve and sparkle. One needs to balance the other in such a milieu. Her first husband brought her to the theater, produced the show and Ruth did everything else. She wrote the script, managed the sets, and shone as his star. Do you understand?"

Amanda nodded. She and Mark. Different, but the same. A balance. A willingness to compromise.

"When Ruth married Lucas, she assumed this joining would be much the same as the last. It wasn't. A lawyer's lot is a secretive one. Lucas's office is as closed as a confessional, his dealings a sacred trust. He didn't discuss his clients and paid little attention to office gossip. Lucas didn't care to entertain, nor did he enjoy socializing outside his home. When they did venture out, their journeys were a disappointment to Ruth. Los Angeles is casual. Ruth's extravagant gowns hung, useless, in the closet. She socialized with club women, rather than moving in the circles of powerful men. Lucas wasn't a counterpoint, he was a millstone who took no pleasure in her attempts to brighten their lives.

"But Ruth kept pushing. She was always at the office, concocting educational opportunities for young people who wanted to enter the law, offering the firm's staff for charity engagements, speakers and such for luncheons. She honestly wanted to make a mark, to help those less fortunate, but, more than that, she needed a life. Ruth couldn't accept that things were different now. Peter Sweeney hated her. Oliver had little love for her. Don Forrester embraced the majority opinion.

"Remember, these were men for whom the firm was a living, breathing thing. It was to be nurtured, not used as Ruth was using it, not opened to the scrutiny of outsiders. But it was Lucas who loved the firm the most. To him it was his life and she was beginning to threaten it in more ways than one."

Kitty rose. She tied the arms of her sweater loosely about her neck and went to the long, shuttered windows. Bright light and bruises were incompatible. She tipped one slat open. A sliver of light wedged itself into the room. Amanda couldn't see the view but she imagined Kitty was contemplating a perfectly mapped garden, a lovely pool, perhaps a man tending to it all. Amanda could have sworn time was ticking away in hours. It was tough to be tolerant. But Kitty had the baton and the score was a dirge.

"Lucas loved that firm from the moment he joined it. In his youth, he was one of those slight men, a bit unsure of himself, terribly intelligent, growing handsome only with age. You know the type." She turned toward them but kept herself apart. "During his years with Dimsdale, Morris and Mott, he became more confident and more powerful. Unfortunately, Lucas never really understood that power.

"To him, the firm was a place of refuge, a place to be held in awe. But he had no capacity to feel for anything outside that work. This was not an arrogant insensitivity to others like Oliver's attitude, it was simply a void. Lucas hadn't the knack." Kitty laid her head back, closing her eyes. The room was shadowy again. She muttered, "It's so hard to explain about these men but you are right. Lucas disappointed Ruth. Terribly. He couldn't be disappointed in her because, once married, he didn't expect a lot from her."

"Mrs. Hedding." Mark waited. He tried again. "Mrs. Hedding?" He had her lethargic attention. "You said Ruth was threatening more than Lucas's comfort level at the firm."

Kitty opened her eyes. She seemed surprised to see these two people in her sitting room. An invalid's disorientation.

"Yes. Oh, yes. The divorce. Ruth. Well." A hand

passed over her eyes. She paced. A book would have been comfortable balanced on her head. "Lucas had accepted Ruth's unhappiness. Though it distressed him because it upset his incredibly balanced life, he was willing to go through with the divorce. But Ruth was angry at her wasted years. A quiet settlement meant the loss of a tremendous opportunity to have a bit of fun. And, when she discovered that there had been an incredible oversight in the business aspect of their marriage, she was determined to have as much fun as possible."

Kitty bit her lip. It was an exceedingly girlish gesture that had a great capacity to annoy if it didn't lead anywhere. Thankfully, it did. She was filling in the blanks.

"When we married our husbands, Mr. Fleming, each of us was required to sign an agreement. Quite like a prenuptial, yet not so pressing. We all obliged without a peep. Actually, Oliver and I had been married some time before it became necessary for me to sign the agreement. He wasn't a partner then, you see, not when we first married. He was only a man with a future then."

"The agreement?" Amanda prodded, trying desperately to find her professional voice. Kitty Hedding offended her. Mark looked distressed. Kitty didn't.

"Yes. Sorry. The agreement was very simple. It stated that, should any of us desire a divorce, the partnership would be excluded from any settlement. The firm, that is. Dimsdale, Morris and Mott."

That was it. The secret. The horrible thing. The hateful thing. They didn't get it and that was obvious to Kitty. She was patient. She was also condescending and made them sit through Divorce 101 before she got to the point.

"In California, a woman suing for divorce is entitled to receive half of all the couple owns together and this includes her husband's business. All profits and assets are included. Much like a doctor's practice, in our case that would include the collective partnership of Dimsdale, Morris and Mott, which would be considered as part of Ruth's settlement." Kitty paused. She underlined the information. "The collective partnership, Ms. Cross. Mr. Fleming. Not Lucas's portion of that partnership."

"Oh, my God," Amanda whispered.

"That could be worth millions." Mark was astounded.

Kitty enjoyed their reactions.

"Naturally, such a settlement would have ruined the firm. Dimsdale, Morris and Mott would no longer exist if Ruth sued and won and there was no question that she would. Fred assured her of that. Case law confirmed it. Legally, Lucas couldn't stop her and financially, the firm couldn't absorb such a shock. Can you imagine how Lucas would have reacted to such a threat? He would have done everything in his power to dissuade Ruth. Everything. Anything."

"But the agreement," Mark reminded her.

Kitty laughed ruefully, "Ruth never bothered signing it. Amazingly, Lucas never followed up. He was sure of her. It was as simple as that. She used the oversight to her advantage."

Kitty was smiling now, remembering her friend's power.

"Ruth had a marvelous, dry wit. A taunting wit when she wished. I believe she tortured Lucas with her position of strength. I believe, in a moment of fury, not knowing what else to do, he killed her. He had always used the law to fight his battles, now the law was saying Ruth was the victor. And to the victor go the spoils. So, in this position, what other weapon did Lucas have except physical force?"

"But this makes no sense." Amanda moved into the middle, rounding Kitty's chair.

"I think it makes a great deal of sense. You heard the tape. Fred is a very good lawyer. He wouldn't make a mistake."

"You inferred that," Amanda challenged.

"I know that, Ms. Cross. Ruth didn't have to fill in the blanks for me. I've followed this drama for quite some time."

"Then why didn't Fred, the good lawyer, come forward after Mrs. Mallory's death?"

Kitty cast a look of pity Amanda's way. "Ms. Cross, Fred's client was dead. He was no longer billing hours. He closed the file and, I'm sure, assumed that, should anyone wish to contact him, they would do so in their own good time. Any attorney worth his salt does not offer to get involved in legal proceedings. They are smarter than that."

"Then why didn't you tell anyone?" Amanda said angrily. "Even if your conclusion were conjecture. Why did you keep that tape to yourself? Why didn't you tell the district attorney about the divorce and the state of the Mallory marriage?"

Kitty turned a cold eye Amanda's way. "You don't know very much about women like me, Ms. Cross."

"I know women," Amanda retaliated.

"You know nothing."

Amanda drew herself up, indignant and speechless. Her attitude made little impact on the older woman.

"If I let myself believe that Lucas was capable of killing Ruth because of this divorce action, then I would have to admit that Oliver was also aware of the situation. That would make him an accessory to murder, would it not? Therefore, I have been married to a monster. I took as my friend, Lucas Mallory, who committed a monstrous act. Could you live with that?" Kitty looked at Amanda. "If it were you, could you live knowing what your husband was capable of?"

"Hell no. I wouldn't have lived with it. I would have been asking a hell of a lot of questions, Mrs. Hedding. I would have been getting to the bottom of things, not hiding my head in the sand."

"I'm afraid I'm not as curious as you."

"It has nothing to do with curiosity. It has to do with selfishness in the extreme. And how about that silly little concept called justice? What about justice. Mrs. Hedding? If not for Nora Royce, for your friend?"

Kitty bristled. Good. A rise out of the ice matron.

"And what good would it have done me to seek justice in such an unjust situation? Would it have brought Ruth back? Would it have made my life better? Of course not. I had just lost the only person who understood the solitariness of this life, the indignation of becoming a nonperson. I didn't want to think about the loss of Ruth or myself. I had learned to stop thinking years ago. By the time I heard that message, I had perfected the art. I questioned nothing. There was a suspect in custody, there was evidence, and my husband seemed satisfied. If I speculated beyond the obvious, I would find myself questioning my very existence. You may be able to pick your life apart, Ms. Cross, find all the ugly little things in it you wish you could change and you may even try to change those things. The ghastly aspects of my life are neatly packed into a cellar in my mind. They remain there, undisturbed, while this face and this body continue on. It is a talent."

"It is sick, ma'am."

"Amanda." Mark half stood. She glared at him and shut

her mouth in disgust. Let Mark deal with Kitty Hedding. Amanda stomped toward the far corner of the room.

"I'm sorry, Mrs. Hedding," he apologized, sympathizing. He knew how it felt to lose oneself. Amanda turned her face away and studied the wallpaper. Kitty inclined her head as if to say the suffering to come would be more intense than this. She leaned forward and reached for the scarf.

"I've changed my mind now, you see. Everything has changed. There is no more speculation. Faced with hard and ugly evidence, I must act. Min is distraught. She will make a scene whether she wants to or not and I would prefer she not be the one in the public eye. I have no choice now but to take your side, Mr. Fleming."

She handed Mark the scarf.

"Min Forrester brought me this. She found it in her husband's tuxedo. I imagine if I thought about it"—a wry glance at Amanda—"I might figure out exactly how it ended up in Don's pocket. But I'm a coward and I'm tired. I'd like you to take it. Min will testify that she found it in her husband's coat pocket if it is necessary. Ms. Cross has the tape. Oh, and this."

Kitty handed him a plastic card. He held it up.

"Nora's room key?"

"It was in the scarf."

"I see."

Mark pushed himself off the chintz sofa. Kitty stood to meet him. He was taller but she gave him a run for his money. They were almost eye-to-eye. Amanda walked to the door of the sitting room. If Mark kissed that broad on the cheek she was going to have a cow.

"Are you going to be all right here?" Mark asked.

"I'm sure I will. Oliver more than likely believes I've

learned my lesson quite nicely. I suppose in a way he's right. It's just not the one he imagined."

Mark nodded. "You have my number," he said.

"Certainly, Mr. Fleming. And thank you."

They parted without as much as a handshake. Mark walked out the door Amanda held open. She couldn't bring herself to leave quite yet. There were a couple of things on her mind.

"Mrs. Hedding?" Kitty raised her head. "If Ruth Mallory sued for half the partnership assets and won you would be destitute. She would have creamed you and the other ladies right along with Lucas."

"Yes. She would have, Ms. Cross."

"I thought she was your best friend."

"Oh. Ms. Cross. Ruth was my best friend and she never would have done anything to hurt me no matter how much she detested the men of Dimsdale, Morris and Mott. Ruth was bluffing, you see. It was only a game. Just something she used to get a rise out of Lucas. We laughed about how really frightened he was—they all were. Ruth had money of her own. She didn't need what he had to offer her. She just waited too long to tell him."

"And my sister?"

"What about her?" Kitty asked, her voice beginning to fail. She was tired of talking, exhausted by the little jaunt around the arid landscape of her life.

"How does she fit in?"

"I suppose she was Lucas's sex partner, Ms. Cross."

"You suppose…"

"I haven't thought much about her, to tell the truth."

Amanda hesitated. There was a lot more to say. She couldn't find the words. "I can believe that, Mrs. Hedding."

Outside, the door closed against them again, Mark and

Amanda stood side-by-side, strangely at odds.

"Weird woman," he muttered.

"Incredible," she added.

Mark held the scarf in one hand, the key gingerly in the other. More than likely, it had passed through too many hands to make the prints worthwhile but one never knew.

Amanda eyed the items. "What do you think?"

"About the key? I haven't the foggiest. Nora must have turned hers in when she checked out because there wasn't one in her purse when the cops got her. Maybe she got this one for Lucas."

"The scarf?" Amanda asked.

"Obviously Nora's. He must have taken it from her room. He had to be setting her up. Maybe the only thing he could think of in the heat of the moment."

"Doesn't make sense," Amanda mumbled. "Had to be premeditated."

"Okay, maybe. I don't know."

Amanda let it lie. Her thoughts were a jumble and she felt strangely sad, harboring a residue of peevishness toward Mark. His empathy for Kitty Hedding had seemed disloyal.

"Lucas did it like she said, don't you think?" she asked.

"I guess. I don't know how. People saw him at that reception."

"People see what they want to see." Amanda kicked at the ground. She fidgeted with the strap of her purse. She was so anxious, so uncomfortable. "I just didn't want it to be this predictable, you know?"

Amanda shivered though it was warm. Mark was there, wrapping his arm around her, stashing the scarf and key in the pocket of his jacket.

"Aw, Christ, Amanda, come on. This is real life. See a

movie if you want something exotic. Besides, didn't you learn anything from her?" He cocked his head toward the house. "Be careful what you ask for. Ruth wanted something more dramatic and look where it got her."

"Yeah." She laid her head on his shoulder, changing the subject because she was a woman and allowed to. "Well, you didn't have to treat Kitty Hedding like that."

Mark shrugged. "I like her."

"Okay. Okay. I'll give it to you but no one else in this mess. Don't you dare feel bad for anyone else except Nora."

"Promise," he whispered. Amanda moved her head to find a comfortable place to rest. "I got what I wanted, though, didn't I? Enough to confuse any jury. Probably enough to have Mallory arrested."

"What are you going to do?"

"Do?" Amanda raised her face and looked Mark straight in the eye. "I should take all this stuff to Leo. He could decide if he should take Mallory into custody. Then the bastard could move for an acquittal posthaste."

Mark laughed. "Now that we know what you should do, what are you going to do?"

"I'm going to court. I'm going to sit through Leo's examination of Lucas Mallory and then I'm going to cross-examine him."

"What about discovery?" Mark reminded her.

"What about it?"

Chapter 23

Nora was fidgety. She hadn't slept much the night before. None of them had. Mark's trailer was fine for an intimate tryst but hardly suitable for a slumber party.

Though Mark insisted the precaution was unnecessary, Amanda was adamant that Nora not be left alone. Oliver Hedding knew Kitty had called Mark. He'd been angry enough to strike out. Lucas had possibly killed. The men of Dimsdale, Morris and Mott were coming out of their shells and apart at the seams. Amanda didn't want Nora in harm's way. She'd already been there long enough.

The night wasn't completely wasted. Nora, the bloom coming back into her cheeks with every passing hour, and Amanda, electro-charged now that her time to shine was at hand, spent the night formulating cross-examination and trying to steer clear of theory. Mark fed them. Scotch and water from a bottle, macaroni and cheese from a box, soup from a can. All the delicacies his larder could provide. He listened, he counterattacked, he was helpful and sharp. They were a team—last night.

Now they were in court.

Leo was finished with Lucas Mallory. All eyes were on Amanda except Lucas's. He stared straight ahead. To look at her he would also have to see Nora. Amanda eased herself from behind the defense table. From the corner of her eye, she saw Mark raise his hand in a sign of support. She smoothed her jacket, hoping it would cover the surreptitious glance she gave to the spectators. Everyone who should be there was. Amanda was ready. She walked into Lucas Mallory's line of sight and faced him head-on.

They considered one another.

She spoke first. That was the rule.

"How well do you know Edward Ramsey, Mr. Mallory?"

"Mr. Ramsey was an employee of Dimsdale, Morris and Mott until three months ago, when he left the firm." Good volley. Not even surprised by the odd opening tack.

"Do you know what he's been doing since he left DM&M?"

Smash forehand.

"I don't."

A weak lob back to her.

"I see." Amanda patted herself on the back with a large mental hand. "Well, he has been working for my firm, Mr. Ramsey. He is a member of the defense team."

Lucas remained silent, his expression implacable, as if to say it was of so little interest to him he wasn't even going to be polite and feign curiosity. Amanda smiled sweetly, not at all perturbed.

"When was the last time you spoke to Mr. Ramsey?"

Lucas's eyes flicked with a strange, mechanical back-and-forth motion. He was processing data, determining the probabilities of infinite outcomes of her questioning.

"I honestly can't remember. He wasn't assigned to my staff. I seldom spoke to Mr. Ramsey."

"Interesting." Amanda moved. She didn't want to risk losing her audience because the visuals were static.

"Objection, Your Honor," Leo drawled. "I see no relevance."

"Sustained. Ms. Cross." The judge gave her the look of subtle disapproval. This was not a real bad thing she had done.

"Of course, Your Honor, though I believe the connection will eventually be made clear."

"Until you can do so," the judge suggested, "proceed with a more relevant line of questioning."

"Yes, Your Honor." Amanda moved to the defense table and picked up a piece of paper. "Mr. Mallory, I would like to show you a telephone bill. Your honor, may this be marked as Defense Exhibit C." With a flourish, Amanda held the paper high. The juror's eyes followed. They were interested. They were hooked.

"Have you shown it to Mr. Riordon?"

"No, Your Honor. I'd be happy to." Amanda handed it to Leo, who reacted as she'd hoped he would. He jumped out of his chair, almost out of his skin.

"This is outrageous. I haven't been advised of this new evidence," he roared, suddenly aware he was going to have to work even though the prosecution had rested.

"There's more where that came from," Amanda muttered, snatching the paper back with a grin on her face but composed again the moment she faced the bench. Thankfully, his honor was going to oblige Amanda this time.

"In the interest of time," the judge droned, "and since the prosecution was so eager to push this trial to its conclusion, the defense may show the exhibit to the witness."

"Thank you, Your Honor." Amanda's eyes twinkled brightly for Leo's benefit, then clouded as she faced Lucas.

She handed it to him. "Mr. Mallory, please tell us if you recognize the phone numbers circled in red?"

Eyes down, paper held between two stiff fingers, eyes up, staring right into Amanda's.

"This is my private number at the office."

"And this"—Amanda took the paper from him, unfolding the top third—"is Nora Royce's phone bill. Your number has been called, oh, seven times in the last month and a half. I find that interesting, Mr. Mallory. Don't you?"

"Miss Royce often called me. I did not return her calls, her affection, or her attention."

"No, I suppose you didn't. In fact, I would venture to guess if we subpoenaed DM&M's phone records we would find that you never once called Nora Royce's home in the last month to warn her to stop harassing you. But I imagine if we did have those records we would find that you often dialed Mr. Ramsey at his home, would we not? And, since we neither have those records nor are allowed to discuss Mr. Ramsey, I ask you why you did not advise the district attorney, or this court, that the lady in question had not ceased her offensive activity? Perhaps you were being stoic, Mr. Mallory? Brave? Stupid?"

"Objection, Your Honor. Counsel is being argumentative." Leo was on top of things.

"Sustained."

"Forgive the speculation, Your Honor." Amanda slid her apology in neatly, giving her undivided attention back to Lucas Mallory. "Given Ms. Royce's obsession, I wouldn't find it odd that she continued to call me. I deemed phone calls during the course of this trial to be irrelevant, since they were after the fact of the crime." Lucas's eyes were as cold as steel. Amanda didn't like looking at them. She imagined she could see Ruth Mallory's reflected there as she lay dying.

"If obsession is what it was, no, I wouldn't find it unusual that she continued to call you," Amanda admitted. She looked thoughtful as if he had provided her with some new outlook on the information.

She had traveled almost to the prosecution's table before turning on her heel. The face she showed the jury was still contemplative.

Amanda made a decision, then walked quickly back to the defense table.

"Perhaps we should leave the question of the phone bill for now and talk about that obsession. Mr. Mallory, since Nora Royce's uncontrolled desire for you is the crux of this case." Amanda rifled through more papers. When she faced Lucas Mallory again, she held a small, rectangular piece of paper against her breast, as if she were going to make him guess what was on it.

"Obsession. It's an interesting thing. One person so taken with another that they can't help but harass them in the hopes of forcing love. The need to be close is uncontrollable. It is a far different thing than a healthy affair of the body and soul. And so, through this trial, we have all assumed that Nora Royce was obsessed with you because that is what you and your colleagues have told us. We believed you because you are fine, upstanding citizens. Yet, Mr. Mallory, in all my investigating, I find that only you four upstanding men seem to have defined Nora Royce's behavior toward you as obsessive. In all my other interviews, not one person commented on Nora Royce's behavior as anything but professional, even if it was somewhat colorful—"

"Objection, Your Honor. Calls for a conclusion as to the opinions of the other people employed by Dimsdale,

Morris and Mott."

Leo didn't even get up to object. He was too busy jotting notes to take time for the niceties.

"Sustained."

"No problem." Amanda smiled again this time at the judge. She wouldn't remind him that he had allowed Don Forrester's speculation on the state of the Mallory marriage when this trial began. She would be kind. She would be magnanimous. She was having fun. "Mr. Mallory, what kind of car do you drive?"

"A blue Mercedes."

"And the license plate number?"

"Irrelevant, Your Honor." Leo again. He was going to start getting tiresome.

"Relevant as to identity, Your Honor."

"Overruled."

"Thank you." Amanda was getting excited. She was on a roll. "Your license plate number, sir?"

"It is a vanity plate. It reads C-N-T-R-C-T-S."

"Your Honor, I would like to have this marked Defense Exhibit D. It is a sworn affidavit by Mr. Stanley Walters, a resident of the town house directly below that of Nora Royce. Mr. Walters can confirm that he witnessed Mr. Mallory's car at Nora Royce's home on at least four occasions before Mrs. Mallory's death. Mr. Walters was unable to be in court today but will, upon subpoena, appear before the bench. Mr. Mallory? Do you have a comment?"

He did but the voice with which he spoke was not quite as controlled as it had been. He faltered, though it was almost imperceptible. He seemed somehow confused as if Amanda was going too fast and her logic was difficult to identify, much less follow.

"I did go to Ms. Royce's home after the difficulty started, to try and reason with her. I told her I was a happily married man and that anything other than a professional relationship was impossible."

"Interesting, Mr. Mallory. And is that why you also special ordered a scarf at the Anni boutique approximately nine months ago—long before that particular scarf was available for sale in the United States? Is that why you gave one to Nora Royce? To try and buy her off with a scarf—or to entice her into your bed?"

"I never gave Ms. Royce a scarf."

"On record, your staff confirms that Ms. Royce began wearing that scarf"—Amanda pointed to the bagged and bloodied scarf on the exhibit table—"or one very much like it, on or about the date indicated on this sales slip from the boutique. A sales slip that is signed by you acknowledging the special order. Ms. Royce's testimony states that you gave it to her on the first night you made love, a night she'll never forget. The same night you picked the scarf up at the Anni boutique in Beverly Hills after it arrived from Italy. All this is corroborated by the staff of Anni. I ask you, Mr. Mallory, if not you then who gave Nora Royce that very unique, very expensive scarf? There were fifteen special orders from Beverly Hills and the only person who ordered one of these scarves who has any relationship to Nora Royce is you, Mr. Mallory. Please, please explain this to me, to the jury. Mr. Mallory."

"I have no idea who might have… I don't know who gave her the scarf." Lucas's lips were tight. He didn't look at Amanda any longer. Instead, his gaze locked with that of Oliver Hedding. His jaw shivered with a tick. Amanda moved in.

"You do know who gave her the scarf, Mr. Mallory. You did. In fact, according to the evidence, you bought two scarves. One, of course, is covered in your wife's blood. The one we all assumed belonged to Nora Royce. I suggest to you that scarf did not belong to Ms. Royce at all. That was the scarf you gave to your wife, Mr. Mallory, and was accessible in your very own suite at the Regency Hotel. I would further suggest to you that you had Mr. Ramsey steal Ms. Royce's scarf when he offered to help her with her luggage the night of your wife's murder. I would suggest it was Mr. Ramsey who, upon entering my employ, called you repeatedly from Ms. Royce's apartment to keep you apprised of the defense situation. Let me show you the second scarf. Let me—"

"Are you suggesting I killed my wife, Ms. Cross?" Fast and cold. The tic was under control. The man had nerves of steel. Amanda's were fraying in the face of such indifference. She opened her mouth. She wanted to shout to the high heavens. Yes! Yes! But she didn't know that he did it. Not for sure, that he had tightened that thing around Ruth Mallory's neck, that he plunged the knife into her chest. There was a doubt, unreasonable though it might be. Amanda couldn't accuse him. Not now. There were so many questions to ask. She questioned him, she attacked him, she couldn't break stride now.

"Did you love your wife, Mr. Mallory?"

That did it. Perfect. The man stiffened. Behind his eyes, panic flared, burning out of control. He reached for the railing that cornered him in the witness box. His mouth dropped slightly, moving, but accomplishing nothing.

"Did you, Mr. Mallory?" Amanda moved in closer. "Love her, Mr. Mallory?" Body tensed, voice rising. "Mr. Mallory?"

"I did," he said.

"Did she love you?"

"She did," he whispered. He was a bad liar.

"Your Honor. Your Honor." Amanda was all motion. Back to the defense table. It was all there. Everything she needed to acquit her sister, to put an end to this madness. In her hand was another piece of paper. "Defense Exhibit E. Please, Your Honor. Please." She whipped over to Leo and shoved the paper under his face. "I submit into evidence the petition for divorce of Ruth Mallory from Lucas Mallory. The suit was filed one month before Mr. Mallory bought two Anni scarves, specially ordered from Italy. One month before Mr. Mallory gave a scarf to Nora Royce. One month before he entered into an affair with Ms. Royce, as evidenced by Mr. Walters, who saw Mr. Mallory's car at Nora Royce's residence, and Ms. Royce's own statement."

Amanda twirled back toward the witness box, holding out the copy of the divorce petition to Lucas Mallory, crushing it in her hand. Her voice boomed with confidence. She was winning. It was frightening. It was wonderful. He crumbled.

"I ask again, Mr. Mallory, did your wife love you? Did she?"

"Your Honor!" Leo was up, pounding on the table. "Defense is badgering the witness. I demand—"

"Ms. Cross, this is…" The judge himself looked perplexed, his hesitation fueled her. Amanda's voice crackled with righteousness. She grew in stature, she felt herself filling the courtroom, ready to shout out the truth.

"Defense will continue to badger the witness, Your Honor, until the witness explains his deceit. Until he explains why he wished to indict Ms. Royce in this matter. Why he knowingly allowed her to be charged with the murder of Ruth Mallory, the wife who desperately wanted a divorce."

The judge sat silent, stunned and enthralled. Amanda was too fast for any of them. She went to the defense table once more. The last bit of evidence. The final nail in the coffin. She closed in on Lucas Mallory. He shrank from her, unable to counterattack in a situation that was not logical and regulated.

"This is a copy of the agreement all partners' wives signed excluding the partnership of Dimsdale, Morris and Mott from divorce proceedings. Ruth Mallory never signed one, did she, sir?"

"I… " Lucas's eyes were dancing in his head. He was seeking counsel, comfort, and there was none to be had. He was a man alone and afraid as his world came tumbling down. Never before had he been so alone, he had always had Oliver. Oliver couldn't help him now.

"Did you love your wife, Mr. Mallory? Did she love you? Did you kill your wife, Mr. Mallory? Did you kill her because she threatened to destroy the thing you loved most?"

"Your Honor!" Leo screamed.

"Come on, bucko," Amanda demanded, angry and mean, ready for the kill. She sneered, low, so only he could hear, "Come on, you asshole."

"Your Honor!"

"Ms. Cross, I will hold you in contempt." The shout came from the bench and nobody heard or cared. Amanda as Joan of Arc.

"No one can hold me in as much contempt as I hold him, Your Honor. I ask again, Lucas Mallory, did you kill your wife? Did you strike her down in your suite at the Regency Hotel and were you willing to allow Nora Royce, your lover, to be charged with that crime? Did you, Mr. Mallory? Did you kill her?"

Amanda's question reverberated in the courtroom. Accusations rained down on Lucas Mallory, fire and brimstone disorienting him with their sting. They waited, all of them in that courtroom, for his answer, but none waited as Amanda did. This wasn't about being an outstanding lawyer, this wasn't about proving herself to Nora or giving Mark someone to admire. This was about being right, about justice, about those damned idiots who thought money and power were just different ways to spell right and truth. She wasn't going to let them make the truth anymore. Amanda was damned well going to shove the real thing down their throats.

Quietly now, she stepped forward. Just one eloquent step. Politely, she asked, "Lucas Mallory, did you kill Ruth Mallory with malice and aforethought?"

Lucas looked her in the eye and those eyes of his were so sad. He was broken. He was lost and in his disorder was defeat. He would tell the truth. Amanda waited, ready for triumph.

"I did not. Ms. Cross."

Amanda was stunned. She fell forward, grabbing for the railing around the witness box. She raised her head, her eyes beseeching him.

"No," she whispered. "No, tell the truth."

Mechanically, he answered, "I am telling the truth."

Indeed he was. Lucas Mallory sat staring over her head and out into the sea of spectators, focused, and told the truth by identifying the murderer with eyes that now looked old and tired. Before Amanda could gather her strength, she heard a voice from the back of the courtroom. A familiar voice.

"Oh, no, Lucas. Oliver, you ass. You swore nothing would—"

Amanda whirled, still holding on to the rail. Her fore-head was slick with perspiration, her heart pounding in her brain. She followed Lucas's line of vision. It went past Oliver, past Don Forrester and Peter Sweeney, and impaled one she never would have suspected. Edward Ramsey stood in the back of the courtroom. Trapped. Terrified. Not so pretty anymore.

"Edward?" Amanda whispered staggering away from Lucas Mallory, unable to believe her eyes.

"They all swore nothing would come of this. They made me do it. Made me do it because of the firm. It was in danger and I wanted a position for life. It was good for everyone. But they watched. Hey, not just me." Edward's hands were up and out, pleading or ready to fight, no one was sure. He pointed, accusing the others. "They watched! All of them. To make sure it was done. I insisted they had to be there... for protection... and... and... Lucas gave his blessing. I swear, Amanda. I swear..."

Edward called out to anyone who would listen, his voice shaking as he pointed to Oliver Hedding, Don Forrester, Peter Sweeney, and, finally, Lucas Mallory. The senior partners of Dimsdale, Morris and Mott reacted in character. Peter pulled himself up and faced Edward, that marvelous military posture of his intact. He was ready for the firing squad and proud of it. It had been a good run, boys. Don buried his face in his hands, his shoulders shaking. His tears meant nothing to anyone. And Oliver. Oliver stared at Lucas, a small smile on his thin lips, amused by such a turn of events.

"They watched," Edward whimpered, then more strongly, "and there was no other way. None. I'll tell you. I just wanted a place, a job. And they set her up!" He looked at Nora with animal eyes, his glibness failing him. No escape, the hunter was on him. "They set her up from the beginning."

"Edward."

Amanda forced her eyes away from Edward, who was half crying, half collapsing as those next to him moved away. The quiet voice that spoke his name was so compelling everyone was powerless to defy Oliver Hedding's call. Edward sobbed and tried to speak.

"That is quite enough, Edward," Oliver insisted, taking a slow dry, death-bed breath. His small eyes glittered. They were surprisingly full of life. How he loved a challenge. Slowly, he looked about, seeing people who admired him, feared and hated him. They were all such fools and none more so than the district attorney. An absurd man defeated by a woman of no consequence. How helpless Leo was. How in need of direction. Oliver kindly obliged.

"Leo, I believe you should move for a mistrial. Then, perhaps, we might all have a little talk." Before Leo could act, Oliver Hedding's eyes were on Amanda. He tipped his head, much like a friend asking what time he should come to dinner. Amanda stared back.

"I do want you to know, Ms. Cross, you were wrong about one thing. There was no malice. Aforethought, most definitely. Malice, no. It was only business. Business—not as usual—but business nonetheless."

Amanda began to speak, needing to answer him, only to find she hadn't the strength. Instead, she turned away, sickened and in need of solace. She collapsed into the first arms held out to her—Nora's arms.

Chapter 24

When Amanda awoke there were two things she noticed: twilight was in full gear and for the first time in a couple of days, she was hungry. She admired the subdued, light show of the former and rolled off the mattress ready to do something about the latter.

Like a sleepy kid, she shuffled through the trailer, still tired, still depressed the way people are after they get what they want and it's not as good as they expected.

The trial was over and it had all ended so strangely. Motions filed, words spoken, reporters, humble thanks, tearful relief, Nora going her own way, Amanda and Mark not quite sure if they were supposed to head into the sunset together or shake hands and say it had been nice. They decided on the sunset and let everything else lie for a while. No questions. No comments. No commitments.

Amanda shivered, waiting for the blood to start flowing again and warm her. Squinting, she peered through the little metal-framed window in the living room, checking out the dusk again just before a plume of smoke obliterated her view.

Food.

She made a beeline.

Mark looked over his shoulder and smiled, waving his spatula. Amanda grinned back and folded her arms, pacing behind him. She gave up waiting for an invitation and wound her arms around his waist, pushing herself gently against his back. His free hand covered hers and he swayed.

"That's nice," he said.

"Yeah. Thanks."

"For what?"

"For holding me up, letting me sleep, cooking for me."

"Steak." The drip and drizzle, fat hitting hot coals. She'd been there before.

"I think this time we'll eat it hot," Amanda murmured.

In one swift motion, Mark managed to move her from back to front without her arms ever releasing him. Her hair grazed her shoulders as she tipped her face up, silently asking whether or not he understood.

"Whenever you're ready, babe," he whispered. Amanda was in heaven.

"It won't be long," she assured him. Tiptoeing, she pecked his chin and moved away. "Smells good."

Mark said nothing. Just flipped the meat.

"I guess I'm still kind of out of whack."

"Don't you think you deserve to be?" Mark Fleming, psychologist. Have theory will travel.

"I guess. Yeah, I do deserve to be." Amanda headed toward the little ridge on the hill and considered the view. She could still see the ocean. The waves were silver tipped, the sky grazed with pink and saffron. When Amanda spoke, she wasn't sure if it was to Mark, herself, or that great spirit everyone else seemed to have such faith in.

"Lord, Edward killed that woman to ingratiate himself to those sub-humans. Goddamn law firm. Can you believe it? Taking a life so coldly, planning it out, meetings, progress reports. It's so sick."

"No sicker than what they did to Nora," Mark reminded her.

"No kidding. Nora was set up from day one and didn't have a clue. Lucas never cared a twit for her. She just fit the bill. I wonder if they knew exactly how perfect Nora was for the part?"

"Of course they did. Those guys had every base covered," Mark assured her. He had the steak on a board and was slicing it paper thin while he talked. "Once Lucas presented Nora with the whole package—personal attention, good sex, inside track—there was no way she was going to turn it down. He understood her ambition. They all did. They wanted something from her; she wanted something from them. It was a game. They were just better than she was."

"You're right." Depression. It came and went as if at will. "Naturally." He waved a fork and made light. He understood being down but he wasn't going to let her stay there. She'd done as much for him. Tit for tat. "Sit down before it gets cold. Potatoes, salad, steak. Macho food. Good stuff for tough lawyers."

Amanda laughed, not quite ready for fun and games but appreciative of his efforts to rouse her.

"Looks good." She came back to him. They sat facing each other on the yellow-and-purple striped chairs. Amanda picked up her wine while Mark dug in.

"I called the hotel while you slept," he informed her after his first bite of steak. "They confirmed the room Nora stayed in was missing a key. Edward's room had all keys returned."

"So?" She picked at the salad.

"So I'd guess that Edward was running too fast for his own good. This is the way I see it. Lucas screws Nora in the afternoon—"

"Isn't that funny how we all assumed Nora had access to that suite on her own? It never occurred to me to ask if someone saw Lucas in the room, waiting."

"Really hilarious," Mark answered dryly. "May I finish my supposition?"

"Be my guest." Another sip of her wine, a quarter cup of butter on her baked potato. She deserved it.

"Thank you. So they get all the goods on Nora in the afternoon. That bite was an incredible touch," he diverged then pulled back quickly so he wouldn't lose his audience. "Anyway, Ruth shows up—we're still not sure if she sees Lucas when she arrives or if he's already wandering around the reception—anyway, she changes and heads for the party. The boys leave Lucas at the party. He might be a prime suspect so they want him seen. Maybe one of them even had enough heart to think maybe Lucas cared enough about his wife to not want to see her die. Anyway, they leave him downstairs and the party's getting bigger, so nobody is really paying attention to who's coming or going.

"Upstairs, Edward's in the room with the other three. Remember our lady with the curlers? She sees one of them going in. They wait for Ruth. She walks in right on time to get her insulin and Edward's got her around the neck with the scarf. But she's a pretty big woman and he's a kind of slight type. She struggles, he grabs the knife off the fruit platter and hacks away at her. Reality is a little grittier than they expected."

"While the good old boys watch. No malice—ha! Those

guys are beyond every feeling," Amanda mumbled through her mouthful of buttery potato.

"So it was messier than they expected but Edward cleans up pretty good, the wounds are clean, and he makes four or five good passes. She's already unconscious from the strangulation. He's hardly mussed. He stashes his coat—the only bloody thing on his body—in a presentation portfolio in his room—cops got it, by the way—and heads for the party. Nora's being pissed off really helped the situation. Edward thinks he's literally going to have to take the scarf from around her neck and isn't sure how to do it."

"She's human, after all." Amanda chuckled sadly. "Angry at Lucas, she leaves the one thing she thinks is a symbol of their commitment in her room. Boy, did she show him."

Mark jumped right back in, forgetting his meal and catching the fever of their triumph again.

"Edward takes advantage of the situation. He takes her key, gets her luggage, is back in a flash. He's whipped the scarf out of her bag and stuck it, and the key, in his pocket. She doesn't think to ask about the key in all the hullabaloo. Edward passes the scarf to Don, forgetting the key is wrapped inside. Don forgets about it and Min has a coronary when she finds the whole kit and caboodle. Hysterical, she runs to Kitty. Kitty knows when Vesuvius is about to blow and tosses in with the winning side. The end."

"Kitty. Good old Kitty. She was as bad as her husband," Amanda intoned attacking a piece of very red meat with one of Mark's dull knives.

"For God's sake, Amanda. The woman was a victim for years," Mark insisted. "You can't equate her deaf ear to Oliver's scheme to protect the firm by murdering one of the senior partners' wives! You're just jealous because I treated Kitty Hedding nicely. Admit it!"

"Jealous? Oh, please. You have the biggest ego—"

"Hold that thought." Mark's eyes narrowed. Amanda looked over her shoulder, her meal forgotten as she watched a car coming up the road, dun-colored dust billowing behind it. Maybe the fat lady hadn't sung yet.

Mark pushed his chair back but Amanda motioned him down. Instead, she stood. Recognizing the car, Amanda waited patiently until both the dust and engine had died. She couldn't see through the tinted glass but had no doubt Nora was watching her carefully from behind it. A few seconds later, the door of the sedan opened and out stepped Nora, head-to-toe gorgeous, lazy-eyed, her old self—almost.

"Hi!" she called.

Amanda walked toward her, shoving up the sleeves of her sweatshirt casually, instead of preparing to duke it out. There wasn't an ounce of fight left in her.

"Hi," Amanda said. Close enough now, they could talk without shouting. They stopped simultaneously, knowing their parameters. Those boundaries would probably never change.

"I couldn't find you at home," Nora explained.

"I haven't been there except to pick up a few things."

Nora nodded, looking briefly toward the trailer and Mark. "This is a good place to be."

Amanda saw just the faintest flicker of envy. Feeling no triumph, she nodded and agreed.

"It's the best place for me."

"I'm glad." Nora's bottomless eyes were back on her sister. That dusky voice had just the slightest hint of humility in it, indicating she had been touched by their experience. Amanda wondered if it would last. "Listen, I can see you're busy and I didn't mean to intrude but I wanted to let you know I'm leaving for a while."

"Any place special?"

"The Caribbean. I have friends there…" Her voice trailed off, leaving Amanda to wonder exactly how sympathetic those friends would be.

"And it's not even Christmas."

That brought a smile.

"Not even Christmas," Nora reiterated wistfully. She brightened. It was forced and didn't sit well on her. She obviously felt uncomfortable. "Listen, maybe this Christmas we could have dinner. We might think about it."

"Sure." Amanda's grin was instantaneous and quashed just as quickly. She'd learned a lot from Nora over the last few months. Protect your flank but leave yourself room to maneuver. "Yeah. I think we should consider it."

"Good." Nora was pleased in her own subdued way.

Amanda grinned. The hell with her flank. Hope would always spring eternal for her.

"Good." Amanda agreed. "So, I'll see you when you get back. You've got my numbers. Office. Home." Nora nodded. "And Mark's?" Another nod. "Have a good time. Take care of yourself."

"You, too. Don't work too hard."

"I won't. We'll talk." Small talk. It felt strange. Amanda wished they were both drunk, their tongues loose. They could cry together or something.

Nora was about to leave but turned back briefly. "I forgot. Here. This is for you."

An envelope passed between them. Amanda didn't even look at it. Her eyes were on Nora. There was something else. She was sure of it. But Nora didn't say a word until she'd opened the door of her car and was halfway in.

"Amanda?"

"Yeah?"

"I think I loved him a little. I must have. I hurt," Nora confessed.

Her expression said more than her words and Amanda's heart broke. She did the only thing she could to help. She said:

"I'll be here when you get back."

"Thanks. For everything." And Nora was gone, driving off into her sunset. Alone.

Amanda watched until the car disappeared before trudging back to Mark. He refilled her wine glass and let the silence extend just long enough.

"Well?"

Amanda glanced at him, trying not to giggle.

"She thinks we should get together for Christmas."

"Really?"

"Yeah. Christmas."

"Can I come?" he asked.

"Some other time," Amanda answered knowing he would understand.

"What have you got there?"

Mark nodded toward the envelope Amanda had all but forgotten. She tore it open and peeked inside. Mark was on the verge of slapping her back to make her breathe again when she burst into laughter.

"What?" he demanded, thoroughly confused, utterly in love.

"Christ Almighty," she laughed, tears streaming down her cheeks. She held up the contents and let Mark have a gander at the check inside. "My fee."

A Look At: The Mentor

A DEADLY GAME WHERE NOTHING IS AS IT SEEMS.

Novice federal prosecutor, Lauren Kingsley, has just been handed the opportunity of a lifetime - prosecuting a militia terrorist responsible for the devastating bombing of an IRS building.

To Lauren, this case is her chance to prove to her long-time friend and mentor, Judge Wilson Caufeld, that she's got what it takes to succeed in the high-stakes world of criminal justice. But when Caufeld is found shot to death, Lauren is in over her head, trapped in a maze of conspiracy, corruption, and secrets leading right up to the U.S. Supreme Court.

Caught in the middle of a fierce tug-of-war between an FBI agent with his own agenda and a colleague whose loyalty is questionable, Lauren must decide who she can trust before she becomes the next mark of a vicious killer.

"With a cast of characters as real as your own next-door neighbors, and an easily identifiable story, the book is impossible to put down."

AVAILABLE NOW

About the Author

Born a Midwestern girl, raised in Southern California, Rebecca Forster earned her MBA and worked in major advertising agencies before she wrote her first book on a crazy dare and found her passion.

Now a USA Today and Amazon best-selling author, Forster is known for her legal thrillers and police procedurals. Over three million readers have enjoyed her fast-paced tales that are known for deep characterization and never-see-it-coming endings.

An avid court watcher, she is also a hands-on researcher. Rebecca is a graduate of the DEA and ATF Citizen's academy, local police firearms programs, and is a Leaders to Sea participant who adds landing by tail hook on the USS Nimitz to her resume in search of authentic details for her books.

Rebecca has taught at the acclaimed UCLA Writers Program and various colleges and universities. She is a sought-after speaker at bar and judges' associations, philanthropic groups and has made numerous appearances on radio and television. Rebecca is also a repeat speaker at the LA Times Festival of Books. She volunteers as a patient/family advisor at Torrance Memorial Medical Center and volunteers at middle schools to bring the joy of writing to students. In her spare time, she plays competitive tennis, and travels extensively counting Albania as her number one destination.

Rebecca Forster is mother to two grown sons, and is married to a Los Angeles Superior Court judge.

Made in the USA
Monee, IL
28 November 2020